Menace

CW01499235

———◆———

Darcy & Lizzy's First Christmas

———◆———

A Pride & Prejudice Sequel

———◆———

The Elizabeth Bennet Series Book 2

GILL MATHER

INQUISITOR BOOKS

Published in 2023 by Inquisitor Books, an imprint of
Write Now! Publications

Cover photograph: Shutterstock
Artwork: Gill Mather

Paperback ISBN – 978-1-912955-45-9
ebook ISBN – 978-1-912955-46-6

To Write Now! – for their ever incisive suggestions

To John – for helping with some technical bits

And to Dan, proof-reader suprême

ABOUT THE AUTHOR

Gillian ('Gill') Mather has been a solicitor for several decades and at various times has worked in most of the basic areas covered by general practice in England (crime, family, employment, civil litigation, wills, probate and property). Gill ran a small solicitor's practice from her home near Colchester until 2020. She is a member of several writers' groups in Essex and Suffolk, including Write Now! Some of Gill's novels were previously published under the pen name of Julie Langham.

Gill has published eight full-length novels on Kindle, the first five being a series of romantic-cum-crime novels set in Colchester around a fictional law firm and featuring the same main characters over a number of years. The last book in the series is also a paranormal romance.

As The Clock Struck Ten, a crime/mystery/psychological drama about an accusation of sexual abuse, is the sixth novel. *The Unreliable Placebo*, a rom-com with a difference, is the seventh novel. And the eighth novel, *Class of '97*, is a mystery/psychological drama.

There are six novellas so far in the Roz Benedict Detective Novellas series. Further novellas in the series are planned.

All Gill's novels are available as both ebooks and paperbacks.

Intrigue At Longbourn is Gill's first historical novel and is a *Pride & Prejudice* prequel. *Menace At Pemberley* is the second novel in the Elizabeth Bennet series.

Gillian Mather – July 2023

'"Do you certainly leave Kent on Saturday?" said she.

"Yes—if Darcy does not put it off again. But I am at his disposal. He arranges the business just as he pleases."

"And if not able to please himself in the arrangement, he has at least great pleasure in the power of choice. I do not know any body who seems more to enjoy the power of doing what he likes than Mr. Darcy."

"He likes to have his own way very well," replied Colonel Fitzwilliam.'

Jane Austen

Pride And Prejudice, 1813

PROLOGUE

ELIZABETH Bennet and Fitzwilliam Darcy are married at last after a relatively short and largely chaste courtship preceded by a long and, at times, uncomfortable period of familiarisation. It is no bad thing in some ways for a couple to verbally spar and even fall out before a greater understanding is reached. It can mean that they have seen the worst of each other and indeed the other's family and friends but nevertheless have arrived at an accord and an acceptance of one another.

The coming of Charles Bingley to Netherfield Park in Hertfordshire at Michaelmas 1797 with his sisters and his great friend Darcy ensured that the party would soon become acquainted with the residents of nearby Longbourn House, the Bennet family, consisting of Mr and Mrs Bennet and their five daughters, of whom Elizabeth is the second.

Now, some thirteen months later and after a degree of adjustment, Darcy is prepared to tolerate the sometimes vulgar and inappropriate behaviour of Elizabeth's mother and other female relations. Elizabeth's older sister, Jane, is the wife of Charles Bingley and *she,* as we know, naturally conducts herself with all the decorum that could be expected of a lady. The demeanour of Elizabeth herself, being well-bred by nature, bears no vulgar words or manners, but the other sisters to varying degrees have not been restrained or disciplined so well as they might have been, allowing for, at times, their comportment to be unreserved and unsuitable.

But Darcy will overlook the shortcomings of Elizabeth's other sisters, although he will never of course countenance any cordial connection with the youngest sister, the flighty Lydia, now married to the infamous Mr Wickham after their scandalous elopement; Wickham, son of the deceased steward of the Pemberley estate in Derbyshire inherited by Mr Darcy, whom Darcy has

1

reasonable cause to hold in strong disapprobation despite their being raised together as friends and almost brothers.

Elizabeth still possesses the letter written circa Easter of 1798 by which Darcy related to her the particulars of Wickham's life of idleness and dissipation and his grossly dishonourable act of persuading Darcy's sister, Georgiana, to elope with him about a year before for her thirty thousand pounds, a plan thwarted just in time by Darcy.

As to Elizabeth's father, Darcy's regard for him grows as a man of books, if not as a provider of the most satisfactory example to his daughters of conjugal felicity.

And Darcy applauds Elizabeth's independent spirit which Caroline Bingley chose to regard as an intolerable air of self-sufficiency.

Elizabeth, in her turn, has had to disregard her first impression of Darcy as a cold and proud individual who once said of Elizabeth in her hearing: "She is tolerable; but not handsome enough to tempt *me*; and I am in no humour at present to give consequence to young ladies who are slighted by other men." This said to Bingley at the first Meryton assembly which the Bingley party attended.

Darcy's proposal of marriage to Elizabeth only the day before he wrote the above-mentioned letter adds extra poignancy to the letter for Elizabeth. Already harbouring a strong dislike of Darcy at the time, she had of course roundly rejected the unexpected proposal. It filled her with astonishment and then anger as, while declaring how ardently he loved and admired her, he proceeded to outline the arguments against a match with her, including his sense of the inferiority of her connections and of relations whose condition in life was so decidedly beneath his own. Elizabeth was forced to enquire why, with so evident a design of offending and insulting her, he chose to tell her that he liked her against his will, against his reason, and even against his character.

She has also had to accept the arrogance of Darcy's aunt, Lady Catherine De Bourgh, who expressed to Elizabeth in offensive terms her violent objections when she perceived that a match might be taking place between Elizabeth and her nephew.

And she has had to turn her face from the sneers of the sisters of Mr Bingley, Caroline Bingley and Mrs Hurst, who spent the greater part of their time living in their brother's household since he arrived at Netherfield Park, as did Darcy, and made no secret of their disdain for the Bennet family, save for Jane whom they allowed to be a sweet girl.

Moreover, it was at Darcy's instigation in collusion with Caroline and Mrs Hurst that Charles was spirited away to his London house in the autumn of 1797. This removal was with the precise intention of parting Charles Bingley from Jane Bennet, Darcy being alarmed, by reason of her family's indiscretions, at Bingley's growing attachment to Miss Bennet.

In his Easter 1798 letter, Darcy freely admitted to Elizabeth having pointed out to his friend the certain evils of such a choice and having persuaded Bingley of Jane's indifference towards him. Further, he revealed that he had later concealed from Bingley the fact of Jane's being in town.

Elizabeth, who was fully cognisant of Jane's great distress at Bingley's sudden departure from Hertfordshire and her huge disappointment subsequently not to have been attended by him during her stay with her Aunt Gardiner at Gracechurch Street, has had to reconcile herself with the knowledge of Darcy having been the means of ruining, perhaps forever, the happiness of a most beloved sister.

Fortunately, the events described did not ultimately prevent a match between Jane and Bingley.

And perhaps the most providential event was the chance meeting of Elizabeth and Darcy during the summer of 1798 when Elizabeth was touring Derbyshire with her Aunt and Uncle Gardiner and they sought to visit Pemberley House believing the family to be from home. Darcy, however, returned a day earlier than expected and, surprisingly, showed every courtesy to Elizabeth and her relations. Indeed, his manner seemed to be so much improved from the Easter proposal that Elizabeth could scarce believe the change.

The good auspices of the reunion were almost foiled when Elizabeth received letters from Jane with the intelligence that Lydia had eloped with Mr Wickham and they were not yet married. Shortly after Elizabeth had read the letters, Darcy came upon her at the Kings Arms at Lambton, finding her in great distress. He very soon absented himself after she told him of the elopement and Elizabeth's assumption was that he would want nothing more to do with her. She and her aunt and uncle immediately quit Derbyshire and repaired to Longbourn.

But with all the tenacity of the ardent lover, Darcy took it upon himself to find Lydia and Wickham and put up sufficient money to bring about a marriage between them in London, and Lydia was married from the home of the Gardiners in Gracechurch Street. Only Elizabeth knew of this most generous act from her Aunt Gardiner, Darcy wishing to maintain secrecy.

Elizabeth had by then begun to comprehend that he, Darcy, was exactly the man who, in disposition and talents, would most suit her. His understanding and temper, though unlike her own, would answer all her wishes. It would be a union that must be to the advantage of both; by her ease and liveliness, his mind might be softened, his manners improved; and from his judgment, information, and knowledge of the world, she must receive benefit of greater importance.

Darcy, Bingley and his sisters returned to Netherfield and, directly, Darcy acknowledged himself mistaken in supposing, as he had done, that Jane was indifferent to Bingley. Having narrowly observed her during the visits he and his friend made to Longbourn House, he was convinced of her affection. And he could easily perceive that Bingley's attachment to her was unabated. Thereby, he felt no doubt of their happiness together as he explained to Elizabeth during a long ramble which they took together.

So it was against this turbulent background that Darcy announced to Elizabeth during this same walk that his affections and wishes were unchanged since last April, and Elizabeth and Darcy settled it between them that they were to be married.

Chapter 1

THE post chaise drew into the front yard of the Swan Hotel in Birmingham. She remembered it well from the family's trip to Buxton in the summer of last year and her tour of Derbyshire with her Aunt and Uncle Gardiner earlier this year. Those other two expeditions had been taken during the summer months but now it was late autumn, November. Fortunately the weather was frosty rather than wet. Frozen roads were easier to negotiate than seas of mud and so the going had been better than it might have been, but the second leg of their journey from Huntingdon had still been gruelling, as travelling always was.

Had it not been for the light from the hotel and the smart town houses along the street, together with some small illumination from the carriage lamps, they would have been in darkness.

Elizabeth turned to her new husband. Observing that his sister was still dozing on his other side, she surreptitiously put out her hand to him below the rug under which they were huddling and he took it. The effect of this small contact was instantaneous, and she tried to still the hammering of her heart and curb the breathlessness which overtook her. In the shadow of the small carriage, he would hopefully not be able to see the heightening of her colour, as she could discern only his dark curls and the general shape of his strong but beautiful face.

"Fitz," she whispered, her secret name for him, less formal than Fitzwilliam or Mr Darcy or Darcy. He had suggested, perhaps, to call him 'Will' or 'William' in public since, he said, the servants had called him 'Master Will' and then 'Mr Will' or 'Mr William' before his father died.

They gazed at each other, wanting more, but both became aware that Georgiana was stirring. She started to exclaim at the attractive street, the frost glistening on the house windows and the road, and Elizabeth and Darcy loosed their hands from one another.

"We had better get down and go in," he said, "and hope for some refreshment before we retire."

It was, of course, very late and they had another full day's travel ahead of them tomorrow.

GEORGIANA had left the dining parlour to go to her room slightly ahead of Elizabeth and Darcy. As had happened at the inn at Huntingdon, they parted on the landing. Elizabeth had mutely indicated her agreement when he had said that it would be better if they waited until they were at Pemberley to become better accustomed to one another. She was well aware that this was a euphemism for the marriage bed and was at first supremely disappointed.

Travelling straight to Pemberley from the Longbourn parish church in the hired carriage had been agreed upon between them. After the joint wedding service of the two couples in the early morning, Jane and Bingley had naturally repaired immediately to Netherfield Park. They had offered Elizabeth and Darcy a suite of rooms there for the period immediately following their marriage but they had politely declined, Darcy saying that he had been away from Pemberley for long enough and had affairs to settle there. In particular, his steward, Campbell, had recently and suddenly quit Darcy's employ leaving a vacuum in the management of the house.

They had briefly stopped at Longbourn House for Elizabeth to change her dress, and then had gone on their way.

Elizabeth's excuse had been a wish to settle at Pemberley as soon as possible, especially as it was mooted that the Bingleys and the Bennets, and probably the Gardiners, would spend Christmas at Pemberley. A deeper, more heart-felt reason had been Elizabeth's repugnance at the thought of having to start her married life under the jealous, possibly hostile, eyes of Caroline Bingley. Further, having her family so close at hand, carried the possibility that they could descend upon her and Jane at Netherfield within days of their weddings.

Since Georgiana was anxious to return to her home, having travelled to Hertfordshire from Pemberley for the wedding, she had concurred in the immediate removal of the three of them to

Pemberley and it was decided. Her presence with Elizabeth and Darcy in the cramped carriage had to be borne, as now did the parting on the landing outside Elizabeth's door at the Swan Hotel.

Darcy bent over her hand and kissed it. His eyes, raised to hers, conveyed everything she needed to know.

"You had better go, Fitz," she said.

He straightened and nodded, kissed her on the cheek and was gone.

As she let herself into the room, she told herself that waiting until they were at Pemberley was sensible, that they should not cause embarrassment to Georgiana who, albeit delighted to have Elizabeth for her sister, was sensitive and shy and still only sixteen. Indeed, apart from the effect on Georgiana of their obviously sharing a bed chamber, the impersonal, unfamiliar hotel rooms would rob the experience of much of its pleasure and allure. Also, the anticipation was becoming quite exquisite in itself and she hugged herself as she quickly fell asleep from the fatigue caused by today's jouncing carriage ride.

Chapter 2

THE morrow, however, brought a change of sentiment to Elizabeth. As the chaise drove through the extensive park, Elizabeth was reminded of her first visit to Pemberley during the summer tour around Derbyshire with her Aunt and Uncle Gardiner. She had been in a state of consternation at the time, most apprehensive lest she had been misinformed by the chambermaid at the Kings Arms at Lambton and it transpired that the master of the house was not really absent. On this occasion, driving through the same grounds, she felt barely less apprehension. The vast responsibility of the position she had taken on as the mistress of Pemberley was beginning to be comprehended, indeed had been threatening to overwhelm her all day, causing a mild nausea to settle on her and prompting Darcy to enquire quietly if she was quite well. She had assured him that she was.

By contrast, Georgiana was clearly excited to be nearly home at last and strained to see as much of the passing view as was visible.

Darcy had taken her hand a number of times. The gesture was comforting and reassuring but in front of Georgiana little could be said. Elizabeth certainly did not wish her lack of assurance to be communicated to her sister, possibly undermining the girl's confidence in her at such an early stage, and she resolved to act with every outward appearance of poise and resoluteness even if it was a struggle to do so.

Moreover, the servants when she met them would sense any weakness. While avoiding an overbearing countenance, she must not allow herself to be an object of contempt such to be taken advantage of.

It struck her forcibly that her life had changed forever. There would be no more lively household of loving parents and talkative sisters, no more strolls to nearby Meryton and no more local, relatively informal events. She began to hope fervently that her family would come to Pemberley for Christmas.

Darcy had been appalled at the society of rural Hertfordshire on first coming to Netherfield with Bingley. He was accustomed, it had seemed, to more sophisticated company, though Bingley had accused him of being fastidious, therefore perhaps she would be quite equal to the company in which she would be moving. She was, she told herself, never usually lost for words. She would have to keep up with the cream of society from now on, to make the best of it and make every effort to succeed at her new position managing a large house. The servants would expect her to be in charge, to be commanded by her. She must rise to the challenge.

A galling notion was that the arrogant Caroline Bingley would very probably have taken on such new duties with no doubts about her abilities or suitability. Elizabeth turned her head and searched her husband's profile for a few seconds.

But he does not love Caroline Bingley; he loves me.

And suddenly there it was, Pemberley House below them, bathed in moonlight, as they topped the hill. Her memory had not deceived her. She was conscious that Darcy was watching her as the chaise wound into the valley and crossed the bridge. She gazed at the house and the lake to the front of it in which was reflected the face of the moon, a smile at last brightening her features.

"Is it as you remember, Elizabeth?" Darcy asked her.

"Oh, very much so."

She leaned nearer the window.

"If anything it is even more handsome and impressive than I recall."

All her misgivings fell away for the time being.

SHE should have expected this. After she, Darcy and Georgiana had climbed the frosty steps to the porticoed front door, Elizabeth was led by Darcy into the vast entrance hall where the whole of the household were lined up to welcome a new mistress. At the carriage, Darcy had instructed the footmen to leave the trunks for now and come up to the house. They had hurried in after Elizabeth, Darcy and Georgiana and stood in line with the rest.

Darcy shook the hand of the butler, calling him 'Patterson', and nodded and said hello to the others who variously curtsied and bowed. Elizabeth wondered what the form was. She decided to smile upon and say a very few words to each person, realising that too much familiarity would make them uncomfortable. They likewise bowed and curtsied to her and replied with "Welcome to Pemberley, Mrs Darcy" without exception as though it was rehearsed, which it probably was.

Mrs Reynolds, the housekeeper smiled at her in obvious recognition from her visit with the Gardiners in the summer. Should she too shake the hand of the butler? She had no idea. Darcy had said something to him. It sounded as though he was arranging a meeting with the man later. She decided merely to say hello. Georgiana smiled at them all and they returned her smiles, bowed and curtsied of course and said "Hello, Miss Darcy. Very pleased to see you again" and similar.

The little ceremony over, the servants dispersed save for Mrs Reynolds and Patterson.

"Mrs Darcy, Miss Darcy and I will take some wine in the blue drawing room, Mrs Reynolds," Darcy said, "however, I would speak to you first, Patterson. We will of course dine in our rooms as we usually do on such a late arrival as this."

He and Patterson walked away.

"Follow me," said Georgiana cheerfully.

MRS Reynolds and Mr Patterson had been summoned to the blue room by Darcy after they had refreshed themselves and Georgiana had excused herself.

"Would you show Mrs Darcy to her rooms, Mrs Reynolds," he had said.

And to Elizabeth: "I'll be along in a few minutes."

He had then walked off again with the butler.

After climbing the stairs with the housekeeper, Elizabeth tried to memorise the way to her rooms. It was not a long walk through the chilly passages but Elizabeth, far from being tired, was having to make an effort to repress her elation and it was clouding her concentration. She did not, during her first days in her new home, wish to enter the wrong rooms and cause embarrassment. In truth, her spirits were so high that she could have skipped along the landing had it been permissible to do so but of course it was not. Soon, she and Fitz would be alone together properly for the first time. She was literally having to swallow down her joyfulness.

The effort not to rhapsodise in the presence of Mrs Reynolds over the suite of rooms when they reached them was considerable. Besides her bedroom, adjoining dressing room and a closet, she was to have the exclusive use of a sitting room with a small dining table, comfortable seating and an escritoire. All the rooms were richly appointed and merry fires crackled in their hearths. The table, already set for two Elizabeth observed, bore covered dishes for their meal.

It was in the sitting room that Mrs Reynolds was about to leave Elizabeth, saying that her trunk had been brought up and unpacked. Her maid, Peggy, she was told, had attended to the stowing of her clothes while they were in the blue room and would come and assist Mrs Darcy to undress. One of the maids, Elizabeth now recalled, had quietly spoken her name as Peggy during the introductions in the great hall. Elizabeth strained to recall her features, yet found she had but a shaky memory of the girl.

"She's a good girl," said Mrs Reynolds, "and quite a clever girl. She is young, but she needs the advancement. I hoped you and she would be a good match for each other."

"I am sure we shall," Elizabeth assured Mrs Reynolds but told her that she would not have need of the maid and would manage for herself tonight and she continued:

"I wished to say, Mrs Reynolds, that I will do my utmost to be a good and conscientious mistress at Pemberley and act in every wise fairly towards you all who serve at Pemberley. I have heard much hitherto of the high regard in which Pemberley is held. I hope that I can continue to foster what is clearly a harmonious household to the benefit of all the inhabitants. And, Mrs Reynolds, I would be most humbly grateful for your assistance and guidance in familiarising me with the ways and methods of Pemberley."

Elizabeth hoped that her small speech would have created the right impression to this servant of long-standing who knew so much about Pemberley; more, probably, than she, Elizabeth, would ever know.

"Thank you very much, ma'am," was the older woman's reply. "It would be my honour to help you in any way that I can. You need only ask."

Mrs Reynolds' lined face betrayed some relief. Her voice, Elizabeth felt, had deepened with emotion. It seemed to portray a degree of consideration for Elizabeth's situation and Elizabeth was likewise relieved. She reminded herself that the servants here would all wonder how a new mistress might perform, whether her arrival would in fact cause them some trouble. As to the emotion, Elizabeth had already perceived Mrs Reynolds to be a kindly woman of good sense. She would doubtless have already reckoned on a young lady, a new wife and a new mistress of such a large house, needing a helping hand and her heart had seemingly been softened by the young lady's entreaty.

"I am most grateful to you, Mrs Reynolds," she said.

The housekeeper smiled and curtsied.

"If that is all, Mrs Darcy, I will take my leave. You need only ring the bell pull if you need anything and a servant on duty will attend you."

"Yes, certainly, Mrs Reynolds."

LEFT to herself, Elizabeth wandered from room to room, touching the fine material of the furniture, curtains and bed hangings, turning the key and pulling down the hinged surface of the escritoire, opening its drawers and compartments, imagining what letters she might write to Jane and others.

She sat five minutes at the dressing table removing the uncomfortable pins from her hair and letting it cascade down her back. Then she stood again and resumed her meandering. Vases and bowl of evergreen cuttings gave the rooms a freshness, as of the gardens and woods.

But what principally struck her were the paintings. A number were of an older man and woman both together and alone. Darcy's father and mother Elizabeth opined. A miniature of a baby rested on the mantelpiece of the sitting room. Would this be Darcy himself? She must ask. The portrait in the gallery of the older Darcy grown to maturity which had so arrested her earlier in the year when she and the Gardiners had toured the house was of course not here. Therefore she fixed her attention on the miniature, a representation of a healthy, pleasing-looking infant with surprisingly alert, dark eyes.

It was before this likeness, in earnest contemplation of it, that she was standing when a pair of strong arms surrounded her waist and a face nuzzled into her hair. Darcy had crept in unnoticed. A smile sprang instantly to her mouth, accompanied by a sharp intake of breath, as his own breath warmed her neck and his lips gently touched her ear.

"Fitz," was all she could say.

"Lizzy, beautiful Lizzy. Do you wish to dine now?" he whispered.

She turned round in his arms and they kissed at least as passionately as they had on their walks together at Longbourn before their marriage, but now there was an increased urgency to their embraces.

Her face buried in his shoulder, she fought to bring her desire under control, but to no avail.

"I would as well eat later, Fitz."

"Then we are of a like mind."

So saying, he lifted her in his arms and walked towards the bedroom.

ELIZABETH gazed lazily around the room from her recumbent position, listening to the faint sounds of her husband at the dining table in the adjoining room, the clink of knife and fork and the pouring of wine into a glass. She had declined the invitation to join him, preferring to languish in the afterglow of their full union.

It had been exquisite, and nought so uncomfortable as rumour suggested it would be on a first encounter. Yes, he had been gentle to begin with, as well as very loving as he kissed her face, ears, neck and then, unexpectedly and, intensely pleasurably, sucked, licked and nipped at her body in various hitherto private places.

She found herself gasping and her back arching at his touch. But once they were coupled, she had spontaneously urged him on, to their ultimate mutual satisfaction.

He had, after a while, expressed himself to be in need of nourishment and hoped she would not object to his leaving her for a short time for the table. Blood streaked the bed linen, Elizabeth observed, when he pulled back the coverlet. Neither of them had given it much attention, so well-established was it that this would happen when a lady's maidenhood was first breached.

In due course, her husband returned to the bedroom and, throwing off his dressing gown, climbed naked into the bed beside her. She too was naked. She had surprised herself by her wantonness, having anticipated being embarrassed and shy to expose herself even to a husband but it had not been so.

Fitz held her affectionately.

"What would it please you to do tomorrow? I was thinking that in the next few weeks, we could spend time walking together. I could take you round the woods, the shrubberies and the pleasure-ground and help you with your riding skills as I perceived at Longbourn that you and your sisters were given little tuition in horsewomanship.

"In a day or two, I must spend some time with my steward, that is my estate steward, but most of the next few weeks I hope we will spend largely in one another's company."

"But will not Georgiana feel neglected?"

"I will see that she does not. She has some friends locally and I will arrange for a carriage to take her to them and bring her friends here. And," he said as he rolled over onto her and resumed planting kisses on her face and neck, "she loves to practise for hours at the pianoforte. And her companion, Mrs Annesley, will be arriving soon."

"Just as you say, Fitz."

Chapter 3

ELIZABETH'S fears of isolation and loneliness in this vast house many miles it seemed from any other notable habitations, it transpired, were largely ill-founded. In the following weeks, scarcely was Elizabeth able to complete a letter to Jane or her family, take an exploratory stroll in the grounds, continue her riding tuition with the groom Thomas after Darcy had turned some of his attention to his estate steward, choose a book from the extensive library or chat to Georgiana, but that a carriage drew into the drive or a horsewoman and her groom cantered up to the front of the house. It seemed as though the ladies of every large house in the country desired to make the acquaintance of the new mistress of Pemberley.

It was not in Elizabeth's nature to be daunted by rank or intimidated by sophisticated chatter. She found that she enjoyed the company and, surprisingly, the higher the rank of the visitor, the less discreet the disclosures made. Gossip, it appeared, was plainly not the preserve of the daughters of Meryton lawyers, but whereas her mother's and Aunt Philips's pronouncements tended to be censorious, these titled ladies of Derbyshire and other counties revelled in scandal.

And they were not above seeking intimate particulars of her married state with Darcy who had been one of the most eligible males for many miles prior to his sudden marriage. Elizabeth struggled to be discreet while avoiding the appearance of a prude who denied her husband the joys of the marriage bed.

Nor were these ladies slow to impart the minutiae of their own marriages, that is if they were already wed and, if not, they still had experiences to divulge. Infidelity was not uncommon it seemed amongst these ladies of high rank. Elizabeth had frequently to stifle an intake of breath at what she was hearing and turn to ascertain that the door was closed lest Georgiana should chance to walk in on any of these incautious communications.

Her mind reeled as to how these ladies avoided the necessary consequences of their actions. There were some dark hints of apothecaries who would put an end to troublesome and inconvenient conditions by administering potions or even the use of surgery.

For those who did not trust the discretion or abilities of the apothecaries or who did not wish to pay their high prices, there were evidently old women in various villages and towns hereabouts to whom it was possible to resort for potions to bring an end to unfortunate conditions. Although it was recounted that some months' absence on some pretext was another recourse.

In a knowing manner, one lady suggested cultivating friends with hothouses. Elizabeth smiled as she wondered what this could possibly mean.

"Upon my word, Mrs Darcy, you must know that lemons have uses other than the culinary," said her visitor and would say no more, leaving Elizabeth to exercise her imagination to its limits.

This talk reminded Elizabeth that she would be expected in the not too distant future to produce an heir and there had certainly been no lack of opportunity to bring such about by the normal means. However, since arriving here, her menses had come and gone. She told herself that there was much time ahead to furnish any number of offspring and was not particularly saddened for she was enjoying this honeymoon period with Fitz. For now, their love was all and more than she could have hoped for.

It was not always possible to predict that a marriage would be happy. She had seen many a couple who were not, or who had made the best of an indifferent match. She thought most especially of her good friend Charlotte in this case, now even farther away than when she had left Hertfordshire for Hunsford in Kent on her marrying the Reverend Collins. Their match was decidedly of the making-the-best variety. She often hugged herself at her good fortune of having married well and to a man she could truly love and respect. The love was uppermost at this time and was to be relished and enjoyed to its fullest.

Of all her callers, Harriet Layham, a baronet's daughter, was decidedly the most likely to become a special friend. A few months younger than Elizabeth, she was as yet unmarried and, blessedly, did not display the worldliness of some of Elizabeth's other new friends.

"My father wishes to effect a match for me with the Earl of Langford but, Elizabeth, I barely know him and he resides at some distance. Papa says he will arrange some meetings, but I...there are other young men with whom I would much prefer to make a closer acquaintance who live hereabouts and who are quite respectable; quite wealthy actually. But I have only been out just over a year. I know I must marry and yet to be wed to a stranger is...an awful prospect. You are so lucky to have many sisters as you have told me. It must...dilute the pressure on one to marry as soon as possible."

"Well, I do not know that it necessarily does. In my family at least, it acts like an echo. Every noteworthy particular on any subject is repeated and passed on, getting louder each time."

And Elizabeth related to her friend the proposal made to her by Mr Collins who was to inherit the Longbourn estate on her father's death, due to the estate being entailed to a male heir only.

"'Tis a common enough arrangement. There was indeed some pressure on me to accept Mr Collins's proposal."

"And you refused? That was exceeding daring of you. I do not know whether I would have had the courage to do so in your position."

"The pressure was from my mother. My father, well, he was disdainful of Mr Collins. We all were as he is such a foolish man, apart from possibly my mother. As my father put it to me with my mother standing there—I will never forget his words—'An unhappy alternative is before you, Elizabeth. From this day you must be a stranger to one of your parents. Your mother will never see you again if you do *not* marry Mr. Collins, and I will never see you again if you *do*!'"

Harriet's eyes opened wide in surprise. Then a broad smile lit her face.

"Your father said *that*. Is your father always given to such eccentric phraseology?"

"Pretty much. We grew very used to it. My poor mother. Even in spite of Papa's attitude, there was a terrible to-do about it. My dearest friend, Charlotte Lucas, I feel, took unfair advantage of the situation. She was twenty-seven and I suppose I cannot really blame her. In no time, she had secured an offer of marriage from Mr Collins to herself. It soured our friendship quite considerably at the time."

Harriet laughed aloud.

"Oh, Elizabeth, I am sorry but you make it sound so comical, as though it were a stage farce."

"Indeed, it was not at the time." Elizabeth, remembering, shook her head. "It was coupled with the intelligence that Charles Bingley, to whom my sister Jane is now married and with whom she was already in love, had left the neighbourhood and it was not known when he would return. This was all a year ago. My mother had high hopes that Mr Bingley would make an offer to Jane any day. The two occasions happening at the same time left her in a most pitiable state."

"And yet it has all turned out so well."

"It might not have. It was mere chance that Fi...William and I met again which led to our marrying. And Jane too."

It brought to mind another event which Elizabeth would just as well not be known abroad, even to her new-found friend, that of Lydia's elopement with Wickham. She wondered if Harriet knew anything of George Wickham having grown up in the neighbourhood. It was best to keep silent on the subject.

"And do please call me Lizzy. Everyone else does."

Except for Georgiana. She would have to attempt to address that sooner rather than later.

"Thank you, Lizzy. In spite of what you say, I still envy you for having a big family. Having no brothers or sisters as I told you, it was very lonely when I was a child. I was actually glad to be sent away to school, and luckily it was a good, happy place. I have heard that there are some which are not. And I am so happy to have you now as a good friend. I find myself impatient to meet your family as you say they are to come here over Christmas. I will persuade my parents to issue an invitation for you all to dine with us."

"I am sure that would be most welcome."

"EDWARD Danvers," said Darcy that night when she told him of her friend's dilemma. Indeed he laughed quietly in the dark after they had extinguished the candles. "She will be a most unfortunate young woman if she is forced to marry *him*."

Elizabeth was mildly alarmed at this news.

"Why, Fitz? Is there something wrong with him?"

"I can't be precisely sure of course, but it is said abroad that his preference is for young men rather than young women."

"I..."

Elizabeth knew not how to respond. Innocent as she had largely been of matters to do with physical love, she had no knowledge of anything other than love between men and women.

Darcy seemed to understand this without being told.

"My love, it is the case with some men that they are not attracted to women."

He left her to draw the obvious conclusion. Elizabeth pondered on this.

"I think I have read oblique allusions to such thing, but I did not understand them. Some people of course remain unmarried," she acknowledged. "But you are suggesting that this man...that he...has carnal knowledge of men rather than women."

"Precisely. Although it is mere rumour. I cannot say if it is truly the case. But if it is, and if she submits to pressure to marry him, the outlook is not good."

"Oh, poor Harriet. I wonder, should I tell her?"

She felt him shrug beside her.

"It is for you to decide. It might not be true."

"Do you think it is?"

"Yes, I do, but I could be wrong."

"How do you know?"

"Oh, hints and japes over the years. And some who say they have actually been...approached by him. Not me, I hasten to say. My rejection of any such advance would have been less than cordial."

Elizabeth laughed softly. "I have no difficulty believing it. So probably I should tell her, then."

"Men so disposed are sometimes referred to as mollies. You should keep it to yourself Lizzy. The act is punishable by death, execution, under the law."

Elizabeth drew a sharp breath. "Oh, my goodness. But she may need to defy pressure on her to marry him. She would be able to tell her parents and thus avert a disaster."

"All I would say to that is that not all fathers are so amiable as your own on such occasions."

"But surely the family will be desirous of an heir and...well...the prospects would seem to be much diminished if the Duke's predilections lie elsewhere than with his wife."

Darcy chuckled.

"Predilections! Yes, that is an excellent way to express Edward Danvers's preferences. But your friend's father, even if he knew about the Earl, which he probably does, may determine that Danvers would be able to manage to service his wife a sufficient number of times to achieve the desired result."

"Poor Harriet. It makes her sound like one of my father's sows."

"Speaking of sows, would you care to accompany me to the farms the day after tomorrow? On horseback. We would come near to Lambton at one point and I could order us a cold luncheon at the Kings Arms to break our little tour."

"Oh yes, Fitz. Nothing would give me greater pleasure," she told him, the subject of Harriet's marriage difficulties for the time being forgotten. "We were not allowed to take much interest in the farm at Longbourn, although Papa spent a good deal of his time there and I suppose still does."

"I would be obliged if you would ask Mrs Reynolds to organise saddlebags of any food which can be spared, indeed to assemble any surplus rugs and thick clothing at this time of year and I will carry them. There are a number of poor cottages on our route whose occupants are always in need of relief."

Elizabeth's mind irresistibly retreated a year or more to her Aunt Philips's drawing room in Meryton and an evening at whist enjoying coffee and muffins, being encouraged to believe that it was Darcy's family and *filial* pride which was the reason Darcy gave his money freely, displayed hospitality, assisted his tenants, and relieved the poor. The cruel inference was that Darcy did this to bolster himself in the view of others and not out of any compassion for those less well off than himself. The person conveying this warped intelligence was Mr Wickham, then the toast of Meryton society, now known to be a liar, a spendthrift debtor and a reckless seducer of young ladies.

"You are most generous, Fitz."

"'Tis nought, as you know, Lizzy. In our fortunate position, we must help others for without such relief some may well perish."

He paused.

"And I am gladdened, Lizzy, that you have found such an eminently suitable friend and so quickly. The family is generally held in good esteem and, although Sir Peter Layham is known to wield a heavier-than-necessary hand over his family, he is not essentially a bad man and Lady Layham works hard to provide much charity in the neighbourhood and I believe Miss Layham assists her."

"Well, it is a small family over which to wield a hand, heavy or otherwise. Harriet has no brothers or sisters. I begin to feel fortunate to have had a large family, whatever their individual follies."

"Follies indeed. And we will renew our acquaintance with all, or most of, those follies you speak of very soon over the Christmas festivities. And I will only have Colonel Fitzwilliam to hold up my end over Christmas."

"Delighted I shall be to see him again. Very especially as he could not be at our wedding. He has, I am sure, no significant follies to speak of."

"I could not vouch for that precisely, Lizzy."

The tone of his voice was light and Elizabeth quietly laughed, squeezed his arm and kissed his shoulder, although she also knew full well that the arrival of her noisy family with their divers foibles and idiosyncrasies would be most likely to ruffle, to some extent, the smoothness and order of life at Pemberley.

Chapter 4

BUT Elizabeth had not to await the coming of her family for her own growing contentment to be shattered. The morrow brought a number of letters for Elizabeth. Darcy was away with his steward and the letters were delivered to her rooms after he left early and were placed on the small table just inside her sitting room.

Elizabeth almost yelped with glee but restrained herself even though no one else was present when she discovered the bundle. She recognised immediately Jane's hand and that of her mother. A letter which must be from Charlotte Collins was a surprise and one from Aunt Gardiner was most welcome. A whole morning of pleasure lay ahead, soaking up the contents of these missives and composing her replies, though there would be little time left before the correspondents, apart from Charlotte, boarded stage coaches to travel to Derbyshire for their sojourn at Pemberley.

And, good heavens! There was a fifth letter, Elizabeth belatedly noticed. And in a gentleman's hand. It took her but a second to determine who was the author of the letter. He had written to her once before and she could not mistake his hand. She was married now as she had not been in June of 1797, had indeed not even met Darcy, but still, her heart beat faster to recall the rector's dark eyes and charming countenance. She thought never to hear from him again. But here it was. A letter from him.

She was powerless to cast it aside and read first her family's and good friend's communications. In a state of high passion, she pulled the seal apart and spread before her Mr Wilde's second letter ever to her, slightly dreading what it must convey. To have written to her at all must signal intelligence of some import.

And as it lay before her now, she could not avoid its full force and effect.

"ST FELIX RECTORY, MARBECH

FRIDAY, DECEMBER 7

DEAR MRS DARCY,

It is a little over fourteen months since I left Longbourn and I often find myself thinking fondly of my short time in the parish and of the kindness and friendship extended to me by you and your family. I read of your recent marriage in the Times and the Courier. I hope that it brings you the happiness and fulfilment which you deserve.

My position here is very satisfactory. The parish is much larger than Longbourn and the duties accordingly more onerous, though very enjoyable. My wife knows the parish far better than I and has been of invaluable assistance in familiarising me with the town."

Despite herself and her most happy situation, Elizabeth could not deny a small pang of jealously towards the fortunate Mrs Wilde. She continued to read.

"Pleasantries aside, Mrs Darcy, I would not have presumed to write to you, especially so soon after your marriage, were it not for the re-emergence into my life of a young lady who you will no doubt remember, namely Miss Helen St Clair, who now goes by the name of Isabella Scargill. The particulars of any marriage she may have contracted are not within my knowledge. I can only assume that she married a man by the name of Scargill."

Elizabeth recalled Helen's departure from Longbourn, her chief emotion at the time having been relief that Helen had left the neighbourhood for whatever reason.

"Mrs Scargill claims to now be a widow. I know not how she met the man nor in what circumstances she was left on her husband's death, but on her own account she now resides in

Nethermill. As you will be aware, this small village is not a huge distance from the Pemberley estate.

It was Mrs Scargill herself who related to me the aforementioned facts in a letter which was pushed through my letterbox very recently, signing herself 'Isabella Scargill, formerly Helen St Clair'. It did not arrive by the post therefore I must assume that Mrs Scargill was in Cambridgeshire and delivered the letter with the specific purpose, so it seemed, of issuing certain threats.

I must at this point acquaint you with the particulars of events which took place while you and your family were visiting Buxton in the summer of 1797 and which are known only to my sisters and me, and of course Mrs Scargill. For the sake of Helen St Clair, as she was at the time, I chose to avert the prosecution which could have taken place. My reasons were twofold. I wished to avoid a scandal and I now wonder if this desire was not misplaced. More importantly, I also had reason at the time to suspect that there was doubt about Miss St Clair's guilt. In addition, I was reluctant to tarnish the reputation and future of a member of my congregation who was young and who I judged, possibly wrongly I now concede, regretted her actions."

What on earth Helen had done, or possibly done, that was so heinous, Elizabeth could not imagine. There was nothing to do but read on and find out, which she did.

"The particulars are thus which I will attempt to summarise. While I was absent from home for nearly a day, my sisters left the house to walk to Meryton. I should explain that the door of the Rectory was never locked. Having found that she had left her shopping list behind, my sister Agnes ran back and discovered that Miss St Clair had entered the Rectory, alone not a major wrong, yet rather disquieting. Agnes saw Miss St Clair descending the stairs and gaining the dining parlour. So far as Sarah and I have ascertained, Miss St Clair did not immediately see Agnes and Agnes now thinks that Miss St Clair may have somehow adulterated my table wine.

Miss St Clair did then notice Agnes and what happened thereafter is somewhat confused. Agnes was quite frightened and had remained standing in the hall. It seems that Miss St Clair tried to leave the house and there was a scuffle or Miss St Clair tried to push Agnes out of her way. Whether Miss St Clair hit Agnes over the head with a heavy statue in the hall, or whether Agnes fell heavily against the edge of a table and injured her head is not clear.

By the time Sarah decided that Agnes had been away for too long and walked home, Miss St Clair had left and Sarah found Agnes on the floor. At first she thought that Agnes was dead and had knocked over the table and ornament when she fell. She ran outside and was some way toward Meryton when she was able to ask a farm worker to go and summon Dr Baldwin.

Dr Baldwin assured my sister that Agnes was alive. He administered smelling salts and Agnes started to show signs of life and tried to talk. Between them, he and Sarah carried Agnes upstairs to her room and put her to bed. She wasn't able to tell them much at that time. There was no blood but Dr Baldwin ascertained that Agnes had suffered a blow to the head or had somehow hit her head. He thought Agnes should rest but that she would recover and left Sarah with some medicine and Sarah sat by her. Agnes was sufficiently recovered after an hour to tell Sarah something of what had happened but she could not be certain that Helen St Clair had deliberately injured her.

When I arrived home, Sarah expressed the wish to call a constable. I dissuaded her for the reasons above-mentioned and I am glad to say that Agnes made a full recovery after a week. However, after taking a few glasses of wine with my meal that evening, I was violently ill for two days.

I would add that I know not why she might have attempted to poison me. She would probably have known that my sisters do not drink wine."

At this point, Elizabeth frowned down at the letter. She found it odd that Helen might have wished to poison Mr Wilde. On the contrary, it was her impression that Helen had been in love with Mr Wilde. But who knew what actions the workings of a disturbed mind might produce or what warped motives might stimulate such a person?

"My sisters and I were saved the awkwardness of meeting Miss St Clair thereafter by virtue of her leaving the area with her sister to visit relatives and she did not return before I departed from Longbourn. Perchance it was during her time away that she met her husband.

Having said thus much, I feel no doubt of your secrecy. Before I close, I must inform you of the nature of Mrs Scargill's threats. I do not know how much your father has told you of the period during which I was endeavouring to ascertain the whereabouts of Alice Carpenter and her child but, as you know, you and I met a number of times on the occasion and Helen St Clair seems to have witnessed and paid particular attention to those meetings between us. Her threats to me in her letter were to inform my wife of some improper association between us and thus seek to disrupt my marriage if she could.

The letter is somewhat rambling. I am sorry to have to relate that it also hints at harm befalling you and your family. She appears to have no motive apart from malice. Her letter contained no demands for money, for example, and she did not during her presumed visit to Cambridgeshire carry out her threats to communicate with my wife.

By the by, I believe the Christian name of Isabella which Mrs Scargill now uses to be a variation of the name Elizabeth."

A shiver ran through Elizabeth at these words. Of course people did change their names and Mr Wilde had not ventured to advance any theory why Helen had done so, if indeed she had at all, but to have adopted a Christian name similar to Elizabeth's had a sinister, almost threatening air about it.

Although, too, Isabella was surely not an unusual name.

Upon my word, thought Elizabeth, Mr Wilde's own horse had been called Bella, presumably also a corruption of the name Elizabeth. Her own cousin, one of Uncle Gardiner's daughters, had been baptised Beth, which must surely be a derivative of Elizabeth.

"Were it not for the above-mentioned events of the summer before last, I might have dismissed the letter as a prank, but the wrong-doing perpetrated by Helen St Clair at that time persuades me that she probably was the author of the letter. I leave it to you what conclusions to draw from this unpleasant tale but I felt it incumbent upon me to warn you in case Mrs Scargill should approach you or your husband or indeed attempt to cause you harm.

I would caution you to take care and wish you good health and every good fortune.

I remain, as ever, your humble servant and friend,

ANDREW WILDE"

Cause me harm, Elizabeth pondered, or both me and Fitz? Harm befalling my family? She sat back astounded and deeply discomfited at what she had read and unable to fully comprehend his account of Helen's trespass into the Rectory. Why would she do such a thing, possibly hitting Mr Wilde's sister and risking the force of the law being applied against her? And poisoning him? Such offences could lead to a gaol sentence or even transportation.

Elizabeth tried to examine the case coolly and logically. The poisoning could have been accidental, or perhaps she had done nothing and the wine had been spoilt without having tasted bad. It made little sense. So far as Elizabeth knew, Helen hugely admired Mr Wilde, although her regard for him had bordered on the obsessive.

Coupled with Agnes's inability to give a clear account of events, she started to comprehend why Mr Wilde had refused to call for the constable.

But the two particulars which dictated in favour of Helen's actions being deliberately pernicious and therefore not merely part of a course of unfortunate, accidental events were the threats to disrupt Mr Wilde's marriage, the mention of harm to her family and the alleged change of name to one similar to Elizabeth's.

And then it struck her that she must of course show the letter to Fitz. She had a duty to do so. Quite why she shrank from this obvious responsibility she found it hard to reason with herself. She had done nothing wrong. But that might not matter. She would have been the medium by which unpleasantness reached Pemberley, even if the threats alluded to or any other difficulties potentially arising failed to come about in practice, and she felt instinctively that Fitz would not appreciate it.

Fitz may be forced to alert some of the servants to possible danger which would no doubt anger him, or was this placing too much importance on the ravings of a damaged person?

Elizabeth sighed to herself. She should perhaps put the letter aside for a day or two, at least until after the ride out which she and Fitz planned to take tomorrow and which she so eagerly anticipated. She would read her other correspondence and then think about it again.

And at least now she had a friend, Harriet Layham, with whom she could discuss her concerns, although the precise depths of her relationship with Mr Wilde would have to remain closed to anyone other than she and the gentleman himself.

"MRS Reynolds."

Elizabeth had asked to see the housekeeper in the blue drawing room because it was a room she used to sit and read being smaller than many of the other rooms used for the reception of visitors or, in this case, to talk to a servant. She had asked the older woman to sit down which seemed to cause her some disquiet but she did so, perching on the edge of her seat.

"I was hoping," continued Elizabeth, "to ask you about visitors who seek entry to Pemberley to view the house as I did with my aunt and uncle in the summer. I believe you recall the visit."

"Of course, Mrs Darcy."

"I wondered how often this happens, whether it happens at all at this time of year or mainly in the summer months and whether people usually come individually or as a group."

Mrs Reynolds took the question seriously and Elizabeth could see her considering how to reply. Happily, she did not question the reason for the enquiry.

"Well, ma'am, 'tis certainly more frequent than it was some years ago that people wish to see the inside of the house. There are more applications in the summer of course but local people are starting to apply. Yes, sometimes there are parties of the gentry or other local groups. Why, just two or three weeks past I admitted a small party of ladies from Nethermill. They were interested in the history of the building as I recall. And the history of the family. They asked about any heirs of the present Mr Darcy —"

Mrs Reynolds stopped. A look of alarm spread across her kindly features, indeed something approaching fear.

"Why, Mrs Darcy, are you quite well?"

Elizabeth realised that she had put her face into her hands. Dealing with the servants of a house such as this was much more difficult than at Longbourn House where servants were accustomed to the frequent hysterics and excesses of her mother and, formerly, the squabbles and high spirits of Lydia and Kitty, and did not flinch at displays of emotion.

Elizabeth raised her head. "Yes, yes, Mrs Reynolds. I am very well. Just a little tired from my walk this morning."

She had taken her other letters out with her and had spent two hours rambling while reading the letters without taking in very much of her family's news, thinking hard instead on Mr Wilde's communications. And now, to hear that a group of ladies from Nethermill had been present in the house so recently was most unsettling.

She observed the relief on Mrs Reynolds's face at her reassurance. Doubtless, the housekeeper would not wish to be found to have been the cause of seriously discomfiting Mrs Darcy. This, again, was another departure from the normal course of events at Longbourn House where gossip of any kind, however riotously received, was actively welcomed, whether from servants or otherwise.

Elizabeth adjudged that she had better bring an end to this interview soonest but wished to explore another particular with the housekeeper before concluding.

"Mrs Reynolds, do you know of a family by the name of Scargill hereabouts?"

Mrs Reynolds did not respond immediately. Perhaps she expected Elizabeth to expand on the reason for choosing a specific name. Elizabeth, not wishing to influence the reply, said nothing.

"Well, Mrs Darcy, it is a common name in these parts. I cannot think of any person of note by that name." She went on to clarify this statement. "I mean, any members of the gentry."

"Hmm," said Elizabeth. Surely if a woman called Scargill had been amongst the party of recent visitors alluded to, Mrs Reynolds would recall without being asked.

"Is any record kept of the names of visitors who are shown the house, Mrs Reynolds?"

The housekeeper looked somewhat discomposed, as though she was being accused of failing somehow in her duties.

"Not as a general rule, ma'am. There is the visitors' book of course, kept in the hall."

"Yes, of course. Well, thank you, Mrs Reynolds. That will be all for now."

The housekeeper's relief at being released from this inquisition was palpable.

Chapter 5

THROUGHOUT the evening meal, Elizabeth felt Darcy casting speculative glances at her. She was of course usually more talkative and she tried to hide her anxiety by asking Georgiana questions about her day. She had little to relate herself than a solitary ramble.

"Oh, Elizabeth, I wish I had known. I am grown stale with so much time indoors practising at the pianoforte and writing lists for Christmas. I would have gladly accompanied you."

"I am sorry indeed, Georgiana. My mind was elsewhere. I received letters today from my mother, sister and aunt, and from my friend Charlotte Collins which I took out with me on my walk."

Darcy fixed her with a searching eye.

"Did Mrs Collins have anything to relate regarding my aunt, Elizabeth?"

"I...er, no, not that I can recall. Of course, Charlotte and Mr Collins are sensible of Lady Catherine's disapprobation of our marriage and doubtless have had repeated to them all the unflattering sentiments which she expressed in her letter to you, William. Hence, Charlotte's letter to me tactfully steered well clear of any mention of your aunt."

Georgiana looked on but said nothing. Despite Darcy's protective nature towards her, not all unpleasantness could be kept from her and she was well aware of the family rift.

"Yes, I suppose so," said Darcy.

"Charlotte did say that the baby William is well."

This much detail at least Elizabeth had retained. Charlotte had been delivered of a son within a week of Elizabeth's marriage, so Mrs Bennet had written to tell her, and the irksome notion could not be avoided that the very baby William spoken of would one day inherit the Longbourn estate. She brushed the thought aside.

Evidently from Mr Wilde's letter, it struck Elizabeth, the rector and his wife had no children as yet or he would surely have made reference to the occasion. But they had been married only a matter of fourteen months or thereabouts. Not a huge amount of time for the event to have occurred. Would she, Elizabeth, be discomposed if she had not produced an heir inside a twelve-month, or at least be carrying within her the next Darcy to enter the world? Darcy's voice cut abruptly into her musings.

"And your family? Are they all quite well?"

"Yes, quite well, William."

"Did they say on what date they hope to arrive here?"

"I don't think they said exactly."

Elizabeth tried to concentrate.

"I rather felt that they will be leaving at the beginning of next week, which should see them arrive here on the twentieth or twenty-first of the month. I have informed Mrs Reynolds."

"Good."

The watchful air remained about him.

"And my Aunt Gardiner," Elizabeth faltered on, "informs me that it is definite that their four children are to accompany them. They will probably set off soon with a view to arriving early next week. Again I have told Mrs Reynolds."

"Children in the house at Christmas! Oh, how wonderful," exclaimed Georgiana. "I will take Jake and Alfred up to the attics to look out all the old toys. You remember, Fitzwilliam, we have a hobbyhorse. They will take great delight in that and all the dolls and the doll's house. If we have snow, they will build a snowman and we can use the sledge to take them about."

"Yes." Elizabeth started to be infected by her sister's excitement. "We have always had wonderful times with the children at Christmas." She smiled at Darcy who nodded.

"Oh, and my other Aunt and Uncle Philips are to come here as well."

Darcy visibly wilted at that. Georgiana smiled, and Elizabeth would ordinarily have laughed, but tonight she had such a burden to bear. She must talk to Fitz later about Mr Wilde's letter.

"If you will excuse me," Georgiana dabbed at her mouth with her napkin and rose, "I must leave you. I am still choosing a gown for the ball on Saturday, despite your help yesterday, Elizabeth. I am so looking forward to it."

It would be Georgiana's first ball, which she was able to attend specifically because Elizabeth would be there. Not having a mother alive nor any other close female relative had rather limited Georgiana's social opportunities. Such assistance as Lady Catherine might have provided in that direction was closed off for the time being. Elizabeth was intending to attempt to rectify this void and further Georgiana's going more into company in the coming months, although the task would not be aided by her own unfamiliarity with Derbyshire society, added to which many of her new friends thus far were more worldly than would be suitable for Georgiana to keep company with.

"Yes, indeed," said Elizabeth.

Elizabeth hoped that, before her sister turned to leave, her own face did not betray her alarm at the sudden mention of the ball at Ashwick Hall in a few days' time. It was the seat of the Duke of Rotherham. She already had mixed feelings when contemplating her first public appearance with Fitz, but now that he might be displeased with her, the prospect of a long night navigating the complexities of the highest society of the country filled her with trepidation. She could only hope that some of her new friends would come to her assistance if necessary.

At least Pemberley's own ball was to be in June, happily some good time away. It had been an annual event until Darcy's mother died and now that Pemberley had a mistress again, it was to be revived. Then she, as the mistress of the house, would have to supervise all the arrangements. For the time being, she dismissed it from her mind.

She already had her own gown for Saturday's ball. Two new gowns had been made for her, her own dresses brought from Longbourn adjudged to be insufficiently grand. Peggy had been a huge help with the measuring and choice of materials and trim. A head-dress had been necessary as well, such as those worn by Caroline Bingley and Mrs Hurst which the Hertfordshire community had found to be the height of elegance.

And Peggy had been ecstatic when Elizabeth had given her a couple of her own old day dresses, as they were of a similar height and figure. She had hesitated to do so in case Peggy might be offended but her reaction had been quite the reverse. Elizabeth had noticed her eyeing the dresses when they were sorting out Elizabeth's clothes together and had made the offer lightly which Peggy had immediately accepted.

"Elizabeth." Darcy called her attention to him once his sister had quit the room.

He moved his chair to be closer to hers and took her hand in both of his, massaging hers gently and at one point bringing it to his lips. She examined the disarray of the table as he did so.

"Lizzy, my love, I know that five letters were brought to you today, yet you told us only of four."

Elizabeth raised her head sharply. So this was what occurred in a fine house. The actions of the wife of the master of the house were spied upon.

"Lizzy, do not be discomposed. I merely enquired after you when I arrived home. You're my wife. I care about you. And Patterson told me in passing that you had received a number of letters, he thought five. Please believe that there was no side to it. And there is none now."

Elizabeth, although she hoped this was how it was, was not wholly convinced.

"I see," she said.

Darcy sighed and looked about him, as though searching for an example.

Turning to her, he said, "I assume that when letters arrived at Longbourn House, everyone was interested. It is quite natural that they should be."

This was true, of course. Letters received at Longbourn were pounced upon and talked about. Nothing could be kept secret for very long at Longbourn.

She smiled at last. "All right."

"But, Lizzy, I know that something has distressed you. It is quite clear to me. And I cannot help thinking that this is due to the fifth letter."

Elizabeth turned her head away again, building up the courage to raise the exact content of the fifth letter and who had sent it. Darcy was evidently expecting her to tell him now, assuming he had settled any disquiet regarding the source of his intelligence, and largely he had.

"Do you have the letter with you, Lizzy?"

"I do. I hoped to tell you, to show it to you this evening when we could be alone. And I may as well let you read it now, rather than tell you what it says."

She pulled the letter from her sleeve and handed it over. Darcy unfolded it and his eye went straight to the end.

"Oh," he said. "The very handsome, the most charming Mr Wilde."

His tone was ironic.

Elizabeth rallied. "I told you about him, Fitz, how he had helped me find out what happened to our kitchen maid's child and how the boy now resides at Longbourn House with the groom and his wife." Somewhat defensively she added: "His charms and appearance were of no consequence."

"Were they not, indeed! At one time, on our arrival in Meryton, I could not move two feet but to be told of recollections of the rector's pleasing countenance. Bingley's sisters were the main channels of this intelligence."

Elizabeth was surprised. She had not known of this.

Darcy looked resigned. "Whatever is the case, I had better read the letter."

There was silence for five minutes at least. Elizabeth could not determine what he thought of the contents, whether he was disturbed by what he read. At length he said:

"Just remind me why you met Mr Wilde in secret as this letter implies."

"I think I told you before that it was because I thought that my parents would not have approved of my having any interest in the kitchen maid. It was they who had thrown Alice out, or allowed that to happen. I assumed they would have had no patience with my wish to ascertain her fate."

"Hmm," he nodded. Then he held the letter out loosely with one hand and, with the back of the other, flicked at a section of the letter a few paragraphs from the end. The gesture had about it a certain air of distaste.

"What," he said, "do you think he meant by this, about your

father and what he may or may not have told you regarding..." he peered down "'...the period during which I was endeavouring to ascertain the whereabouts of Alice Carpenter and her child.'?"

"I wondered the same thing, Fitz. I have no idea. My father told me that Mr Wilde intended to quit the parish and marry. Soon after that, the boy Peter came to Longbourn House and was placed with the groom and his wife and we left for Buxton. Mr Wilde must have first told Papa about Peter, for I did not."

"Well, you'll be able to ask your father soon. Do you really think this Helen or Isabella or whatever she's called could seriously cause any harm?"

"You never met the St Clair sisters, Fitz. They left Longbourn before you arrived in Hertfordshire. I am a poor judge of those with troubled minds, Fitz, who would do harm to others, but when I accepted an unexpected invitation to call on Helen shortly before Jane and I visited our Aunt and Uncle Gardiner in London, she rather frightened me. She pressed me to become one of the parish ladies who assisted Mr Wilde. It may sound innocuous enough, but her air of intensity was most disquieting. It was clear to me that she was in love with Mr Wilde. Although, so were half the ladies of Meryton and Longbourn."

"So it would seem," he said dryly.

"But, Fitz, I did ask Mrs Reynolds about visitors to Pemberley, about groups seeking access to see the house and she told me of a party of ladies from Nethermill a few weeks ago who were interested in Pemberley's history and that of the family. They also wanted to know if you had any heir."

"Did they, by God!" His brow creased and he seemed to take the matter seriously for the first time. "Were any of these ladies of the name of Scargill?"

"I do not know. I did not wish to ask Mrs Reynolds outright. I had asked her if the name Scargill was prevalent hereabouts and I suppose I thought she would say if she recalled a Mrs Scargill in the party. She alluded to the visitors' book when I inquired after any record kept of those visiting, but I have not looked at it yet."

"Well then, my love, come, shall we go and do so now?"

"Yes, indeed. Thank you, Fitz."

He thrust the letter into his pocket and took a candlestick from the table from which he lit a lamp on the mantel. Holding her hand, he led her out of the small family dining parlour. The visitors' book was kept on a table in the grand reception hall. The chandeliers were not lit at this time and, despite the candles in sconces, the table was still dimly lit. Darcy held up the lamp while Elizabeth opened the book and turned the pages. Together they scrutinised the last few entries assuming that any by the Nethermill party would be amongst them.

It took but a short time to find a number of signatures in an entry dated 29th November 1798. Some of the signatories gave their addresses as Nethermill. A few did not.

"These," pointed out Darcy, "are villages near Nethermill."

One of the signatures looked like Isabella Scargill, said to be of Nethermill.

"Well," said Darcy, his voice even but she detected some steeliness in his tones, "we will have to see what to do about this. First, I will get the attorney, Waring, of Lambton on to it. He will find out anything there is to find."

THAT night Darcy came to her bedroom with her, the room she had come to regard as *their* bedroom, but did not remain after their congress, throwing on his dressing gown and leaving her with a light kiss, saying that he would spend the night in his own room, not even in the adjoining dressing room. Elizabeth was so shocked that she failed to question this at first and in an instant he was gone. And he had taken the letter with him.

Despite Darcy having dismissed any notion that the servants would spy on her for their master, Elizabeth could not herself entirely banish the idea that this would happen, perhaps not as a deliberate practice, but at least in the normal course of things. Very likely, for a house the size of Pemberley, it would be entirely customary for the head of the house to be made aware of all that went on. Patterson would simply tell Darcy everything. He might fear for his job if he did not.

As she had thought of Mrs Reynolds, these servants wished to please in every respect and avoid to displease at every turn. If this was the case, then Elizabeth did understand, but it was not an easy knowledge to bear, that everything that happened to her was likely to be reported to her husband, even minor events. She almost wished she had made Fitz aware of the letter earlier, so that she would have remained ignorant, for now, of the implications of Patterson having told Darcy.

Knowing how cold and distant Darcy could be from his first few months at Netherfield, indeed until his manners seemed to have improved so astonishingly by the time of her tour of Derbyshire with her uncle and aunt that summer, she cried herself to sleep.

Chapter 6

ELIZABETH did not accompany Darcy around the farms the next day. She passed word to him via Peggy, who came to help her dress, that she was indisposed and he did not enquire after her. Could it be that their delightful honeymoon period had ended already and so unfairly? She had done nothing wrong. Apart from having enlisted Mr Wilde's assistance to discover the kitchenmaid's fate, she had had no control over the events of last year, of much of which it seemed she must be in ignorance judging from the reference to her father in Mr Wilde's letter, but still she was to be blamed.

Her only recourse would be to ask her father. He would be here soon enough. She and Darcy would just have to await his arrival.

The ball loomed frighteningly close, only three days away, including today. Elizabeth took out her gown and admired it. Despite the simple, high-waisted design, it was otherwise an elaborate garment with a heavy bow at the back, fine lace trimming, and jewels sewn into and gold thread weaved through the green brocade material. She held it up to herself in front of the looking-glass and saw how it brought highlights like emeralds to her eyes which were of dark blue in most situations. The colour of the dress must be reflected in her eyes. It was quite striking.

As she examined her reflection, she thought of Fitz dining alone and possibly glumly at the Kings Arms at Lambton. Should she feel a little sorry for him? But why should she? He had deserted her last night and made her feel unloved.

Quite suddenly she recollected herself. If Fitz wished to cast aside their young love and become like a stranger to her, then let him. If necessary she abruptly, and probably rashly, decided, she would return with her family to Longbourn after Christmas. She would not have to invite their pity. They need not know the real reason. No doubt she would tell Jane, but some plausible excuse would have to be concocted for the rest of her family.

An urgent inquiry, perhaps, into Helen Scargill, née St Clair. Yes, that would probably do. If her heart was broken in the process, then no one else need know.

But first there was the ball to get through. It was a great event. She must enjoy it. She *would* enjoy it and dance with as many men as sought her hand, seek out her friends and make sparkling conversation.

And she was as proud as he, Fitz. Above all, she must not let Fitz see how hurt she was. She would not keep to her room. She must show herself to the world, or at least to this household. She would visit Harriet tomorrow and have a cosy chat with her, never letting her friend know how unhappy she was.

She peered at her red-rimmed eyes in the glass then walked over to the wash-stand and splashed her face with water, patting it with a towel afterwards. A little dusting powder applied around her eyes saw away the redness and, using delicate movements, she brushed it free of her thick dark lashes with a moistened fine-toothed comb. It was her luck that hours of weeping did not render her face swollen and the skin unevenly blotched with red patches as it did some of her sisters. She was possibly a little pale. That was all. She pinched her cheeks and bit at her lips, bringing the blood to the surface.

She took up a pair of kid gloves and a bonnet and her eyes gleamed with renewed vigour as she rushed to the door, pulling it open. She nearly fell over backwards as, at the same time, the door flew towards her, pushed from the other side.

"Lizzy," Darcy caught her arm, steadying her and smiling. "Why such a hurry?"

She swallowed. "Oh, Fitz. I thought you would be in the inn at Lambton by now."

"Hmm. It did not appeal to me any longer. I will have to recompense the innkeeper. Where were you going?"

"Just out to take some exercise."

"May I join you, then?"

She could hardly refuse.

"One moment." He drew Mr Wilde's letter from his pocket and laid it on the table inside the door where it had rested the previous day with the others. "Let me return this. I took it with me to give the particulars to the Lambton lawyer."

"Of course."

They walked together along the corridor, down the wide staircase and to the boot and coat room. He seemed to be excessively attentive. He helped her on with her cloak and knelt and laced her boots, looking up at her, while she sat. Then he put on his own coat and they proceeded directly outside through the door which gave onto the side of the house.

"Lizzy," he said as they passed arm in arm along a path leading away to the wood. "I must explain."

"There is no need. I quite understand," she replied. "I have, or may have, brought some sort of dishonour on Pemberley. It is because of me that you have had to visit an attorney and may have to alert servants to the possibility of some harm being visited upon us. I am a nuisance therefore, not an asset. I quite see why you should be angry."

He stopped and turned to face her, compelling her to pause as well.

"Lizzy! It is not that at all."

She shrugged. "Well, I am resolved to make the best of it," she said with far more conviction than she felt.

"You are looking very beautiful today, Lizzy, as always, of course."

"You are very kind, sir."

"Lizzy, please do not be formal. It is my fault for last night. I am sorry, very sorry."

He touched her face with a gloved hand. "You must be able to see why I would be...disconcerted."

"Yes. I have become a hindrance."

He lowered his hand. "Do not say that. It is not true. It is...him, the Reverend Wilde, the most personable man ever to have set foot in Hertfordshire. Lizzy, were you in love with him?"

Her astonishment was great. This was the last thing she had imagined. Such a direct question was difficult to avoid.

"Why would you say that?"

"Lizzy, credit me with some sense. It appears from what I

heard that he was wildly attractive to women. You were meeting the man in secret. You only told me of the letter because of the menacing content, because you felt you had to."

She frowned. "Not only that. Although he would not have written to me at all were it not for Helen's communication." They were still standing facing each other, not far from the door. "Fitz, can we continue to walk."

He sighed. "Of course." And they resumed their stroll. "But Lizzy, may I speak plainly?"

This conversation was very strange, very difficult.

He hurried on. "I have to say that I was much surprised at how readily you...took to married life. It was a shock. Very pleasing of course, but still a shock to me."

They paced on. Elizabeth turned this over in her mind. She could not avoid her cheeks colouring. Naturally, he would have noticed her enthusiasm the first night and since, although his own approach to the joys of the marriage bed had hardly been awkward or fumbling. At last she said:

"Fitz, I hope you are not suggesting what I think you may be."

"I don't know. You tell me."

"Tell you what, Fitz? You are saying...Fitz you must know that...I was a maid when I first came here."

"I hope so, of course. Though I dare say such things can be faked."

"How could you even consider the possibility that I was not...chaste."

Her face flushed, more in anger than embarrassment at the turn the conversation had taken. She removed her arm from his and quickened her pace, striding ahead of him. The action did little to quell her anger which built with every step. He caught up with her and took her arm, turning her so that they stood facing one another again. She glanced up at the house.

"Fitz," she said, "someone may see us."

"I don't care. Tell me this at least. Did he ever make any improper advances towards you?"

"Indeed, he did not." This, at any rate, was the truth. She hoped he would not press for more particulars regarding her feelings towards the man, but her affirmation seemed to satisfy him.

"Good. And again I apologise for last night. It was as hard for me as maybe it was for you."

She looked down at the ground. "I was bereft without you, Fitz."

"Oh, Lizzy. I am a fool. You know how much I love you. Do you love me still?"

He caught her in an embrace.

"Of course I do. More than anything, ever"

He kissed her discreetly on her cheek which faced away from the house.

"Can we then regard this as a lovers' tiff? I barely saw half the farms today nor had time to go to the cottages as I had to visit the lawyer and also wanted to come home to you. Will you come with me tomorrow as we planned to do today? I must get round to the other farms. And the warm clothing and food still has to be handed out. It would be most beneficial for you to be able to hand over relief to these people so that they can see the excellent new mistress."

Happiness filled her heart. His bad mood was due merely to jealousy of another man, which was very sweet in its way. It did not result from any censure on her for indirectly causing possible trouble at Pemberley. It was as well to have the reason for his actions last night and this morning openly expressed than left to simmer quietly.

She smiled broadly as she clutched him to her. All thoughts of visiting Harriet the next day were dispelled.

"It would be delightful. I would love to come with you. And thank you, Fitz, for being so kind and understanding."

Chapter 7

THE morrow dawned fine and bright. They breakfasted early in her sitting room, *their* sitting room as she liked to think of it, after which she put on one of her new riding habits. She chose the grey one. The other of bright scarlet she adjudged too ostentatious to go amongst the poor. Darcy agreed. Her hat was without plumes and her cravat very plain.

They set forth with two saddlebagsful of food on Darcy's horse, and cloths and clothing in saddlebags carried by Elizabeth's horse.

She was getting to know her mount, a placid little bay called Annie, and she sometimes visited Annie in the stables with treats. Annie had started to look out for her.

The Pemberley estate was extensive consisting of many small farms and some very large ones. After leaving the park, they travelled on roads in quite good condition which, Darcy said, he had to maintain as they were part of the estate. The smaller farms were tenanted. The larger ones were managed by his estate steward, a refined and affable man of middle years named Sanders whom they visited first.

Sanders's house, to Elizabeth's eye, was quite grand, almost the size of Longbourn House. So, George Wickham, son of the now deceased previous steward, must have grown up here, Elizabeth thought, as she cast about the large entrance hall, and well-appointed sitting room whence they were ushered by a maid on their arrival.

"I'll go and tell Mr and Mrs Sanders you are here, sir, ma'am."

Within a minute, Mrs Sanders rushed in to greet them and offer them refreshment. Having been on horseback for an hour, Elizabeth gladly accepted, as did Darcy.

Mr Sanders was not long behind.

"I believe, Mrs Darcy," said Mr Sanders after the formal introductions were made and they were seated, "that your father is a gentleman farmer who oversees his own working farm, similar to Pemberley."

"He is indeed, Mr Sanders, though comparisons with Pemberley are somewhat deceptive. Our estate is very much smaller. But I regret that I have played no role in the workings of the farm and have no significant knowledge of it at all, a shortcoming which I would be happy to redress now that I am here. My father spoke to us once or twice on the subject or, more correctly, on the benefits falling to us, his family, of the farm. He is lucky enough to have a very good farm and estate manager, Mr Gilbert, who took over last year after the previous manager died. Mr Gilbert was a farm worker before but very capable. My father holds him in very high esteem."

"Why, Mrs Darcy, that is very unusual, for a farm worker to rise to the rank of an estate steward. Your father must be a very forward-thinking man."

"My father is certainly a kind man. But Mr Gilbert is a clever man, he just did not have the formal education and social position, or indeed money, necessary to better himself. My father noticed his proficiency."

Darcy watched this exchange, evidently with approbation. Mrs Sanders also looked on with great interest it seemed to Elizabeth. Addressing her, Elizabeth said:

"We hope to travel round the whole estate and to all the farms today, and possibly visit Lambton as well."

"Then you have a full day ahead of you, Mrs Darcy," said Mrs Sanders. Elizabeth detected a trace of the local Derbyshire lilt in her speech. "It is a lovely estate. It was a beautiful place for our children to grow up, though they were quite well grown already when we arrived here. Now, two of them are full grown, a son in the Navy and another taking holy orders. Our daughters are yet only thirteen and fifteen."

Elizabeth turned to the window and silently admired the view, thinking of her own future children being brought up here. A rush of joy filled her at her good fortune.

Darcy rose. "We must leave now, Sanders, Mrs Sanders, if we are to make our full rounds today."

Elizabeth also rose as did the Sanders. "I am very much obliged to you for your kind hospitality. I hope we will meet again soon."

"Oh, you must visit whenever is convenient for you, Mrs Darcy," said Mrs Sanders.

"Thank you, Mrs Sanders. That is very kind."

Darcy nodded. "We will talk again next week, Sanders. We will see you in church if not before."

"WILL they be at the ball on Saturday?" asked Elizabeth as they rode away.

"No. It may seem unnecessary prejudice to you, but farm stewards are of course not members of the gentry, not of sufficient rank to be invited to such an occasion. Though they would attend local events."

Elizabeth considered this. "I think my father would happily have had the Gilberts to dine with us, but my mother would never have heard of it."

"A forward-thinking man, as Sanders said."

"I do not think it is even that. He likes the Gilberts very much. And he told us that Mr Gilbert had practically run the farm for a decade or so due to the old manager's inadequacies, but the old manager was a former friend of my father's towards whom he felt a residual loyalty."

"It would have been a difficult matter for your father, I am sure," Darcy said. "But Lizzy, we are come upon some of the cottages. There." Darcy pointed to their right. At first Elizabeth could see nothing but a tangle of brambles. Then, a small gap appeared and Darcy started to hack at the briar with his crop.

"I have been too much away in the last year," he said. "Areas have become overgrown."

"Does not Mr Sanders deal with all that?"

"It is a large estate, Lizzy. He cannot do everything."

"Could you not employ someone to assist him? An under-manager perhaps?"

"That is an excellent idea. Lizzy, you are already becoming an asset to the estate." He said this lightly but Elizabeth was pleased with the sentiment. He continued: "Although I must have some occupation myself. I cannot sit about and take my ease."

Visions of Mr Hurst, Bingley's brother-in-law, sprawled on a sofa, snoring with his mouth open, swam before Elizabeth. Perhaps the same thought occurred to Darcy for she saw him smile to himself. She could scarcely say so, but it reminded her:

"I wonder why Caroline Bingley and Mrs Hurst will not be coming here at Christmas. Jane did not say in her letter."

"Last year, they were in town — as you will recall. Mayhap they will spend Christmas there again this year."

Elizabeth did recall. Darcy, Caroline and Mrs Hurst had persuaded Charles Bingley to leave Hertfordshire to avoid a growing attachment to poor Jane, and Bingley, trusting Darcy's judgement and being of a pliable disposition, had agreed. Jane, in her own quiet way had been heart-broken. This was a very touchy subject for Elizabeth still and Darcy had been the prime mover. She should let it rest, but she ventured at least to ask:

"And did you remain in town with them over Christmas or return to Pemberley last year? You never did tell me."

"Georgiana and I returned to Pemberley. But as to the estate again, it is necessary for me to be vigilant. There are many on and about the estate who have interests and may seek to advance them, possibly to my detriment. I must be here permanently so that those with purposes of their own will be deterred from exercising an advantage. I cannot afford to be duped, Elizabeth, and must be more watchful."

"But surely you trust Mr Sanders, Fitz?"

"I do. But there are others." He ceased to hack at the overgrowth, and they sat side by side atop their horses so that he could better make his point. "By way of example, some of the farms are let and an agent places them with suitable tenants when a farm becomes free. It would be a simple matter for an agent to prefer a griping fellow known to the agent for a tenant, instead of an honest man.

"And also there is a water mill on the estate and a fast-flowing river which could be put to far better use. I must attend to these things. Only an owner can make the best of the opportunities available. And now, I have **an assistant, a wife, a guide** in every plan of utility or charity for Pemberley; someone who would make Pemberley and all about it a dearer object than it has ever been yet."

"I am delighted to be such, Fitz."

It occurred to her for the first time that Darcy may have come south last year and spent so long away from Pemberley in order to find a wife. As she understood events, Bingley had sought Darcy's approval of Netherfield Park before it was taken. Perhaps it was a deliberate choice of Darcy's to fix on a property a considerable distance from Derbyshire, knowing that he would become part of Bingley's household for a time. It raised the possibility that Derbyshire held some sort of disadvantage for him in the marriage market, although of course the same could be said of Bingley. Yet an alternative explanation would be the convenience of being nearer to London and to Lady Catherine de Bourgh in Kent.

Further, it was to be expected that a wealthy young gentleman would seek to broaden his knowledge of the world but, as he said, he had been too much away from Pemberley. With his father some years dead, the estate, and indeed the house, must have been left to be overseen by others in a piecemeal way.

And a mill. The word struck a chord with Elizabeth. Mr Wilde had rescued Peter Carpenter from a cotton mill in Nottinghamshire, the next county to Derbyshire. Would Fitz consider developing such a manufactory which employed child labour? He would probably expect her to know nothing of such things and a discussion with him would mean mention of the Reverend Wilde again.

These were all subjects for some consideration. Elizabeth would have to put them aside for later and her husband was speaking again.

"Of course, when we have children, Lizzy, I would wish to be more at home and then perhaps would be the time to hire an under-manager. Or another way might be to split the duties of the estate manager and create a new situation. With our children, I would like to be more often present, to be a father more akin to your own father."

"My father! Fitz, you astonish me. He was very negligent in

48

many ways. You even wrote to me of his want of propriety."

"Indeed I did. I fancy however that he was always near at hand, whereas my own father, though a good, kind and fair man was somewhat distant. I suspect that George Wickham, who was a favourite of my father as you know, if he could ever bring himself to speak the truth for once, would tell you the same thing. It is my impression that your father was more...approachable."

"Well, to own the truth, with five daughters in a house many times smaller than Pemberley, there was little opportunity for my father to be at all remote." She found herself laughing aloud at the notion and Darcy joined her. "The best he could manage was to hide in his library.

"But," she continued, "More seriously, I would trust that you would exert yourself to restrain any wild tendencies, for how grievous was the thought earlier this year that Jane had been deprived of happiness by the folly and indecorum of her own family!"

"I hope that we could strike a happy balance in our own family, Lizzy."

Yes, thought Elizabeth. With their so recent restoration of harmony, he would not now hazard to mention the unhappy defects of her family; her mother, with manners so far from right herself, having been entirely insensible of the evil caused by the imprudence of Catherine and Lydia.

"It has become my view," said he, "that being brought up largely by servants is all very fine. I would be the last person to deprive these people of their jobs and it saves the parents a deal of trouble. But I wish that my own parents had been available much more often to me and Georgiana, and I would certainly aspire to be with and about my own children a great deal more, or for them to be with and about me."

It was undeniable that Darcy and his sister were uncomfortable in company. Perhaps that was the reason, that they had been paid insufficient attention by their parents, spending most of their early years in a nursery, remote from the rest of the house, cared for by nursemaids, seeing their parents only briefly at bedtime. By contrast, the Bennet girls had been paid a great deal of attention, even though this was hardly by design, more coincidentally the result of the boisterous ambience pervading Long-bourn House. Yes, there were nursemaids, but the children, five of them coming in quick succession, had of necessity spent much of their time out of the nursery and in various parts of the house with their parents.

"Fitz, as you are desirous of a more...informal way to bring up our children...when the time comes...there is a matter I would raise with you regarding our own present family. Oh," she said, seeing his brow furrow, "it is nought very serious. I merely wished to ask you whether I could invite Georgiana to address me as Lizzy."

"Oh," he said, smiling, "I had never considered that—"

Further thought and discussion was brought to an end as a group of small, ragged children ran out of the gap in the brambles, dodged round the horses' legs and disappeared into the wood on the other side of the track.

The horses, startled, began to tread sideways, backwards and forwards. Darcy and Elizabeth brought them under control.

"I think we must dismount," said Darcy, "and make our way on foot through this tangle as best we can to the cottages."

He held back the briar with his crop, allowing Elizabeth to walk Annie through the opening, arriving at a small clearing, and Darcy followed with his own horse.

THE condition of the cottages seemed reasonable according to Elizabeth's untrained eye, so why were the occupiers poor and in need of relief? Certainly the land surrounding the small dwellings which could have produced vegetables in the summer was overgrown with weeds. No goats or hens or other stock foraged in the open space. A thin, mangy dog was digging a hole and took no notice of them.

"You'll have to knock on one of the doors," Darcy told Elizabeth, "and go in if no one answers."

As Darcy had hinted, her knock at the first door produced no response. Tentatively, she therefore lifted the latch and pushed her way into the house. There was some resistance resulting from a pile of unidentifiable rubbish which had accumulated immediately inside. She walked farther in and covered her nose with her hand. The stench in the place was grossly unpleasant. There was no fire in the hearth and it was barely warmer in here than outside. The single room held some sort of a mattress in the far corner on the floor with straw spilling out of it, a couple of stools and little else. On the mattress languished a person of indeterminate age and sex covered in sacks. She or he had long unkempt brown or grey hair and a face and hands covered in sores. The talons of the hands grasped the sacks to the bony, pointed chin.

"Is she...or he...ill, Fitz," Elizabeth whispered.

"'Tis a woman to my knowledge, by the name of Jones."

"Does she have some disease?"

"A disease of the mind perhaps," he said.

"Does she have no one to look after her?"

"The other cottagers I dare say help her. They are likely related to her. But there is very little wrong with her body. Whatever ails her renders her unwilling to do much to help herself."

Elizabeth steeled herself and moved towards the bedding, holding out a rug in one hand and a cloth bundle containing bread and cheese in the other. The woman, although she had her eyes open and looked at Elizabeth, made no move to take the proffered goods, so Elizabeth laid the food still wrapped in the cloth on the floor near the bed and gently placed the rug over the top of the sacks. A grunt came from the recumbent form but no other reaction.

"Come on," said Darcy, "we might as well go."

Elizabeth let him lead her out into the cold air.

"These are the worst of the poor cottages on the estate. The tenants here are worse off than elsewhere because, to speak the truth, they largely make things worse for themselves. They will not take employment. They could be employed seasonally on one or other of the farms but they will not accept any work. If they come by any money, the men, and frequently the women too, spend it on spirits. They will not work the land with their dwellings or breed any stock. Anything given to them is often sold for money for spirits. The rug you left in the Jones woman's hovel is liable to be taken by one of the others and sold. It is to be hoped that they will leave her the food."

"How can they survive, Fitz?"

"In the main by foraging in the woods around here. That is probably what the children were going to do. Or some may go to the town to beg."

"Is foraging not tantamount to poaching, Fitz? Do you allow it?"

"On such a large estate, Lizzy, it would seem very hard-hearted to deny those who live on the estate the taking of minor game and hedgerow fare, berries and so forth. It is only allowed in some areas and then only rabbits and pigeons. It is certainly allowed here, but I very much doubt if the wildlife hereabouts is in any great danger from the Joneses. They are too lazy to make sufficient effort to catch vermin."

"What about those who come onto the estate from outside to pilfer?"

"Gamekeepers, three of them and their helpers, apprehend the trespassers. Granted it is a full-time job for them. We will pass their cottages on our way."

"What is done, then, with these trespassers?"

"They are ejected of course. If they are persistent, then they are reported to a constable." Seeing her anxious expression, he said:

"It does not happen often."

"But can nothing be done to stop this hopeless way of life of the Joneses?"

"Turning them out would put a stop to it. But they would probably die. They all have the family name of Jones. They have been here for several generations, always showing this complete lack of initiative. But do not distress yourself. The cottagers here are unusual. Most others, even if poor and without employment, make efforts to improve their lot and hence are granted more relief. With the Joneses it is pointless, apart from keeping roofs over their heads, maintaining the hovels to a certain standard. At least they know that if they try to sell off any parts of the cottages capable of being taken away, they will be charged with theft and likely deported."

Their voices had been heard. Creaky doors had started to open and heads then bodies, mainly women, began to emerge.

They stayed some paces from Darcy and Elizabeth.

"Hello there," Darcy called. "Come forward."

They clearly knew who he was and toothless grins spread over their faces, seeing the cloths and food being drawn from the saddlebags. Darcy and Elizabeth proceeded to hand out mainly food. Darcy whispered to Elizabeth to give them only the small rugs and a few children's clothes.

It was probably pointless, but Darcy introduced Elizabeth as his wife and the new mistress of Pemberley.

"Thank yee Master, Mistress," they rejoined as they took the food and textiles. "Thank yee, thank yee."

This appeared to be the extent of their conversation.

Darcy led her away, through the gap in the brambles, leaving the small group to pick over the offerings and argue between themselves. Elizabeth thought of Mr Wilde's visits on her behalf to the workhouse in Meryton and what he had told her of the poor. Now she had experience at first hand.

"So Lizzy you have seen the worst of poverty in this area, though these people we have just seen do nothing for themselves. As I said to you earlier, even I cannot be idle. Everyone has to do some work. Even George Wickham, curse him, has to occupy himself fighting for his country. I hope it serves to improve him. Come on, let me help you mount and we can be on our way again.

"Oh and, in case I forget, please do invite Georgiana to call you Lizzy if you wish. I have no doubt she will be delighted."

Chapter 8

IT WAS Saturday, the day of the ball or, more correctly it was the early evening. A half-moon was rising over the lake. The sky was clear of cloud, allowing it to shine clearly over the frozen landscape. Turning away from Peggy who was stowing in a trunk the ballgown, slippers and various adornments and articles of finery, Elizabeth pulled the curtain aside and peered out of her bedroom window at the visible grounds of Pemberley. They appeared as a magical scene from an illuminated manuscript, the bare tree branches, hedges and paths edged delicately with silver frost.

She would change later at Ashwick Hall. Her second ballgown was also in the trunk in case the first somehow or other became ruined. Elizabeth hardly thought this was necessary, but it was what Peggy had been taught to do by Mrs Reynolds.

Peggy would not be accompanying her mistress. It was understood that a lady's maid would be provided at the Hall.

Darcy was presently in his own room being dressed by his valet. They would be spending the night at the Hall, which was just into the next county of Yorkshire, and would travel home tomorrow. To speak the truth, although her apprehensive mood was tinged with excitement, Elizabeth would later have happily climbed into the carriage at any hour of the night or early morning and made the journey home. Tonight's outing would be far removed from anything she had experienced heretofore, much grander even than the ball in London she and Jane had attended when staying with Aunt and Uncle Gardiner or the ball at Netherfield hosted by Bingley, both of which events had taken place the previous year.

Traditionally, at Ashwick Hall the guests ate, danced, played cards and discoursed most of the night, enjoying a hearty breakfast not long before the sun came up, then slept for much of the remainder of the day.

As she walked to the carriage with Darcy, the cold hit her. There must be snow soon. Within a day or two, Elizabeth's family would be setting out for Pemberley. Georgiana looked forward to snow at Christmas, but it was to be hoped that the snow would hold off until the family arrived. Becoming stranded at some remote place en route would be a disaster and a horrible way for them to spend Christmas, not to mention the great disappointment for her and Georgiana, Darcy no doubt somewhat less so.

It saddened Elizabeth, naturally, that Lydia would be unable to form part of the lively family party, but Lydia would be the most likely member of her family to cause disruption and unpleasantness, with her careless tongue and her wild, untamed behaviour. She would be bound to flirt with Colonel Fitzwilliam and with as many gentlemen as possible at any functions they attended and Darcy would be horribly embarrassed.

By contrast, the Colonel, she suspected, having observed his easy manners during her stay earlier this year with Charlotte Collins at the parsonage at Hunsford, would very probably have found any such attentions absurdly amusing. Darcy and he had been at Rosings visiting their aunt and Mr Collins's patroness, Lady Catherine de Bourgh, at the same time. It was at the parsonage, in the course of this visit, that Darcy had made his first disastrous proposal to Elizabeth.

With Wickham's regiment being in the North-East, their journey to Pemberley would have been shorter than that of the Bennets, yet to have invited them to Pemberley would have been out of the question given Wickham's attempt to elope with Georgiana less than two years ago, to say nothing of his and Lydia's scandalous elopement earlier this year. No, Mr and Mrs Wickham would never be received at Pemberley.

"FITZ my love, can you tell me more about the Duke of Rotherham and Ashwick Hall, the sort of people who will be at the ball. Do you know him well?"

"Not well, no."

"Upon my word, you surprise me."

"The Duke and Duchess spend much of their time in town

and when I have been in town, our paths have not frequently crossed. The Duke is fond of gambling which I am not, and the Duchess seeks her own amusement. I expect we shall mingle with their friends and others from London, possibly writers, politicians, others of note, as well as local gentry. Probably no royalty though."

Elizabeth drew a breath. "Indeed!"

"I and others like me, senior county gentry, as well as aristocracy from hereabouts, are invited for our local connections. If I wanted, say, to go into parliament, I might assiduously solicit the Duke's attention by making it known that I support any causes which he espouses, or otherwise make myself prominent in local affairs. However, I have no such ambitions, Lizzy."

"I am pleased to hear it, Fitz."

The nickname had slipped out twice in spite of Georgiana's presence in the carriage with them, as had the shortened version of her own name. Elizabeth looked at her and she smiled, her golden hair shining in the bright moonlight slanting through the carriage windows. They would get dressed together at the hall and have their hair dressed together, as sisters. Elizabeth caught her hand under the fur coverlet and squeezed it, feeling a returning pressure.

HAD Elizabeth not visited Chatsworth during her family's stay in Buxton, she would have been quite overwhelmed by the splendour of Ashwick Hall. It was on a similar scale to Chatsworth and equally ornate. No wall or ceiling of the great entrance hall was without lavish friezes and works of art, family portraits or large tapestries. The stairs leading up from the main hall were magnificent.

However, the way to their rooms for the night was through more plainly decorated passages and she was glad to arrive at their bedroom and sit in a chair for five minutes. Fitz had an adjoining dressing room should he decide to take advantage of it and Georgiana was led to her own room nearby. Fitz was not here though, having remained in the entrance hall to re-acquaint himself with old friends.

A worm of anxiety within her threatened to spoil the first

flush of excitement. It had been only five days since their major argument, as she saw it, when he had withdrawn from her to his own bedroom and left her broken-hearted. He seemed to have recovered his good humour very quickly, but Elizabeth could not avoid the apprehension that some of his reserve would return tonight and that he might leave her largely to her own devices. Indeed, his sterner side may reassert itself by reason merely of his tendency to be uncomfortable in company. What a pity Colonel Fitzwilliam was not here with them tonight. He would not abandon the ladies and let them fend for themselves.

Well, if Fitz did so, she must summon her own reserves and adopt the course she had decided upon those several days ago and seek out and make merry with her new friends.

But all those misgivings, serious though they were, could not quite destroy the pleasure of the adventure.

Elizabeth sat down at the dressing table and examined her flushed face in the looking glass. Having assumed that she and Georgiana would dress together, she was disappointed to realise that this may not be the case tonight. A knock came at the door and a maid entered.

"I was told to bring you this package, and that Mr Darcy has sent it up for you, ma'am."

The maid scuttled out. Evidently, she was not the maid who would be dressing Elizabeth.

This was most unexpected. A present from her husband, perhaps. A smile crossed her face as she pulled at the wrapping, took out a small, flat box, parted some cotton wadding and drew a breath. A delicate silver bracelet encrusted with jade lay inside. It would match her dress perfectly. Was it, she wondered, a family heirloom or rather a recent purchase especially for tonight? Was it a peace offering for their falling out a few days ago, or rather for his withdrawal of his favour for a few hours? Miserable, tear-filled hours for her. Whichever it was, the beautiful gift buoyed her spirits and she felt less inclined to think that he would ignore her this evening. Though, indeed, she must learn how to make her way in this society.

As she drew the bracelet from the box, a note fluttered to the floor and she bent over from her chair to pick it up.

'*To my only love. Fitz*' it read in his unmistakable hand. Elizabeth was almost driven to tears by the thoughtful gesture. She put the thin band round her left wrist and fastened it. Then she held it up to the light of the candles in the sconces either side of the dressing table and turned it this way and that. As with the green dress which she had held up against her front a few days ago, the bright green jewels seemed to be reflected in her dark blue eyes, giving them the appearance of a cat's eyes, the pupils large in the rather poor light and her thick, dark lashes framing her eyes, heightening the effect.

She wondered if Darcy had sent up a present for Georgiana also. She rather hoped he had as the three of them were out tonight together and she did not want her sister to feel excluded or overlooked.

To pass the time, she ran her brush through her dark hair time and again until it seemed to double in volume and gleam in the candlelight. There was another knock at the door and a second maid entered.

SOME considerable time later, wearing her gown and jewellery, her shining hair piled up, a very tiny bit of rouge on her lips and her favourite scent dabbed on her neck and wrists, Elizabeth thanked the maid and asked her to find out if Miss Georgiana Darcy was ready and if so to invite her to Elizabeth's room.

Within five minutes, Georgiana had slipped in and by the time the two had finished admiring each other, showing each other Darcy's gifts, for which Elizabeth was grateful, making minor adjustments to dress and hair and debating whether to go down on their own or send a message to Darcy, there was another tap on the door. It opened to Elizabeth's call. It was Darcy, turning to thank someone, presumably for showing him to their room. Facing them, he looked them up and down.

"What a privilege it is," he smiled, "to be able to escort two such beautiful ladies to the ball."

This was so unlike Darcy, that Elizabeth laughed heartily, causing Darcy to chuckle in response and Georgiana to appear somewhat surprised.

"You are all politeness, sir," said Elizabeth, "and we are all gratitude." She glanced at Georgiana, bringing her into the joke.

"We are indeed. I thank you for the compliment, William," said Georgiana, at last catching their mood.

"Come now," said Darcy, extending his elbows for them to take an arm either side, "let us go and join the assembly."

"Indeed," said Elizabeth.

Before she put her arm through her husband's, she wafted her left arm gracefully in front of him.

"A hundred thanks, a thousand, Fitz for this elegant bracelet. I adore it."

"Oh, and thank you so much for my earrings." Georgiana smiled broadly. The blue gems brought out the aquamarine of her eyes and matched her blue gown.

"Mere trifles for such worthy subjects," he said. "Now come. There are guest here already waiting to make your acquaintance both, and hoping to mark your cards for dances later."

Elizabeth laughed again. It promised to be an enjoyable evening.

COMMENTS were reaching Elizabeth's ears once she and Darcy, and Georgiana and her first partner left the dance floor. As soon as they reached the ballroom, Darcy had introduced Elizabeth and Georgiana to a young man by the name of Matthew Rankin who had immediately sought Georgiana's hand for the next dance. Georgiana was clearly enchanted. Elizabeth took the floor with Darcy.

"You must not dance with me out of a sense of obligation, Fitz," Elizabeth had said, spotting Harriet Layham out of the corner of her eye sitting with an older couple who must be her parents, and thinking how satisfactory it would be to start the evening off with a long chat to her friend over a glass of the punch being handed out by footmen.

"Naturally, I wish to dance first with the prettiest girl in the room," Darcy had said and Elizabeth was charmed into immediately accepting.

"DARCY has made a love match, I hear. And one can see why." Elizabeth caught this and similar sentiments from the men standing around the dance floor gossiping like old women, though the old women themselves had different ideas.

"Mr Darcy's new bride is passing pretty, I suppose, and one has heard that she has brilliant eyes, but it is still a mystery why he did not seek the hand of..."

Elizabeth strained to hear the names of the several girls whom the ladies, ranged on sofas around the large room fanning themselves, declared would have been ideal matches for Darcy. But the matriarchs' voices dropped and their fans covered their mouths as soon as she and Darcy came within many feet of them.

"Harriet," cried Elizabeth, arriving at the sofa she was sharing with her parents. Elizabeth had the impression that the father at least, sitting stiffly erect, was reluctant to take part in the social discourse around him or for his family to do so.

"Harriet, may I introduce you to my husband, Mr Fitzwilliam Darcy of Pemberley whom I believe you have not yet met."

Darcy bowed to Harriet.

"How do you do, sir," she said. Then, remembering her manners, she introduced her parents to Elizabeth.

"My pleasure," Elizabeth said.

"And Sir Peter and Lady Layham, may I too present my wife to you, Mrs Elizabeth Darcy."

"A great pleasure," Sir Peter mumbled.

"My dear, we are delighted to welcome you to Derbyshire," said Lady Layham warmly.

"Sir Peter," said Darcy, "we are looking forward to welcoming you to Pemberley for our annual shoot after Christmas, and Lady Layham."

Faced with Darcy, Sir Peter was inclined to become less taciturn. "Indeed, we are delighted to have been invited once again. It is a fixture of the County's calendar, greatly anticipated all year."

"Oh indeed, Mr Darcy," Lady Layham smiled sweetly up at him. "We can hardly get through Christmas for anticipating the joy of another event at Pemberley."

Sir Peter sighed at this exaggeration but said nothing.

Elizabeth smiled. She liked this woman.

"I hope, Sir Peter and Lady Layham," said Darcy, "that you

will allow my wife to bear your daughter away for a short time, as I know she is desirous of re-kindling their friendship from those few weeks ago when Miss Harriet was kind enough to call on my wife very newly arrived at Pemberley. Mrs Darcy much appreciated her visit."

"Well—" began Sir Peter.

"Upon my word, of course, Mr Darcy," exclaimed Lady Layham. "Mrs Darcy shall have Harriet's full attention."

"Thank you, Mama," Harriet smiled at her mother.

"I am obliged to you, Lady Layham," Elizabeth said.

Knowing when he was out-flanked, Sir Peter resignedly crossed his arms over his chest and sat back.

"And we must go and see how Georgiana is faring," Elizabeth reminded Darcy as they walked away with Harriet.

"Pretty well, I would say," said Darcy, and Elizabeth saw that Georgiana had another partner for a Cotillion and was talking and laughing prettily with the young man opposite her.

Good, thought Elizabeth. That is good, that she is able to mix in society so much more easily than formerly.

Darcy loosed his arm from Elizabeth's. "I will wait for Georgiana to finish her dance with that young man who is known to us I am glad to say, while you renew your acquaintance with your friend."

Elizabeth led Harriet off to a table bearing refreshments. They took plates and glasses and sat down some distance from Harriet's parents.

"This is Georgiana's first ball," Elizabeth explained to her friend. "And she is only yet sixteen years. Fortunately, she seems already to know some of the young men present.

"Now tell me," continued Elizabeth, "how are things regarding the Earl of Langford? And what about the other young men you mentioned, respectable and quite wealthy you said, who might interest you? Are any of them here tonight?"

Harriet turned her head. Through the throng of dancing, drinking, talking bodies, Harriet's gaze rested on a group of men. One of them was taller and somewhat older than the others gathered around him, although the contrast was mainly because the others were so young, little more than boys. The tall man was also flamboyantly dressed and foppish in his mannerisms. Elizabeth had never before encountered a man who favoured the society of men

over women as explained to her by Fitz, but she knew instinctively that the individual on whom Harriet's gaze alighted was such a man.

"So, that is the Earl of Langford."

Harriet nodded.

"Fascinating. His behaviour and mannerisms are excessively affected I notice."

Harriet laughed. "Are they not."

"He puts me in mind of some characters from literature and dramas which I have read about. A popinjay. Have you spoken to him tonight? Do you find yourself any less averse to a match with him, Harriet?"

"No. I mean we have not spoken tonight. He is, you will see, much diverted by his friends."

She must try to find an opportunity tonight to warn her friend about the Earl. How was she to word such intelligence when Harriet may be as innocent as she herself was on the subject of 'mollies' before Darcy had enlightened her. For a quarter of an hour, she therefore let Harriet discreetly point out to her the other young men who took her fancy, telling Elizabeth what she knew of them and how well she knew any of them. Not well at all, it seemed, so sheltered a life did her father impose upon her.

Nonetheless, Harriet's descriptions of the men were humorous. Most of them were the sons of families known to the Layhams; brothers of young ladies who were friends of Harriet insofar as her father allowed her to mix in local society. It sounded as though most invitations were refused and very few extended to other families. Afternoon tea seemed to be the most frequent social opportunity available to Harriet when her mother entertained and was entertained by ladies of her acquaintance and at least Harriet was able to be present. And of course the sons of the houses would often appear for a time when their mothers were doing the entertaining.

Elizabeth did not wish to upset her friend or in any way alienate Harriet's parents, but she felt that she must raise the subject of the Earl and be honest about him.

"I see that your father and the Earl show no sign of talking together tonight. I am surprised that your father is not taking this opportunity to further your family's connection with him."

"Oh, no. All the negotiations are between Papa and his father, the Duke. And the Duke is not here tonight."

"Of course, but if you are to marry him, you must be better acquainted with him. Tonight would be an ideal occasion on which you could meet and talk together."

"Father is old-fashioned, Lizzy, as you may have discerned. And...I fear that the negotiations are not faring as well as they might."

"What do you mean, Harriet?"

"Only that there are others who are vying for a match with the Earl."

"I don't doubt it. But it is you, my friend, about whom I am concerned. I..."

Elizabeth hesitated. Harriet's expression was quizzical.

"You must know that it is said abroad that the Earl is...not attracted to women. He seeks out the company of men, as you see now, as companions."

"Yes, he has friends, Lizzy. We all do."

"But...the men he associates with are more than friends. To be completely open, they are more akin to the mistresses of men."

Harriet's brown wrinkled.

"What you say is impossible."

"So it should be, but it is not."

Harriet stiffened.

"I do not think we should be talking of such sinful behaviour. I had better return to my parents."

"Harriet, don't go. I am merely trying to warn you. If you were to marry the Earl, if your father is successful in bringing about a match, your life would be miserable. He could never love you."

Harriet stood. "I am going now. And I am sure you know that love is overrated and often absent from marriages."

"Very well, Harriet. But think on what I have said and watch the behaviour of the Earl tonight. Decide whether your observations tell you that he is a normal man and would make a loving husband to a woman. No one can force you to marry against your will and surely if the Earl was interested in you as a wife, he would pay you some attention tonight."

Harriet glared down at Elizabeth and then stalked away.

"LIZZY, why so serious?" came a voice from behind her chair and a hand lightly gripped her shoulder. Despite her disappointment at having lost a good friend, she presumed, she smiled at the gentle but firm pressure of her husband's hand. Indeed, the reassurance it gave her caused her to feel that she had been right to warn her friend. Nothing could be more desirable than a happy marriage to the man she was sure had been made for her. Anything else would be a pale imitation. And, she realised, she had neglected him for at least half an hour in the interests of protecting her friend.

Elizabeth cast her eyes down at her hands clasped in her lap.

"Yes. I am afraid so. I told Harriet of the Earl's preferences. She would not have it. I can only hope that if she won't take heed, that at least the Earl's father and Sir Peter will fail to reach an accord. I gather from Harriet that there are other contenders for the Earl's hand in marriage. To my regret, our friendship appears to be over before it has begun."

"I am sorry, Lizzy. We can talk of it later. And you will see Harriet again at the shoot."

"Yes, if the family will still attend."

"Let us hope so. But come, we should enjoy ourselves for the rest of the evening. And naturally, Georgiana craves your company."

"Yes, of course." She had left her husband's side for too long.

"We are to go into dinner soon and before that I must introduce you to our host, the Duke of Rotherham. There will be cards later. As I told you, the Duke is a keen gambler, though I trust the stakes will not be high tonight."

"No." Elizabeth's eyes widened. "I assume the Duke would not wish to send his neighbours and guests home bankrupt on such a night."

"No, indeed. I expect there will be some other games. And more dancing. Many gentlemen are desirous of making your acquaintance, Lizzy, and taking the floor with you; also ladies of your recent acquaintance hoping to have your attention. Indeed, other guests of the Duke, about whom we spoke, writers, artists, politicians. The night is yet young. I will introduce you to some interesting people, Lizzy."

At last Elizabeth felt able to smile and be genuinely happy. If Harriet wished to be unreceptive to the truth, then Fitz and Georgiana should not suffer for it. And she must not avoid the opportunity to enter into this society on account of her friend's obduracy.

THE rest of the night passed in a haze of laughter, chatter, more scandalous indiscretions from her new friends, more serious intellectual discussion, dancing of course, winning a little money at cards, losing a little, feasting, walking in the extensive hothouse admiring the lush plants and rare fruits; of necessity being introduced in the first place to the Duke of Rotherham and separately to the Duchess.

The Duke was of medium height and thin and bony, save for a large paunch. He wore a heavily powdered wig and had bad teeth and pale skin. He was vague in his speech, did not appear to concentrate when spoken to, but when faced with a hand of cards, he sharpened up miraculously.

The Duchess, when Elizabeth was introduced, was much younger, very pretty and her dress and jewellery had to be worth many thousands of pounds. She was much more interested in the artists and writers than the ordinary guests and soon drifted off to a group of men almost as flamboyant at the Earl of Langford, although he was not among them. One of the 'men' however, stood out. Elizabeth was sure the person was a woman dressed as a man.

"It is Emma Black," whispered Darcy behind her. "She paints mainly miniatures and teaches painting to the aristocracy. She is unmarried. She is, possibly, the female equivalent of the Earl of Langford."

Elizabeth gasped.

"Upon my word, Fitz," she replied in similarly low tones, "is such a thing even possible?"

"Many say that it is," he said softly, his lips touching her ear. The frisson this produced, both Fitz's suggestion and his proximity, caused the blood to rush to Elizabeth's face and she resisted a quiet exclamation which would have been more of a cry. Momentarily she closed her eyes, then recollected herself.

"I see that Langford is making the best of the evening, out no doubt to make new conquests amongst the innocent young men present. It is likely an ideal hunting ground for him."

"Oh," Elizabeth's eyes widened. "The picture you paint is reminiscent of a lion out hunting. A predator."

"Yes, indeed."

"Upon my word." Elizabeth fanned herself at the pinkness which touched her cheeks at this further astounding proposition. Her knowledge of the world was certainly being expanded this evening.

Elizabeth did not dare to be included in the card games in which the Duke took part, but watched from behind a row of spectators and was astounded at his mastery of the game or perhaps good fortune, especially in the rubber, the third deciding round when he invariably won. She sought out other less disquieting games until the company almost spontaneously grew restless and moved away from the tables towards other entertainments.

There were magicians and jugglers who suddenly appeared, attracting crowds around them and fascinating the watchers with their skills, sleight of hand and dexterity. Elizabeth put her arm through Georgiana's as they viewed the entertainment. The men seemed to be able to do these elaborate tricks endlessly, without rest.

Georgiana yawned eventually. Darcy miraculously appeared next to Elizabeth.

"What is the time, Fitz?" she said.

"Probably time that we should retire for a few hours. I'll wager the dawn will be coming up quite soon — or would be if it were not mid-winter. And we must keep our energy in reserve for a hearty breakfast."

THEY saw Georgiana to her room but then on impulse, instead of retiring themselves, at the sounds from below, they made their way back to the assembled company. The orchestra had returned to their dais and dancing was again in progress.

Elizabeth caught Darcy's arm and they took the floor together for several lively reels, by contrast to the more sedate, stately scores on offer earlier on. The company had found its second breath. Increasingly, the loud clatter reached them of dishes being set as breakfast was served somewhere nearby and many flocked in that direction. The Duke and Duchess did not seem to be amongst them. Nor were they anywhere else so far as Elizabeth could see. Indeed, the artists, writers and politicians with whom she had discoursed so eloquently, she felt, hours earlier, had, save one or two, dissolved as though they had been mere figments, imagined, not real. The Earl of Langford and his young entourage had similarly vanished.

"Where *are* all those people," she asked Darcy, casting her eyes around the ballroom and the breakfast room.

"Better we should not know," Darcy replied.

Elizabeth raised her eyebrows at her husband's evasion.

"If they wish to engage in unnatural and probably harmful practices, then let them," Darcy continued.

Elizabeth knew her husband was trying to protect her from, probably, the awaredom of undesirable practices, yet she yearned to know what it was that these people did to amuse themselves that Darcy considered too scandalous for her to have cognisance of.

"But I want to know," she said, somewhat plaintively she recognised.

"Of course you do," he sighed. "Then you shall. They most probably indulge in fornication, both natural and unnatural. Various forms of debauchery. They possibly take drugs of various sorts in order to enhance their experiences or, as artists and writers, to enhance their artistic abilities. It is not an area with which I am familiar either, Lizzy, so I suggest we enjoy our breakfast. Do not worry on Georgiana's account, there will be plenty left and fresh servings later. We can join her in a second helping before we leave." He paused.

"Lizzy, I hope you have enjoyed yourself tonight."

"Yes, indeed. Thank you for your careful guidance. And, I am pleased to say, as I saw Harriet leave earlier with her parents, she raised a friendly hand to me. Therefore, I have every hope of seeing her with her family at the shoot."

"That is excellent news, Lizzy. And, I confess, I find myself wearying. I would as much prefer to retire now and take a second serving of breakfast later, or even a third."

Elizabeth yawned. "I would as well do so too, Fitz."

Leaning on his arm, she allowed herself to be led towards the grand stairs and thence to their room, glad and sad in equal measure that the ball was almost over.

Chapter 9

ON the following Tuesday, Elizabeth had the pleasure of receiving Mr and Mrs Gardiner, arrived earlier than expected with the object of taking a longer time over the journey if necessary and to make sure they arrived safely with their children. Mr and Mrs Gardiner were greeted most heartily by Elizabeth and Darcy, both ever sensible of the warmest gratitude towards the persons who, by bringing Elizabeth to Derbyshire in the summer, had been the means of uniting them.

The Gardiner children, two girls and two boys, were very happily received by Elizabeth and Georgiana. The toys Georgiana had spoken of and more had been brought down from the attic rooms and in the week or so since it was confirmed that the children would be coming to Pemberley, a space had been rearranged as a place where the children might play near their own bedrooms and their parents' rooms. Georgiana's and Darcy's old nurse, Batchelor, who had not many years ago ceased to care for Georgiana and who still lived in the house was to watch over the children during their stay, assisted by a cheerful young maid, Nancy. Batchelor was overjoyed to be brought out of her retirement to look after children again.

Georgiana showed the boys and girls the little theatre which had been made for her at which, as a child herself, she had occupied many hours concocting plays and having the puppets perform them. Elizabeth was struck by the fact that Georgiana as a child had largely had to make her own entertainment. The little Gardiner girls in particular, Beth and Julia, were fascinated and they, Georgiana and the boys enthusiastically expressed their desire to perform plays for the family this Christmas.

More than ever, Elizabeth was convinced that it would be better for children to be among their parents as Fitz had suggested than spend rarefied hours and days by themselves in isolation with servants. However diligent and kindly Batchelor had been as a nurse, she could not have replaced the society of parents and siblings in a busy household.

INDEED, Georgiana, too, was not ignorant of the part played by Elizabeth's aunt and uncle in the present happy situation for her, her brother and his wife. Neither had Mr and Mrs Gardiner's good breeding gone unnoticed by her during the evening spent by them at Pemberley after her arrival there with Mr Bingley and his sisters in the summer. She could only have hoped that a deeper acquaintance might have been forged between them had not the sudden news of Lydia's elopement with Wickham intervened, casting all their intentions asunder.

She had never spoken of it, but the intelligence of the elopement had forever changed her view of George Wickham, leaving her sure that she would henceforth be quite inured to the charms he had exercised over her last year, should they ever meet again. Now, she was able to recognise him not as an attractive suitor, a man she might have loved, but as a man who would ruin a woman's reputation in order to have his way with her for a short time, for she was sure that Wickham would not have married Lydia unless some accommodation had been made for him to enable him to live well, at least for the time being. She knew not how such accommodation had been achieved, but she was sure it was so.

As to whose intervention had made it possible, then Lydia's own family was the obvious agency, though if not her family, Georgiana's mind irresistibly strayed nearer to home to identify the benefactor. Darcy had certainly disappeared last summer after the report of the elopement had sent Elizabeth hurrying back to Hertfordshire and the Gardiners back to London.

Well, whoever it had been, she rejoiced in her own escape from the prison which would have been hers had not her brother rescued her from her own planned elopement with Wickham.

WHEN the children, their excitement overcome eventually by tiredness, were put to bed after their tea, Mr and Mrs Gardiner, Darcy, Elizabeth and Georgiana together with Mrs Annesley assembled in the blue drawing room before a roaring fire and talked over the preceding months and what was known of the Bennets', the Bingleys' and the Philips's arrival. Very little it seemed beyond the letters received by Elizabeth last week.

And Colonel Fitzwilliam?

Darcy shrugged. He would probably arrive on his own steed at some time.

Elizabeth added for her aunt's and uncle's benefit: "He hopes to bring with him a friend, we understand, a lieutenant colonel."

At this, Elizabeth celebrated the fact that the result would be an equal number of gentlemen and ladies at table and dancing, that is if one did not take account of Mary who, in any case, detested dancing and would be happier performing on the pianoforte that others might dance.

"It must be strange for Kitty and Mary," Mrs Gardiner observed, looking mainly at Elizabeth, "to have such a reduced family now that you, Jane and Lydia are all married and gone."

"Yes, indeed, Aunt," observed Elizabeth, "but it is a change most families have to undergo at some time. Parents cannot go on breeding children forever to provide succour to and company for those who happen to be left with their parents."

Her aunt knew nothing of Wickham's attempted elopement with Georgiana, and Elizabeth tried covertly to observe Georgiana's reaction to the mention of Lydia, whom it was common knowledge had run off with Wickham and lived with him for a fortnight before their marriage took place. She was pleasantly surprised to see that Georgiana displayed no signs of distress, since the last time she had witnessed Wickham being indirectly referred to in Georgiana's presence, the allusion to him then had rendered Georgiana speechless. This was in the summer when Elizabeth and the Gardiners had been invited to visit Pemberley.

The person responsible at that time had been Caroline Bingley whose motive had been spite towards Elizabeth, the former designing to diminish the latter in the eyes of Darcy. The plan had not succeeded, leaving Miss Bingley vexed and disappointed.

Before long, they were called to dinner in the smaller family dining room. Over their meal, they talked over in more detail the arrangements for Christmas; the greenery to be cut and brought in to decorate the house, the yule logs waiting to be brought in, the gifts they had brought with them and were making or had made for those yet to arrive, the trips to be taken to Lambton to buy more gifts, the parties they would be attending.

Suggestions flowed and hints were given for gifts as yet not decided upon. Georgiana was very obviously excited at the prospect of a large family party in the house.

"Upon my word," she said, "how delightful it will be to use the large dining room when everyone is here."

She turned to Mr and Mrs Gardiner. "I hope that the children will be able to spend most of the time with us."

"Oh, yes," came the reply from Mrs Gardiner, "I am pleased that you wish it so. We will have to devise games to keep them occupied."

"Indeed, I have been looking in books and magazines for suitable games and Lizzy tells me of some which you have all played at Longbourn.

"And Lizzy, how old is your sister Catherine?"

"She is not long seventeen, Georgiana."

"So, nearly the same age as me. I will be seventeen early next year."

"I had not considered it, but yes, it must be so." Elizabeth glanced briefly over at Darcy. Was he perhaps meditating that Kitty may not prove to be the best of influences on Georgiana? If he was so minded, the same thought had occurred to her, but also conversely that Kitty could provide the stimulus Georgiana needed to become more comfortable in company. And Kitty certainly needed a friend and ally now that Lydia was no longer at home.

"Does she play the pianoforte, Lizzy?"

"A little. Not half so well as you, Georgiana."

"Oh, I must help her practise. How very agreeable to have a sister here the same age as me."

"I am sure she would appreciate that."

"What other pursuits does she follow, Lizzy? Does she draw?"

Elizabeth laughed. "Well, not very obviously. To own the truth, Kitty likes to trim bonnets and thinks a great deal about the fashions of the day; that is when she cannot play cards and dance."

"I should like to become more proficient at cards. As the more interesting games require four people, there has been scant opportunity to practise. Does Mary play cards?"

"She does not care to, Georgiana. She spends many hours in fact as you do practising at the pianoforte. She also reads a good deal and she is not at all interested in dancing or fashion."

Mrs Gardiner smiled. "As sisters, they could not be less alike."

Georgiana clapped her hands and laughed. "It will be an interesting Christmas, then."

"I do hope so," said Elizabeth.

"I DO not think I have ever seen Georgiana so happy and so animated as she was tonight," Darcy later observed to Elizabeth.

"I trust you are happy for her, Fitz."

"Yes, indeed. But I would not wish her spirits to be elevated only to be crushed later if...things go amiss for some reason. She is not accustomed to a great deal of excitement. Apart from the Wickham episode, her life has largely been lived quietly up to now. I don't want her to be hurt."

"Of course you do not, Fitz, but she is young. It may be equally bad for her if her life is *too* sheltered."

"You are hardly an old matron yourself, Lizzy."

In the darkness of their bedroom, she heard the smile in his voice.

"I grant you, Fitz, that your saving her from Wickham's clutches was nought if not fortunate. Nevertheless, for her to have had the experience may be no bad thing. It may ultimately prove to have strengthened her character."

This declaration was met by silence and Elizabeth feared she may have offended Darcy.

"I see," was all he uttered eventually.

"As my father put it more than once: '...a girl likes to be crossed in love a little now and then. She gains a sort of distinction among her friends.' Or something like that."

"That sounds very much like your father. On what occasion

did he say this, Lizzy?"

"Oh, well, I think he was referring to Jane when Bingley disappeared to town before last Christmas and we knew not when he would return."

"You said, my dear, 'more than once'. I hesitate to enquire what was or were the other occasions giving rise to your father's assertion."

Elizabeth silently castigated herself for mentioning her father's words. Fitz would be imagining the other occasion having been directed towards her and attachments to either George Wickham or Mr Wilde, or even both of them. Her face grew hot in the darkness and she knew not how to respond, especially as she was not convinced that he had no past himself in the realms of romance. To cover herself, she said:

"We were talking of Georgiana and what happened to her. In truth, at the mention this evening of Lydia being married, which implicitly included reference to Wickham, I detected no discomposure on her part. I think, I hope that she may have recovered from the incident."

"Very prettily side-stepped, Lizzy. I too hope that may be the case." He turned towards her and drew her to him, causing her breath to quicken. "Do not be unsettled, Lizzy. You know me to be a jealous man, especially now that we are married, but I accept that you have some past. Certainly, I should not make trouble between us over a chance allusion to your father's whimsical pronouncements which may or may not be in connection with you and some other man at some former time."

She fancied he was playing with her, yet still felt all the embarrassment of the moment, mingled with the effect his proximity always had on her. She stretched her neck so that her tongue and her lips found his own willing mouth and any slight difference between them was soon washed away.

Chapter 10

THE next two days were occupied taking brisk walks with and without the two wolfhounds who normally lay idle in the house most of the time, slumbering in front of fires, and with the gun dogs, playing ball games with the children and making paper decorations with them. Beth, Julia, Anthony and David were delighted with the dogs, hurling sticks for them and chasing after them.

On Wednesday, Darcy was away for most of the day, saying that he planned to visit Matlock and the Cromford Mill. He rode off early and returned after dark. Elizabeth would have liked to have accompanied him, but he said it would be too far for her to travel on horseback and a carriage would have slowed him down. In any case, there was too much for her to do at home.

It was a busy period and Elizabeth only found one opportunity on the Thursday morning to take herself off for a short ramble through the woods to clear her head, think on the events of the last few days and relish the peace of the outdoors. She could not stray far, and after half an hour she had to turn round to retrace her steps. As she did so, she was startled to see a woman close by. She had certainly not been aware of anyone following her, but was relieved to see that the woman must have emerged a moment ago from a side path. She was further reassured to see that the woman, poorly dressed, clutched a large cloth, doubled over, from which twigs protruded. This was the usual method of collecting kindling. The woman must be of a very low order to be doing this job. Though Pemberley did not employ children, usually a child of one of the servants would be sent out on such an errand, or possibly a general outdoor servant.

The woman halted and flattened herself against a tree lining the path. Elizabeth couldn't see the servant's face or whether she was young or old as she wore a cloak with a hood and had lowered her head respectfully. Irritation momentarily overtook Elizabeth as she passed the woman at this act of abasement. Housemaids did this in the house as well, flattening themselves against a wall if she encountered one when moving about the house, though they would smile rather than hide their faces. This had never happened at Longbourn. That certain of the Pemberley servants were trained to act with such obeisance was personally abhorrent to Elizabeth and she decided to talk to Fitz about it once Christmas was over and their visitors had departed.

She was soon indoors again, seeking out Mrs Reynolds to discuss this evening's dinner.

Everyone kept a lookout for carriages sweeping up the drive to deliver the Bennets, the Philipses and the Bingleys. They were rewarded instead on the Thursday by the sight in the distance of two horsemen. As they drew nearer, the vivid red of soldiers' tunics confirmed that it must be Colonel Fitzwilliam and his friend. Darcy, Elizabeth and Georgiana gathered at the top of the steps to greet them.

As their horses were led away in the growing dusk with soldiers' bags strapped to their sides to be brought in and unpacked by a footman, the colonel hurried up the ornate external staircase to shake Darcy's hand and bow over Elizabeth's and Georgiana's hands. The lieutenant colonel, a little younger by the looks of him, ascended more slowly.

"Welcome, Fitzwilliam," said Darcy. "You travel light, cousin. And, Lieutenant Colonel, welcome. Come in, come in."

Colonel Fitzwilliam gestured to his friend. "Allow me to introduce Lieutenant Colonel James Harvey."

Lieutenant Colonel Harvey bowed.

"My family, Harvey: my cousin Fitzwilliam Darcy, Mrs Darcy his wife and my cousin Miss Georgiana Darcy."

"At your service ma'am, sir, Miss Darcy."

"You are looking well, Darcy," Colonel Fitzwilliam continued. "Married life obviously suits you. And Georgiana, you are truly a young lady now. And," directed at Elizabeth, "how delightful it is to see my fair cousin again."

The expression was so reminiscent of Mr Collins's blandishments to Elizabeth, that the smile which curved her mouth resulted as much from its comical effect as for the pleasure of seeing him. He was as she remembered him at Rosings at Easter, not handsome, but very pleasant in his countenance, enquiring after those who would be making up the Christmas party as they walked through the grand hall.

"A jolly time we shall have, to be sure," he said. "Harvey loves to dance, don't you? He is a firm favourite at our regimental soirées."

The lieutenant colonel smiled. "Favourite or not, 'tis quite true that I enjoy dancing."

"How very excellent," said Elizabeth. "I certainly hope we will be able to entertain ourselves with many dances over the festive period. Even William, you will be pleased to hear, Colonel, is now much less reluctant to take the floor than hitherto. Ladies are no longer in danger of sitting down for want of a partner."

The colonel looked momentarily confused.

Darcy turned to him. "She means me, Fitzwilliam. You will recall how she loves to tease."

"Yes, I do. What a happy state of affairs to see that marriage has not blunted your humour, cousin." This addressed to Elizabeth.

Elizabeth took the opportunity to observe Lieutenant Colonel Harvey during this exchange. He was certainly handsome, with fair, not quite brown, hair and had spoken with a deep, clear voice. Elizabeth fancied that he might well have a good singing voice, a tenor or baritone perhaps, which promised more entertainment for the family over the coming days.

As it was late afternoon, Darcy asked for tea to be served in the blue room and the others were called.

LATE arrivals after midnight were Mr and Mrs Bennet with Mary and Catherine and, in a separate carriage, Mr and Mrs Philips. Darcy quickly donned a nightshirt and threw on his dressing gown on being roused by poor Patterson, himself in a dressing gown and tasselled night cap. Elizabeth followed him down as soon as she could make herself decent.

Mr Bennet was effusive in his explanations and apologies.

"Our carriage hired from Ashburn lost a wheel just after Wirkworth. We had to walk back and shelter in the inn there while the coachman fetched help."

Mr Philips nodded vigorously. "And of course we were not going to come on ahead of them."

"No, quite. But," Darcy said as Elizabeth joined him, "You are safely here now, and very glad we are to see you."

He extended his hand to Mr Bennet, Mr Philips and Mrs Philips in turn, as Elizabeth hugged her anxious mother, then her father, sisters and aunt.

Darcy then stepped forward, placed his hands on Mrs Bennet's arms and bent and kissed her cheek.

"Mother," he said, "we are delighted to see you."

Mrs Bennet drew a sharp breath. "Mr Darcy," she squeaked.

"William, please," he smiled on his mother-in-law.

Mrs Bennet's mouth silently opened and closed, so astonished was she to be thus addressed by the stiff, unfriendly Darcy as she thought of him.

"And Mary and Catherine," he added, "welcome to Pemberley."

The girls were looking about them in wonderment, as was Mrs Philips — and they were only in the blue room.

"We will show you round properly tomorrow," Elizabeth said. "Mr and Mrs Gardiner and their children are here already and Colonel Fitzwilliam arrived this evening with a friend. We hope Jane and Mr Bingley may arrive tomorrow. But now you must be very fatigued."

She noticed Mary rather sourly observing the surroundings. No doubt tomorrow she would express her disapprobation of the excessive wealth in the hands of one man. Well, thought Elizabeth, she must think as she would. Mary had been satisfied enough with Chatsworth on their visit last year and that house was a good deal larger and grander than Pemberley, though both houses were built in the same Baroque style. Darcy was at least as good a master as the Duke of Devonshire. Mary had applauded the fact that Chatsworth was open to visitors and, it was said, once a month gave a dinner to anyone visiting the house. Being less well known than Chatsworth, visitors to Pemberley were not so large in number. But those wishing to see the house were rarely refused and were hospitably treated as she herself had experienced with her aunt and uncle earlier in the year.

Mrs Reynolds bustled in at that moment, fully dressed.

"Oh, Mrs Darcy, Mr Darcy, I do apologise for not being immediately ready to receive Mrs Darcy's family."

"No, Mrs Reynolds," Elizabeth assured her. "You could not have known."

"Thank you, Mrs Darcy." Mrs Reynolds turned to the new arrivals. "On this winter night, may I arrange for you to be brought refreshments, cold collations, fruit, wine, ale and cordials?"

"Oh, please do not trouble yourself," said Mr Bennet. "I am sure we will manage until breakfast."

Elizabeth was relieved, thinking of the poor maids who would be woken up to plate and serve the food, and then had to be up again at four in the morning to light the fires and begin the cleaning.

"Oh," said Mrs Philips, "I could certainly eat a small amount."

"Yes," echoed her husband. "We were served very ill at the inn at Wirkworth."

"A moment, please."

Elizabeth took Mrs Reynolds aside and whispered with her for a minute. Returning, she told her family that there was some fruit, cheese, wine and probably some bread left in the small dining room which she and Mrs Reynolds would bring to their rooms. There was no need to wake more of the servants at this hour.

"Quite," said Mr Bennet.

Darcy took up a candlestick and gestured to Patterson.

"Come, follow us to your rooms," he told the Bennets and the Philipses.

ELIZABETH sighed, having settled her family and being in the course of undressing again. The activity of the last hour had torn from her all desire to sleep for now. Darcy sat at their dining table, still in his dressing gown. She threw on her own and sat with him. For some minutes they drank a glass of wine together and quietly talked over the events of the last few days. She told him of her hopes that Lieutenant Colonel Harvey might entertain them all with songs.

"It occurs to me, Fitz, that I have never heard you sing."

"And never shall you."

"I cannot believe it. Even when we are in church, you just mumble. The world is possibly being robbed of one of the greatest pleasures man could ever know."

"Even those with no musical sense whatever would recognise something so grossly disagreeable to the ear, I assure you, and run in the opposite direction."

"Well, I would risk it. But if no performance is to be forthcoming, even for my private listening, 'tis as well that we share so much pleasure in other ways. Fitz, I am not tired for now if you are not."

He stood and, taking her hand, raised her to her feet.

"Let us not then waste our time. I feel sure that we can exhaust our remaining reserves of energy very satisfactorily, as always."

Chapter 11

AT LAST Jane and Bingley had arrived yesterday evening, Friday, with just enough time to become settled by Christmas which was on Tuesday. Jane, her colour high, looked the picture of health as she tripped off to her room, and today Elizabeth determined to spend as much time as possible with Jane and find out all her news.

They had been unable to wait any longer to show the family around the house and had done so yesterday well before the Bingleys arrival. Mrs Reynolds and Mr Patterson assisted Elizabeth and Darcy in the task. Bingley, of course, was already familiar with Pemberley, but Jane had never visited. Her tour would have to be undertaken therefore another time.

Yesterday's tour took in almost every room with the exception of private bedrooms and the servants' bedrooms. Elizabeth herself had not yet seen some parts of the house and was just as interested as the rest of her family. Some parts of the house were virtually closed off. They held furniture but were obviously unused with dust covers and the curtains closed. The kitchen was visited in some haste so as not to discompose the cooks and kitchen servants.

Kitty and Georgiana, already the best of friends, were away to Lambton together this morning with a footman to chaperone them. Darcy had been reluctant to call for a curricle for them and had suggested sending Mrs Annesley with a list of wares they were hoping to buy, herself accompanied by a footman, but the sisters had begged to be able to go themselves, Kitty pointing out that the Bennet girls had taken frequent trips to Meryton with their sisters or sometimes alone.

Darcy had sought Elizabeth's counsel before agreeing.

"It is only a few miles. They will travel with a footman. Surely the freedom would be good for Georgiana. And it is true, as Kitty said, that my sisters and I frequently walked to Meryton.

Lambton is not so dissimilar to Meryton."

"Very well," said Darcy. "I cannot guard her forever, I suppose."

Twenty minutes later they went together to see off the girls.

"Where are the rest of them?" Darcy, speaking as the curricle disappeared, sounded resigned to have had his house invaded. He had breakfasted early and had ridden out to see Sanders, returning in time to receive Georgiana's and Kitty's entreaties to be allowed to go to Lambton.

"So far as I know, my father is in the library and Georgiana has given Mary full permission to practise on the pianoforte. I believe Colonel Fitzwilliam and Lieutenant Colonel Harvey are practising their swordsmanship and hope to exercise their horses later. My mother and Aunt and Uncle Philips were still in the breakfast room when I last looked. They appeared very settled, drinking coffee, happy for the servants to clear up around them. As to the others, let me think.

"Oh, and we have been so busy, I have not thanked you yet, Fitz, for your welcome to my mother on Thursday. It was excessively kind of you. She is still reeling from the shock."

"Well, she is my mother now, is she not?"

"Indeed she is. How fortunate for you!"

"I am sure we will come to understand each other very well as time progresses.

"Now," he continued, "Mr and Mrs Gardiner and I plan to take the children out with the dogs before luncheon. The children are much entertained by them. And here comes Bingley. He seemed interested to join us and stretch his legs after several days of travel."

"How very convenient as I have every intention of monopolising Jane for most of the morning. Nearly two months apart must have stored up a deal of news for each of us to impart. And then," her expression towards her husband held a measure of significance, "I must spend a little time with my father with a view to learning more of the mysterious events of last year."

Darcy nodded but made no comment and they loosed their clasped hands as his friend came upon them.

ELIZABETH had not forgotten the great pleasure of having Jane to herself, to receive the benefit of the other's calm countenance and sensible, restrained view of the world.

They were sitting in her own sitting room, the scene of so much love between her and her husband. This room, and their bedroom beyond, had witnessed the full and varied ways in which their deep attachment had been satisfied. She had no way of knowing whether other couples experienced the same heights of passion, the same sorts of physical congress as she and Fitz. Was any of it unusual or sinful? She could not tell.

Did Jane and Bingley act similarly? She would like to know but could never enquire.

What she was told almost immediately filled her with surprise.

"Oh, Lizzy, I have been burning to tell someone and you are the only person in whom I can confide. Charles and I are going to have a child."

"Upon my word, so soon? Why that is wonderful."

"Yes, though it is uncomfortable. I feel constantly queasy, as though I may vomit. It is not pleasant, but to be having a child is the greatest gift."

"How do you know, Jane? What signs are there? I should like to know for when I may fall with child myself at some time."

"Well, of course no menses. Not since the wedding ceremony, Lizzy. Then almost immediately, I felt as though I was becoming full."

"Full?"

"Yes. Full all over, like a pig's bladder being inflated. Well, not quite so bad as that, but it is the nearest likeness I can express. My clothes have become ill-fitting. I must soon have new dresses made. And, as I have said, thinking every minute that I may vomit. But I have not done so yet. If I eat something, cake for the most part, the feeling goes away for a time."

"Oh, Jane, we will certainly order cake for you. I am so happy for you."

"I thank you, Lizzy, but there are some disadvantages. It is not all a bed of roses."

Elizabeth could not imagine what might be the problem.

"Elizabeth, Charles is...reticent since knowing of my condition."

Elizabeth frowned. "Reticent?"

"He will not...continue as we were. He is frightened of damaging me and the child."

Elizabeth understood now. She looked aside. What could she suggest? There was nothing she could suggest. She could only hope that if she fell with child, that her own marriage would not be so afflicted. It would be a bitter blow, so much had she come to rely on her closeness to Fitz. One thing occurred to her.

"Jane, of course you must share this news with the family while you are here if you wish. I was just thinking that if our mother knows you are with child, she may well start to exert pressure on me to perform equally. And nothing has so far come about and I think it is something one cannot control one way or the other. Of course, Fitz and I wish for children, but for now we are very happy indeed."

"I am surprised Mama has not noticed. She must have experienced every sign of pregnancy there is to know. But at breakfast today, she said almost nothing. It is quite unlike our mother."

"I think she is overwhelmed just by being here. And, on their arrival, Fitz kissed her on the cheek, addressed her as 'Mother' and asked her to call him William."

"Fitz?"

"Well, it is what I call him. Call Darcy."

Jane laughed. "You have tamed a bear, then."

"Not exactly. Our father expressed to me over a year ago that he perceived that there were two types of person. Some appear hard and unfriendly, whereas their true natures may be quite at variance with their appearance. Others appear cordial and charming, but have an iron core. He meant Mr Wilde who was determined to pursue his chosen profession above all else, even if at cost to himself. Papa said that one day I might meet a person who is the opposite, someone with a stern and reserved countenance, proud even, and yet find within a soft and generous core. I found him, Jane. None of us realised, least of all me, to begin with."

Jane was speechless for a time. Then she rallied.

"Lizzy, please believe that I have no intention of informing anyone, apart from you and Charles, of my condition. I do not wish to be treated like a fragile china ornament. If Charles chooses to treat me so, I do not like it but there is little I can do about it. But I do not want everyone else dancing attendance around me. I am perfectly well."

"Of course, you certainly appear in excellent health. Charles always loved you so very much, Jane. That was evident from the very first. I am sure his...reserve...will dissolve before long and all will be agreeable between you again."

"Lizzy, I begin to feel queasy again. I think I will return to my room."

"Yes, yes. I will walk with you and have some refreshment sent to you."

Jane hugged her. "Lizzy, you are the best sister. I believe the sickness does not last for more than the first three months. I will soon be fully myself again."

ELIZABETH, on returning to her room, stood at the window for a time. The milky sky was more wintry-looking than ever. Surely snow would fall soon.

She took some time to reflect upon what Jane had told her. The news of a baby coming was of course wonderful without question. That the occasion gave Bingley cause to retreat somewhat from the joys of marriage was a surprise indeed. Her father's words came back to her again. Bingley had always been eminently charming and cordial. He was all ease and cheerfulness. Yet he had withdrawn his favours from his wife at the first sign of her being in the least indisposed. It seemed that his nature was not quite as it appeared. His inner core was perhaps not hard, but it seemed that there was a seriousness within with which she would not have previously credited him.

Faced with the same circumstances, she knew that she would have made her feelings clear to her husband. She knew that quite likely Jane had not. The sisters were very different in their reactions. Jane probably did not voice her objections. She never did show her true feelings to any degree. Her calmness had almost destroyed her chances of securing Bingley's attachment. Darcy, it seemed, had been easily able to persuade his friend at one time that Jane was not partial to him when nothing could have been further from the truth.

Shouts and cries from outside caught her attention. The party of adults, children and dogs, still some distance away, were coming towards the house. They stopped at an opening in the wood which gave onto a path off to the side through the trees, leading away from the house. There was a brief discussion. Elizabeth saw the Gardiners, the children and the wolfhounds start again towards the house. Darcy and Bingley raised their hands to the others as they turned onto the woodland path with the gundogs.

Did men, Elizabeth wondered, as her husband and Bingley disappeared, discuss intimate matters as she and Jane had done? Probably not.

"I SEE that you and Mrs Darcy have developed a very satisfactory intimacy in such a short time."

Darcy detected some bitterness in his friend's tone as they forged further into the wood and the tree branches closed over them.

"Indeed, we are fortunate to find that we are very much...in accord."

"That is very evident, Darcy."

"Come, come, Bingley. You and I married the two prettiest girls in Hertfordshire. I cannot believe that your marriage is not at least as happy as my own."

"Well, since you have always seen fit to involve yourself in my life and loves, there is no reason why you should now be ignorant of the complications of my marriage."

"Upon my word, what ails you, my friend?"

Darcy spoke lightly, imagining some minor difference in the choice of carpets, for example.

"As you know," Bingley replied, "Jane is delightful and charming and gentle and kind. It is her gentleness which I find is something of an impediment. And now she is with child — yes, Darcy, already we think, though I would be grateful if you would keep it to yourself for the moment, except that she is bound to tell Elizabeth—Darcy, I don't want to hurt her, or the child, of course."

"Ah, I comprehend. I can understand your quandary. Yet people have been reproducing for millennia. Babies have survived their parents' amorous activities to be born fit and healthy. If you and she wish to be intimate, then I think it is unlikely the baby will come to any harm."

"I expect you are right. But Jane herself is so fine, so fragile I sometimes feel."

"Charles, she is Lizzy's sister. Two more robust girls I never saw."

They came to a place where the path divided.

"Let us take the right-hand fork," said Darcy. "It will take us more quickly back to the house."

They walked on, the dogs frolicking towards them and then away again into the undergrowth. Bingley was silent.

"I think, my friend," said Darcy after a time, "that it would be a great mistake to allow this state to become...settled, entrenched, so that it may prove to be permanent and be impossible to eradicate."

"But do not you recall how unwell she was after she rode over to Netherfield in the rain to visit my sisters?"

"I recall that she was confined to bed for a few days, that everyone made a great fuss of her and that the whole incident was almost certainly contrived by her mother in the hope of securing an early proposal of marriage from you."

"Quite possibly, although you ensured that it would not come to pass."

"I cannot deny it. However, the reality is probably that Jane was already sickening for a cold, not that she is so delicate that she could not undertake a short ride in the rain without falling ill."

"I suppose I talk not so much of Jane's constitution. The fineness is more in her nature. One would not wish to desecrate a valuable manuscript or wrestle with a fine piece of china. That is how I see her."

"I feel sure she would not see herself in that light, Charles. Think of her upbringing, in a crowded, noisy household, with a mother and aunt—I speak of Mrs Philips of course—given to such vulgar words and behaviour at times, though I grant you, they have been more reserved of late."

"I credit you, Darcy, with accountability for that happy change. They are in such awe of you that they cannot be themselves."

"Perhaps. And what of her sister Lydia, one of the least discreet girls one could encounter, ready to run off with that scoundrel Wickham? I think your Jane is no piece of fine china beneath her calm exterior. Try to picture her instead as an ordinary pewter jar, filled with rough country ale; or a gossip sheet rather than a manuscript."

Despite his anguish, Bingley laughed at his friend's characterisation of his lovely wife.

"Charles, she is a flesh-and-blood woman, not an ornament as perhaps you have come to regard her. And beneath her serene exterior, I expect she is very similar to Lizzy. 'Tis a certainty indeed that she will desire your full attentions quite as much as you desire her."

Darcy was happy to see Charles smile in spite of his apparent inner consternation.

"There speaks a man of the world, eh, Darcy."

"Hardly."

"Don't forget, Darcy, I was there."

Darcy hacked at some overgrown shrubbery with his stick.

"You mean Clara, I presume," he said, straightening up.

"Indeed I do."

The men walked on.

Darcy turned his head towards his friend. "I had no idea she was married, you know, whether you believe it or not."

Bingley assumed an air of nonchalance. "It matters not to me, Darcy."

"You know how it was. She just appeared. And just as soon disappeared when her father left to continue on his lecture tour. Everyone was entranced by her."

"Yes, but it was you she chose to occupy her days with in Cambridge."

"Days indeed. It is like a dream."

"And if I recall, there was no shortage of females in Derbyshire hoping to catch your eye before we left to go south last year. I am not convinced that none of them succeeded."

"All the more reason, then, to have escaped to Hertfordshire."

They rounded a bend in the path.

"Come along, Darcy, we are almost at the house. I thank you, my friend, for pointing out the obvious and simplifying the formerly seemingly impenetrable. I speak figuratively, of course."

"Of course."

"I will go and see Jane now."

"Stand with me for a moment, Bingley, if you would. I hope you will not object to my troubling you with a problem of my own."

"Certainly not." Bingley fixed his eyes on Darcy with interest.

Darcy summarised the contents of the letter received by Elizabeth from the Reverend Wilde.

"I instructed a lawyer, Waring of Lambton, to make enquiries about this woman. I saw him on Wednesday. I have said nothing to Lizzy yet. I did not wish to alarm her and ruin her Christmas with her family. This is what he reported to me..."

Chapter 12

MR BENNET, as Elizabeth had predicted, was to be found in the extensive library. Two newspapers had been read and discarded on a side table. When Elizabeth walked in, Mr Bennet had settled in a chair drawn near to the fire and was engrossed in a book.

"Papa," she said. "I hope I am not disturbing you. However, there is a matter which I would discuss with you."

He looked up. "My dear, you are of course interrupting me. But it does not follow that the interruption must be unwelcome."

Obviously, she *was* disturbing him but nonetheless she wished to find out soonest, following Mr Wilde's letter, what had gone on last year of which she was in ignorance. She had told Fitz she would speak to her father and she must do so. There was a little urgency. The woman formerly known as Helen St Clair had possibly injured Mr Wilde's sister and had possibly poisoned Mr Wilde last year. More recently, she had issued threats to Mr Wilde and for him to have alluded in the same sentence both to Helen and what Mr Bennet may or may not have told Elizabeth about events last year, must mean that the two were in some way connected.

Helen had left Hertfordshire and was believed to be now living not far from Pemberley. She had assumed a Christian name similar to Elizabeth's own name which was a strange thing to do and was distinctly unnerving. She had visited Pemberley three weeks ago with other local women who had enquired about the Darcy family and any heirs of the present owner.

Elizabeth told herself there was no immediate need to panic. Nothing had happened, no harm had come to anyone, but the situation had to be addressed.

"What are you reading, Papa?"

He peered at her over his spectacles. Perhaps he sensed some disquiet in her manner since he appeared to be scrutinising her face. After some seconds, he gestured to a nearby chair.

"This is a fine library of your husband's Lizzy. There is a large section devoted to science. I wonder if he reads them all. And there are more books, newly arrived, as yet unpacked."

He pointed to several piles in a corner, still in wrapping paper tied with string.

"But I prefer something lighter on this winter day. It is 'The Vicar of Wakefield', Lizzy, as you see, by Oliver Goldsmith." Leaning forward and keeping a thumb in his book, he partly closed it so that she could see the title on the front cover. "Draw up a chair to the fire, Lizzy, and sit by me."

She did as he suggested.

"A very good choice, Papa. I would not have thought that it would be a book to greatly interest you, though I have read it several times."

He opened the book again and let it rest on his knees. "I dare say you have. I, too, thought it would probably not suit me, but now I have read several chapters, I like it quite well. And I can think of no more pleasant way to spend one's time as Christmas approaches, in such opulent surroundings, being waited on, knowing that one's two eldest daughters are so admirably settled, and having not a care to interfere with one's sense of well-being."

And here she was, she thought, about to introduce a subject of some menace. She would not, she decided, show him Mr Wilde's letter. She would merely summarise the contents and try to find out from her father what he knew of the events relating to Peter Carpenter's rescue from the Nottingham cotton mill, since this seemed to be the point of her father's contact with Mr Wilde.

"So, Lizzy, what is it that is exercising you, for I can see that something troubles you?"

"Oh, Papa, I simply wished to tax you on a matter relating to Mr Wilde. You will recall the Reverend Wilde who was our good friend for nine months last year."

"Of course, I do indeed. A very good friend, as I recall. A very good man."

There was some meaning in her father's voice. Whether it was directed at her own attachment to the rector, she had better ignore and get on with her task.

"Well, Papa, he wrote to me recently and—"

"Did he indeed! And does this doting husband of yours allow gentlemen to correspond with his wife?"

"I...he...it wasn't like that." What it was not like she was not exactly sure, but she hurried on. "He wrote to me to warn me."

Mr Bennet raised an eyebrow. "This sounds somewhat ominous, Lizzy."

"I expect it does. But it cannot be of any importance, I am sure. I formed the opinion last year that Helen St Clair, if you recall her, was obsessed with the rector. She seemed to be jealous of me for some reason. She evidently wrote to him recently and threatened to disrupt his marriage and his warning to me was that she may attempt to disrupt mine. She must have thought that the rector and I were...close, and I suppose she intended to somehow use that intelligence."

He removed his spectacles and sat back. "That girl, Lizzy, is wrong in the head. Dangerous even, in my view."

"Papa, what can you mean?"

Mr Bennet shook his head. "Well, I've probably said too much."

A shudder ran through Elizabeth at her father's words.

"Papa, please tell me what you mean. There is more, but I did not want to alarm you. If I tell you, please promise not to say anything to the rest of the family." Elizabeth felt herself becoming overwrought. "This is terrible. We have asked you all here for Christmas, and now this happens. I had not intended to, but I feel I must show you Mr Wilde's letter for you to understand."

She produced it from her sleeve and handed it to her father whose face held understandable astonishment.

"Read it, Papa. And then you will see."

He didn't immediately react, staring at the letter as though it held some curse. Then he reached across, grasped it from her and, placing his spectacles back on his nose, started to peruse the epistle. It took him at least five minutes to read to the end, punctuated by sighs and shakes of his head and short periods staring out of the window.

"Lizzy, my dear," he said at last. "I have been attempting to forget that whole period of my life. I am not proud of my actions at that time. I behaved like a fool."

This told Elizabeth nothing. Her astonishment at his words was great and she longed to urge him to explain himself but, not wishing to break his train of thought, she remained silent as she took back Mr Wilde's letter.

At length, he resumed.

"I must have been going mad, Lizzy. I concocted a ridiculous scheme to take the Gilberts' next baby, which we reasonably assumed would be a boy, and supplant him in our own family as though he was our own child. Then, when I died, there would be a male heir to inherit the Longbourn estate and you, your sisters and your mother would not be thrown out of Longbourn. Between us, Richard Gilbert and I devised an elaborate plan to render it credible that your mother had given birth to a baby boy while most of the rest of the family and all the servants were in Buxton."

Elizabeth struggled to comprehend what he was saying.

"But Mrs Gilbert gave birth to a little girl."

"She did indeed. But that was not what we expected, Lizzy, given that all the Gilberts' children were boys."

"So Mr Wilde knew of this scheme?"

Elizabeth cast her mind back to September 1797 and her last meeting with Mr Wilde.

"Oh!"

Realisation dawned. Her announcement to Mr Wilde that Mrs Gilbert had been delivered of a healthy baby daughter had given rise to extreme mirth on his part which she had not at all understood at the time. Now, it made sense. So, she reasoned, Mr Wilde must have known of the scheme.

Did this also mean...?

"Was Mr Wilde part of your scheme?"

"Oh, no, no, no, Lizzy. Most certainly he was not. He found out about it, I think from Mrs Gilbert."

"So...why did you not go ahead with the scheme? Oh, of course, the birth of a little girl would have thwarted it for sure."

"It was already abandoned by that time. You will recall that we were going to take the servants to Buxton with us and hire a house rather than lodgings, but then did not and left the servants at Longbourn. The scheme was already finished by then. Mr Wilde had found out about it and, being the man he is, was of course appalled. I had to relinquish the scheme. By the way, your mother knew nothing of the scheme. Only the Gilberts and I and Mr Wilde know of it. And now you."

Thoughts churned around in Elizabeth's mind like a pudding mix. It was still not making much sense to her and she voiced one respect in which she found herself bewildered.

"I simply cannot fathom, Papa, what this has to do with Helen St Clair."

"Ah, well, Lizzy, that is another matter. She accosted me after church one Sunday and made it clear that she had been watching you. She gave me particulars of meetings you had with Mr Wilde. She seemed to believe that you and Mr Wilde were meeting in secret and drew the obvious conclusion, or thought I would. Of course, I rebuked her and sent her away. As I've said, I formed the view that she was wrong in the head and probably dangerous.

"But Lizzy, to my undying regret, I too was observing you. I too formed the view that you and he were conducting a secret courtship, knowing nothing of the quest to find Peter Carpenter. I challenged Mr Wilde. In fact I threatened him with his removal from the benefice and he, not unnaturally, countered with his knowledge of my venture to defraud the real heir to the entail."

"You mean Mr Collins would have been disinherited? Oh, Papa."

For the first time in this interview, Elizabeth found there was humour to be had. She put a hand in front of her mouth and stifled a laugh.

"Oh, Papa," she said again, "just think of Mr Collins's reaction if the plan had worked and a baby boy had come along to oust him. The disappointment, his consternation and dismay."

She laughed aloud this time at the picture conjured up of a deeply indignant Mr Collins.

"Aye. 'Tis a comical notion to be sure. But it must never come to light. It would have been a crime, Lizzy, and I cannot now imagine how I could have countenanced such a plan and attempted to make it happen."

"Well, at least I know now what Mr Wilde meant in his letter when he said he did not know how much you had told me. That was what I wanted to find out from you. But we are still left with the spectre of Helen St Clair or Isabella Scargill and what she may attempt to do, if anything."

Her father was drawing breath to reply when a high-pitched scream reached them through the semi-open library door, echoing down the hallways, bouncing off the stone walls, pillars and high ceilings. They both rose immediately and rushed out in the direction of the sound. More screams and sobs could be heard. It seemed as though more than one person was giving vent to their anguish and it sounded like the cries of children.

They followed the noise to the blue room and hurried in. The door was open and the Gardiner children were kneeling down. Their parents and Batchelor and Nancy stood over them in various attitudes of horror. One of the wolfhounds was standing. The other lay still on the hearthrug before the fire, its body rigid.

Beth and Julia, Anthony and David were consumed by grief.

"She's dead," Anthony sobbed looking up at Elizabeth and Mr Bennet. "Lady's dead."

Chapter 13

DARCY entered the room and took in the scene. The adults seemed to be petrified by the sight of the dead animal and the screams of the children.

"What has happened?" he said.

No one answered.

He bent and touched the motionless animal and looked her over. Then he put his hand on Anthony's shoulder.

"Don't be too upset," he said softly. "She was quite old. I'm sure she didn't suffer."

"Really?" The boy swallowed his cries and looked up at Darcy.

"Oh yes, I'm sure."

The other children calmed down at this.

He straightened and turned to the Gardiners.

"You brought Lady and Caesar back to the house. What happened?"

Mrs Gardiner was the first to recollect herself.

"No. We didn't bring them directly to the house. A footman, I think he was called Michael, came and met us and took the dogs away to the back to clean them up and feed them. He has done this every day since we arrived. We've taken the dogs out every day." She added quietly: "The children so love to be with them."

Darcy nodded.

Reassured, she continued, "I'm not sure if he brought the dogs to this room. They always seem to find their own way here. We went upstairs to tidy ourselves. We came down and — found this."

"Anthony," Darcy seemed to summon the reserves of his memory for the names, "Beth, Julia and David, we will get a puppy tomorrow or Monday. Lady would have wanted another dog to take her place. And Caesar will welcome a new friend."

"Do you really think so?" said Beth.

"Oh, yes, definitely. It is always the way. Now, it is best that you all go and wait elsewhere until luncheon is served. We will soon be along to the dining room ourselves. About half an hour I should think."

"Yes, of course we will," said Uncle Gardiner. "Thank you, Darcy. Come along children. It will all be all right."

WHEN they had gone, Darcy rang the bell for Patterson and Mrs Reynolds. They attended promptly and Darcy gave orders for a footman to be summoned to take away the dead dog.

"And please," he said, "tell them not to dispose of the dog's body. Keep it somewhere safe. The children may wish to bury her properly. And," he lowered his head, "as you know, she was my mother's pet."

"Yes, Mr Darcy."

"And Patterson, can you see if you can find a puppy nearby that needs a home."

"Yes, sir."

"Patterson, I must speak to Michael since it was he who took the dogs away. If you would not object, I would use your room for the interview. It should not take long. I had better see him alone."

"Of course, Mr Darcy."

"Would you send Michael to your room."

"Of course, sir."

The butler and housekeeper hurried away.

"Will you wait for me in my study, Lizzy?" Darcy said.

"Papa knows," said Elizabeth. "About Isabella Scargill."

"I see," said Darcy. "So does Bingley. I will summon him as well and then we must all decide what to do after I've spoken to Michael."

THE four faced each other in the large room used by Darcy as his study. Three walls were lined with bookcases and a large desk stood near the back of the room. In the open area nearer the door, easy chairs and tables gave the room a less formal look and the four were seated here around a table. Bingley and Mr Bennet had each poured themselves wine from a decanter. As yet, Elizabeth and Darcy hadn't taken a glass.

Darcy cleared his throat before he addressed his wife and guests.

"You all know about Helen or Isabella Scargill, and her threat to the Reverend Wilde, as well as his account of her trespass in his house, her possible attack on his sister and that she may have poisoned him. I suppose you don't still have Wilde's letter, Lizzy?"

"Yes, I do. I was showing it to Papa when the children's cries alerted us."

"Would you let Charles read it, Lizzy? He is the only one who has not seen it."

"Yes, of course." She found she was still clutching the letter. Smiling faintly at Bingley, she leaned over and handed it to him.

Darcy resumed. "Mrs Scargill is believed to be in this area and my dog appears to have been poisoned. I suppose she could have died of natural causes but it does not seem so to me."

Addressing principally Mr Bennet and Bingley, he said:

"Once I had seen the Reverend Wilde's letter myself, and Lizzy and I had looked at the visitors' book and seen that Isabella Scargill had visited Pemberley with a group of local women, I decided to instruct a Lambton solicitor, Waring, to make enquiries about Mrs Scargill. I must tell you what the solicitor Waring said about her

He flung down the solicitor's letter.

"Take a look at that, but it says very little. Mr Waring, quite sensibly, was not prepared to put in writing what he couldn't verify, therefore he asked to see me and gave me a verbal report on Wednesday—"

"You saw him on Wednesday?"

"I did. I'm sorry, Lizzy, I didn't want to tell you and possibly upset you before Christmas. Now this has happened, I cannot keep it to myself."

"I see," she said, casting an eye over the document.

"DEAR SIR,

I regret that intelligence regarding Mrs Scargill is very limited. She is of course known of in the village of Nethermill where she maintains a residence. She has also not been long in Nethermill, having arrived some three months ago, it is said following her husband's death. Little is known about him. He had not lived in the house since inheriting it from a distant cousin some years ago. He died before Mrs Scargill came to Nethermill.

The above-mentioned facts are all that is reasonably certain. The remainder of what I have been able to discover regarding Mrs Scargill I regret results from rumour, gossip and supposition and I have to leave it to you what reliance to place upon it. As you know, I am an attorney dealing mainly with property and wills. I do not practise in the courts. However I have many clients, professional colleagues and friends who have wide interests and I have made discreet enquiries of them.

If you would care to attend me at my office at nine o' clock on Wednesday the 19th inst. I will acquaint you verbally with such intelligence as I have been able to gather regarding Mrs Scargill. I apologise for the early hour, sir. I act as clerk to the parish council and I am obliged to attend a meeting at ten o' clock. If you wish for an appointment the following day, then I could see you at any time which suits you but I understood your enquiry to be urgent.

I REMAIN SIR," &C. &C.

As Darcy had said, it told one almost nothing of any importance.

"I take it," said Elizabeth, "that you rode on to Matlock afterwards."

"I did."

There was silence to allow Bingley to read the parson's letter which was considerably longer. While he did so, Mr Bennet looked over the solicitor's letter then passed it along the table for Bingley to peruse which he did, thereafter placing both letters on the table.

"Hmm," was Bingley's only comment.

"Now, as to what Waring told me. I stress that it is all rumour of course. He said that some of his informants have connexions in other parts of the country, so it is not all Lambton and Nethermill tattle.

"There is talk that Scargill's death was suspicious. It is said that Mrs Scargill uses disguises and aliases, assumed names. She poses as old women and young men. She is said to accumulate intelligence about people and extort money from them for their secrets to remain so. This may be her principal source of income. It is not known whether her husband was wealthy or otherwise. Particularly worrying is the suggestion that she studied for a time under an apothecary.

"In former times, she might have been suspected of witch-craft. People are wary of her, although conversely, she is reputed to be able to easily gain people's confidence.

"These are the main points of Waring's verbal report to me and of course all or any of it may not be accurate."

Elizabeth touched her husband's arm. "What did Michael say about the dogs?"

Darcy's chair being close to hers, he folded his arm around hers and placed his other hand over hers. She felt all the closeness, comfort and reassurance which the gesture conveyed.

"He said that he took the hounds to the pump outside the kitchen door, washed them down and dried them. Afterwards, he left them for fifteen minutes or so to eat their food, which he brought them. This is what he always does. Then he let them into the house after which they usually go and lie before a fire as they did today in the blue room.

"I also had a word with Mr Gardiner who told me that while they were out with the dogs, all the dogs ran off into the woods from time to time if a stick was thrown into the trees."

Darcy looked around at the others.

"I am anxious not to make hasty assumptions. I think that Lady almost certainly died of poisoning, but it is quite possible that she took some bait left in the woods to kill a fox or other vermin. The gamekeeper is not supposed to leave poisoned bait anywhere near the house, or only such as to kill rats and so forth and there are known situations where this may be done where the dogs are not likely to be affected. But it is not infallible, and some other animal may have taken bait which was further afield and then dropped it near the house.

"Or Lady may have found something near the kitchen door left there by mistake."

"Or," said Mr Bennet, "some person might have crept to the back door and mixed poison in with the dogs' food or just Lady's."

"It's possible."

"If I may say," Mr Bennet spoke again, "I had some dealings with the young woman, Helen St Clair, before she left Longbourn which was in the summer of last year so far as I can recall. Her father is a friend of mine and a good man. But Miss St Clair or Mrs Scargill is a strange girl in my opinion. As I've told Lizzy, I think she may be dangerous. I did think that I had frightened her off last year by warning her that the nonsense she was uttering was defamatory and actionable in law. She certainly seemed to be alarmed."

"William, I will have to tell you later the occasion to which my father alludes."

Elizabeth addressed Darcy who nodded. Then turned to her father.

"Papa, I was hoping to ask you when we were in the library what Helen's parents have said of her movements since she left Longbourn. They must have known when she married and where she went to live. According to the solicitor, she has only been in Nethermill three months."

"To speak the truth, Lizzy, I took little interest in what I was told about her. I did not like her and was glad she had left the area. But I understood that initially she went to visit relations. I think Simon, her father, said that the relations were in Norfolk.

"I do not know anything of her marriage. You could ask your mother. She may know. I am not aware that her parents attended a wedding but Simon was becoming unwell over a year ago. In any case, as you probably recall Lizzy, Mr and Mrs St Clair left Longbourn about six months since because Simon was ailing. Mrs St Clair has a cousin in Bath and they went there for Simon's health and their elder son, Simon, remained at their house.

"All I would say is that if Helen Scargill is able to live comfortably, she must have some source of funds and the most likely source would be a husband, whether alive or now dead. And, as the solicitor said, extorting money from people."

"Well," said Darcy, "a decision has to be made what to do. In my view it is far too early to alarm the servants and our guests by telling them that the dog may have been deliberately poisoned by an ill-wisher. I know that extra servants have been taken on for the Christmas period." He turned towards Elizabeth. "I will have them brought before us, Lizzy, to see if you recognise any as Helen St Clair in disguise. Indeed, any new servants employed in the last three months should be scrutinised.

"I will also ascertain whether any servants have disappeared suddenly.

"Apart from newer servants, what I suggest is that Lizzy and I summon all the servants, and that they are told that I have received reports of robbers in the area and that all the outer doors are to be kept locked at all times, day and night. It is inconvenient, I know, but Pemberley must be kept safe from interlopers. It should be rendered less problematic by virtue of the fact that we have only one service wing with the majority of the servants confined to the ground floor. I will insist that Patterson and Mrs Reynolds see that these instructions are followed and I will be vigilant myself as to their observance."

Darcy paused and thought for a moment.

"Or we could tell them simply that, with guests in the house, we wish for extra security, which would be no bad thing in any case. If we say that instead, we can later revert to the story of robbers in the area if necessary."

"Of course," said Mr Bennet, "Mrs Scargill, if she is bent on mischief, having entered the house at some time, may be hiding inside the house even now. We observed on our tour that there are a great many places in which someone might conceal themselves."

Darcy's posture, more than anything he said, showed his irritation at the suggestion.

He sighed. "Then, we will have to think about having the house discreetly searched, but I do not think it can be exhaustive. It would take far too long and upset the whole household. Everyone will have to be told to be vigilant. The ground-floor and first-floor windows will have to be inspected daily for example."

"What about our guests, William?" Lizzy asked. "What do we tell them?"

"Well, if we merely tell the staff that we are increasing security because of guests then, if we have to tell the family anything, we can say the same thing to them. And on second thoughts, when we speak to the servants, we should see them in small groups, about ten at a time, to see if you, Lizzy, recognise Helen Scargill. We can ask to see groups of more recently employed servants and then those of longer standing. That way, we will avoid having to say anything about a possible intruder."

"Yes," said Elizabeth thoughtfully. "I think that is probably the best idea. I do not wish to cause distress to my mother or aunts or Jane, nor indeed my other sisters or uncles. As to the soldiers...I don't know. I suppose they should be able to look after themselves quite well."

"Let us assume so for now," said Darcy.

"And I think, if I may say so, Papa, that searching the house is too extreme. If any strangers were to have been seen lurking in the house, I am sure the servants would have reported it. Anyone in hiding would have...needs and be bound to show themselves eventually."

"As you wish," said Mr Bennet, "but just bear in mind what I have said about Helen Scargill. Indeed, what the solicitor reported."

"Of course," said Darcy. "Therefore, are we agreed that the four of us in this room will keep what we know to ourselves?"

There was general assent.

At that moment, the sound of a horse-drawn vehicle could be heard at the front of the house.

Darcy stood and went to the window. "Very well. So to the

dining room. And it seems that Georgiana and Kitty have re-turned."

Chapter 14

LUNCHEON might have been a muted affair, had it not been for Georgiana's and Kitty's chatter on the subjects of their trip to Lambton, their purchases and the news that next Saturday there was to be a ball at the Assembly Rooms at Lambton.

Naturally, they had been told of the death of Lady, though without any suggestion of poisoning or other unnatural cause of death. Georgiana in particular expressed her sorrow at the fate of the family pet and agreed that a decent burial was desirable, but the girls' high spirits could not be contained for long.

"Yes, I did know something of it," said Darcy, when told of the Lambton event. It would of course be a small, local affair.

"Oh, Fitzwilliam, may we go?" asked Georgiana eagerly. Kitty, being still wary of Darcy and awed by the splendour of Pemberley, was less vocal, but her enthusiasm for the evening was no less evident. Elizabeth took note of her bright eyes and her glowing complexion. Indeed, if Elizabeth was not mistaken, she had grown prettier since Elizabeth had last seen her at the wedding in November. And she had not heard Kitty cough once since the family's arrival. She also noticed Lieutenant Colonel Harvey glancing frequently at her sister. If he became an ardent admirer over the course of the Christmas festivities, they would have to research his background and means.

Oh dear, she thought, not another military man in the family!

But this was perhaps thinking too far ahead. A few stray glances hardly amounted to a suit for Kitty's hand and she saw comparisons with her mother in her train of thought. How very undesirable in most respects that would usually be to her. However, she must recognise that girls had to have husbands and the more wealthy and more gentlemanly, the better. Lieutenant Colonel Harvey certainly seemed to fulfil the second requirement, as he conversed cheerfully with Mrs Bennet seated next to him, she as ever enthralled by a red coat.

As to the first, Elizabeth was vaguely aware that it was a lieutenant colonel rather than a colonel who took a more active part in wars and fighting, the colonel's role being largely administrative. There were obvious dangers for a soldier in action and therefore for a young wife to be left a widow. And wasn't it a colonel's rank rather than a lieutenant colonel in which Mrs Bennet during her reflections at Longbourn had expressed an interest for her daughters? Maybe, accordingly, they should not encourage any match.

"Perhaps we could all go," exclaimed Georgiana looking round the table and recalling Elizabeth to the present.

Darcy drew a breath, his eyes straying to Elizabeth at the other end of the table. They were in the large dining room, there now being twenty in number to seat, including Mrs Annesley and the four children.

"Lizzy and I will discuss it later or perhaps tomorrow after church. It depends, too, on Kitty's parents."

He said this kindly with a smile towards Kitty whose eyes widened, and towards Mr and Mrs Bennet.

"You are quite right...William," Mrs Bennet responded. "The matter requires some thought."

"And," Darcy continued, "we are to enjoy singing and dancing here tonight. It will provide an opportunity for those of us who are not well acquainted to become more so. Perhaps everyone for now would give some consideration to Saturday's ball."

Conscious of her duty to support her husband, Elizabeth followed this with:

"Quite so. And Mary has kindly agreed to play for us tonight so that we may dance."

Mary, for once, smiled her assent and looked pleased to have been acknowledged.

"And I believe that Georgiana intends to play and sing for us."

Georgiana nodded.

"I may attempt to do so as well," said Elizabeth, "and we are hoping that one or more of the gentlemen may render a ballad or two."

"Mrs Darcy," said Colonel Fitzwilliam, "I do not recall your performance on the pianoforte during Easter at Rosings as being anything other than polished and that Darcy declared that no one admitted to the privilege of hearing you—now what did he say?—could think anything wanting."

Elizabeth was conscious that both of her parents had suddenly jumped to attention, ignorant as they would be of the full events at Rosings earlier this year. No doubt her mother knew something of Darcy's presence at Rosings from Lady Lucas who would have been informed by Charlotte, but those exact words of Darcy would be unlikely to have been related. Mrs Bennet regarded Darcy with new interest. Her father merely frowned his confusion.

A raised eyebrow and sly smile from Jane conveyed her understanding. Kitty appeared perplexed. Georgiana did not seem excessively surprised. Mary, as usual, showed no reaction.

The colonel smiled his triumph.

"Is that not so, Mrs Darcy?"

"Elizabeth, please, call me Elizabeth as we are cousins," said Elizabeth, somewhat warmly, recalling the occasion and Darcy's first proposal soon thereafter to follow, of which presumably Colonel Fitzwilliam, and everyone else, apart from Jane, was ignorant. "You flatter me, sir. As to my voice, you and others will have to judge tonight."

"Fitzwilliam," Darcy called with good humour across the room to his cousin, "you toy with us. I pray you would desist."

"As you wish, Darcy."

The children then clamoured to be allowed to stay up and put on a puppet play.

"We have been practising in the afternoons. We have made it up ourselves," said David. "It is about King George and Prince George and some ladies of the court and Napoleon. We have had to alter the Prince of Wales puppet to make him fatter."

There was laughter at this.

"But we do not know what Napoleon looks like so we used the devil puppet for him."

"Good choice," said Colonel Fitzwilliam.

"And I should like to dance," said Julia, the eldest, aged twelve. "I know all the steps."

"So do I," cried Beth, aged seven.

The boys seemed less interested in dancing.

Elizabeth looked at Aunt Gardiner and back to the children. "It is for your Mama and Papa to decide."

"I see no reason why not," her aunt replied, "if everyone else agrees."

"I would be highly diverted by a play about the Prince of Wales," said Aunt Philips.

There was general concurrence and the children clapped their hands together in satisfaction.

Darcy had been at least ten minutes behind everyone else coming to the dining room and, as discussion of tonight's entertainments filled the room with chatter and laughter, Elizabeth was debating with herself what his lateness could mean. Had he spoken to someone else? Their eyes met over the plate, glassware, silver and candles. Naturally, she was anxious to know of any developments and resolved to speak to him as soon as the meal was over.

For the moment, she was filled with the satisfaction of a mistress of the house who finds her guests in joyful and congenial intercourse and felt not the need to enter into the discourse herself. She caught Jane's eye. Jane's appetite had certainly increased, especially for the small sweet tarts which were a speciality of their under-chef who would be delighted to be able to produce so many little delicacies this Christmas. Jane returned the look with one of her secret smiles which Elizabeth so missed.

As she watched her sister, she saw too that Charles's expression towards his wife showed all the indulgence of a husband in his position. Unquestionably, he would make a devoted father.

Elizabeth's cogitations led her to imagine how delightful it would be if the Bingleys moved to Derbyshire. Was it possible that Darcy might consider suggesting to his friend the purchase of a house nearby since it was known that Bingley had intended at one time to purchase his own estate? To have her sister nearby would, Elizabeth thought, complete her own happiness, however it was hardly a suggestion to be made in the presence of the family. Mama in particular would doubtless be greatly discomposed at the thought of a move by Jane away from Netherfield.

Feeling a light pressure on her arm, her musings were interrupted and she turned to her father seated beside her.

"Papa?" She found herself whispering.

"Lizzy," his voice was also lowered, "has it escaped your notice that that woman must have turned up in Derbyshire about September, therefore around the time your engagement was announced? Do not you think it is more than a coincidence?"

A shiver ran through Elizabeth despite the heat from the fire, the chafing dishes and so many bodies in the room.

"It is certainly something to think on, Papa."

A possibility which had been at the back of her mind came now to the fore, and she might as well voice it to her father.

"Mr Wilde wrote of suspicions that Helen had tried to poison him. I did wonder, though, whether, rather than harm him, she had administered some sort of love potion but it performed badly. I think she was fanatically in love with him. If that was the case, then there is less cause to believe that the dog, Lady, was deliberately poisoned, rather than that she took poison by accident as William suggested may have happened."

"Think that if you must, Lizzy. I believe her to be at the least unpredictable and that you and Darcy should be on your guard."

A stirring of those round the table was taking place and Elizabeth saw that Darcy had risen.

"I apologise that I cannot remain to take port with the gentlemen, but I have business to attend to. I look forward to this evening's entertainments.

"Lizzy," he said, "could I have a word?"

THE very short discussion took place in Darcy's study.

"I thought it was only fair to take Patterson and Mrs Reynolds into our confidence about Mrs Scargill. We will have to tell your father and Bingley, of course. Patterson suggested locking the doors to all the unused rooms and areas of the house, which I think is an excellent idea."

"Oh it is, Fitz. How very clever of him. It largely avoids a search."

"I hope that it will. He will do it later when we have seen the servants in groups. I estimate that ten minutes for each group will be more than sufficient, so that we may accomplish the task within less than an hour. Seeing and talking to the servants engaged on outdoor pursuits will of course be more difficult. But the main thing is the locking of the outside doors.

"And neither Patterson nor Mrs Reynolds are aware of any servants going absent or taking leave, Lizzy, which is reassuring."

"Mrs Reynolds must realise now why I questioned her about the name of Scargill and visitors to Pemberley."

"Indeed."

"Oh, and Fitz, I must tell you briefly of the last year's events of which I was unaware involving my father..."

And, to a raised eyebrow and some head shaking on the part of Darcy, she proceeded to summarise the abandoned plan to pass off a son of the Gilberts as Mr and Mrs Bennet's own.

"It must be kept completely secret Fitz."

"Of course. Upon my word, that is quite a story. Now my love, the servants are being assembled, so shall we go and address the first group?"

ELIZABETH stirred at a sound from the next room. She had not intended to fall into a slumber after she and Fitz, unusually, took to their bed in the late afternoon and had enjoyed a quiet, less energetic, but wholly satisfactory coupling. But she had become fatigued from the exertions of the last few days and anxious following the death of the dog, the unexpected news of the attorney's report and the interviews with six groups of servants. Thereafter, the relief that the ordeal of seeing and inspecting the servants was over for now, had relaxed her to a considerable degree.

There were, in fact, more servants than were strictly necessary at Pemberley in order to reduce the individual burdens of these people, but nevertheless their hours were long and their work arduous.

The servants had largely looked baffled at being told about the extra security. Such a thing had never been proposed before. Most ordinary folk did not lock their doors even at nights, although larger houses, such as Pemberley, did have the doors locked and bolted before the servants retired.

She and Darcy stood, while the servants were seated, their chairs staggered, so that she should look down on them, the object being to attempt to make her inspection less obvious and so that taller servants would not obscure shorter servants from her view.

There had been much frowning and some slight shaking of heads. This was, after all, rural Derbyshire. While Fitz had told the assembled men and women what was required, she had tried to concentrate on people's faces and what she remembered of Helen St Clair. None of them remotely resembled the pinch-faced look of the girl she remembered from Longbourn, seeing her in church, at functions and once in Helen's own drawing room.

Furthermore, of course, she had to consider that some disguise might be employed.

There certainly were no hunched, white-haired old women which is how Elizabeth pictured such a false appearance being achieved. As to young men, she tried to imagine Helen in a manservant's clothes, usually clean but of poor quality, and with her hair pulled back in a rough queue. She was thin and tall enough to pass as a young boy or young man, though probably not sturdy enough for a mature man.

She and Fitz would stand at the door as the servants filed out after the talks in order that Elizabeth should see them face to face.

The servants did not seem very convinced at what Fitz was telling them, and of course most of them were used to taking their orders from Patterson or Mrs Reynolds or filtered down to them via lower servants. When these upper servants, Patterson and Mrs Reynolds, spoke out next, after Fitz had given his own short talk, it seemed to Elizabeth that the men and women at last stiffened to attention.

And when Fitz called upon her to say a few words to the first group of servants, she hardly knew where to begin. She was acutely conscious that it was her presence here which had brought about this need for change, although the servants would be unaware of this.

It was also the case that in order to attend church tomorrow, the servants were going to have to work extra hard to prepare food for tomorrow as well as for tonight, and for a larger number of people than on most weeks. It was no wonder that they appeared restless. Very probably they were desperate to return to their duties.

Summoning every ounce of her courage as she stood in the servants' hall composing herself, she forced herself not to waiver in her speech and dragged from her worried mind some suitable words and phrases to support Fitz's calls for extra protection, although she couldn't use that word. Indeed, every word which entered her head seemed to reek of some sort of danger.

Smiling at the upturned faces, she began:

"Pemberley is a large house with many points of entry and as Mr Darcy has said, we are asking for your help in providing a little more security here at Pemberley during my family's stay, especially as my family includes children. We are well aware that it is as a result of your excellent service that my family's stay has been made so comfortable and I thank you wholeheartedly for that. I am sure it will continue to be the case.

"Your hard work at all times does not go unnoticed. To be absolutely clear, the minor changes we are making are in no way a reflection on your service which is always of the highest standard as befits a house like Pemberley. The additional security is of course intended to benefit all at Pemberley, that is you as well as the family, and may well continue once our Christmas guests have departed. We are all concerned for the smooth running and safety of Pemberley and I know you will all give your full support to the new measures."

This was the gist of the speech she rendered to each group of servants and by the time she delivered it to the last group, she was almost word perfect.

It had not been so difficult as she had anticipated, but still she was glad to see out the last of the servants and leave Patterson to traipse round the house and lock all the doors to all the dormant rooms and parts of the house in accordance with his suggestion, and also to verify that the outer doors had been locked.

The sounds in the next room continued, then footsteps approached the communicating door. Momentarily, Elizabeth experienced a surge of fear, bearing in mind today's events, but recollected herself. There was no cause to expect Helen Scargill to be inside the house lurking near her bedroom — or at least not quite so soon.

It was of course Fitz who appeared. He carried a bowl of tea for her, and sat on the bed on her side, holding it while it cooled.

"I had better go to my room to dress with my valet, and Peggy will no doubt come to you."

"I am sure she will. What time is it?"

"Nearly six o' clock."

"I had no idea it was so late, but the rest has done me good. I feel much refreshed. Mrs Reynolds has arranged for other maids to assist my mother, aunts and sisters.

"Thank you for what you said today, Lizzy. I think it was couched in exactly the right terms. Let us hope for a pleasant evening."

DINNER was to be served at eight o'clock, with the play first thereafter and then music, singing and dancing in the large saloon, into which the pianoforte had been moved a couple of weeks ago, ready for Christmas. It had since been re-tuned by a gentleman brought from Lambton.

A tap on the outer door was answered by Peggy who was finishing Elizabeth's hair. Elizabeth went out to the sitting room into which Peggy had admitted Kitty who was swirling around in a smart evening dress of blue silk.

"What do you think, Lizzy? Jane has given me some of her dresses as they no longer fit her well, and of course Bingley has bought her many new dresses. Do you think it suits me? Of course I have had to take it in a little, but I have had no shortage of time to myself. There has scarce been anything to do at home now that you, Jane and Lydia have gone, apart from the few invitations we have had to Netherfield. Do you like it on me, Lizzy?"

Kitty gave a few more twirls.

"And my hair? Molly has dressed it exactly as I asked. These little flowers come from the conservatory, she said. Mary did not wish to have help dressing or with her hair, so Molly is dressing Mama now."

"You look very well, Kitty. The dress fits you perfectly. And your hair is beautifully dressed."

Indeed her sister did look very becoming. Quite a beauty with her golden hair with hints of copper, the only one of the sisters whose hair was not chestnut or auburn in colour. Tonight her hair had been brushed until it gleamed. It would do no harm to tell her so. In the rather harsh hierarchy often employed within families, Kitty had not been a particular favourite of anyone and Elizabeth knew that Kitty felt this, if not deeply or bitterly, then in a spirit of resignation which was, if anything, worse.

"Kitty, you look more than well. The word does not do you justice. You look beautiful."

For a moment, she feared that Kitty might burst into tears, causing her face to swell and become red and mottled for the whole of the rest of the evening. But happily, Kitty's surprise turned to delight. She smiled broadly, and came to Elizabeth to embrace her warmly.

It seemed a suitable point at which to mention George Wickham and the advisability of keeping his name out of any conversation.

"Oh, Kitty," Elizabeth said as they parted, "you spoke of Lydia. It would be better not to speak her name if you can avoid it and certainly not Wickham's for William heartily disapproves of him."

"Yes, Georgiana told me so today."

Elizabeth tried to hide her astonishment, but could not resist delving a little deeper.

"Oh yes, Kitty? In what connection did his name arise?"

"She told me that he had persuaded her to elope with him last year, but Mr Darcy, William, found out and prevented it. How scandalous!" Kitty giggled. "I am quite envious of her. Of course I am to say nothing of this to anyone else but I imagine you know already from...William. She does not love Wickham at all and knows he only wanted her money, as with Miss King at Longbourn. Georgiana thinks that he must have been paid money by someone to have agreed to marry Lydia. Or else, perhaps he does really love her."

"Hmm. Well, as Georgiana says, no one else should know about it. It would damage her reputation as I am sure you are aware."

Kitty's face at once became serious.

"Of course, I would tell no one," she said warmly. "Georgiana is my dearest sister. She is far kinder than Lydia. I feel so happy that we are here this Christmas. It will be wonderful."

Elizabeth sighed, hoping that this would prove to be the case. "Indeed. Now, Kitty, I had better let Peggy finish dressing my hair. Tell Molly that I said she has done very well."

"Yes, Lizzy."

AS her hair was piled higher by Peggy and threaded with tiny pearls on a string the exact colour of her hair, Elizabeth could not help reflecting on Kitty's revelation. Darcy must be told of Georgiana's confidence and that any partiality she had harboured for Wickham had passed. That should be a relief to him, but Elizabeth was not so sure it would be. At least if Georgiana was a little broken-hearted, it may have acted as a warning to her resulting in her being in less danger from any other adventurers she might encounter.

But Elizabeth failed to see how they could weaken the girls' friendship. Indeed, in her opinion, it would be cruel to attempt to do so. Darcy would just have to be persuaded to her view, as previously expressed, that Georgiana would fare better if she was not over-protected. In any case, the friendship would be naturally interrupted near the end of January when the Bennets' stay at Pemberley would be at an end.

That Kitty should be envious of the foiled elopement was not strictly desirable, but Elizabeth was thrown back on her father's words of last year: that for a girl to be crossed in love gives her a sort of distinction among her companions. How was it that her father understood such things? And why should Georgiana be deprived of some satisfaction in her singularity or Kitty of her appreciation of the other's experience?

She saw that Peggy had stepped back to view her mistress's hair. Elizabeth looked at herself in the mirror noticing, as she did, the reflection of the unmade bed, the linen and coverlet carelessly tossed and rumpled and, moreover, strewn with her shift and stockings and Fitz's stockings and breeches. Other garments had been thrown over chairs, somewhat more neatly.

Peggy had offered to tidy the bed when she first came in, but Elizabeth had said no matter, Peggy had already made the bed once, though when she left, she could take away anything which needed washing. The girl had surveyed the disorder, discreetly saying nothing, her face completely blank and certainly appropriately devoid of humour. But Elizabeth knew full well that the servants would almost certainly discuss the master's and the mistress's bedroom habits, and the fact that they slept together every night would no doubt be the subject of gossip in the servants' hall.

Elizabeth thanked Peggy and praised her skills at which her maid smiled broadly and left happily. Peggy had said nothing of the new measures or the speeches to the groups of servants earlier, in one of which of course Peggy had been included. Hopefully this meant that the measures were not resented nor that the calling together of groups of servants was found to be particularly strange.

In truth, though, Elizabeth was still feeling her way as the mistress of this large household, not quite sure how acceptable it was to be at all familiar with the servants or any particular servant. Having only Longbourn as an example was not especially helpful to her. Her only near experience with important families, indeed members of the aristocracy, had been Lady Catherine De Bourgh, Fitz's aunt, and Lady Rose, the mother of Julius Fairweather. Neither was a good example.

Elizabeth had met Lady Catherine in the spring when staying with her friend Charlotte and Charlotte's husband, Mr Collins, the Rector of Hunsford, the Rectory being in the grounds of Lady Catherine's home, Rosings. It was clear immediately to Elizabeth that the aristocrat was so puffed up with her own importance, so prone to interfere in the lives of anyone with whom she came into contact and so arrogant as to be scarcely conscious of the place of servants. They were now estranged from Lady Catherine due to her having written to Darcy in extremely abusive terms on the subject, at the time, of his forthcoming marriage to Elizabeth.

Lady Rose was a special case. The daughter of an earl, she was married to an industrialist. She and the rest of the family behaved with unusual informality, but they were now in any case in America, having departed from Hertfordshire over a year ago after Julius was wanted for holding up stagecoaches and had himself disappeared.

There was, of course, their house guest for the Christmas festivities, Colonel Fitzwilliam, who, as the younger son of an earl, bore no title but was entitled to be address as The Honourable. He was as easy in his manner as any man of her acquaintance. His informality had extended during her visit to Rosings to indicating that a younger son must be inured to self-denial and dependence and that he could not marry where he liked without some attention to money. As he had paid her considerable attention during her stay at the rectory with the Collinses, she had wondered at the time whether his words had been intended as some sort of warning-off towards her.

Whether they were or not, his words, though not hugely indiscreet, demonstrated his willingness to talk openly when he had only known her a week or two. She had chosen not to take offence at what he had said. Was this because she had failed, in her naivety, to comprehend the social gulf between them? Others might have—taken offence. Was his familiarity towards her, she now wondered, because of what Darcy had described to her later in the day during his disastrous marriage proposal, namely the inferiority of her connections and of relations whose condition in life was so decidedly beneath his, Darcy's, own? Did the Colonel feel able to address her so because he, being a member of an aristocratic family, perceived her to be inferior and therefore of less account?

The notion was disquieting and, for the moment, Elizabeth preferred to ignore such implications and prepare for the pleasantries of the evening to come. She would return to these ideas later if it became necessary to do so.

She dawdled into the sitting room to wait for Fitz to come and take her down and perhaps on the way whisper to him of

Kitty's disclosures.

Chapter 15

THE popular folk song seemed to go on interminably in a rather melancholy way. Elizabeth wished it would come to an end, although afterwards, there would be another song, and another, and perhaps a fourth if those gathered in the saloon called for an encore as they were quite likely to do, if not from any real appreciation of her skills at the pianoforte or the quality of her singing, then from the quite high spirits in which the party found itself after the comedies of the children's puppet play.

The girls and boys had portrayed the Prince of Wales chasing ladies of the Court, King George showing signs of returning madness, Queen Charlotte lecturing King George and Napoleon falling overboard and nearly drowning. The audience were amazed at the children's grasp of events.

Aunt Gardiner felt the need to apologise on behalf of her children, lest their ridicule of the royal family caused offence.

"It is the caricatures in the newspapers which they see," she said.

Everyone protested that the short plays had been excellent and they wished for more another night. The children had taken their bows and then it was time for the music and singing to allow everyone's stomachs to settle after dinner and before the dancing commenced, hence Elizabeth being first at the pianoforte.

She knew the tunes and the songs almost by heart and thus was able to cast about the room, rather than be forced to read the music and words. As the mistress of the house, she could not but be satisfied at her guests' evident gaiety in some quarters and contentment in others. She did not expect to be listened to attentively, would indeed have been discomfited by all eyes on her and a strained silence. Rather like a string quartet at a soirée, she felt her function to be to supply music to act similarly to the scenery of a play. Those present would be conscious of her but not concentrating on her.

Most had someone to talk to and those who did not appeared relaxed, perhaps even sleepy, as was Uncle Philips, his eyelids drooping. Darcy, sitting alone, regarded her tenderly with a smile which she returned through her singing. Colonel Fitzwilliam at turns watched Darcy and Georgiana. Georgiana was sitting with Kitty, the two girls huddled close together, whispering.

Mary sat separately on the edge of her seat, no doubt eagerly awaiting her chance to perform.

Lieutenant Colonel Harvey was again talking to her mother. Aunt Philips sat with them and both women were laughing at something the soldier had said. Jane and Bingley were nearby. At intervals, the Lieutenant Colonel glanced across at the two girls, whether at Kitty or Georgiana, Elizabeth could not tell, but suspected his attention was directed at Kitty.

Card tables had been set out and her father, Mr and Mrs Gardiner and Mrs Annesley had formed a four for whist. The children sat at another table playing some game of their choice.

As Elizabeth came to the end of her first piece and reached for the score to the next song, Colonel Fitzwilliam stood up, walked over to Darcy and sat down next to him. Darcy would no doubt take this opportunity to tell him of Georgiana's disclosure to Kitty. As Georgiana's other guardian, he was of course entitled to know. Elizabeth wondered what the Colonel would make of it and whether Darcy would discover anything of Lieutenant Colonel Harvey's background and prospects.

"DARCY, this is indeed a pleasant family party. We, I mean the lieutenant colonel and I, could not have hoped for a more congenial Christmas sojourn. Thank you so much for your invitation. I know that Harvey is especially grateful given that his parents are both dead this last six or seven years and he has no other close family."

"I am sorry to hear it. Perhaps he should take a wife as I have done and then he may find himself far from short of relations."

The Colonel laughed at the joke.

Darcy continued more seriously. "I guess, though, that he has some means behind him to have been able to buy himself a commission."

"I believe there is some sort of trust, set up by an uncle or some relation or other. And he inherited the family home, Brownham Hall, a mansion house in Staffordshire. I went there once with him. It is a gloomy place in some disrepair. I am not surprised he does not wish to spend Christmas there alone."

Darcy was on the point of telling his cousin of Lizzy's suspicion that the lieutenant colonel may have taken a fancy to Catherine, but he decided against it. If Lieutenant Colonel Harvey turned out to be a suitor of reasonable means and the colonel for some reason disapproved of a match, Lizzy would not thank him for having alerted the colonel. No doubt any strong partiality would become apparent soon enough, but there was no point in giving the colonel advance warning. Instead, he moved on to intelligence which he felt it was his duty to communicate to the colonel. He lowered his voice and leaned in to the colonel.

"I should tell you that Georgiana divulged to Catherine that Wickham attempted to elope with her. I am told that Catherine is sworn to secrecy and can be trusted. She is very fond of Georgiana, so Elizabeth says."

The colonel turned his head in the direction of Kitty and Georgiana, still talking quietly, their fair heads close together.

"That is somewhat unfortunate."

"Which? The disclosure of the attempted elopement or the girls' friendship?"

"Both, I should say. Would not you?"

"Well, what is said cannot be unsaid. And it is Elizabeth's opinion that Georgiana's best interests are not served by protecting her to a great degree. From all I see, Georgiana is flowering in Catherine's company and doubtless Catherine benefits from Georgiana's...interest in culture. But above all they are young and to have a good friend is beyond value, priceless."

The colonel fixed his cousin with a speculative gaze.

"I must say you have changed, Darcy."

"If you mean that I have discovered that happiness is ultimately more rewarding than submitting to what our Aunt Catherine would no doubt refer to as 'the claims of duty', then, yes, I have changed."

The colonel bit his lip, turned away and then back towards Darcy as though deciding on his next words.

"You know, Darcy, many were surprised at your marriage to Miss Elizabeth Bennet, as she was."

"Surprised? How?"

"Come, Darcy. Your father married the daughter of an earl. With your position and means, you could have married a titled lady. Many hereabouts, girls with fortunes I would think, and in London, would have made excellent matches. I feel sure there would have been no shortage of mothers pushing their daughters in your direction."

"For my position and means, according to you."

"Of course."

"I believe I was aware that ambitious mothers had their sights set on me from the time I left Cambridge and I must say that I largely found their overtures quite repugnant. It is as well, then, that my mother-in-law certainly did not seek me as her son-in-law in any obvious way; quite the contrary."

Darcy smiled at the recollection of Mrs Bennet's previous rudeness towards him, of which, of course, the colonel would know nothing.

"Nor did Lizzy marry me for my position and means."

"How can you be sure of the latter, Darcy? You cannot look into her mind."

"I know beyond any doubt that she did not. And with that, I am afraid, you will have to be content, Fitzwilliam."

He could be entirely certain because of Lizzy's refusal of his first proposal. If she had merely sought a marriage for its material benefits, she might have decided that a match with him could be tolerated despite his harsh words at that time, now much regretted. He knew she had also refused Mr Collins notwithstanding his position as the heir to the entail in which the Longbourn estate was held and the serious urgings of her mother. He again smiled to himself to think of his wife's stubbornness, resistance to intimidation and independent spirit.

Glad for now that he had said nothing of the lieutenant colonel's suspected liking for Kitty, Darcy saw Lizzy watching him and the colonel. He raised an eyebrow and they exchanged a smile. If it was truly the colonel's opinion that he, Darcy, had married beneath him, his cousin would quite possibly discourage the lieutenant colonel's liking for his wife's younger sister.

GEORGIANA played beautifully. Kitty turned the pages for her and the room fell silent in its appreciation.

Elizabeth had spoken to Lieutenant Colonel Harvey yesterday, inviting him to sing tonight if he felt so inclined and he had expressed himself delighted to have been asked. She had made a note of the songs he professed to know well and Georgiana selected those with which she was familiar. Again the gathering listened appreciatively to the performance.

Georgiana of course played effortlessly and Harvey sang confidently in a clear tenor, having no trouble with notes high or low, such that at the end of the recital, the audience applauded. He invited Georgiana to take a bow with him which marked the point at which dancing would soon begin.

By now it was quite late, about eleven o' clock, and a light supper had been laid in the dining room to which those with the appetite repaired. Elizabeth saw Georgiana and Kitty move in that direction on the arms of the lieutenant colonel, followed by the children. Her mother and Aunt Philips accompanied Colonel Fitzwilliam and Mr Philips, the older man having roused himself for the purpose of eating. The Bingleys walked off as well and the card-players stayed at their table. Mary took the seat at the pianoforte and started sorting musical scores. Elizabeth and Darcy remained in the saloon.

"I informed Fitzwilliam that Kitty now knows of Georgiana's history with Wickham. He did not seem pleased and I rather gained the impression that neither did he favour the girls' close friendship," Darcy told Elizabeth.

"That seems very harsh, Fitz. I sometimes wonder about the colonel, suspect his motives."

Darcy sighed.

"It is surprising that he is unmarried," continued Elizabeth.

"Yes. I do not know why, although he may have had to expend large sums on his regiment in the past."

"During my stay at Hunsford in the spring with Charlotte

and Mr Collins, the way the colonel spoke to me causes me to now suspect that he regarded me as socially inferior, such that he could speak with an informality he would not employ when addressing someone of higher rank. It did not occur to me at the time, although his allusion to his need, as a younger son, to marry a wealthy woman discomfited me somewhat. This was during a walk in the park at Rosings. It was as though he was warning me that as a girl of no means, I should not expect him to make any offer to *me*, of which I assure you I had no expectations at all in spite of his having paid me quite some attention."

She spoke with some warmth and Darcy placed his hand over hers.

"Do not upset yourself, Lizzy. I know the colonel is not exactly as he seems. He is all affability on the surface, but there is a stern, ruthless side to him, not surprisingly I suppose given his military career."

Another man, Elizabeth mused, within whom lurked her father's suggested trait of hiding his true character.

Darcy squeezed her hand. "It may be that he would not approve of any match between Lieutenant Colonel Harvey and Kitty, but as yet we know not whether either of them favours the other.

"I did find out, however, that Harvey's parents are dead, that he has no close relations and particularly welcomes his invitation to this Christmas gathering at Pemberley. He has a mansion house in Staffordshire which Fitzwilliam described as run-down and gloomy, and he benefits from some sort of trust fund."

"So you must have told your cousin of my fancy that Harvey is attracted to Kitty."

"No, not at all. I merely remarked that Harvey must have some means to have been able to buy himself a commission and he volunteered the intelligence about the house and the trust fund."

"I hope the lieutenant colonel does not think that Kitty is of a wealthy family, with any fortune of her own."

"I doubt that. The colonel is bound to have told him something of your family's situation. As to Fitzwilliam, when we were at Rosings last Easter, he quite failed to comprehend that I was so violently in love with you. Maybe Harvey's liking for Kitty, if he does like her, will equally pass him by."

"Fitz, how can I put it? You did not exactly display your emotions at that time."

"I speak in jest, of course. I can only be grateful that my actions at that time have been forgiven. Or at least tolerated."

"Fitz, let us not dwell upon it."

She placed her free hand on his. "But anyway, poor Kitty would certainly benefit from having an admirer. She has never been a favourite of either of our parents. With five children, it is difficult for parents to love them all equally. I think she has grown to be so much prettier since we left Longbourn, or perhaps I simply did not realise before that she was so pretty."

"A little of both, I would say."

"Fitz, everyone is returning and Mary is dying to play." She turned to him mischievously. "Am I to be in want of a partner tonight and have to remain sitting? Though I also hope you will favour others with your hand. My mother, perhaps?"

"I think your poor mother would be struck down in terror at the prospect of taking the floor with me. No, if I am ever to partner her in anything, I think it must be at the card table."

"MISS Kitty, do you play any musical instrument yourself?"

"Why, sir, I am not proficient in anything at all, reading, drawing, playing, not as is dear Georgiana."

"Then you do play some instrument, I suspicion."

"Very ill, sir. I have been practising on the lute since my sister Lydia left Longbourn House earlier this year and married a lieutenant in the regulars. Though it is not popular, I find it produces a very pretty sound."

The lieutenant colonel observed his dancing partner's modesty and, did Kitty but know it, found it most appealing.

"The lute is a very pretty instrument. I should like to hear you play, Miss Kitty."

He looked into her eyes and Kitty found there a sentiment which she had never seen directed at her before in the expression of a gentleman.

She blushed scarlet and lowered her gaze to the floor, though not for long. Mary was already playing the introduction to the next dance and the reels were too lively to allow for much discourse. The lieutenant colonel had sought her hand for the next dance also and so she hurried on:

"I did not bring our lute with me to Pemberley, but I...there is, I think, a lute in the music room here at Pemberley. I could see if it suits me, its weight is right for me. Though I am sure Georgiana would play it far better than I."

"But it is you I wish to see and hear at this lute."

"Tomorrow perhaps, then, after church."

"Yes, tomorrow, Miss Kitty."

IN TRUTH, few of the gathering would ordinarily have danced. But the informality of the party induced Mrs Gardiner to take the floor with Colonel Fitzwilliam and Mrs Bennet to promenade with Lieutenant Colonel Harvey with whom she seemed to have formed an immediate rapport.

The children cavorted to every single dance, sometimes partnering each other and sometimes being taken onto the floor by an adult.

Elizabeth had never seen her father dance, although he was neither elderly nor infirm. When Mary struck up a minuet, a short slower dance for two, she decided to persuade him to partner her, sending Fitz to seek the hands of variously Georgiana and Mrs Annesley. Her father seemed pleased to be asked and surprised her with his grace and style.

Three such dances however were enough for him and Elizabeth sat with him for some minutes, seizing the opportunity to tell him quietly that the butler and housekeeper had been taken into their confidence in the matter of Mrs Scargill and that Patterson was to lock the unused rooms and parts of the house at his own suggestion.

"Well, that is something," he commented. "Let us hope it is enough, with the locking of the exterior doors."

"I suspect," Elizabeth replied, "that keeping the outside doors always locked is not going to be very practical. There is much coming and going. Food and other goods have to be delivered. It is a large household. Even at night, I understand that the gamekeepers often finish their rounds at the house and come into the kitchen for tea and something to eat."

"I am impressed, Lizzy, by your grasp of the running of the house."

"I have made it my business since arriving here to find out as much as possible about the house and how it operates, without actually interrogating the servants. My maid Peggy of course likes to gossip and tells me things. Mrs Reynolds the housekeeper is always prepared to help me. And, of course, I can ask Darcy anything."

"I am happy for you, my Lizzy, that your husband is such a good partner for you, in all ways it seems."

"He is, Papa. But he is not a conjuror. I do not see how anyone can fully protect this house. Outside doors are bound to be left unlocked and unguarded some of the time. Patterson cannot be everywhere at once and he needs to sleep sometimes."

"It seems likely to me, Lizzy, that others will have to be told, especially if there are any more incidents. Footmen perhaps who will assist Patterson. Younger men who can fend off some attacker or intruder or run after them if necessary. I doubt if your Patterson is capable of breaking into a run."

Elizabeth looked away, considering what her father had said. It was starting to dawn on her how difficult it would be to properly protect Pemberley from a determined ill-wisher and how serious the situation actually was. But this was dismal talk for a family party three days before Christmas.

"Papa," she forced herself to smile and her voice to adopt a lighter note. "There is something I would like you to do for me. Or for Kitty really. She is looking so pretty tonight. I hoped you might tell her so."

"Well, young Harvey certainly seems to have a liking for her. Yes, of course I will tell her. The next time she is sitting, I will ask her to dance. How's that?"

"Excellent, Papa."

They were interrupted by the cries of the children standing near one of the windows gazing out in awe at the falling snow which none of the adults had so far noticed. Those of the adults who were not dancing rushed over to stand with the children, including Darcy and Georgiana.

Anthony looked up at Darcy. "Does this mean that we will not be able to go to church tomorrow?"

"Probably not. The snow will usually have stopped by to-morrow morning and the footmen will be out early clearing the paths and lanes."

That, thought Elizabeth, would mean even more comings and goings and render it even more difficult to protect the house.

The church was within the grounds of Pemberley and only a short walk from the house. It was already arranged that the vicar and his wife and family would join them at the house after the service tomorrow.

More people had come over to watch the mesmerising spectacle of falling snow on a bright night, almost a full moon which the cloud cover could not totally obscure. The snow had not melted away as it sometimes did, but had settled. There was a thick white blanket coating the ground already.

"Oh, botheration," said Anthony. "What a pity we won't miss church. I hate sermons."

"It will do you good," said Mrs Gardiner.

Lieutenant Colonel Harvey was standing close behind Kitty. Elizabeth could see that Kitty was affected by his proximity and was barely taking any interest in the scene outside. She hoped that the young soldier would not take things too quickly with Kitty. They knew so little about him, though Elizabeth also saw that Harvey himself appeared captivated by the scene.

"I wonder if it means we shall not be able to go to the ball at Lambton on Saturday," said Georgiana.

"About which, if you will recall, a decision has yet to be made, Georgiana," replied Darcy.

"Of course, William. But you said we might go. Or at least you didn't say we cannot. And before that we have the Wirkworth party on Friday to attend."

"We will see. Now come everyone. Let us enjoy our final dances. Lizzy, I see you are not engaged. Would you do me the honour?"

"Certainly, William."

"And, Kitty," called her father, "I was hoping that you may

have saved the next dance for me. I would value the practice."

"Indeed, Papa. What a compliment."

Mary needed no second prompting to rush back to the piano and strike up the opening chords for a cotillion.

Chapter 16

THE SCENE before her was familiar, but lacked authenticity somehow. She had been here in this bathhouse before, over a year ago, the steam rising from the surface of the water, the architecture having a Grecian quality, the stone pillars with their carved Corinthian capitals of curling acanthus leaves, the ripples of the water reflecting off the walls and ceiling in the yellowish light, the ladies in their slips languishing in the shallows and on the steps.

The ambience was relaxing, calming. Yet as she walked away along the stone corridor to the ladies' dressing room, screams rent the air. It was Lydia's voice relating something to do with Aunt Philips. Had she slipped on a stone step worn smooth by the passage of feet over the few years since the baths had been opened? Not very likely. Or had slime built up rendering the steps hazardous?

"Lizzy," the voice called, "come quickly."

Abruptly, Elizabeth's mind foggily registered instead her own bedroom at Pemberley as her eyes opened, with Fitz beside her, holding onto her, not wanting her to leave the warm bed. But Lydia's voice continued to call insistently.

"Lizzy."

The yellow light had disappeared and the room was almost completely black, the only illumination coming from the remaining embers of the fire in the grate. Maids crept stealthily into most of the dark bedrooms before dawn and lit new fires for the comfort of the occupiers, but Fitz had ordered that his and Elizabeth's room should always be left for later. He made up the fire before they retired and usually their room remained tolerably warn until they were awake and he would throw more coal into the grate and return to Elizabeth under the coverlet.

How could Lydia be here? It would never be countenanced. And she and Wickham were in the North of England. They could not have travelled here and somehow gained entry into the house.

The cries, which had sounded so like Lydia, eventually resolved into those of her mother, Mrs Bennet's and Lydia's voices being so similar.

There was a muffled curse from Darcy and a "What now?"

He had no doubt recognised her mother's voice before she had!

Elizabeth rapidly dressed herself in her nightgown and overthrew her dressing gown. Darcy similarly and quickly attired himself in his equivalent, though seldom used, nightwear and made up the fire. Taking up and lighting a candlestick, he grasped Elizabeth's hand and led her through the sitting room in which the fire *had* been lit and onto the landing where the shrill tones were louder, leaving them in no doubt in which direction to go. Candles in sconces assisted the going though most were by now spent or nearly so.

"Which is my Aunt Philips's room, Fitz?"

"Not much farther." He pulled her along gently and they reached the source of the sound.

Mr and Mrs Bennet's and Mr and Mrs Philips's rooms were adjacent to one another. The entreaties seemed to be coming from the rooms occupied by the Philipses. More than that, a low moaning, as of a girl in pain, reached them through the open door.

Darcy looked at Elizabeth and together they entered the Philips's bedchamber. The first person they saw was Mrs Bennet standing not far into the room.

"Oh, Lizzy. You are come. Thank heavens. And William. Your Aunt Philips is unable to talk through fear. I heard a crash and came in and found this."

She pointed dramatically to a maidservant collapsed on the floor.

"She must have tripped over that—thing, there. I ran back out onto the landing to call you Lizzy."

The thing alluded to was a large, furry, motionless shape.

"Oh, my God," said Darcy. "It is Caesar."

He loosed his hand from Elizabeth's and put it over his

mouth in horror. Then he went over to the inert form and touched it, holding the candle over it for it was still dark in this room. The fire hadn't yet been lit. The maid's candle must have been snuffed out when she fell.

"He's dead," said Darcy, "stiff, though not quite cold yet."

Recollecting himself, he went to the maid and spoke to her.

"What...are you in pain? Where does it hurt and how painful is it? If you would say, we can decide whether to summon a doctor."

The girl groaned and sat up.

"Can you stand?" asked Darcy.

She looked up at the master in awe.

"I think so. I came in quietly to light the fire."

Darcy nodded. Elizabeth went over to the window and pulled one of the curtains aside an inch or two. It was still pitch black outside.

"Then I fell over...the dog. I am sorry, sir. I never expected it to be there."

"No. Of course not."

Mr Philips wasn't in evidence, presumably in the dressing room next door, probably still fast asleep. Mrs Philips must have recovered sufficiently to cry out:

"Upon my word! It might have been me who fell, if I needed...to get out of bed in the night."

"Indeed it might," said Darcy.

And, thought Elizabeth, that could well have been the intention. It must have been a strong person to have carried the dead weight of the dog up here and placed it on the floor of this room. It was highly unlikely that the dog would have found its own way up here and collapsed; also unlikely that Caesar had taken poison at the same time as Lady but that it there had been a delayed effect in the case of the male dog. Caesar had seemed well enough when the household had retired to bed at about one o' clock. The mischief must have been done in the three hours since then.

Her train of thought was arrested by her father entering.

"What on earth is going on?" he said.

"We are not sure, Papa, other than that the other wolfhound

is in here, dead, and that the maid fell over him in the dark."

Mr Bennet shook his head in evident dismay.

"I had better summon help," Darcy said. His expression was grim as he walked over to the bell-pull. "Would you step outside with me, Lizzy, Mr Bennet?"

"Mama, will you be all right? We will be immediately outside the door." Elizabeth asked her mother. Mrs Bennet responded with a faint nod, not prepared, obviously, to go against Darcy.

They were half a dozen paces from the door before any of them spoke.

"Once again," Darcy's voice was low, "this is an episode which may or may not be the work of an intruder. If it is, perhaps that is the object. To disconcert us, but not physically harm any person. It makes it more difficult for us to summon a constable. Two dogs have died. It would not be taken seriously."

"I tend to agree with you, Darcy," said Mr Bennet.

Elizabeth addressed herself principally to her husband. "Surely a woman could not have carried that dog all the way up here, Fitz. She would have needed help."

Her father raised an eyebrow at the sobriquet but did not remark upon it.

"I agree," said Darcy. "But the dogs were both very tame and trusting. It is quite possible that someone could have lured Caesar up here with some treat and fed it to him in the bedroom," said Darcy. "We must try to think of everything, but again, as I said earlier before lunch, not necessarily assume the worst.

"Ah, here come two footmen. They can remove Caesar and take the maid to her room. Mrs Reynolds will have a look at her ankle tomorrow morning. It may only need binding up and rest. I suggest we go back to the ladies and that I reassure them by apologising and telling them that Caesar was elderly and sometimes wandered about and got lost. That he probably suffered an apoplexy or something of the sort. Sadly, too much excitement in the last few days."

ELIZABETH went back to bed but of course was unable to sleep. Darcy dressed quickly and roughly and went off downstairs. He returned after a time with the news that Patterson was already up and had settled a point which had been preying on Darcy's mind.

"As I told you before, my steward, Campbell, who managed the house and the servants, left just before I returned to Pemberley with you. I wrote to him, telling him of my forthcoming marriage and my intended return to Pemberley. He replied with a letter giving me notice. He said that his father was very ill and he wanted to leave immediately to go to him. He asked to be excused his full period of notice which was six months and then, according to Patterson, he just left at the beginning of November without waiting for my answer. I was going to discuss it with him as soon as we arrived. My letter to him is still here in Campbell's office.

"And at the moment, we don't know where he is. He left no address. No information about future employers. The only address we have for him is that of his former employer before he came here, but that was seven or eight years ago. I was meaning to write to them at some time to ask whether they have a family address for him, but it did not seem urgent until now."

"Are you planning to replace him?"

"Probably not. I have been away previously for lengthy periods and Campbell was invaluable in my absence. Now I don't propose to be much absent. I suppose I rather half-suspected that my marriage was also part of the reason for him wishing to leave. That he might have thought that it would change things."

"What makes you think it is more urgent now? To contact Campbell?"

"I asked Patterson outright whether he thought Campbell's story of an ailing father was genuine and he thinks not. He was not aware of Campbell having living parents, and neither was I. He thought rather that Campbell was having some trouble with a woman but he couldn't be more specific than that."

"But he must have had reasons to suspect there was a woman."

"Oh, things such as staying away overnight, letters to Campbell delivered here which smelled of scent. He thought that Campbell was upset and worried about something and he appeared short of money."

"Was Campbell unmarried?"

"Yes. As far as I knew. He was always so reliable, or seemed so. Now I don't know. He was employed originally by my father when he became unwell."

"Are the letters from a lady still in his office?"

"No."

"So you're thinking that the lady in question might have been Isabella Scargill?"

Darcy shrugged. The whole thing was so nebulous, built on vague suspicions and very little else.

"Surely Campbell will need a reference at some point to obtain fresh employment."

"One would assume so. The fact that he has not asked me for a reference makes me further suspicious that his life is in some disarray, maybe because of a woman as Patterson said."

This seemed logical. Elizabeth sighed.

"I am sorry to cast question after question at you, Fitz, but do you really think Caesar was poisoned?"

"I would guess that he was, as I believe was Lady."

He paused.

"Oh, and I have given orders for menservants to be positioned around the house as they were in former times before the bell-pull system was installed. We will have to say that the bell-pulls are not working properly. I am not comfortable about continually lying to people, but there seems to be no alternative for now. It is pointless alarming people when there is possibly no threat at all."

"No," replied Elizabeth lamely. "Will you come back to bed, Fitz?"

"I think not, Lizzy. I find it difficult to settle after what has happened and the uncertainty. It will be light soon and snow is no longer falling. The men are already out clearing the paths and roads. I think I will join them. I feel the need for activity and to be out in the air."

FOR FITZ to have joined men working on the estate in a manual task was a surprise indeed. It was dawning on Elizabeth that somehow his passion for her and their marriage were changing him, both his behaviour and his values. There was his allusion to his upbringing and wishing to have their children around them in due course; his mention of a mill on the estate and his visit to Matlock, about which she had yet to find the time to discuss with him; his friendly, open acceptance of her family, including her uncle in trade.

Left to herself for a couple of hours, Elizabeth relaxed in the warm, comfortable bed and allowed herself to contemplate, as often, the remarkable events of the last nine months and the huge good fortune which had brought them together.

However inept had been Fitz's first proposal of marriage at Hunsford at Easter, it was probably inevitable that it would make a not altogether negative impression upon her, and would have done so even apart from his letter pushed into her hand the following day apprising her of Wickham's shortcomings. It was not possible for a handsome man to look into a woman's eyes and inform her how ardently he admired and loved her without such an event having at least some favourable effect, even if barely perceived at first.

Thereafter, she could not help but dwell, not for the first time, upon marriage and what it essentially entailed. The marriage bed and what pleasures or pains it might hold; the physical closeness of another person; that he, Darcy, had wanted to share the rest of his life with her for better or for worse. His face, his intense expression and the words spoken frequently floated before her, softening over the months her dislike of him. The impact of his action in separating Bingley from her sister and the reasons for it became, if not forgivable, then more understandable.

And Darcy's visual appeal could not fail to touch and affect the areas of her mind and body which, over the previous year or so, had become increasingly more desirous of intimacy with a man. Before the proposal, there were only two other men whom she had liked, about whom she was able to compare her feelings for Darcy; they were the Reverend Wilde and George Wickham, both good-looking, outwardly charming men.

Mr Wilde had no imperfections that Elizabeth could divine. He was kindness and generosity all through. He had never deceived her or led her on. His resoluteness was such that he had adhered strictly to his ambitions, regardless of his own feelings.

Wickham, of course, had turned out to be a flawed character and she was surprised that she had not apprehended this at the time when he first came to Meryton and had immediately emphasised his hardships and blackened Darcy's name. It was obvious to her now that neither assertion was a noble or gracious stance for Wickham to have adopted which should have warned her immediately of the weakness of his nature.

By contrast, save that he had, during a dance with Elizabeth at Netherfield, thrown doubt on Wickham's ability to retain friends once made, Darcy had kept his criticisms of Wickham to himself. That was until forced by Elizabeth to defend himself and tell her the truth about Wickham. This he did in his letter to her, trusting her to the extent of revealing his beloved sister's near elopement with Wickham.

Neither had he trumpeted his saving of Lydia's reputation and, thus, that of the whole Bennet family in the form of providing a substantial financial incentive to Wickham to marry Lydia. He had instead involved the Gardiners alone and it was only because Lydia had let slip that Darcy was at her wedding as well as the Gardiners, that Elizabeth had appealed to her Aunt Gardiner for an explanation. Still, he had not told Elizabeth of his part in Lydia's redemption. He had put her under no pressure to agree to marry him as such a benefactor might have done. It had been *she* who had spoken of it to *him* to thank him on behalf of her unsuspecting family.

"I believe I thought only of *you*," he had responded.

Neither Wickham nor Wilde could have touched her mind in the way that Darcy did. With his mingled vulnerabilities and strengths, she began to feel an empathy with him, a certainty that he would not ultimately disappoint. And indeed he had not. He had remained steadfast in his devotion to her, ill-expressed at first to be sure, but evident in his demeanour towards her since her accidental and, to her, excruciatingly embarrassing meeting with him at Pemberley. Those perceived qualities of his had played on her mind until she had hoped, she thought probably in vain, for a renewal of his addresses to her. Her desire for him must have shone through her diffidence and modesty for they had become betrothed against, probably, all the odds.

And might not have become so had it not been for the Easter 1798 proposal and the effect it had upon her.

Chapter 17

THE SERMON droned on. The presence of the Darcys, Bingleys, Bennets, Philipses, Gardiners and the army officers had considerably swelled the congregation this Sunday, causing the Reverend Carmichael's chest to expand with enthusiasm so that his interpretation of the Gospel According to Saint Matthew filled the modest dimensions of the parish church and bounced around the pillars and beams.

Elizabeth let her mind wander to the return of her husband this morning from his physical endeavours. He had been refreshed and cheerful after two hours out in the cold helping to shift the snow. And the paths and ways were remarkably clear now.

"That is until the next downfall," said Fitz.

"Did the men mind you being there?"

"To begin with. But then they almost forgot about me. It's heavy work. And I learned something too. I didn't ask them anything. They started to jest about the unmarried gamekeeper, Walker, that they thought a woman has been visiting him."

His expression had been significant when he looked over at her before going off to his own room to shave and wash and be dressed by his valet.

"Are we to believe, then," Elizabeth said in reply, "that Isabella Scargill has been liberally spreading her favours among the menservants of Pemberley to further her ends, whatever they may be?"

"It is of course too early to say. My fellow workers who knew anything about it did not see the woman well. Indeed, their descriptions could probably apply to at least half the women in England."

Elizabeth suddenly recalled the woman she had seen collecting kindling in the wood before her family arrived. But they both had to ready themselves for breakfast and there was no time to tell him about it.

"I should say," Darcy told her, "that a gamekeeper's life is a lonely one. Even for those who are married with families; they find they are very isolated. It would not be surprising for an unmarried keeper to find comfort where he can."

As the service proceeded, Elizabeth saw from the corner of her eye that Anthony was yawning with abandon. The sight drew a smile to her lips which she had quickly to hide, though not before Jane had noticed and treated Elizabeth to one of her secret conspiratorial looks.

The text was from Matthew: Chapter 6, not manifestly tedious, but not very interesting either.

"Behold the fowls of the air," the Rector declared, "for they sow not, neither do they reap, nor gather into barns; yet your heavenly Father feedeth them. Are ye not much better than they? Which of you by taking thought can add one cubit unto his stature?"

Well, thought Elizabeth, this did not stop men from holding shooting parties, one of which would be taking place at Pemberley on 27th December. Indeed, the only man she had ever encountered who did not seem to feel the need to take up a firearm at regular intervals and blast birds from the sky and set dogs after hares was Mr Wilde. He had harboured no such murderous tendencies.

Inevitably, these reflections reminded her that the Reverend Carmichael's most agreeable young wife had come to their rescue today by telling Elizabeth and Darcy before the service began of their large litter of field spaniels which had just been whelped and needed homes. On the spot, Darcy had agreed to take three of them.

The Gardiner children had been beside themselves with grief earlier to be told of the death of Caesar.

"He must have died of a broken heart," cried Julia, with which sentiment, it was quietly suggested by Darcy, they should probably conveniently agree.

The dogs would be buried that afternoon and it was hoped that the Reverend Carmichael might be persuaded to say a prayer or two over their grave. Three spaniel puppies were expected to considerably soften the effect of the loss of the old wolf-hounds.

"Take heed," boomed Carmichael, "that ye do not your alms before men, to be seen of them: otherwise ye have no reward of your Father which is in heaven. Therefore when thou doest thine alms, do not sound a trumpet before thee, as the hypocrites do in the synagogues and in the streets, that they may have glory of men. Verily I say unto you, They have their reward.

"But when thou doest alms, let not thy left hand know what thy right hand doeth: That thine alms may be in secret: and thy Father which seeth in secret himself shall reward thee openly."

Just as Fitz had nobly behaved in the summer by paying off Wickham in secret.

Elizabeth affectionately took her husband's arm and looked up at him. He smiled down at her indulgently.

THEIR contentment was short-lived. As they arrived at the house in a large group on foot, the rector and his wife and family to come before long with the puppy dogs, they heard raised voices emanating from the rear, where the kitchens were situated.

"Do go in," Darcy told their guests at the foot of the steps, "I will be in shortly after I have ascertained what may be the problem."

Elizabeth followed him.

Contrary to Mrs Bennet's earlier supposition that Darcy had two or three French cooks at least, there were no French cooks at Pemberley. Two were from the south and one was a young Yorkshireman in training under the other two. They were assisted by a number of kitchen maids. The two southerners had trained in London and Darcy considered himself lucky to have been able to engage them. Notwithstanding, the men were no less excitable than any Parisian chef might have been.

"It is not my fault," one of the cooks was heard to say, as the maids huddled against the outside wall of the kitchen.

"Then, whose is it I'd like to know?" asked the other.

The dour Yorkshireman said nothing but stood watching in an agitated manner.

At the sight of Darcy, the men and the maids all straightened.

"What seems to be the trouble?" he said.

"It is the white soup," said the younger cook, almost in tears. He held in his hands a large tureen of red liquid.

"They are all like this, sir. It is ruined!"

"Do you know how this happened?"

"No!" The man's voice rose hysterically. "Sir."

"Do you know what was used...to make it red?"

"It must be a prank. An evil trick. We have beet-root stored in the cellar. It will be that, boiled to make the white soup red, sir."

"You will recall," said Darcy, "that only yesterday I ordered that the outside doors were to be locked at all times. So how is it that some person could have entered the kitchen and so adulterated the soup?"

Neither cook had an immediate answer. At length, the older cook spoke up:

"It is extremely difficult, sir, to keep the outer doors locked when we have fresh food arriving all the time and waste having to be taken out. We have to bring in water for boiling. I do not know how it can be done."

Darcy addressed one of the maids. "I am sorry, I do not know your name, but would you go and fetch Mr Patterson and Mrs Reynolds and tell them about the red soup."

"Yes, sir." The maid curtsied and scuttled away into the house.

"When did either of you last see the white soup before this happened?"

The London cooks looked at each other.

"Last night—"

"It was left in the cold room overnight—"

"I was in here until two in the morning at least with two of the maids, sir," said the Yorkshireman, "washing plate and glass and polishing silver after your evening party." He spoke politely though Elizabeth thought she caught a hint of resentment. "And I saw nothing untoward."

"Would you give us a moment."

Darcy drew Elizabeth aside.

"This cannot go on," he said. "I will have to order the whole meal destroyed."

"But—"

"Elizabeth, we cannot have your whole family, or mine, or anyone else put at risk of poisoning. Perhaps the adulteration of the soup is merely a prank as the cook said with nothing more harmful than beet-root, but we cannot take the risk."

"The rector and his wife and family are to dine with us," cried Elizabeth. "How are we to feed everyone?"

"It cannot be helped. Someone is in this house bent on causing harm and mayhem. All the food will have to be thrown to the pigs and see if *they* show signs of poisoning. The animals will have to be brought to the stables nearby, and all food in future tested on them first. I will order all the outer doors of the house to be guarded and the kitchen guarded at all times. It will mean taking on more men, but there are plenty hereabouts who will welcome the work.

"And we have to tell your family what is possibly afoot and give them the option to leave if they wish to do so. It is only fair. And we must address all the servants as well so that they may be aware of the danger of a warped intruder, up to mischief and heaven knows what else."

Elizabeth could not contain the hot tears which built behind her eyes, nor the desperate howling which quietly wrenched itself from her.

"This was supposed to be our happy family Christmas together. It is ruined," she sobbed.

Darcy's arms encircled her and he let her cry until Patterson and Mrs Reynolds appeared, when he released her and she turned away.

"I am sorry, Patterson, Mrs Reynolds," Darcy said, "I underestimated the possible risk to the household."

He repeated more or less what he had said to Elizabeth and that the two senior servants had his authority to inform the rest of the servants of the potential danger from Isabella Scargill until he and Mrs Darcy had the time to address the servants themselves.

"Furthermore, please arrange for menservants to be present in the kitchens and ancillary rooms and the corridors leading to them to guard all the ways to the food preparation and storage areas at all times. Take on as many extra men as are needed for the task and as soon as possible. If the food we and all the servants eat is not safe, then how are we all to survive?"

"Of course, sir," replied Patterson, completely unperturbed it seemed.

"Mrs Reynolds, as the food already prepared is to be thrown out, do you have any idea how we can provide the family and our other guests, the rector and his wife and family, with a decent meal this luncheon?"

"Think nothing of it, sir. I will see to it."

"Mrs Reynolds, you are magnificent!

"And I am afraid that I will probably have to inform a constable of our situation, although I fear there is little that can be done with so little information. Our guests include two soldiers. Perhaps they can assist us to root out this unpleasant person."

As Darcy led Elizabeth away, he told her that he would make the announcement to the family members and guests once the rector, his wife and children had left to go home after lunch.

And there they were now, walking along the path from the rectory, bearing baskets in which no doubt squirmed the three spaniel puppies.

Darcy whispered to Elizabeth. "We will have to do our best to keep these three little innocents safe from harm too."

THE meal was inevitably delayed, with apologies to the family and guests. With over an hour to fill, Elizabeth spoke to Aunt Gardiner and asked her to rally the children to perform a short puppet play which they agreed to do with pleasure. She could only hope that the Reverend and his wife would not be offended by anything the play portrayed.

"Lizzy, you are looking pale," said Aunt Gardiner. "Is everything all right?"

"No, not really, but we will tell the whole family what is wrong after lunch when the rector and his family have left. But now I must go and see what other entertainments can be arranged."

She came upon Kitty in the music room preparing to play the

lute and sing for Lieutenant Colonel Harvey, apparently. She persuaded Kitty to perform in the large saloon for everyone present. Kitty was reluctant but must have glimpsed Elizabeth's desperation. In the event, her recital was charming, the medieval songs wistful and moving and the lieutenant colonel in particular was transfixed.

Mary, of course, needed no encouragement.

"Please, Mary," Elizabeth whispered to her, "play something jolly."

Mary examined her sister's face but, unlike Aunt Gardiner, made no comment.

After the entertainments were exhausted, somehow one hour and a half had passed and, as games were being played, Mr Patterson came to the saloon to announce that the meal was served.

The meal was the best that could be expected. No doubt the rector and his family were a little surprised to be served cold, preserved meats and other preserved foods, but the cod (probably, Elizabeth thought, from salted cod which had been soaked) in shrimp sauce with potatoes, the tarts and the fruit, gathered fresh from the hothouse, were excellent. Fresh barrels must have been broken open and wine decanted, for wine aplenty there was, together with weak ale.

It was gone four o' clock by the time the clergyman and his family departed, their lanterns swinging in the dark as they made their way home on foot along the paths of the estate. It would be a few hours yet before the moon rose.

Everyone was asked to return to the large saloon, save Beth and Julia, Anthony and David who were herded off to the blue room, where the puppies had been taken, to be looked after there by Batchelor and Nancy. The footman Michael who would be caring for the puppies and training them would also be on hand. Elizabeth and Aunt Gardiner went with them to see that they were settled. The children's shrieks of joy followed them away along the passage. As they passed a window at the rear of the house, Elizabeth's attention was drawn to some activity outside.

"You go on, Aunt. I'll be along soon."

She was amazed to peer down upon a line of ragged men

waiting at the servants' entrance. By the light of a few lanterns placed on upturned crates, they anxiously turned their caps in their hands and looked about them. Evidently word had already gone out that there was work to be had at Pemberley House. Winter was a lean time, particularly for agricultural workers.

The line snaked off into the darkness and she couldn't see the end of it. Those men looked as though they would need to be fed a decent meal themselves before they could be given the job of protecting the food of others. They would probably be appalled at the thought of all the food being thrown to the pigs.

She didn't envy the task of poor Patterson who would have the job of weeding out those who were suitable and rejecting those who were not. It was a sad thought and Elizabeth hoped it would not stir up more resentment, because she was beginning to believe that resentment must be at the root of the recent events.

It occurred to her, too, that she would probably be required to inspect the new recruits for similarities to Helen St Clair in disguise.

In the saloon, Darcy had asked everyone to sit. She trusted that he would already have acquainted her father and Bingley with the most recent events. She took the empty chair beside him.

Darcy's account was as brief as he could make it but it still took at least thirty minutes by the time questions had been asked. There were varied reactions. To the suggestion that people had the option to leave Pemberley and return to, respectively, Hertfordshire, London and the soldiers' military camp, most of Darcy's audience did not seem able to take this in. Kitty however exclaimed: "No, no, I do not want to leave. I am happy here."

Georgiana clasped her arm.

"No, William. She cannot leave."

Aunt Philips, by contrast, crossed her arms over her chest in her normal gesture of determined decision-making. She turned to her husband.

"I think we should consider going home." Her gaze slid quickly over to Mrs Bennet. "What say you, sister?"

"Well, I do not know. But Lizzy, are you certain it is Helen St Clair doing these things?"

"No, Mama, how can I be certain? It is just Mr Wilde's letter saying that Helen had written to him and made threats to him and what she is suspected of doing last year. And her change of name to Isabella and that she had been here to Pemberley only weeks ago. Her signature is in the visitors' book. What the lawyer found out about her."

"She was jealous of Lizzy, you know," said her father. "Of that I have no doubt."

"Was she? Why Lizzy?" asked Kitty.

Elizabeth drew a breath. It was a subject she did not like to raise in front of Fitz. Her dear father came to her rescue.

"She thought that Lizzy and Mr Wilde were close, that he favoured Lizzy, which was not true."

"Well, what of it?" Kitty persisted.

"She, Helen St Clair," Mrs Bennet told the gathering, "was...interested in the rector herself. She conspicuously chased after him at functions. It was very obvious to me."

"Oh," said Kitty.

"Hold on there," interjected the colonel. "You told me, Darcy — I beg your pardon, Bingley — that Caroline Bingley was smitten with you and probably herself very jealous of Elizabeth. And yet are we to find her here on the sly killing dogs and trying to poison people?"

This surprised Elizabeth. Darcy had never given the least indication in her presence that he was aware of Caroline's partiality to him even though it was so obvious.

"I would say, Fitzwilliam, that 'smitten' is entirely the wrong word and I do not think I ever used that word to you. I believe I told you that her countenance suggested some partiality. That is all."

Bingley's face was resigned. He must know Caroline's character as well as anyone and no doubt his main worry at the moment would be his wife and their baby-to-be.

Elizabeth found herself to be uncomfortable with the subject under discussion, of other women jealous of her by reason of various men's apparent attraction to her. It made her feel like the heroine of a second-rate novel. Her cheeks reddened and she cast her eyes down at her hands twisting in her lap.

And she could not escape the notion that all this was all somehow her fault.

Darcy at the same time became impatient.

"We are getting away from the point. We have evidence of threats and of a person taking an unhealthy interest in this house and its residents, coming to Derbyshire at about the time Elizabeth and I became engaged. Two dogs have been poisoned, of that I am sure. One old dog might have died of the excitement of the last few days, but I doubt two would have. I had a friend at Cambridge who was interested in animal doctoring and one of the things he told me was of substances, a mere dram of which, could be used to poison large dogs and cause them to die very quickly. And now, today, someone has frightened certainly Elizabeth and me by tampering with our meal.

"I failed to mention before that my steward who has disappeared is reported to have been probably meeting a woman. *And* the same is suspected of one of my gamekeepers, an unmarried man. I would remind everyone that gamekeepers have access to poisons."

"So what are you going to do?" said Fitzwilliam.

"I have told you of the measures I have already taken. What I would like to do as soon as possible is visit the gamekeeper's cottage before he goes out on his nightly rounds and question him. I hoped that you, Fitzwilliam and Lieutenant Colonel Harvey would accompany me. Further, I am going to have to report this matter to a constable and one of the local magistrates, and also visit Isabella Scargill's house. And not necessarily in that order."

"Do you know where she lives?"

"As I said, the name of the village is Nethermill. Her house is called Payne Lodge so the lawyer told me."

"That's more like it, Darcy." The colonel rubbed his hands together.

He and the lieutenant colonel both sat erect, alert, evidently eagerly relishing the prospect of action.

BY THE time Darcy and the officers had ridden away, orders having been left to serve dinner at eight o' clock whether they had returned or not, the saloon had largely cleared of people. Footmen were carrying coal around the house for maids to make up the fires and the room was a little stuffy, especially after being so full of people. At length Elizabeth found herself alone with her parents. She hardly knew what to say to them. She feared to raise the possibility of their leaving Derbyshire by the next available stagecoach to make the cold, uncomfortable, potentially hazardous journey of several days back to Longbourn.

She felt as though she was in the middle of a bad dream, trapped in an impossible situation, every avenue blocked by some insurmountable obstacle.

Kitty had made it clear that she would stay here unless absolutely forced to leave which would be bound to cause a major stir, or at least that was how it presented itself to Elizabeth at the moment. Yet perhaps she was envisaging too many problems, ones which would not actually come to pass.

"Lizzy," her mother broke into her reverie. "Lizzy, I did not wish to say this in front of everyone and contradict you." This in itself was astonishing, that her mother should make efforts to spare anyone embarrassment. "But I fancy that all this business about Helen St Clair must be mistaken. Her mother is not any special friend of mine. As you know, I found her as peculiar as Helen. But I am sure she told me at the beginning of the year, and some months before she and Helen's father left Longbourn, that Helen was settled and happy and had married a vicar in Norfolk. Not a rich man by any means, though someone at least with a living."

"But did Mr and Mrs St Clair attend the wedding, Mama?"

"I think not. Mr St Clair had become too ill to travel. Helen was over twenty-one and would not have needed her father's consent. There was some mention later that Helen was with child and Mrs St Clair wanted to see her before going to Bath."

"Did she, Mama? Visit Helen?"

"I do not know. I could write to Mrs Long and ask her what she knows if you think it would help?"

Mr Bennet's laugh was without humour. "There is no doubt,"

he said, "that that woman knows the business of the entire neighbourhood. However, whether you could phrase an enquiry so as to avoid putting Mrs Long on alert for further tattle, I would not be so sure."

"Or," said Mrs Bennet, "I could write to Mrs St Clair herself. I have her address. I could quite naturally tell her a little of our news and ask after her family. She would be bound to tell me if there is a grandchild."

Another obstacle seemed to Elizabeth to rise up in front of her.

"But Helen might lie to her mother, Mama. If Mrs St Clair has not actually been to Norfolk and seen Helen's circumstances with her own eyes, she could tell her mother anything."

"Well, as I said, she may at least have managed to visit Helen in Norfolk before moving to Bath."

Yes, and Mrs St Clair may invent some happy news to save face.

"One other thing, Lizzy, is that I gained the impression that Helen and her sister Anne had fallen out. It was not so much that anything definite was said. It was more what was *un*said."

This was not helping, Elizabeth thought. Instead, she raised the subject she had dreaded.

"Mama, Papa, have you thought any more about leaving to return to Longbourn?"

"We would not countenance it," said Mr Bennet. "And leave you in possible danger here? Absolutely not."

"No, certainly we would not," repeated her mother.

"Oh," said Elizabeth faintly. "I thought you might feel as does Aunt Philips."

"Your Aunt Philips," said Mrs Bennet, "has no children. She can afford to think only of herself."

Elizabeth was more moved than she could express.

"Thank you, Mama, Papa." Tears sprang to her eyes for the second time today. "You are most kind. As you have seen, William is doing all he can to resolve the situation. I wonder how they are getting on."

Chapter 18

THE cottage, when the three horsemen arrived, was in complete darkness, more so due to being almost completely surrounded by trees and encroaching vegetation. Notwithstanding that tonight was a full moon, little light penetrated the cloud cover and thick branches hung with ivy. The shutters of the small single storey building were closed and no candlelight showed through the gaps in the wood. Darcy jumped down and rapped on the door with his crop. He waited and did so again and then a third time. He tested the door.

"It's open," he called to the others. They dismounted and followed Darcy into the cottage.

Darcy peered around in the gloom. The cottage consisted of only two rooms, this room which was effectively the parlour, with any cooking carried out on the open fire, and the adjoining bedroom, the door to which it was just possible to see was shut. The impression in the darkness was that the parlour was sparsely furnished. Darcy cast about, going over to the hearth and stirring about with his boot. In the grate, there were the remnants of a fire which must have been out for some time. Wood and lumps of coal sat on the hearthstone with some kindling twigs. The room was as cold as the outside, with the smell of neglect and bodily functions.

The cottages on the estate were all largely of the same basic design, two rooms with a fireplace and whatever refinements and improvements the occupiers made. The present smithy, for example, had built himself a decent-looking range and when he married had sought permission to extend the cottage which Darcy had granted with some extra land added for growing food.

The man's predecessor had kept to the original two rooms and made no enhancements after his wife had died giving birth to their first child, also deceased. But as a boy, Darcy had been fascinated by the workings of the forge and could not resist frequent visits which the taciturn old smith tolerated and had eventually seemed to gain a liking for the young master.

Usually, the single men took little care of themselves as in this grim place.

"Darcy, there's nothing in here." The colonel interrupted his recollections. Darcy could hear him but barely see him. "Are you going to see what's through there?"

He must mean the bedroom and Darcy walked over and pushed the door open. The smell in here was much stronger. He felt about with a gloved hand but there was nothing, in particular there was no candle to light which was odd. He pulled a handkerchief from his pocket and, cursing to himself at having brought no means of illumination with them, felt his way back into the parlour to the fireplace on the opposite side. Bending down, he picked up pieces of kindling and wound the kerchief around it and then bound it tightly with string which he had about him. He dug in a pocket and pulled out a flint which he sparked on the stone hearth and eventually got his makeshift torch to light.

He saw the shape of a chest against a wall. Lifting the lid, it was clear that the lock had been broken. He made out firearms inside, including a pistol and some pots containing possibly poisons. Darcy has to assume that something had been taken. Perhaps that was why there were no candles in the place. Stolen.

"Bravo, Darcy," called Fitzwilliam, still in the bedroom with Harvey. "There's something in here. It feels like..."

Darcy went through and held the spluttering torch high. On the bed was a dark shape. He made out the gamekeeper, Walker.

"I hope to God he's not dead. Here, hold this, Fitzwilliam," he said, passing over the torch.

He removed a glove and touched the man. He thought he discerned a faint stirring and felt about for blood or obvious signs of injury but there were none that he could detect.

"He's warm. We'd better get him back to the house to see what can be done for him. We'll have to sling him over one of the horses. I suppose it had better be mine."

THIS was their second trip out after leaving the gamekeeper on a

152

cot in a sickroom with a maid who had some nursing skills. The soldiers were full of energy and enthusiasm, whereas Darcy would quite like to have stayed at home, eaten a meal and gone to bed.

Nethermill was some three miles beyond Lambton, which was itself five miles from Pemberley. They passed through Lambton but Darcy decided to press on to Nethermill for now and not seek out a constable or one of the magistrates. It was possible that the gamekeeper was merely dead drunk. There was certainly a smell of volatile liquid about him though not a recognisable spirit.

When they rode into the village, there were no more than twenty mostly modest-sized dwellings, well spaced apart, ranged around what was presumably a green under all the snow with a well in the centre. The clouds were breaking up and moonlight at last provided illumination. One house alone stood out among the others, being imposing, three-storeyed in large grounds with a high stone wall and tall iron gates which were closed. There was no one about. The snow lay thick on the ground and had not been cleared away but was well trampled.

Payne Lodge sounded as though it might be quite grand though it turned out not to be the large house. It was itself a small house surrounded by a little land enclosed with a low stone wall. It looked to be no more than three rooms up and down. No candlelight shone in any window and no smoke rose from the chimney.

Darcy's rap on the front door produced no response. He tried the door which must have been locked or bolted. He followed the officers who had marched on round the house to the back. The back door was similarly locked or bolted. Darcy turned to the soldiers.

"I suppose we'll have to leave it there for now," he suggested.

"Come now, Darcy." Fitzwilliam raised a booted foot to kick in the door. Darcy moved to block the action.

"Hold on, Fitzwilliam. This is not a deserted hamlet in rural France or Ireland during one of your military campaigns. It's an English village, not far from a well-populated town. We can't just break into people's houses."

The pair of them haggled for half a minute until Harvey, who had walked right round the house and was just coming back to them, stopped and called out.

"Quick. Someone has climbed out of a window. He's getting away."

The three of them ran back to the street where they could see a figure tearing off over the snow-clad green.

Harvey was mounting his horse. "He won't be able to get away if we follow him on horseback."

The others mounted their horses and they all gave chase.

It should have been easy to run him down, but the man was resourceful enough to sprint to the gates of the large house and scramble over them, disappearing into the grounds, leaving the horses to stamp their hooves outside.

Colonel Fitzwilliam jumped to the ground. "The gate is not locked. Two of us can drag it open while the other attempts to follow the man."

Darcy stayed on horseback "What do you propose, Fitzwilliam? That we gallop through the shrubbery, flatten the rose beds and trample their kitchen garden?"

They looked over at the house. Light shone from the windows with obvious activity inside and what appeared under the snow to be well-laid-out gardens to the front of it.

"We could call at the house and seek permission to carry out a search of the grounds. Maybe there's a back way to the house."

"There looks to be woodland behind the house, no doubt fenced or walled-in fields. The man will be well away by the time we have disturbed the owner and been told to be on our way or otherwise."

Lieutenant Colonel Harvey watched the cousins verbally sparring with some amusement.

Darcy was reminded again of his boyhood, the times he and his cousin had met and played together at Rosings in Kent. Fitzwilliam was several years older than him but Darcy was big for his age and already assertive by nature and the pair were pretty well matched. Fitzwilliam had been all for venturing onto land outside Rosings' boundaries and scrumping for the tastier apples there. Or worse, stealing into the glass houses of others to come away with grapes and other treats.

Darcy had always resisted. In his own county of Derbyshire he knew of cases whereby children were thrown into gaol for such crimes. Quite possibly the cousins' elevated stations in life would have saved them from any judicial action, but at any rate it was not sensible to take the risk so unnecessarily and he would stomp off back to the house and leave Fitzwilliam, who would eventually follow him.

"Very well, Darcy. The voice of reason as usual," said the colonel somewhat moodily. "It's your call."

Regaining his horse, he wheeled round looking to be ready to charge away but he waited while the other two turned their horses and kicked their flanks and the trio set off silently in the direction they had come.

"At least we know there was a man living there," said the lieutenant colonel at length.

Darcy didn't respond for at least half a minute.

"Or visiting. And the solicitor said that Mrs Scargill poses as a young man sometimes."

"I don't think it was a woman, Darcy," said Fitzwilliam. "The build and the gait were all wrong."

"The person who escaped left the window open. We could go back and search the house for anyone else without having to break in." At this suggestion of Harvey's, Darcy's heart sank. He was sick and tired of the whole thing. The lieutenant colonel was right of course, though it was the last thing Darcy wanted to do.

"I suppose so," he found himself saying.

"Splendid," said Fitzwilliam, his spirits apparently lifting in a moment.

It took hardly any time to canter back to Payne Lodge.

"I would be obliged," Darcy said to Fitzwilliam, "if you would wait outside with the horses and Harvey come in with me."

"I hardly think that is necessary," said Fitzwilliam. "We can tether them."

"Fitzwilliam, consider how foolish we would look if the person or persons we seek, whoever that or they may be, were to creep to this house and loose our horses, slap their rear quarters and send them off into the night. In this weather, with the going as it is, we might arrive back at Pemberley on foot by dawn."

Fitzwilliam grunted but tethered the horses to the gate and stood by them without another word.

"I'm asking you to stay outside, Fitzwilliam," Darcy whispered, "because I judge you better suited to fighting off any attackers, and your superior rank and commanding manner more liable to impress. And, as you said earlier, it's my call."

The soldiers still wore their uniforms after church.

"Come along, Harvey," said Darcy, taking up a knapsack tied to his saddle and hefting it onto one shoulder. "I'll give you a leg up."

THIS time Darcy had not left his tinder box at home and had packed candles and brass candlesticks in the sack which were easier to carry, to light and to handle than lanterns. However, as luck would have it, orange embers glowed in the hearth of the small parlour and he noticed that the house wasn't freezing cold.

"Harvey, would you go round and close the shutters."

He waited until this had been done before igniting a wooden spill from his box and lighting a candle apiece.

"What exactly are we looking for?" asked Harvey.

"Anything unusual, any weapons, anything connected with poisoning, personal papers of the person living here, anything to tell us what the person is up to."

They searched both floors and found no other person in the house.

A thorough search was difficult by the dim light and having to be careful not to set fire to furnishings and burn the house down. Darcy rifled through the books in a bookcase but there was nothing of interest.

A table in the small dining parlour had been set for two and upstairs one of the bedrooms contained a made-up bed, the covers disturbed. The room held a woman's clothes and accoutrements. The other two rooms appeared to be not in use but a few men's clothes were strewn about. Therefore the conclusion to draw was that a woman was living here alone, but may have had male visitors.

Darcy looked again for books which might contain information about poisons. He found nothing until he went through the escritoire in the parlour. Luckily it wasn't locked and in it he found a number of substances he couldn't readily identify in small labelled boxes, a handbook in which was scribbled various lists which might have been recipes for potions, a bundle of letters and some more official looking documents.

He was about to start reading the letters and documents when he heard a scuffling below the open window.

"Darcy," came Fitzwilliam's voice in a stage whisper. "I think we must go. Some men have appeared from round the back of that large house and are coming over here. We can't assume they are friendly."

Darcy tended to agree. He called to Harvey who was still upstairs, while he stuffed the items he had found including the letters and documents into his bag, wet his fingers and doused the candle, shouldered the bag and was on the sill of the window ready to jump down by the time Harvey entered the parlour.

"Put your candle out Harvey. Wet the wick. The candles and sticks can go in my bag. I don't want to leave anything of ours behind."

Fitzwilliam had the horses ready. They leapt onto them, glancing over at the men now running towards them with sticks over their shoulders and left the village at speed.

It was nearly midnight by the time they got back to Pemberley. Darcy went first to the kitchens and was pleased to note that all the rooms were guarded. He walked round to most of the exterior doors and found them likewise guarded.

In the sickroom, the same maid was dozing on a chair. When roused, she said the gamekeeper, Walker, had stirred once or twice. She had tried to spoon ale into his mouth and thought he had taken a little. He hadn't said anything but appeared to be sleeping peacefully. Darcy told her to retire to her own room and went to find a spare footman to keep watch over the gamekeeper for the night.

He found Fitzwilliam and Harvey in the dining room where food had been left out for them. He bade them good night expressing the hope that they could save any discussion until the morning. Taking a plate of food with him and his knapsack which he still held, he wearily made his way to his and Elizabeth's rooms. Footmen at intervals on chairs were everywhere he went. The most determined would-be intruder should surely be deterred and thwarted, he thought with satisfaction.

Please God, the house would be safe tonight and there would be no more unpleasant surprises tomorrow.

Chapter 19

DARCY yawned and dragged himself out of bed. He and Elizabeth had been sleepily exchanging their respective accounts of the previous day. Most importantly, there were no reports of sickness from the food.

Elizabeth had told him what her mother had said about Helen St Clair.

"Damn Fitzwilliam!" Darcy complained, "It's a miracle that he has never found his way into serious trouble. Or led me into trouble."

"You must have seen some of the new footmen last night," said Elizabeth. "Only the most suitable have been allowed upstairs alongside the permanent footmen. The rather less, er, refined of them have been put to work guarding the outside doors. Indeed, none of them actually refined at all but I am glad to say that they have been cleaned up and are all polite. There was no sign of Helen St Clair in disguise when I inspected them."

Upon the whole, they were a cheerful collection of men, happy no doubt to have secured employment, a bed to sleep in and regular meals. Elizabeth had learned much of the state of the poor in the last eighteen months. The men's hastily assembled uniforms fit well in some cases; less so in others.

"I did," said Darcy. "I hope we have now secured everyone's safety. I do not see what else can be done but I am wondering whether it is necessary to inform one of the magistrates, especially if Walker, when and if he comes round, tells us of an attack upon him. I will go and see how he is before breakfast.

"Now," he continued, lifting his knapsack onto the bed and starting to remove the contents, "let us see what we have here."

Elizabeth leaned forward curiously.

"These look interesting." She picked up some of the small boxes of substances and opened the notebook. "I wonder what they are used for."

She thought back to the Physic Garden in Oxford, visited last year on the way to Buxton, wishing she had taken more notice of the various plants and their medicinal qualities. Her Aunt Philips had said that she was interested in herbs. Perhaps she could be consulted later, that was if she wasn't already planning her escape back to Meryton.

"I might visit an apothecary in Lambton today and seek an opinion," Darcy told her. "There is a gentleman named Fox who has a good reputation. I think I will make a list of the labels which I presume are the names of the substances and ask Fox for his advice about them."

"Why not just take the little boxes?"

"It could be the case that Fox was the supplier of the substances. He would surely recognise his own labels and handwriting and would probably know who his recent customers have been."

"Yes, of course, better that you are not connected with searching someone's house."

"Would you like to go to Lambton this morning with perhaps some others in a carriage? I will ride. Or I suppose if enough people wish to go, we could use two carriages."

"I am sure many would wish to visit Lambton. We can ask them at breakfast. Though we need to return in time to help with the decking of the greenery."

Traditionally this was done on Christmas Eve. Menservants would be out today collecting holly, ivy, yew and laurel cuttings, together with mistletoe if there was any, which would be hung in the grand hall, the reception rooms and on the landings. More greenery would be arranged in bowls and vases in various rooms. Mr Patterson, she had been told, insisted on making the large kissing bough which would be hung in the saloon.

"Yes, of course."

Darcy had undone the ribbon around the documents and was spreading them out as Elizabeth wondered whether it would be wrong to read someone else's personal letters, even if the someone was up to no good.

"The Deed to Payne Lodge, I imagine." He unrolled and flourished a large piece of vellum.

Then another. "And a will. We will have to find a way to return these to the rightful owner.

"And here is the lady's marriage certificate if I am not mistaken."

His head was down and Elizabeth could not see his face.

"Good heavens," he said at length, raising his eyes to hers, "look at this."

Elizabeth took the proffered document.

It recorded the marriage in June of Isabella Anne St Clair to Ebenezer Joseph Scargill in the Parish Church of Saint Nicholas by licence. It was by licence because the parish in Norfolk was not the home parish of either the bride or groom. The certificate recited that the bride had attained the age of 21 years, as indeed had the groom according to the certificate.

Elizabeth was astonished. "I did not know that Anne's first name was Isabella. So perhaps my mother was correct, that this all has nothing to do with Helen."

"It is very puzzling. The Reverend Wilde's sister appears to have believed that they were visited by *Helen* St Clair."

"Well, I recall that Helen and Anne were very similar in appearance so I suppose Mr Wilde's sister might have been mistaken and simply assumed that it was Helen. She was far more active in the parish than was Anne. By the time Mr Wilde received the letter from Isabella Scargill, if my mother is to be believed, Helen may have been obviously with child, or even have recently been delivered of a child. She would probably not have been able to travel to Cambridgeshire, merely to post a letter through a letterbox.

"But why Anne would have threatened Mr Wilde, I cannot imagine. Or me and my family. My mother did say that she thought Helen and Anne had fallen out. Perhaps Anne did it out of spite for Helen."

"Lizzy, if my memory serves me, the letter he received gave Helen St Clair's name as the former name of Isabella Scargill, but it cannot be. There is perhaps more mischief afoot here than we thought. Whoever wrote the letter and included a vague threat towards you and your family, must have intended that Mr Wilde would inform you, thereby sowing the seeds of our distress these last ten or eleven days. And indeed, if that was the plan, it has worked. Now, with the house so well guarded, I hope we do not have to fear any further unpleasantness.

"But in the immediate future, I must somehow contrive to get these documents back to Mrs Scargill. Damn Fitzwilliam and his escapades. I wish we'd never gone back to Payne Lodge."

Darcy's brow furrowed as he considered the problem.

Elizabeth thought too.

"Oh," she said. "Could not you take them to Mr Waring the Lambton lawyer and ask him to arrange it? He could tell Mrs Scargill that they were found in a bag discarded in a ditch somewhere between Lambton and Nethermill."

"Yes, I suppose he'd do it. And I'm sure he would keep my name out of it."

"And I will not read the letters. I feel that it would be wrong to do so. I will copy out the marriage certificate and some of the notebook before you have to hand them over to Mr Waring."

"An excellent idea, Lizzy."

ELIZABETH and Darcy decided to keep to themselves for now the mystifying knowledge that Anne St Clair and not Helen St Clair must be Mrs Scargill of Nethermill and say little of last night's events in Nethermill beyond the intelligence that there was no one at home at Payne Lodge. There was little point creating more confusion for the family. Darcy made sure to speak to the officers before they arrived in the dining room.

Everyone was jolly. The general feeling that no more harm could be caused to the residents of Pemberley House lent a festive mood to the family at breakfast. And tomorrow was Christmas.

"And while we are in Lambton," Darcy said, "I will, if anyone still wishes it, obtain tickets for the ball on Saturday."

The soldiers, although they did not wish to visit Lambton today, expressed a hearty desire to attend a ball.

Of course Georgiana and Kitty were delighted and Mary condescended to attend. Mrs Annesley agreed to attend as did Mr and Mrs Bennet and Jane and Bingley.

Although Mrs Philips was coming to Lambton today, she and

Mr Philips would, she informed Darcy, forego the pleasures to be had on Saturday evening, evidently all thoughts of returning to Hertfordshire abandoned for the time being.

Mr and Mrs Gardiner would also stay at Pemberley today and on Saturday. Though Aunt Gardiner had spent her childhood near Lambton and loved the town, the children wished to play with the puppies today and take them outside and on Saturday evening she would prefer to be at home with the children. This was especially as most of the family were to attend a big party on Friday at a large hall near Wirkworth and, after the Saturday ball, there were other parties to attend elsewhere as well as being hosted at Pemberley for the whole of the rest of the twelve days of Christmas.

"Lizzy and I will of course attend the Lambton ball. So I shall need to obtain...twelve tickets," Darcy said. "We will probably have to take three carriages."

Elizabeth smiled. The seven Bennets had often all travelled together in their single carriage. At least to local events.

"Harvey and I will ride, Darcy, therefore two carriages may be sufficient," said the colonel.

"We will take our own carriage," said Bingley, "therefore two Pemberley carriages for the others should definitely suffice."

Today, as Darcy had predicted, two carriages would be necessary to take Elizabeth, Georgiana, Kitty, Mrs Annesley, Mrs Bennet, Mrs Philips and Jane and Bingley to Lambton.

"Mary?" Elizabeth said, "would not you welcome a trip to Lambton today? It has a good library."

"Thank you, Lizzy, but I would prefer to read in the library here and perhaps accompany Aunt and Uncle Gardiner and the children when walking with the dogs."

"You would be most welcome, Mary," said Aunt Gardiner. "We will go out as soon as everyone has departed to Lambton."

"Thank you, Aunt."

"Good. That is settled," said Elizabeth. "Do write a list, anyone, if you would like me to buy anything for you when we are in Lambton."

Before breakfast was finished and everyone quitted the dining room to either ready themselves for the expedition to the nearby town or take themselves off to their chosen pursuits for the morning, Colonel Fitzwilliam narrowed his eyes.

"What, if anything, did the gamekeeper have to say this morning, Darcy?"

"That he was disabled an hour or so before we found him. He often sleeps for some hours during the day as he has to patrol the grounds at night. He woke on his bed to find someone pressing a rag soaked in some volatile liquid, possibly ether, over his mouth and nose. He tried to struggle and then remembers nothing. Ether would not have kept him comatose for a whole night, therefore I suspicion that he must have had some other substance forced into his mouth. I suspect laudanum or something similar."

"Why, for heaven's sake?" said the colonel. "What could someone expect to gain?"

"Possibly the theft of rat poison. His head aches but otherwise he seems recovered and he will leave Pemberley House shortly. And at any rate, he must prepare for the shoot here on Thursday."

What Darcy did not say in front of the family, which Elizabeth knew, was that when told by Darcy of the breaking of the lock on the chest in his cottage, Darcy and Walker together concluded that possibly one or two of the firearms may have been taken, and that Walker was disabled for that purpose. Walker would have to go back to the cottage to check. Indeed, he believed that poison had been stolen in the preceding two weeks, hence he had locked away his firearms and poison. He had never before had to worry about pilfering. Theft of any kind was very rare despite the poverty because the penalties were so severe.

In addition, he had confessed shamefacedly that he had been meeting Mrs Scargill and that he had given her money, usually riding to Nethermill to see her.

The administration of ether and laudanum alone was a sober subject for breakfast on the day before Christmas despite the withholding of the most worrying intelligence, and Fitzwilliam did not ask anything else.

BINGLEY offered to ride with Darcy and was lent a tall chestnut stallion. They cantered along to begin with to get ahead of the carriages, then slowed to a walk and Darcy was able to acquaint his friend with last night's events, the revealing marriage certificate and Walker's information.

They came to a full stop at one point by the side of the road and Darcy gave Bingley the marriage certificate to read and Bingley made the obvious comment.

"Now that we know that Helen St Clair isn't Mrs Scargill, it rather suggests that anyone could have written the letter which Wilde received."

"It does. Lizzy and I thought that the reason it mentioned harm to her family was to render it most likely that Wilde would inform Lizzy. Thereby, we would be caused alarm. However, as it transpires, we have been more than alarmed, we have actually been harmed. Although now that the house is so well guarded, I am hoping that the person will be deterred and give up."

Bingley returned the document and Darcy stuffed it in his saddlebag.

"Well, whatever is going on, I can assure you, Darcy, that Jane and I are having a splendid time. I feel sure that others are of the same mind. If anything, the unexpected events have provided at least a diversion. And I would say that the soldiers are relishing the excitement." He laughed. "They could hardly keep to their seats yesterday afternoon at the prospect of expeditions to the gamekeeper's cottage and to Nethermill."

"Yes, well, they are obviously accustomed to actions not words. And thank you, Bingley. It is most gratifying to know that Christmas at Pemberley is proving to be a success, regardless of someone's efforts to cause distress. When we arrive in Lambton, would you take a jar of ale with me at the Kings Arms, my friend?"

"I would be delighted. I am not due to meet Jane until midday."

"Let us make haste, then," said Darcy, digging in his heels.

DARCY examined the brass plate next to the front door on the main road of Lambton. Mr Ebenezer Fox boasted a number of letters after his name. Darcy had no way of knowing whether they denoted any useful skills. Vague noises from inside indicated that there was someone at home, therefore he knocked on the door and waited.

At length the door was opened by a maid. He stated his name and business and was admitted to an ante-room which looked as though it was set up for seeing patients or clients, with chairs, a couch and a desk, writing materials, a ledger, scales and a couple of mahogany cases which might have held surgical instruments. One wall was lined with books and two others with labelled boxes, jars and bottles. A few glass jars contained preserved specimens. There were possibly more tools of the trade in cupboards and drawers beneath the shelves.

While he waited, Darcy stood and peered at the specimens, frankly fascinated. One, he was sure, was a human foetus. He was leaning in for a closer look when a door to the interior was wrenched open and a tall, cadaverous-looking young man dressed in black entered. Despite his unpromising appearance, his face wore a friendly smile. He advanced and bowed. Darcy nodded.

"Mr Darcy," said the apothecary. "How can I be of service to you?"

"I thank you, Mr Fox. I hope that you will oblige me with information about the uses of these substances."

He handed over his list which the other man scrutinised.

"Hmm," he said, looking up. His expression held guarded curiosity.

"Mainly, these are herbs. May I ask, Mr Darcy, why you have an interest in these particular plants?"

Darcy would have preferred to disclose the absolute minimum to this man but had to give some plausible explanation for consulting him. If he was too evasive, it would look odd.

"Well, the fact is that two of my dogs have been fatally poisoned. And some food from my kitchen adulterated."

"And this list? Is it in your own hand?"

"It is. A list was found in the grounds of Pemberley, my house. It was soaking wet and in danger of falling apart, therefore I copied it onto fresh paper. I may have made some mistakes in the transcription. The names are in Latin, I believe."

"I see."

Mr Fox must be a careful man. Darcy had the impression that he was not believed, but that Mr Fox was striving to conceal his disbelief.

"I ask because these substances are mainly plants used to treat various medical conditions."

Fox hesitated.

"Do go on," said Darcy.

"Many common plants have medicinal qualities. The plants in your list include things like purgatives, drugs to reduce pain and induce sleep, to reduce swelling, to stem bleeding or alternatively thin the blood, to combat infection and inflammation. A few are thought to have aphrodisiac qualities; you might call them love potions. Some of them have been employed for centuries for common ailments and other uses."

Darcy sighed. "And what else is there?"

"Well, these are the common names." Reluctantly, so it seemed, Fox proceeded to list a number of plants some of which were familiar to Darcy, others not.

"Wormwood, rue, salvia, liquorice root, mint, pennyroyal, calendula, nightshade, tansy, hellebore, juniper."

"And what of it?"

"They are sometimes referred to as –" Fox looked away and his pale cheeks reddened slightly – "'herbs for delayed menses'."

Darcy started to comprehend, but he wanted the man to spell it out.

"Could you just tell me what that means exactly and what is the main purpose of these plants."

"They are plants you should ensure that your wife avoids if she is with child. They may bring an end to the condition. They are effective to a greater or lesser degree, but that is what they are often used for."

"I see. But they are not poisons, you seem to be saying."

"They are not, yet they may be fatal in some cases. Also your list includes mandrake which is very poisonous, but it can be used in the right quantity to treat stomach and some other complaints. However it is not the sort of thing one would use to kill a dog. You would need something like *nux vomica* for that. It acts on the nervous system. It acts quickly. Principally, though, in small quantities *nux vomica* is used in rat poison and to poison other vermin."

Darcy decided that he liked this man. Of course, he may be leading Darcy, who knew little of the subject discussed, a merry dance and Darcy would not know the difference. But he thought not. He had learned quite a lot today. In particular that the powders and dried plants in Mrs Scargill's little boxes did not contain poisons suitable to kill large dogs. Therefore, if she had killed the dogs, she must have kept more noxious material elsewhere than in her house. It would have to be looked into.

Had Mrs Scargill stolen poison from Walker's cottage? Had she, a woman, disabled him yesterday with ether and laudanum? She might well have possessed these substances, but to have overpowered a big man? It seemed unlikely — unless she was visiting him for some other purpose, for some amorous purpose, or Walker thought that was why she was there and he was caught off his guard. Yes, that was a distinct possibility.

And if it was not her who had disabled Walker and stolen from him, then who?

For now, he would pay his bill and meet up with Lizzy.

"You are not a physician, Mr Fox."

"Sadly, no."

"Why is that, when you are so knowledgeable about medicinal substances?"

"My father died, sir, when I was a boy and my mother struggled to feed us, still less educate us, my brothers and me. I could not afford to train as a physician. I chose this profession instead. It makes a satisfactory living I am pleased to say and I am able to provide my kind mother with a home."

"You are not married then?"

"Indeed I am, with three children."

Darcy smiled. "If I need advice on some ailment, I will know where to come."

HAVING already obtained the tickets for Saturday night's ball and visited the attorney's chambers, Darcy went to find Elizabeth.

He met her coming out of the lending library with Kitty, Georgiana and Mrs Annesley. Kitty and Georgiana were clutching novels. Darcy and Elizabeth drew ahead.

"I hope those are suitable," Darcy whispered to Elizabeth.

She smiled. "Well, I have read them."

"Is that any recommendation though?"

"Of course. You must know that all girls' heads are filled with frivolous notions. My father could deliver a lecture on the subject. I assure you it is all quite harmless."

"Happily, it appears not to have done you any lasting harm."

"I am much obliged to you for the compliment, sir."

Their laughter turned heads in the street.

THE SOLEMN procession wound slowly along the pathways of Pemberley that afternoon until the mourners reached a small clearing in the woods. The snow had been cleared away and, earlier, a fire had been lit to temporarily thaw the frozen ground. A deep rectangular hole had quickly been dug, slightly longer than it was wide and, at one end, a cross fashioned from wood had been driven into the ground. In clear lettering, the words *Caesar and Lady* had been carved along the wide T bar of the cross.

May they rest in peace forever together was inscribed in smaller letters underneath.

The lettering would be painted black later in better weather.

The footman Michael, at the head of the group, pushed a handcart in which rested two stiff shapes wrapped in white cloth. Darcy, Elizabeth and Georgiana followed him. The four children came next, then their parents and Bingley. The soldiers brought up the rear.

The party congregated round the grave and the soldiers stood near the head of the grave, one on either side, providing a Guard of Honour, with their swords held aloft and crossed over it.

At Darcy's nod, Michael lowered the bundles into their grave. As those assembled threw handfuls of soil onto the bodies, Darcy, in the absence of the Reverend Carmichael, read a short passage from the Book of Common Prayer.

Forasmuch as it hath pleased Almighty God of his great mercy to take unto himself the souls of our dear friends Caesar and Lady here departed, we therefore commit their bodies to the ground; earth to earth, ashes to ashes, dust to dust; in sure and certain hope of the resurrection to eternal life, through our Lord Jesus Christ; who shall change our vile body, that it may be like unto his glorious body, according to the mighty working, whereby he is able to subdue all things to himself.

Would the Reverend Carmichael have approved? Darcy wondered. Possibly not. But without this small service, of necessity delayed from yesterday, the children might always feel dissatisfied that they had not said their farewells to the pets and that the passing of the two innocent dogs had not been properly marked.

"Come," he said to the small congregation. "It grows colder and will be dark soon. We should return to the house. And thank you, Michael."

"Thank you," muttered the others and left the footman to complete the burial.

Chapter 20

THE family spent Christmas morning in a jolly mood, exchanging presents. Darcy gave Elizabeth a beautiful sapphire necklace which, he said, had belonged to his mother, together with a pair of sapphire earrings and a brooch which he had bespoke specially made to match.

Elizabeth offered him in return a silk waistcoat which she had been embroidering prior to and since her arrival at Pemberley. It included, at intervals, the Darcy family crest. Her neatness, both as to the embroidery and the sewing of the seams, was remarked upon.

Georgiana and Kitty, amid their laughter, exchanged bonnets, gloves and shawls.

Mary's and Georgiana's presents to each other comprised a number of musical scores and both declared themselves to be delighted and to have wished for many years to play those tunes.

The children were given toys and books.

Darcy handed Mr Bennet a wrapped parcel. He broke it open to find *The Life of Samuel Johnson*.

Mr Bennet gasped. "Darcy, you are too kind. I will treasure this."

Elizabeth looked on enviously.

"Yes, and you must read this, my dear, before I bear it off to Longbourn at the end of our most enjoyable stay."

"I will certainly do so, Papa, for I have not had the opportunity to read it yet."

As her father's present was admired, Elizabeth turned to Jane and passed her a wrapped parcel, suggesting that she should open it later when she could be alone.

"A fine christening shawl," she whispered to Jane. "It is of Darcy's family. Do not worry, there are many more, should the need arise. Darcy's parents hoped to have a large family, but sadly, it did not come

about."

Darcy's presents thereafter to the family were mainly trinkets.

Elizabeth lost count of the presents after that, save that she caught sight of Kitty receiving a small square object from Lieutenant Colonel Harvey. Elizabeth tried not to stare as Kitty opened the little casket and drew out the article within. Elizabeth fleetingly espied the sparkle of jewellery, ruby perhaps, and then had to look away as her mother called her attention to a fashionable cloak she had been given by Aunt Gardiner.

Was it jewellery she had seen, a ring perhaps? How would Lieutenant Colonel Harvey have known that he would meet a girl here this Christmas whom he might wish to favour with a ring?

But, yes, it was a ring, Elizabeth saw. The lieutenant colonel was placing it on the third finger of her right hand. It looked like an eternity ring to Elizabeth, a circle of small red gems, perhaps garnets, in a pretty filigreed band of silver, very medieval, in keeping with the lute and the songs Kitty had sung.

Jane noticed, as did Mrs Bennet of course who pulled a face at Lizzy and Jane but did not comment. Kitty looked delighted, astonished and embarrassed all at the same time. Her face flushed scarlet, then she laughed up at the lieutenant colonel as he smiled down at her. Elizabeth saw them whisper to each other. She had trusted that Kitty would have learned a lesson from Lydia's escapade earlier this year, but now found herself fretting in case they were planning some tryst later when everyone was abed. Elizabeth determined to herself to find the time to have a quiet talk to Kitty shortly.

Kitty nodded at something the young man said. Lieutenant Colonel Harvey turned towards Mr Bennet and Kitty nodded again. Thereafter, Elizabeth's attention was caught by Darcy.

He announced to everyone that the shallow marshy area to one side of the lake had frozen over as usually happened and had been adjudged safe for skating. There were, he said, more than sufficient numbers of skates for everyone who fancied their skills — or boots for any who would care to watch others take the occasional tumble!

Georgiana laughed and clapped her hands. It was obviously not a new experience for her. The soldiers both applauded. Bingley laughed too. As he was from the North of England, he no doubt had skated on ice before.

There were gasps from the older family members who had never thought of skating on ice. Elizabeth was entranced by the idea and wished she had taken lessons before now, as she had on horse-riding, though without ice, she reminded herself, it would of course not have been possible.

"Do not worry," whispered Darcy, "I will hold on to you."

"Shall we," he continued to the family, "avail ourselves of the skating after lunch?"

It was agreed that they should.

THE sky was turning grey by the time the meal was finished and they made their way, muffled against the cold, down to the icy marshland. Mary had declined the strange new pursuit, saying she would rather read in the library and practise her new tunes on the pianoforte.

More warm clothing was handed out and tables had been set out on the snow-packed shore for punch-bowls, with glasses and plates piled with sweet-meats, cold meats and other treats. Lanterns hung from lower tree branches creating a fairyland appearance. Braziers burned merrily on the shore to keep the skaters and the watchers warm.

Elizabeth laced her skates with Darcy's help and stepped out onto the ice, assuming, watching others, that she would be equal to the task. It turned out that she was not and she felt her feet disappearing from under her in a most alarming way. Darcy caught her before she fell onto the hard surface.

"Try to take small steps, spread your feet. Look at Georgiana."

Elizabeth looked over to her sister-in-law. She was having no difficulty staying upright. Colonel Fitzwilliam partnered her and they laughed together as they covered the circle of ice which had been determined to be safe. They slowed and beckoned to Mrs Annesley who ventured gingerly onto ice. The pair placed themselves either side of Georgiana's companion and held her up as they moved across the ice. Elizabeth fancied she saw Mrs Annesley stumble once or twice.

Lieutenant Colonel Harvey helped Kitty around the icy surface. They laughed together. Elizabeth decided that she should take more care and at length she found she was able to stay upright, holding hands with Darcy, holding his arm when necessary, and slowly negotiating the circle of ice. She found herself laughing too, exhilarated by the new experience.

The children had no difficulty, whether through experience or natural ability. And Aunt and Uncle Gardiner, she saw, skating as though they had been doing it all their lives.

"The Thames sometimes freezes over," Elizabeth was told later by her aunt. "And the Serpentine. Or sometimes an area is flooded with shallow water and left to freeze. And of course we have to take the children to enjoy the entertainments which are set up, and the roasting sweet chestnuts and the like."

Bingley declined to skate and sat with Jane, though Darcy told Elizabeth that his friend was more accomplished than anyone he knew.

Elizabeth enjoyed a rest, while Darcy expertly circled the ice, nearer the centre than the others who hugged the sides. She was beginning to be concerned that the ice would be thick enough to support him and at the same time, as the sun sunk below the tree line, she had started to realise how cold it was when her father sank into the chair beside her. Both thoughts flew from her mind for the present as she hugged her arms about herself to quell her shivering.

"Such a gay pastime, Lizzy. I never would have imagined that we would be treated to such a sight this Christmas as your Uncle Gardiner promenading on ice. He puts me to shame. I dare not set foot on such a smooth surface. 'Tis like a sheet of glass. I would wager, though, that your uncle's, er, figure seems to act as an advantage."

Elizabeth laughed. She too had noticed that her uncle's girth appeared to aid rather than hinder him. The sight was not graceful but it was evidently effective. Conversely, Aunt Gardiner glided gracefully by her husband's side, like a swan on a lake. This skating was a skill she hoped to learn to master, if not by the time there was a thaw this spring, then during the winters to come.

Joy filled her heart at the pleasure given to her family by the events this Christmas, the gruesome deaths of the dogs aside. Yesterday, the men had hauled in two enormous yule logs of elm, cut down two summers ago and allowed to season in a barn since then. One was blazing away in the saloon, its warmth spreading beyond the room. The other burned in the large fireplace in the grand entrance hall. The logs were expected to last several days.

Elizabeth was surprised to see that the kissing bough, which she expected would be in the saloon in view of everyone, had been hung near to the back of the great hall. If any couple disappeared for a time tonight, she would suspect them of taking advantage of the ancient custom.

And tonight there would be feasting, singing, dancing and games and tomorrow more of the same, with walks and skating again for those who chose to do so.

Tomorrow, traditionally, the servants would be given the day off, or those who wished for it, to rest or go away to visit their families as they chose. Darcy hoped that many of the new servants would wish to stay to guard the house and they would be well rewarded for doing so.

On Thursday, many from other grand houses in the neighbourhood would be here for the shoot. The womenfolk would mainly stay indoors while this went on. Darcy had told her that cottagers would come later in the day to receive a large part of the game for their own tables.

Sir Peter and Lady Layham and Harriet would be attending, Elizabeth hoped, despite her quarrel with Harriet at the ball at Ashwick Hall. Elizabeth was greatly looking forward to seeing Harriet again.

"Lizzy, you should have put on thicker clothing," her father said, recalling her to the present. "Let us take our chairs nearer to the fires."

"An excellent idea, Papa."

They re-settled themselves next to a brazier which hadn't yet been surrounded by the Philipses, the Bingleys and Mrs Bennet.

They must be out of earshot of the others, but nevertheless Mr Bennet leaned nearer to Elizabeth and said quietly:

"You know, I expect, that the soldiers are due to leave next week?"

"Yes. 'Tis a pity that they could not stay longer, especially as Kitty and Lieutenant Colonel Harvey are on such friendly terms."

"Indeed so. The lieutenant colonel asked me for permission to correspond with her. He would also like us to take her to see his house in Staffordshire if possible while we are here. He told me that a couple look after it for him and that if I agree, he would write to them and tell them to expect us. What do you say to that, Lizzy?"

"Oh! Upon my word! What a sweet overture. I rather thought something more serious could be afoot."

"I suppose you saw him give her that ring. He said it was his mother's and that he has carried it with him everywhere since her death to remember her. 'Tis a pretty object, to be sure."

"I was worried some sort of betrothal was taking place. But she is so young."

"Yes, he mentioned that himself, her age, with a vaguely expressed wish not to rush into any firm or binding arrangement. He seems an honourable young man. And of course he will not be here soon. We know not when we may see him again. I wondered if you knew anything more about him other than that he has a house."

"Colonel Fitzwilliam told Darcy that Mr Harvey has no close relations, that he inherited the house and benefits from some sort of trust fund set up by an uncle possibly. He said the house is neglected and gloomy, but of course that may be an exaggeration. From all we know, Colonel Fitzwilliam owns no house at all himself, being a younger son."

"Do I detect a degree of disapprobation in your tone, Lizzy? I confess you surprise me."

Elizabeth wondered whether to deny the sentiment altogether. Indeed, she knew she had little basis for her feelings.

"Oh, it is nothing, Papa. Merely a fancy of mine that the colonel may be a little resentful. It is not important."

"I see," said Mr Bennet thoughtfully. "Well, I gave Harvey my permission. Kitty seems to like him and writing to one another can do little harm. If it comes to anything more serious, I will have to enquire further about his means, such as how this trust fund falls to be disposed of in the event of his death, given his role as a soldier."

"Yes, I thought of that, that he follows a dangerous occupation."

"Lizzy, you are still cold I can see. It grows dark and everyone is making ready to return to the house."

"Indeed, Papa. And here comes Darcy now."

She still wore her skates. Darcy bent and untied them and the party gathered together and turned in the direction of the house.

As the family strolled away, lanterns swinging, she noticed that Mrs Annesley was limping and holding Georgiana's arm.

Chapter 21

THE day after Christmas was a day of rest for the servants. Thereby the family spent the day eating cold meats and leftovers. The servants did as they pleased, save for those who wished to work for the reward on offer including those who stayed and guarded the house.

The family enjoyed walks and more skating. The sleigh was brought out and rides around the grounds were enjoyed. Mrs Annesley, it transpired, had twisted her ankle and stayed indoors. She would no longer be able to attend the ball at the Assembly Rooms on Saturday, so there was a spare ticket and an idea took hold in Elizabeth's mind.

THURSDAY dawned fine and bright, cold but clear, an ideal day for shooting, Darcy said with satisfaction as he and Elizabeth rose early, Elizabeth to speak to Patterson and Mrs Reynolds, and Darcy to address the gamekeepers about the purpose of the day, the sport.

Elizabeth had to pay attention to the arrangements for the provision of refreshments for the guests, both those who would largely remain indoors, and those who would be outside for most of the daylight hours and needed to be kept plied with food and drink.

Darcy had to discuss matters such as where the markers would be placed for the guns, how the beaters would be ranged throughout the woodland and scrub to best effect, who would control the dogs, that sufficient heed had been paid to the safety of the guests, the beaters and anyone else who might come and go amongst the guests and servants. And where the majority of the game would be left for the local people to collect later for their tables. And many more decisions on a proceeding which could pose dangers to those participating.

Often enough on such occasions, people had been injured or

killed by mischance. Darcy did not wish to send any of his guests away in a mortuary wagon.

These events, these shoots, happened periodically, and Darcy supposed that some might call him fastidious. Bingley had certainly applied that adjective to him in the past, though in relation to less potentially deadly recreations. Firearms, by contrast, were dangerous and Darcy wished to be as scrupulous as he could in the arrangements for his shoot.

Elizabeth having the far easier task of overseeing the food and drink, once she had ensured that all was in hand, looked forward to a delightful day of chatting to her sisters and her friends and furthering her aims in certain directions before the men finished outside.

"LADY LAYHAM, Harriet, how delightful it is to see you again. I understand that the game is excellent this year and I am sure that Sir Peter will be quite impressed."

"Let us hope so," said Lady Layham, with a meaningful smile.

Elizabeth laughed. Harriet raised an eyebrow.

The man was obviously a tyrant. Elizabeth decided that she should make her suggestion as soon as possible so that some measure of agreement could be reached with Lady Layham, whom she perceived to be an ally, before the men came in and Sir Peter bore his family away early, as Elizabeth fully expected him to do. It was a risk as she had not had any opportunity to seek the wishes of Harriet herself.

"Lady Layham, Harriet. We are to attend a ball at the Assembly Rooms on Saturday, and, as luck would have it, a spare ticket has become available. We, I, hoped that Harriet may wish to take up the ticket and favour us with her presence and accompany us to the ball. I do not know, Harriet, whether such an event would entertain you?"

"Mrs Darcy," said Lady Layham, "I do not doubt that Harriet would be delighted to attend, but, as I think you know, Sir Peter is not in favour of events of this nature."

"I do not doubt it. But please think upon it, Lady Layham. We would of course chaperone her and send a carriage for her on the day. Naturally, she could come to Pemberley for the night and return to you on Sunday."

Elizabeth felt all the discomfort of discussing her friend's arrangements as though she was not present. She hoped that Harriet understood and would concord. It was hard to discern. Harriet sat very still, watching the exchange. At length, Elizabeth had to leave as the gentlemen started to come in and Elizabeth realised that dusk was falling and the shoot would be finished.

THE yule logs still smouldered in the hearths of the saloon and the great hall, complemented by smaller logs added today and yesterday and together they blazed merrily. The saloon and dining room were bright with the light from the chandeliers, candlesticks and the sconces. The dining table was set with plates of small foods such as cold, sliced roast beef, ham and tongue, small pies, salads, biscuits, cakes, puddings, fruits, cheese and bread. The guests could thereby spend their time mingling and chatting and renewing their acquaintance as well as eating.

There would be games in due course, followed by dinner later and then dancing. But today's purpose was mainly the shooting. It was not the start of an elaborate house party. Most guests lived locally and would travel home tonight. A few who lived further afield would have a bed for the night at Pemberley.

"DARCY, tell me, Sir Peter Layham, what is his rank? Is he a baronet or rather a knight?"

"As you ask, he is a baronet."

"And has he a male heir?"

"He does not."

"Therefore his title will go to the next male heir in line, if there is one."

Darcy said nothing.

Silence reigned for a time.

"Come on, Darcy. Do not be obtuse. What of his fortune? Does that, too, go to the next heir in line?"

"So far as I understand, the title and Sir Peter's estate are not tied to one another."

"Meaning?"

Darcy sighed. "Sir Peter is free to dispose of his lands as he sees fit. They are not tied to his title. Some ancestor acquired the lands quite separately."

"Interesting."

"To some, maybe."

"And Harriet Layham, is she the eldest daughter?"

"The only daughter. Only child."

"Is she spoken for?"

"Not to my knowledge, Fitzwilliam."

"Are the baronet's lands...extensive?"

"I believe so."

"Larger than Pemberley? Smaller, perhaps?"

"Fitzwilliam! If you like the girl, of what account is that?"

"'Tis all very well for you, Darcy, to ignore the practical side of life. But for me, I must consider such things."

Darcy glanced over at the Layham family, talking together quietly but fairly earnestly it seemed to him.

"The estate is possibly about two thirds the size of Pemberley," he told his cousin.

"Thank you, Darcy. Does she know of my rank?"

"I have no idea."

AS THE feasting and jollity proceeded, Elizabeth watched her cousin by marriage making obvious overtures toward Harriet, who seemed, to Elizabeth's surprise, to be much taken by the pursuit, as Elizabeth saw it. She noticed, too, Lady Layham, observing her daughter and the colonel. A red coat could, of course, turn many women's heads. She wondered who had introduced Harriet to the colonel.

Elizabeth, returning from a talk with Patterson and Mrs Reynolds, found Harriet seeking her out.

"Lizzy, you are here at last."

"Yes, indeed. I am sorry that I spoke out about the spare ticket to the ball at the Assembly Rooms without first discussing it with you. I had no chance to do so and I thought that if I posed the possibility in your mother's presence, she might feel obliged to accept on your behalf. I hoped you might wish to avail yourself of a ticket and join us for the night. That is of course if you wished to attend. I know it is difficult with these things."

"Tell me, Lizzy, will the colonel be attending?"

"Oh, yes, he will."

"Well then, I wish that I could attend, if my father will allow it. My mother is attempting to persuade him now."

Elizabeth was silent for a time.

"And what of the Earl, Harriet?"

"You told me how it is with him, and I think you are right. I have heard whispers that the colonel is the son of an Earl himself."

"Indeed he is. He is a second son."

Elizabeth knew how charming the colonel could be. Indeed, he had paid great attention to her those months ago while he and Darcy were at Rosings at Easter, when Darcy, in company at least, contributed little to the conversation at the time.

"The colonel is all ease and politeness," Elizabeth said. "How do you like him?"

"He is very much the gentleman. I like him very much, Lizzy."

Elizabeth, struggling rather to hide her consternation, could see by her friend's expression, her shining eyes and glowing complexion, that this was true. Of course, that Harriet might have a fancy for the colonel should not have been unexpected. If Elizabeth was honest with herself, her doubts sprang from her own mixed feelings about the colonel. On Darcy's account, Fitzwilliam was impetuous. Her own impression was that he was somewhat arrogant in his view of those beneath him, although she had to admit that he did not show this side of himself very obviously.

But these were not heinous qualities. Enough of this, Elizabeth scolded herself. She had effectively discouraged her friend's prospective match with the Earl of Langford. She should cease her interference.

"By the by, Harriet, who introduced the colonel to you? I assume someone did."

"Upon my word, Lizzy," Harriet smiled broadly, "it was your kind and handsome husband while you were absent somewhere. Mr Darcy brought him over and introduced him to me and my parents. I am bound to say that Papa seemed to take a great liking to the colonel." She laughed. "And then Mr Darcy led us round to all your relations and introduced us. I am envious of you, Lizzy, for your large and varied family. It must be great fun."

"Well, Harriet, it is entertaining at times."

THE day and evening wore on. Informal piano recitals and singing preceded dinner and Kitty played on her lute. She and the lieutenant colonel had, between them, found a number of songs and music suited to the lute. Harvey's sweet tenor tones and the delicate plucking of the lute, the words of medieval love songs and the obvious rapport between the young performers lent a plaintive air to the recital.

Harriet surprised Elizabeth by playing the pianoforte very competently and singing prettily. Music was not a subject they had so far had the opportunity to discuss. The colonel of course applauded the loudest.

Elizabeth and Darcy exchanged looks.

Elizabeth was pleased to be spared the task of performing tonight. Others were entertaining the gathering quite well enough.

Georgiana gave a brilliant performance on the piano and then it was time for dinner after which Mary played for hours and the dancing became more and more lively. Laughter echoed round the large saloon and those who did not dance clapped heartily in time with the music.

It was not the most stately of parties but it was, Elizabeth ventured to say to Darcy, one of the most enjoyable parties many of the guests would have attended. Even Sir Peter looked on mildly. His mouth twitched upwards and his shoulders shook from time to time. It must be, Elizabeth decided, his version of laughter.

Fitzwilliam and Harvey, naturally, monopolised respectively Harriet and Kitty.

The party broke up about midnight. Lady Layham came over to Elizabeth ahead of Sir Peter and Harriet and thanked her for the kind invitation to Harriet to attend the Assembly Rooms with the family on Saturday. Elizabeth was sure that this was leading up to a rejection of the offer and was so surprised when Lady Layham said that they would be delighted to accept on Harriet's behalf, that she found her eyes wide and eyebrows raised and had quickly to adjust her expression. To cover her reaction, though she knew full well what the answer would be, she said:

"And shall we see you at the Hamiltons at Wirkworth tomorrow? My family are looking forward to the outing."

"I regret not. We were invited, but..." She shrugged. "I am so glad that Harriet will enjoy herself on Saturday."

"Likewise, Lady Layham. We will send the carriage for her in the morning."

"You are so kind, and such a good friend to Harriet."

"Indeed, she is my very best friend in Derbyshire, Lady Layham."

Chapter 22

MRS Bennet alighted from the carriage, or more properly she was helped down by Mr Bennet and a footman. Kitty and Georgiana quickly followed and the four of them stood gazing at the attractive building near the centre of Lambton with its fine portico and elegant sash windows from which streamed a blaze of light.

For Georgiana, this was hugely exciting. She had never been to an event at the Assembly Rooms and now she was here with her new family which made the experience exceedingly enjoyable. She smiled broadly and put her arm through Kitty's.

For the Bennets, to come to a function at an assembly rooms was not a novel experience and this public building was little different from the one in Meryton which served the same purpose.

But Mrs Bennet, too, was overflowing with happiness. This sojourn at the home of her new son and her second daughter, his wife, was a wonder to her. That Darcy had turned out to be such a loving and sweet-natured husband and son was little short of miraculous. Of course, she was still in awe of him. His bearing had not changed greatly. He was still correct in every mannerism, but he smiled a great deal, he laughed. And he treated Lizzy with open affection. Even today, in the saloon after lunch, they were standing together and Lizzy had said something which made him laugh. He had clasped her round the waist and had drawn her towards him. It looked for a moment as though they might kiss, but they had not, of course. It would not be seemly.

Harriet Layham, Mrs Bennet noticed, watched her friend's husband with interest. She sat next to the colonel at the early dinner and smiled prettily up at him. Was Harriet wondering whether the colonel would make as loving a husband as Darcy? Mrs Bennet, alert to all such things, had not failed to notice the colonel's obvious partiality to Harriet which it appeared she returned.

Even Jane and Bingley, whom she had previously regarded as the most affable of men, did not appear so happy. Mrs Bennet tried not to mar her happiness tonight by thoughts of regret that her own marriage had never been so intimate. Certainly it had never been like Darcy and Lizzy, although in truth the early years of her marriage had been devoted to the overwhelming effort, sadly unsuccessful, to produce a male heir

The remark of Darcy's, repeated by Colonel Fitzwilliam at lunch on Saturday a week ago, had been playing on her mind: That no one could think anything wanting, this said of Lizzy evidently during the Easter stay at Rosings. Mrs Bennet had been aware that Darcy was present at Rosings at the same time as Lizzy was staying with Charlotte Collins. Lady Lucas, Charlotte's mother, had wasted no time boasting of it to Mrs Bennet, that the latter should be in no doubt of the elevated company her daughter, Charlotte, was keeping. She had even teased Mrs Bennet that it was Charlotte's opinion that Mr Darcy had some fancy for Lizzy. Mrs Bennet had dismissed the notion as a rather cruel taunt by the other woman.

But it must have been so. That he was already in love with Lizzy. The young girl still in her heart thrilled at the idea of that stern man harbouring romantic feelings for her daughter before anyone was aware of the fact.

And now, he had so well and so thoroughly organised the guarding of Pemberley House against some strange person wishing to do harm that there was no longer any need for fear. The remainder of their stay could be enjoyed to the full.

The strains of piano playing could be heard emanating from the building and braziers burned in the street outside to keep the coachmen warm. One man played an accordion. The horses drank from buckets or had their faces buried in nosebags. One or two horses were dozing off. There was a festive air even before they had set foot inside the building.

The soldiers had arrived and were leaving their horses with the ostler at the Kings Arms for the evening. From there, it was but a short walk to the Assembly Rooms. The carriage bearing Darcy, Elizabeth, Harriet and Mary was drawing up, followed shortly by Jane and Bingley's carriage and Mrs Bennet began to be impatient to go inside.

HARRIET was no less excited to be here than was Georgiana. She contained her elation as best she could, attempting to converse with Mary on the way here, but finding her unreceptive and quite the opposite of garrulous. Eventually, Mary admitted that she had been deeply interested in a book she had been reading earlier and could not stop thinking about it.

"Mary loves to read all the time," Elizabeth assured Harriet.

"Well, Mary," Harriet felt bound to say, "perhaps you should consider writing a book yourself."

Elizabeth laughed, but Mary's eyes widened and, without saying anything, she turned her head to fix Harriet with a stare which was difficult to interpret. Then she looked away and appeared to fall into a reverie from which she only emerged as the carriage drew up outside the Assembly Rooms.

By that time, Harriet and Elizabeth were discussing the forthcoming evening, with the occasional interjection from Darcy. Harriet was dying to ask Elizabeth more about Colonel Fitzwilliam, but could not until they were alone.

AS WITH Pemberley House, the entrance hall and the main room had been hung with greenery and the mood was festive. Darcy's party had stowed their cloaks and taken up glasses of wine by the time Fitzwilliam and Harvey arrived. The soldiers were flushed from the cold and both cast about the attractive room, seeing Darcy and the others and smiling their joyful anticipation of the evening to come.

"They are coming over," whispered Harriet next to Elizabeth.

The soldiers bowed towards the ladies and first addressed Darcy, Bingley and Mr Bennet.

"'Twas a bracing ride," said Fitzwilliam.

"An understatement, I am sure," answered Darcy.

"The weather is turning even colder," Harvey told them.

Their red coats were catching the attention of the assembly and admiring looks were coming their way. Indeed, Darcy and Bingley being tall and distinguished and not having attended the

Assembly Rooms before were also the object of looks and whispered comments.

Elizabeth did not recognise anyone. None of her new friends seemed to be here. But some of the men hailed Darcy and he responded by raising his glass.

The band had been tuning up for some time and, with a rising note, they suddenly struck up God Save the King. Everyone ceased to chatter and stood up straight, singing their loudest to the domed ceiling.

Good, thought Elizabeth, dancing will start soon. And so it did.

Fitzwilliam whisked Harriet away and Lieutenant Colonel Harvey took Kitty's hand for a *boulanger*. It was a suitably lively dance to begin the evening.

Jane sat down with her parents and Mary; Bingley asked Georgiana to dance. Thereby, seeing that Georgiana was not neglected, Elizabeth and Darcy felt it reasonable to take the floor together. Thereafter the eight dancers changed partners between themselves and kept to the floor for an hour at least.

A tall gentleman with a lady on his arm walked towards their set as they stood out the next dance.

"Mr Darcy, may I present to you my wife, Mrs Mary Fox."

"Good evening, Mr Fox, Mrs Fox."

Darcy proceeded to introduce Elizabeth to Mr and Mrs Fox and then the rest of his family, Darcy singing the praises of the young apothecary, while avoiding allusion to having consulted him over the substances found in Mrs Scargill's house. He trusted the professional discretion of Mr Fox to remain silent on the subject himself. The group stood chatting for some time. Mr Bennet walked over and was introduced. Others of Darcy's acquaintance came over and were introduced to the Bennets. Mrs Bennet, Mary and Jane joined them and it was a large group which made their way to the room where refreshments were being served. After a time, Elizabeth and others, including her mother and Mary, gravitated towards the card room.

The stakes were very low and the games most absorbing. Elizabeth found herself winning and stayed on longer than she would normally have done. She started to understand why card-playing was such a popular diversion. Darcy joined at one point and then left. In due course, music resumed for dancing. Elizabeth, passing by the ballroom at one point on the way to and from the water-closet, glanced into the ballroom and saw her father enjoying a lively country reel with Kitty. She smiled to herself and hurried back to the card table.

DARCY once again found himself cornered by Fitzwilliam.

"I see that your charming wife takes a keen interest at the card table. I had not realised she was a lover of gaming."

"You are right. She does not play often and would not do so tonight if the play were high."

"When I looked in, she appeared to be winning. Perhaps you should encourage her in the higher-stakes games. You might find some profit in it."

"I trust you are jesting, Fitzwilliam. Neither I nor Elizabeth would countenance serious gambling."

"And is Sir Peter, Harriet's father, a gambler?"

Darcy should have realised, he told himself, that his cousin would start to fish for more tattle about the Layhams.

"Not to my knowledge."

"Well, all to the good. Gambling is certainly an excellent way to dispose of one's fortune. Or heavy spending in other directions. Sir Peter would not be the first baronet to lose his fortune by making risky investments or other unwise expenditure."

"Fitzwilliam, you have only known the girl a few days. Is not it a little early to be planning to inherit such fortune as her father leaves her?"

"I think not. At any rate, there is no harm in seeking your opinion. As you know, Harvey and I will be leaving soon. Miss Layham is a lovely, lively girl and I like her a great deal. As you imply, it is far too soon to make her any offer but at the very least, it would be cheering to think pleasant thoughts of future happiness while I am away."

Darcy found himself softening at this sentiment, even though it seemed to him that Fitzwilliam's aims were as much mercenary as they were romantic.

"Well," he said, "Sir Peter is, I would say, anything but a

spendthrift. I feel sure that while battle is raging about you that you could reasonably comfort yourself that Harriet's inheritance is not being frittered away."

"I thank you Darcy, not only for this intelligence, but for having us here at Pemberley this Christmas. We merely looked forward to pleasant company and a restful sojourn. I could not have foreseen that both Harvey and I would meet girls whom we might one day marry."

The colonel's interest in Harriet Layham must have killed off any disapprobation he may have harboured over Harvey's attraction to Kitty.

Darcy sighed. "Life, it seems, is full of these unpredictable events. We must make the best of it all."

This was, Darcy realised, a poor and somewhat trite observation on the vicissitudes of life, but it would have to do for now. Lizzy must soon be emerging from the card room and he wanted to be free to dance with her when she did.

BY the time Elizabeth had had her fill of cards, it was getting late and she returned to the ballroom; the floor was crowded. She happily took the floor with Darcy and the band played on for longer than she had expected. Eventually though, the music stopped and the hall started to clear. Darcy called everyone of their party together to ready themselves for the carriages to be called for the return to Pemberley. The soldiers stood waiting for the others to leave.

"Where is Papa?" said Mary. Her voice was low against the raised voices of her family, in high spirits.

"Fetching his cloak, perhaps?" said Jane.

"Oh yes. That will be it," said Mrs Bennet.

"I will go and look for him," offered Darcy.

He returned within five minutes, frowning. "I have not found him. He is not in the building. I have looked outside but there is no sign of him. Who saw him last?"

Darcy's expression was bland and his voice held no obvious alarm but Elizabeth sensed that he was worried, doubtless due to the events of the last week.

"Well, he must be here somewhere," said Mrs Bennet, not answering his question.

Rather more sharply, Darcy said, "Hopefully, but who saw him last?"

"William, I saw him dancing with Kitty earlier," said Elizabeth.

"Yes," said Kitty. "Then he walked off to dance with...Jane?" She looked over at her sister.

"No, he did not dance with me," said Jane. "He came over to me but he was hot and said he would go and splash some water on his face."

"Did he return to you? What time was that?" Darcy asked, his face beginning to show his concern.

Jane shook her head. "No, he did not return. I thought he had probably gone to take some refreshment or to the card room. I do not know for sure what time it was. Perhaps an hour ago? Maybe more," she ended weakly.

Elizabeth, too, was alarmed by now. It was past one o' clock. How long did one wait before admitting that someone was missing?

She reached for Darcy and tugged at his arm. "We should go and search for him, William, and ask people if they have seen him. It may be nothing, he may have gone to the carriage to get something for example and fallen asleep but we should not assume that all is well."

"You are right, Lizzy. Bingley, Fitzwilliam and Harvey, come with me. Everyone else, wait here for now."

A TENSE half an hour ensued. Servants were clearing the tables and sweeping the floors. Most of those attending the ball had left or were leaving. A few came up and enquired what was amiss. There were mixed reactions to Elizabeth's declaration that her father had disappeared. Some were sympathetic. A few of the men Darcy had seemed to know raised an eyebrow suggestively. Elizabeth looked away to hide her anger at the imputation that her father was off somewhere up to no good.

Mr Fox solicitously offered to be of assistance should it transpire that Mr Bennet was lying injured somewhere.

"Do bring him to my consulting rooms," he offered. "if you

cannot call a physician. It will be an hour or so before we retire, but you must rouse us at any time if necessary. My wife is an excellent nurse."

"You are very kind, Mr Fox," Elizabeth told him, her face pale and her voice shaking. She had begun to fear the worst. Someone who would kill two healthy dogs and bring anxiety to a large household by tampering with the food might be equally ready to injure a man if the chance arose. If the person was wrong in the head, who knew what they might be capable of?

Darcy came back in. He was clearly in a dark mood and somewhat dishevelled. He had cast off his slippers and was wearing a pair of boots. He must have brought them in the carriage.

"Ladies," he said shortly, "I think it best that you travel home to Pemberley. There are seven of you therefore two carriages should suffice. You will be safe enough with the footmen. Bingley and I will take the horses hitched to the third carriage which will have to remain at the inn. We will arrange its collection some other time. The soldiers already have their horses here in Lambton. The four of us, therefore, will ride out and search further afield. We will return to Pemberley later."

"But I wish to remain here," cried Elizabeth.

"I regret that is not possible. It is all in hand, Lizzy. The two carriages are being brought round now. If you would all please –"

"But what of Papa? Is there no sign, no word at all?"

"Lizzy, *please*. There is no time to lose. Bingley, the soldiers and I have run round the town and he is not here. We will return to Pemberley later, please God with Mr Bennet or, if he cannot be brought, we would arrange for him to stay at the inn and one of us will stay with him. Now if you please ladies, I beg you would fetch your cloaks and come outside, for the carriages will be waiting."

Elizabeth told Darcy what Mr Fox had said, to which he merely nodded.

The rest of the ladies were already collecting their cloaks. Elizabeth swallowed her ardent desire to be part of the search for her father. She knew, of course, that Darcy was right. She briefly hugged him and then accepted her cloak which Jane brought her, and the seven ladies made their way out and were helped into the carriages by footmen. Darcy had already disappeared.

It quickly became obvious how cold the night had grown. Elizabeth wrapped her cloak around her as her carriage bore her away with Harriet, Kitty and Georgiana. Jane had agreed to travel with Mrs Bennet and Mary.

Scratching the rime from the inside of the carriage window, she peered out disconsolately at what had been a jolly, welcoming scene five or six hours earlier. She must hope that by some miracle her father would be found and safely delivered home.

Chapter 23

THE cold was eating into him. He could hardly move for being so cold. He was unable to feel parts of himself at all. He wanted to sit down but he was roped, standing, to some sort of post, the bonds tight, the rope thick and wound around his legs as well as his body. And round his neck, firmly under his chin, keeping him rigidly upright.

He was dressed only in his indoor clothes from last night. Breeches, stockings, shirt, stock, waistcoat, thin coat, light shoes, slippers almost, though he was still wearing the gloves he had pulled on to go outside. His memory started to make a return. Last night he had been at some sort of entertainment; dancing, music, cards, noise, chattering. It was all a blur as to the exact sequence of events, but he knew he had been at the Assembly Rooms at Lambton, that the event had gone on for a long time, the room had been hot and about midnight he had stepped outside to get some air. Had he danced? He could not remember. Possibly, as he had been warm enough to go out by a side door, not wishing to encounter the drunken revelry, which often accompanied these events, of those less fortunate who congregated at the front of the building hoping for a coin or two to be thrown their way when the gentry and professional classes emerged.

Certainly he was not warm now and his head hurt, throbbing painfully. He could smell vomit from close by, possibly on his own clothes.

He was in almost complete darkness. A circle of feeble, hazy blue light came from nearby, moonlight probably, not sunlight, and a brisk, freezing wind blew into this place from outside.

His head itched and he instinctively moved to raise a hand to scratch the place, but the bonds prevented him from doing so. Instead, he tried to turn his head round to agitate the ticklish spot against the hard surface of whatever it was that he was bound to. It was impossible and the movement made him dizzy and caused a shard of pain to sear through his brain. He groaned and wanted to be sick.

"Be quiet, you horrible old man," came a voice from the inky blackness, a voice which he did not recognise. It was a man's voice and sounded educated, of good family.

"What," he croaked, "is going on? Why am I here?"

The effort of asking these questions made him breathless.

"Look at you. Vomit on your clothes. You have pissed in your breeches. You are disgusting."

Perhaps he had — wet his breeches. And the vomit was almost certainly his own.

"And yet you pretend to be so superior, so much better than me, than others indeed. Able to bestow and withhold favours at your will. Though still your bladder fails you. You are no better than a dog."

Mr Bennet started to comprehend through the freezing cold of this place and the numbness of his body that he was in the presence of a madman, someone who would not be amenable to reason. Someone, perhaps, who would poison two dogs and otherwise attempt to intimidate a household. At least, he decided, his own brain was still working and his best prospects lay in trying to humour this man and find out what it was that he might have done, if anything, that was so offensive to this person, and hope that in due time someone would come to rescue him.

"You may be right," he said through chattering teeth. "What, pray, could I have withheld? And from whom? From you? Do you think you have been treated unfairly in some way?"

At least the concentration necessary for this small speech kept his shivering at bay. He wiggled his fingers to try to bring some blood back into the veins. He could at least now see his breath in the air before him. His eyes must be adjusting to the gloom.

"You cannot comprehend the ill you have done me. Why should I waste my energy telling you the results of your cruelty?"

"Whoever you are, it is possible that you may derive some satisfaction from doing so," Mr Bennet haltingly told this person. "If you plan to kill me, as perhaps you do, then at least I will know why I deserve the fate, in your eyes."

These words were increasingly difficult to enunciate as Mr Bennet's facial muscles began to seize up with cold as those of his body had. Mr Bennet wondered if the man was actually able to understand what he, Mr Bennet, was saying. If the man would not tell him soon what ill he was supposed to have visited upon him, he feared that he would fall into unconsciousness. He would never know himself what he had done, and the man would never know what Mr Bennet's defence may have been to these charges.

"You do not even know who I am, do you?" said the man.

"I regret not," said Mr Bennet, as economical with words as he could be. "It is very dark in here."

"My name is Paul St Clair. You refused to recommend me for the benefice at Longbourn as Mr Wilde was leaving. I am the son of your friend but you denied me this simple advantage."

Ah, so this was it. And yet it was a regular occurrence. Young men sought all the time to be preferred for an incumbency and, if refused, they would move on to the next person they knew of with an advowson, and the next, and so on.

He did recall Paul St Clair applying to him and that he had considered the young man completely unsuitable to take holy orders. It was his opinion at the time that even if he did recommend his friend's son, the bishop would probably refuse to proceed. He searched his brain, fast seizing up as his body had already done, for a suitable reply.

"Did you try elsewhere, Mr St Clair?"

"Why should I tell you?"

Mr Bennet dug deep into his almost depleted reserves of energy to utter a convincing reply. It might help, might get him out of this place.

"If you did not, then I am surprised. I have always tried to prefer young men with a university education, or if not, then those with experience. Had you been employed as a curate for several years, then I might have been able to recommend you the next time a vacancy arose."

"Yes, and how was I supposed to obtain employment as a curate?"

"Did you try?"

"I am not disposed to tell you my business, you vile old man. You had not a care for me and my...kin."

"Your family? What is it to do with them? Your parents are in Bath, your brother still in Longbourn. Your sisters...I am not sure. What is it to do with any of them?"

Mr Bennet's voice was weak now. He knew he could not continue this conversation for much longer.

"I am talking of the lady I was to marry."

"I did not stop you from marrying anyone, Mr St Clair."

"I had no income, nowhere to live. I could not marry her."

"I am sorry, but I fail to see why. Could not you continue to live at Pollards?"

"My brother Simon would not have me. Especially if I had a wife and child. He wishes himself to marry."

A child. Mr Bennet started to understand better this young man's wrath and resentment. So far, St Clair, wherever he was in this black hole, had not moved. Now Mr Bennet heard a scraping of feet and suddenly a face was thrust before his own, a few inches from him, the eyes close together, the face of a weasel as he recalled. The other man's breath was foul. He smelled as though he had not washed or changed his clothes for weeks.

"The woman who would have been my wife died in the workhouse at Meryton giving birth to our child, and the child died with her. It was because of you. Because you refused me the living which should have been mine."

"I...When was this?"

"Not four months past. Just as you were arranging the most advantageous marriages for your own daughters, my lady and child were passing away."

Mr Bennet tried to make sense of this. It had been August or September the previous year when St Clair had appealed to him for the living.

"I see," he said faintly. What he saw was that St Clair must have begat the child some months after failing to secure the benefice at Longbourn, despite knowing full well of his situation. And yet he held Mr Bennet responsible. St Clair was the author of his own downfall, or that of the unfortunate young woman

197

who had allied herself to him. Of course, reasoning with the man would achieve nothing, therefore he decided on a change of subject.

"Why did you come to Derbyshire?"

In reply, St Clair spat in his face.

Mr Bennet blew the foul spittle out of his mouth and persisted. "I believe that one of your sisters may reside nearby, at Nethermill."

"I had nowhere else to go."

"So you are staying with her."

"No."

"I do not understand."

"Look. This has gone on long enough. I wanted you to know what your selfish actions led to. How people like you stride through life ruining other people's lives without a care. Now I intend to leave you here to die. Yes, die old man, *die*."

"You will hang for this, St Clair."

But he was talking to empty space. The crunch of boots on a hard surface was his answer. St Clair was striding away. The feeble blue light coming from what Mr Bennet presumed was the entrance to this place was partly obstructed. The light quickly returned and St Clair must be gone. At length, the light seemed to fade and a bitter, howling wind whistled into this cave, stronger than before. Incredibly, snow started to be blown in on the wind and build up around his feet. A horrified Mr Bennet submitted to a spasm of violent shivering, lowered his head as far as he could and wept.

BY the time he had ridden a mile or so from Lambton with the dead weight of the inert Bennet slumped uncomfortably in front of him over the horse, it had begun to dawn on Paul St Clair that what he had done was not hugely clever, greatly limiting his choices.

He had ventured into Lambton after learning of the ball to be held at the Assembly Rooms, hoping there might be food left about or thrown out or some that he could steal, coins accidentally dropped on the ground or the opportunity to pick a neglectful pocket, or indeed some kind souls throwing coins asunder for the less fortunate to scavenge. Or, if nothing else, then braziers before which he could warm his freezing hands and body.

But there was very little of any kind of comfort to be had and he could not, a stranger, venture too near the activity outside the Rooms for fear of being recognised as such and driven away. It had entered his mind that the Bennets might be attending the gathering and by the time the old man had emerged, very late, from a side door of the Assembly Rooms and leaned against the wall, evidently taking the air, St Clair had become frustrated by the paucity of reward for his trouble in walking to the town. He would give the old man, the cause of all his misfortunes, a shaking up and then go on his lonely way back to the freezing mill where he could at least light a fire and eat the remains of a scrawny rabbit he had been able to snare and cook for himself. These were the depths to which his life had descended.

All he had wanted to do was to drag Bennet round the back of the building, stick a pistol under his nose and force him to listen to his, St Clair's, woes. Perhaps take any coins in his pocket, perhaps rough him up a bit. But the old fool had put up a fight and St Clair had been forced to hit him hard over the head with his pistol. On impulse, he had seized a horse and hauled Bennet onto it. At least no alarm appeared to have been raised, no shouts of 'Stop him!' reached his ears.

Now it was too late to give up. He had already wounded the old man, possibly seriously, he had stolen a horse and had ridden off with Bennet. He could tip the old fool off the horse and leave him on the frozen road. But Bennet would be discovered by the first carriage or rider which came along and, if he wasn't overridden and killed, then he would give St Clair away.

St Clair reasoned that people had probably seen him about the Pemberley estate and in the neighbourhood when he had not been disguised, a relative stranger. Best to ride on and see what transpired.

Why should not this man and his family be caused alarm and consternation, so he had reasoned a few weeks ago? A letter pushed through the letter box of the Reverend Wilde would have been sufficient, warning of harm to the Bennet family and threatening to disrupt the marriages of Bennet's daughter and of the clergyman himself. His sisters had spoken volumes about the Reverend and Elizabeth Bennet meeting in secret, especially Helen who appeared to have been obsessed with the clergyman.

He had taken little notice of their tattle until Bennet had refused him the benefice at Longbourn, whereby his life was suddenly pitched into a headlong dive towards ruin. All his hardships stemmed from that uncharitable act.

Hence, he had wished this man ill for over a year. When the very worst had happened and the woman he hoped to marry and their child died penniless in the workhouse and he had been powerless to help, he had come to Derbyshire with a view to living off his sister Anne for a while, but she had not been agreeable. En route, he had stopped in Cambridgeshire to deliver the letter to the Reverend Wilde's home. It seemed to him to be a master-stroke to have penned the letter in the names of both Helen and Anne, creating confusion and implicating both of them; making it seem as though it was Helen who had married Scargill when it was actually Anne, who had decided to use her first name of Isabella so as to, she told him, start a new life after her husband's death.

He reasoned that the Reverend would probably communicate the threats to Elizabeth Bennet and then she at least, the daughter of his enemy, would be caused disquiet. He recognised that it was a fairly feeble retaliation, but there was nothing else he could do. That was until he had found that the man was here at Pemberley on this Christmas sojourn with his family. It was a gift, providence; without doubt it was meant to be.

By this time, his sister having thrown him out, he at first tried to obtain food and shelter from a row of cottages occupied by a family of idiots on the Pemberley estate. However, far from providing him with succour, they expected relief from *him*, no doubt assuming that his refined accent and good clothes marked him out as a member of the gentry. When it was clear he had nothing to give, they became violent and he was forced to flee.

Thereafter, he was reduced to living in an abandoned mill-house not far from Lambton and stealing to survive, occasionally appealing largely fruitlessly to his sister for money. His resentment had increased, especially as the weather grew colder. To pass the time, he explored the many caves and disused mines hereabouts, dreaming of what might have been, owning a big house, living in comfort. It even crossed his mind to somehow arrange the death of his older brother, so that he, Paul, would become the heir and would have the house and the income from the estate when his father died which was becoming distinctly likely as Mr St Clair's health deteriorated.

Of course, he would not do the act himself. He would enlist the aid of another who would be promised a large reward when Paul inherited the estate. Such hopeless dreams kept him from going mad. Or perhaps they were the result of his actually having gone mad, to be planning the death of his brother.

Even before Bennet and the rest of them had turned up at Pemberley, he took to loitering near the house and on the estate, dressing up as a poor old woman collecting kindling. He was never approached or challenged. So many were poor that his actions and appearance were commonplace.

Killing the dogs had been an excellent idea. No human had been hurt. It was, he found, very easy to gain access to the house. Creeping to the second floor during the night, enticing the dog with meat laced with *nux vomica* stolen from a gamekeeper's hovel, had been heart-stopping, but exciting. He had noticed old Bennet peering out of an upstairs window earlier on, and hoped he had found the right room in which to leave the dying dog. He would never know.

Contaminating the white soup with beet-root dye had been another master-stroke, with no person having been harmed. He knew how ladies valued the white soup, serving it up at their dinner tables. His mother had done so when the maid of the moment had been sufficiently trained to reliably prepare the delicacy and when the ingredients had been available.

But that wretched man Darcy had put an end to all the fun by having the house guarded like a fortress. Prior to riding off into the night with Bennet, his last act had been to attack the same gamekeeper who lived alone and steal more poisons, two pistols, a couple of knives and powder. He had used ether stolen from his sister's house, and laudanum. He hoped he had not fatally harmed the man.

Now, having left Bennet in the freezing cold, tied to a prop in an old mine working, his options were limited. He had the stolen horse. He had better make haste away from this county. Bennet was right; he would hang for what he had done. Yet there was nothing to connect him, Paul St Clair, with Mr Bennet's disappearance. Though a few people had probably noticed his presence around Pemberley and Lambton, no one hereabouts knew his name. His sister used her married name of Scargill. If anyone was suspected, it would be her in view of the letter to the Reverend Wilde, perhaps acting with an accomplice.

Despite the urgency, torpor seized him and he was fit for nothing. These balls went on until the early hours. No one would probably have missed Bennet yet. A couple of hours of sleep at the millhouse and a rest for the horse would enable him to escape far away from this county.

In which direction, he was not sure. But escape he must.

Chapter 24

THE ladies had gathered in Elizabeth's sitting room adjoining her bedroom almost before dawn broke. They were all pale from lack of sleep and had red-rimmed eyes from crying apart from Georgiana who was of course upset, but could not be expected to be so deeply affected as the others. She comforted Kitty instead. They wore their dressing gowns. None of them could take the trouble to dress properly and they certainly would not go to church today.

Mrs Bennet had not thrown a fit of hysterics on this occasion as she might have done, but sat wringing her handkerchief and uttering the occasional small cry. Jane and Kitty looked bleak. Even Mary sat with head bowed.

The Gardiners and Philipses put their heads round the door a few times, enquiring if there was any news. But the Gardiners, of course, had to be with their children who again wanted to take the dogs out.

Elizabeth had tearfully seen off her friend Harriet in a Pemberley carriage, though in truth she was relieved at her friend's departure. She had not the strength to entertain a friend on this very worst of days.

She could not help but feel that it was all her fault, as it was she who had particularly wanted to invite the family to Pemberley for this Christmas. Why could she not have waited until next year? Why could she not have acceded to the suggestions of Jane and Mrs Bennet that she, Darcy and Georgiana should have travelled to Netherfield instead for Christmas?

And the Gardiners could so much more easily have travelled to Hertfordshire from London than to Derbyshire.

It was foolish pride, she decided, conceit on her part.

It did help in some ways to blame herself. It took the sharp edges off the fretting she would otherwise have indulged in; the horrible visions of her father in the clutches of some maniac and what might be happening to him. That is if he was still alive. The alternative she wasn't yet prepared to admit to herself or the others.

Darcy, Bingley and the soldiers, together with any number of men employed in the house and on the estate, had been out all night looking for Mr Bennet. More men were still guarding the outside doors and kitchen. They had been back twice for refreshments and to ask if anything had been heard, which it hadn't. No ransom demand had been received, which was not to say that the person responsible for the abduction might not be composing a note at this very moment calling for a small fortune to be paid in order to gain Mr Bennet's release.

The men were exhausted, but refused to stay at home and take a couple of hours' rest. Constables had also been drawn into the effort and if nothing came of the search, handbills were to be displayed in Lambton and the surrounding district.

One of the magistrates with whom Darcy sat on the bench, Terence Standing, was in charge of the operation. They were concentrating their efforts on the estate to begin with, given that the episodes of dog-poisoning and food-tampering had taken place at the house. So far they had found nothing. Mrs Scargill's house had, of course, been searched by constables but there was no indication whatsoever that someone had been held captive there. No firearms had been discovered.

A report had already come back to Pemberley that she had complained that last Sunday evening men had broken into her home, had searched it and had taken away various documents as well as medicinal substances which she used in connection with her growing business as a herbalist. The items had been returned a few days later via a lawyer, having been found, it was alleged, in a ditch by the side of the road between Nethermill and Lambton.

There had been no trace of Mr Bennet last night at the Assembly Rooms or anywhere nearby. When it emerged that a horse was missing and an hour had passed in fruitlessly hunting for him throughout the streets of Lambton, the unhappy conclusion was reached that Mr Bennet must have been taken and carried away somewhere. This was supported by a report that one of the coachmen waiting outside had noticed some sort of scuffle between two men round the side of the building earlier on. The coachman had failed to raise the alarm at the time since such altercations were not uncommon and he had not thought it important.

Elizabeth had suggested a thorough search of the cottages occupied by the Joneses which Darcy had shown her on their ride together round the estate. It had seemed to be a promising suggestion but no trace had been discovered and the Joneses, using single-syllable words and grunts, had denied any knowledge of an older man being brought here last night and hidden or any stranger loitering near their homes in the last few months. Darcy, on one of his return visits to the house before dawn, expressed doubt to Elizabeth whether they were to be trusted. If anyone had paid them money, they would probably say anything, however there was no course but to accept what they said.

Breakfast had been brought into the sitting room at half past eight and the ladies made desultory efforts to eat something.

And they waited, and they waited, talking over the events of last night and, before they knew it, it was half past nine and still there had been no word. Elizabeth went over to the window and stood observing the freezing conditions. There was considerable activity and noise from outside and some from inside the house. Shouts could be heard; the sound of horses' hooves, footsteps, doors banging. This had been going on periodically all night and since daylight, as men returned to change horses, take a little refreshment and so on. She cried silently into her handkerchief at the thought of her poor, dear father freezing to death out there somewhere.

AT ten minutes after ten o' clock, Mrs Reynolds knocked on the door and entered the sitting room, saying that someone was here wishing to see Mrs Darcy. A visitor at this time was surprising. One of her new friends would be unlikely to call without first sending a card, especially on a Sunday. She was about to make an excuse, when the housekeeper told her that the caller was Mrs Isabella Scargill.

Elizabeth drew a sharp breath at the news. That the woman

should present herself *here* at such a time was quite astounding.

"Do you know how she got here? Did she walk, Mrs Reynolds?"

"She appears to have come in a chaise with a footman, madam."

"I see," said Elizabeth, wondering how Mrs Scargill could have achieved this.

"Do you wish me to accompany you, Lizzy?" said Jane.

The visit was so unexpected that Elizabeth barely knew how to respond. "I don't know. I suppose...I had better see her alone. I don't want her to be intimidated in case she can tell us anything to help find our father.

"Mrs Reynolds, would you show her into the office next to Mr Darcy's. The one the steward used to use. Please arrange for a fire to be lit in the room and tea served in about fifteen minutes. And please ask Peggy to come here."

"Certainly, Mrs Darcy. And Peggy is waiting outside."

ELIZABETH dressed quickly and, unusually, her hair was tucked into a lace-trimmed mob-cap. It would have taken too long for her hair to be dressed properly. She drew a deep breath and walked into the study with as much composure as she could summon.

"Good day, Mrs Scargill, although I have always known you as Anne."

She regarded the other woman warily. She certainly looked a lot like Helen, but was not so very thin and hence was prettier.

Mrs Scargill was standing stiffly with her hands on the back of a chair. The fire had already been lit and the room was starting to warm up. A tea tray sat on the desk.

"Do sit down."

"Thank you, Elizabeth. I have been using my first name of Isabella since...well, since leaving Longbourn. Although now..."

Elizabeth decided not for the present to question the reason for her visitor's enigmatic unfinished comment. She took another chair to the front of the desk opposite Mrs Scargill. It would probably seem unfriendly to go and sit behind the desk as though it was a formal interview. She had no particular liking for this woman but did not want to alienate her when her father's fate might rest on some information Mrs Scargill could provide.

"As you have probably observed from the commotion outside, Isabella, we are in some disorder here at Pemberley. My father is missing and it seems has been the subject of an abduction. He was taken, we think, from outside the Assembly Rooms in Lambton last night where a horse was also stolen. We know not where he may be. All attempts to find him have so far come to nought."

"So I have been told, by constables who woke me before dawn and searched every inch of my house. I know not why, except that I have heard that my name has been blackened in the neighbourhood as a poisoner, the reports having evidently come out of Pemberley this past week."

Isabella sounded angry. Her voice shook.

"And my house was entered Sunday evening past and a number of items taken, private documents and tools of my trade which, granted, have since been returned to me. I was actually in the house at the time. Of course I was frightened for my life and had to conceal myself. I have been told that two of the men were soldiers and it is said that you have two soldiers staying here at Pemberley. What can account for such unlawful behaviour?"

Elizabeth bridled at the woman's tone and her indignation. She would not be intimidated. What Mrs Scargill said was no doubt true, but there had been every reason to suspect her of wrong-doing.

"It is clear to us, Isabella, that you are not blameless. We have it on good authority that you or your sister Helen committed a heinous crime a little over a year ago by trespassing in the house of the then rector of Longbourn, Mr Wilde, badly injuring his sister and poisoning his table wine. Or perhaps both you and Helen conspired to do those things. We have more recently been threatened with harm and your name was mentioned. You have evidently been in this house which seems very sinister. Your name and I presume your signature appear in our visitors' book at the end of November."

Mrs Scargill's attitude changed somewhat and she began to

look uncomfortable.

"Yes, I came to view the house with other ladies. I am not long in this neighbourhood. I am attempting to make a name for myself as a herbalist. I arranged the trip as a treat for ladies who may at some time wish to consult me."

"There is already an apothecary in Lambton, Isabella, a Mr Fox."

"There is, but many women would prefer to consult another woman."

"I was informed by our housekeeper that the visitors asked after any heirs of the present Mr Darcy."

"Well, it was not me who asked. I knew full well from my mother's letters that you had only just married and there would be no children yet. I confess that as we are acquainted and are both former residents of Longbourn, I was curious to see Pemberley House."

"Be that as it may, two of our dogs have been poisoned to death and food intended for this household has been tampered with. We know that you have been meeting one of our gamekeepers who was attacked last Sunday and suspect that you were also meeting the steward at Pemberley House who has since left."

Elizabeth paused briefly to take a breath and was pleased to note Mrs Scargill's eyes widening.

"Elizabeth, I assure you that this is only the second time I have been to this house, the first being the group visit in November. I am not responsible for harming dogs or adulterating food."

"Well, somebody did these things. We have had to take extreme measures to guard and protect the house and the people in it. Regrettably both my own family who have been staying here and all the servants have had to be told of the reason for these steps being taken and inevitably they were told your name as the likely perpetrator as we had every reason to suppose that you were involved."

She had not intended to become so angry but now found that she could not stop herself from raising her voice and glaring at Mrs Scargill.

"And now my father has been taken. And you have the impudence to present yourself here and complain of a legitimate search by constables. It is best that if you know anything about our father's abduction that you tell me now so that perhaps my father may be found before..."

Elizabeth could not say the words and found that her rage was exhausted and she feared she might shame herself by shedding tears in front of this woman.

Mrs Scargill said nothing for a time and Elizabeth used the interval to recollect herself.

"Well," she said, "do you know anything, Isabella?"

"Perhaps," Mrs Scargill said. "I don't — "

She stopped.

"Tell me. *Please*. Whatever it is."

"I can only think it is my brother Paul. May I ask, how do you know of the difficulties last summer with Mr Wilde?"

Loathe as she was to provide this woman with further intelligence, Elizabeth had to do what she could to extract any useful information from her.

"Mr Wilde wrote of it and to warn me," she said. "He told me of a letter he had received signed 'Isabella Scargill formerly Helen St Clair'. So naturally we thought at first that Helen was Mrs Scargill, but now I see it is you. And my mother thinks that Helen is married to a vicar in Norfolk and may have a child."

"That is true. We both went to Norfolk to stay with relations and she was lucky enough to meet her husband. She fancied herself in love with Mr Wilde and marrying a clergyman, albeit not Mr Wilde, seemed to make her very happy. I also met my husband. He was a little older than me but a very pleasant man and I did love him. Unfortunately he gambled. He lost absolutely all of his money and shot himself one night. I had no money and I had no alternative but to come to Nethermill to claim his house, Payne Lodge, and to live there."

"What happened with Mr Wilde and his sister?"

"It was I who went to his house. Helen persuaded me to go. She had obtained some sort of love potion from a woman in Meryton and wanted me to put it in his wine. I thought there would be no harm in it. It seemed quite a lark. I had no idea it

209

would poison him. And his sister came back and tried to stop me from leaving the house. As I struggled to get past her, she fell and I think banged her head.

"I was furious with Helen when I found out that Mr Wilde had become very ill and that his sister had been rendered insensible. That was why we both hurriedly left Longbourn. I became interested in herbs myself after that and persuaded an apothecary in Norfolk to teach me what he knew. I have to earn a living for myself, Elizabeth, but I assure you it is not from poisoning people — or dogs. And I have had some help from...gentleman friends. I don't deny that your gamekeeper and steward have been friends of mine."

So, Elizabeth thought, she has been selling favours to men, a fate, she admitted to herself, which might easily have befallen her sister Lydia had Wickham not been persuaded to marry her; that she might have been forced to come upon the town. Perhaps that was the extortion of which the solicitor, Waring, had spoken to Fitz; that men would pay money, more money, to avoid their wives knowing that they had been visiting a woman. Indeed, if she had treated ladies for various ailments and conditions, she would be in their confidence; she would know their business intimately and might take advantage of that.

The lawyer's intelligence was starting to make some sense now. Mrs Scargill had openly admitted to her having studied under an apothecary and why she had done so. Further, for her husband to have shot himself could certainly seem suspicious. As to adopting disguises and assumed names, perhaps these were elaborations on the part of the lawyer's informants.

Mrs Scargill continued:

"As you probably know what happened on Sunday past when men searched my house, because I think one of them was your husband, I will tell you that the gentleman who escaped out of the window of my house was one of my friends who was visiting me."

"I see. And the chaise you travelled in today belongs to one of your friends, does it?"

"Yes, it does. I am not proud of myself, Elizabeth. I have had to do these things to survive. My parents are no longer at Pollards, but in Bath. My older brother Simon wants the house to himself as he wishes to marry. My other brother Paul had some woman friend, I believe. That all seemed to go wrong for him but I do not know the particulars."

She leaned forward.

"Elizabeth, I think it must have been my brother Paul who wrote the letter to Mr Wilde naming me and Helen. He has been here, I mean in Derbyshire. I let him live in my house for a short time as he had nowhere else to go, but I had to force him to leave as I think he was stealing from me. One of my friends helped me persuade him to go. I know he is troubled, he always has been, but quite why he would harm you or your family, I cannot say. It must be some grudge or other."

Elizabeth, of course, remembered Paul St Clair. To her he had simply been a member of another local family in Longbourn. Her contact with the St Clair sons had been minimal. Mostly it had been Helen and Anne and Mr and Mrs St Clair whom the Bennets had known. She may have heard her own father at some time making some derogatory comment about Paul, the younger son, but she had taken little notice, and what it may have been now escaped her.

Perhaps Paul St Clair was the root of the lawyer's allusion to disguises as a young man or an old woman.

"So you do not know where he is, then, Paul?"

"I do not."

"Oh, this is terrible," Elizabeth cried, and she did shed tears this time. "My father will die in the conditions as they are. Oh, God, where might he have been taken?"

She bent and sobbed into her lap. The tea sat untouched at the edge of the desk. Mrs Scargill muttered words of sympathy. She became aware of footsteps in the hall outside the door but did not raise her head.

The door opened and Darcy entered. He went straight to Elizabeth, stooped and put his arm around her shoulder.

"What is happening here?"

Elizabeth sniffed and looked up. "This is Mrs Scargill, William. She thinks her brother Paul is responsible for the poisonings and taking my father. It is not her, of that I am pretty certain. But she does not know where he might be."

Darcy, sounding angry, said: "Why she thinks her brother is the culprit, we can examine another time. But have you no idea, Mrs Scargill, where he is? If he is not living with you, and I take it he is not, then where might he be? Who does he know in this neighbourhood?"

Mrs Scargill's face showed her fear. This man now questioning her was a magistrate, a rich man, a powerful man and Elizabeth could see that he fully intended that she should apprehend this. Mrs Scargill swallowed. "I know of no one."

"We are talking of Paul St Clair, I take it."

"Yes, William," said Elizabeth.

"I think I may have seen something of him around Meryton when we were there. I think I would recognise him."

Breathing hard, her eyes wide, Mrs Scargill addressed Darcy. "Mr Darcy, I was telling Elizabeth that I had to throw him out of my house for stealing from me. That was three weeks ago. I can only assume he has been living roughly somewhere. There are many caves hereabouts, around Lambton. Old mines. I can think of nothing else. Except that the few times he has visited me to beg for food or some money, he has left and walked in the direction of Danemill."

Elizabeth looked up at Darcy.

"Danemill is a village outside Lambton. There is also an old, disused mill nearby," he said. "I had better change my horse and take some men there. As to a cave, there are hundreds thereabout. It would be...well, at any rate I had better go, Elizabeth. I will see you later."

He was out of the door in seconds, glancing at Mrs Scargill as he left.

Elizabeth heard her husband enter his own study next door. He was in there a short time, then his footsteps receded away along the passage.

Chapter 25

DARCY called for the soldiers, Colonel Fitzwilliam and Lieutenant Colonel Harvey, to be found and summoned if possible. He then sat for some time deciding on a course of action. After leaving Elizabeth in his steward's old office, he had gone into his own office and withdrawn a large sum in coinage from his safe. It seemed to him that if they, he and the soldiers, found Paul St Clair, that the man would need some incentive to take them to wherever he had secreted Mr Bennet.

Otherwise, St Clair might just as well deny having abducted Mr Bennet. It would certainly be in his interests to do so and there would probably be little evidence of him having done so, if Bennet was never found. And that, thought Darcy, would be the worst possible outcome. A probably dead father-in-law, for whom he now felt all the love of a son by blood. A distraught wife, whose father may be alive or dead, left to wonder for the rest of her life what had become of him. Carried away by gypsies? Eaten by wolves? Except that there were no wolves in England. Taken and cast into a deep chasm or a fast flowing river or down an old mine shaft?

No, that would never do. St Clair must be given a solid reason to lead him to Mr Bennet and money was the most obvious inducement. And if he did lead them to Mr Bennet...?

Darcy didn't consider what would happen after that, whether he would give St Clair up or not. Certainly he would if Mr Bennet was found dead. If found alive, he was not sure.

DARCY and the soldiers rode first to the disused millhouse at Danemill, assuming this would probably be St Clair's hiding-place. They were all armed and were accompanied by a footman driving a flat-bedded wagon filled with straw and blankets in case they had to convey Mr Bennet back to Pemberley, alive or dead. It was the best that could be devised in a short time. The riders had to slow down at intervals to allow the footman to catch up with them.

Darcy had of course related to the soldiers what he had learned of Paul St Clair and his possible whereabouts. He had not told Fitzwilliam of the money he carried with him and had tightly twisted and bound the bag in which it was held to prevent it from rattling. He knew there would be strong objections from his cousin whose instincts would be to beat St Clair almost to a pulp and then still expect to get some sense out of him. It might work, but since St Clair faced the gallows if Mr Bennet was dead, he might very well prefer to be beaten to death than undergo a prosecution and an execution by hanging.

Darcy's priority was to recover Mr Bennet alive if at all possible. He would deal with Fitzwilliam's anticipated protests later.

It must have been about two o' clock by the time they reached the old millhouse and the light would be fading soon. Snow had fallen earlier this morning. It was ferociously cold and becoming colder. That part of the building which anyone could usefully occupy was very small and it took no time to search it. They could see the remains of a fire on the floor and some charred animal bones. A pile of rags signalled where St Clair had probably slept if this had been his refuge. Darcy removed his gloves and felt about among the material. Surprisingly, it was warm.

"I think he has not long departed."

SHORTLY after Darcy had appeared and left again, Elizabeth called for a servant to see Isabella Scargill out of the house. Both women rose and, while they waited, Elizabeth asked her visitor whether she knew why Campbell the steward had quit Pemberley so precipitately.

Mrs Scargill smirked rather unpleasantly.

"He told me he had got a Wirkworth girl with child. I think he did not want to be forced to marry her or have a bastardy order made against him. He was forced to flee. Where he went, I do not know."

Elizabeth stared at Mrs Scargill with disgust. The poor girl; the poor child. She was reminded of her family's kitchen maid, Alice, and her little boy, Peter, recovered from the cotton mill at

214

Lowdham. Campbell did not want to support his child and yet he had paid money to Mrs Scargill for her favours and Mrs Scargill had accepted the money.

"Do you know the girl's name?"

Mrs Scargill shook her head.

Darcy would be appalled when Elizabeth told him. She watched through the window as Mrs Scargill's chaise drew away from the house, hoping never to have to do business with her again.

The woman's manner suggested that she still harboured resentment at having been suspected of poisoning and at the searching of her home. Elizabeth in her turn could not but feel huge anger at the grave trouble visited on her family by the St Clairs.

The encounter had kept her grief and worst fears at bay for an hour or so. She left the study to seek out Jane and talk over what she had found out.

JANE was more than willing to take some exercise and fresh air when Elizabeth suggested it. Bingley accompanied them.

"What do you know of this fellow, St Clair?" asked Bingley.

"Very little," said Elizabeth. "William said he thought he had seen him about when in Hertfordshire and would probably recognise him."

"I do not know how that would have been," said Bingley, "though I believe we knew of their house, Pollards."

"I think Mama said at one time that he was interested in taking Holy Orders," Jane offered.

"Did he approach our father?" Elizabeth said.

Jane sighed. "I am sorry. I do not know. We could ask our mother but I would prefer not to at this time."

"No, of course. But if he asked Papa and Papa refused him, that might be why he has taken our father now."

"It seems a mean reason to commit a possibly hanging offence," said Bingley. "And the present rector who married us has been in place since about the time we, Darcy and I, came to Netherfield last year, therefore if St Clair's motive was that he had been refused the benefice, he must have waited over a year to exact this revenge, if that is what it is."

Elizabeth found this eminently logical and regarded Bingley with respect. This discussion, she found, was warding off her desperation for now. Jane never did exhibit strong emotion to the world, though Elizabeth knew she would be thinking all the same things. She saw that Jane and Bingley both looked ragged from lack of sleep and Bingley, who had been out on a horse all night, was dishevelled.

She should suggest that they took a rest and have hot water and food delivered to their room. The same with the rest of her family. She looked over at where Mr and Mrs Gardiner and their children were playing with the dogs, the puppies gambolling madly in the snow and hurling themselves at the older gundogs which bore the attention patiently. The snowman stood abandoned nearer the house, though someone must have brushed the latest fall of snow from its coat. Elizabeth could not prevent herself from irreverently comparing the snowman's figure with that of Uncle Gardiner. The bell-shape must provide stability for standing objects as well as for skating men.

The attempt to build a snow house had not stood the test of the prevailing north wind and had it collapsed in a disorderly pile of packed snow, sticks and old sacks.

She had the task as yet to be undertaken of cancelling all their forthcoming engagements both at Pemberley and at the homes of others. The weeks either side of Christmas were traditionally times of feasting, dancing, balls and parties and she had been looking forward to providing her family with all these entertainments.

Harriet would know full well that it was impossible for Elizabeth and her family to visit the Layhams as had been planned next week, but Elizabeth would still have to write formally to Sir Peter and Lady Layham, and she would write a personal letter to Harriet. She had dreaded sitting down for hours composing apologetic notes for footmen to ride off with to those hosting events and to the many guests who would no longer be coming to Pemberley. But it could not be delayed any longer and she walked off towards the house to make a start on the correspondence.

Elizabeth wondered how Darcy and the soldiers were faring. She could do nothing in that regard but wait. She felt completely helpless.

Chapter 26

DARCY had assumed that St Clair would have taken himself out of the neighbourhood as soon as possible. If, Darcy thought, I had committed a probable hanging crime myself, I would not wait to be apprehended. But it seemed as though St Clair had come back here and slept. It was incredible!

"There are fresh tracks out here leading roughly north-west," shouted Harvey from outside.

The others joined him. The tracks were clear in the pristine, hard-frozen snow.

"We had better follow them then," said Darcy.

To the footman with the wagon, he said: "Please wait here and rest the horses. I hope we will be back before long. Keep the lanterns ready to light. We may have to explore caves or other dark places once we have some idea where Mr Bennet was taken."

"Yes, sir."

The tracks led in the direction of Manchester, Darcy thought. He shrugged.

"He makes for Manchester, it appears."

"Indeed," said Fitzwilliam. "You do not think that he has taken Mr Bennet with him?"

"I think it most unlikely. Do not you? If he had kept my father-in-law with him, it would have created considerable difficulties for him. As far as we know, St Clair has only one horse."

"But by taking him away, it would lessen the chances of our finding Mr Bennet. Thereby St Clair could keep him and use him to demand money repeatedly."

"His sister said he had nowhere to go though, hence his living in the old millhouse. I would assume that he took my father-in-law to somewhere nearby and left him incapacitated. He may have seriously injured him. Almost certainly ensured that he could not escape, by tying him up, I imagine. It has been fourteen hours since he went missing and there has been no ransom demand. It is surprising that St Clair did not immediately leave the area, but it appears he went back to the millhouse to sleep."

"Mr Bennet may have been at the millhouse with St Clair, and is with him still."

"If that is so, though I do not think it is, we had best make haste to pursue him. Or we could instead go now and search the hundreds of caves hereabouts."

Fitzwilliam grunted.

"It is to be hoped that if we catch him, he will take us straight to where he has left my father-in-law."

"Yes," said Fitzwilliam. "And if he will not, then I will be happy to persuade him."

"There will be villages on the way," said Harvey. "We may have difficulty following the trail."

Neither of the others replied. There was little point, but there appeared to be no other riders or walkers about to disturb the fresh hoof-prints and cause confusion. It was Sunday and most folks, rich or poor, would have attended church and then spent the day with their families.

Darcy dug his heels in and the others did likewise. It would be hard going, he assumed, and uphill, towards the Peak. They rode in silence for maybe half an hour when they saw that the tracks suddenly veered off to the left. It appeared that the rider had attempted to jump the stone wall running alongside the road, possibly to take a short-cut over the field or merely to get away from the road.

On the other side of the field there was thick woodland. Perhaps that was where the rider had been heading however no prints led away from the wall on the other side of it. Instead, a mound was visible some yards into the snow-covered field where the snow had been churned up. It was difficult to see exactly what it might be. The snow and the poor light played tricks on the eyes.

Darcy dismounted.

"I hope it is St Clair, and not some other fool who was dossing in the millhouse and decided to possibly cripple his horse by taking a run at a stone wall in these conditions."

The others jumped down and they all peered over the wall at the shape in the field.

"We had better take care," Darcy continued. "If it is him, he may be armed. It is likely that firearms were taken from the gamekeeper's cottage."

"Thank you for telling us now, Darcy," said the colonel.

"Perhaps, then, you would stay with the horses, Fitzwilliam, and Harvey and I will go and investigate what it is over the wall."

"Hold on, Darcy. We should all go. I would say that our best plan is to creep up on him, disarm him between us and give him a severe beating. Then force him to take us to wherever he left Mr Bennet."

"That is what I was afraid of. That you will wish to attack him. I would remind you that if he is rendered totally incapable, or indeed if he is shot, he will be unable to show us where he has left my father-in-law. My absolute priority is to recover Mr Bennet. I am not interested in injuring St Clair in the process."

"Darcy, you cannot treat these people with kid gloves. Only harsh treatment will give a result. It is the only language they understand."

"I repeat, Fitzwilliam, I do not want him injured, not at this point."

They all watched the lump in the field which now appeared to be moving. Something that might have been horses legs started to paddle the air, spreading snow asunder, and suddenly a dark-coloured horse regained its feet and shook its head. The fool, whoever had brought the horse here, must have left the road to take his chances in the deeper snow of the field which could hide a variety of hazards.

"Please both stay here," said Darcy. "I'll go and deal with him."

"Darcy, this is madness."

"No, it is not. I am confident of persuading him to be sensible."

The colonel frowned. Harvey said nothing.

Darcy climbed the wall. "Come over if I shout."

The snow, though no doubt deep, was so hard that it formed

a surface like a sheet of steel for a man to walk on with just a light covering of loose snow from this morning. But the horse's hooves had obviously sunk into the snow under its weight. Darcy strode over towards the horse which, seeing him coming, tried to walk towards him but something stopped its progress and a muffled cry issued from the snow. Darcy saw a depression and a tangle of arms and legs. He drew his pistol and walked to within a couple of feet of the floundering shape.

"What ails you?" said Darcy.

"God, man," came the reply, "can you not see my foot is trapped in the stirrup?"

"Tell me your name, please."

He was almost certain it was St Clair. The man was lucky not to have been trampled or crushed by the horse. He was fortunate indeed that they had come upon him so quickly after his fall. In these temperatures in the snow, a man might succumb and die within a few hours.

"Simmonds. If you would do me the courtesy of disengaging my foot from the stirrup..."

Then he saw the pistol. An instant later, he looked at Darcy's face and obviously recognised him. Darcy in his turn saw that it was St Clair.

"Now tell me your real name."

"Why do you point a pistol at me?" St Clair blustered, trying to sit up, but since the horse had risen, one of his legs jutted out, straight up towards the stirrup where his still booted foot was caught. He was forced to remain on his back, unable to reach up and free his foot.

Darcy kicked the man's leg hard. The man gasped in pain.

"*Your name.*"

The man didn't reply and Darcy kicked him again.

"Very well," he said quickly. "I am Paul St Clair."

"You know who I am St Clair and why I aim a pistol at you. I will not tolerate any further argument. I will help you out of the stirrup. Then you must take me to wherever you have left my father-in-law, Mr Bennet of Longbourn, missing from the Assembly Rooms in Lambton since about midnight last night."

"I do not know what you are talking about."

"Yes, you do. If my father-in-law dies, you will hang. Now I will give you an alternative. I have with me two hundred and fifty guineas." Darcy took a few coins out of his pocket and held them up for St Clair to see. The gold was bright against the background of snow and trees. "The rest is in my saddlebag. A tidy sum. Enough for you to buy yourself a house and to start some sort of useful life elsewhere. I will give it to you if you take me to my father-in-law. You will take me forthwith. Throw your weapons out onto the snow. Your horse seems uninjured. Get up and lead him to the end of the field there, where there is a gate and I will ride with you to the place where you have left my father-in-law. Is all that clear enough for you?"

Suspicion, surprise, cunning and greed all chased themselves across St Clair's thin face.

"I do not have any weapons."

"Look, man, I would happily shoot you dead now were it not for my father-in-law. Do not tempt me. And have some sense. I am not going to bend over you to free your foot from the stirrup if you are armed. Throw your weapons out. If you try any games, my comrades," Darcy indicated the soldiers at the wall who had drawn their pistols, "will kill you for certain."

For the first time, St Clair seemed to notice Fitzwilliam and Harvey. He grunted, felt about his clothing and hurled a pistol some feet away from him.

"And any knives too."

St Clair swore and produced a small dagger, of the sort used to gut game.

Darcy kicked the weapons farther away.

"What is that bulge in your coat?" he said.

"A few spare clothes. I have nothing else."

"Open your coat and show me."

"This is nonsense."

"Oh, I see. Is it your assertion that you did not take my father-in-law, because if so, I might as well shoot you now?"

St Clair was shivering and his teeth had started to chatter.

"My fingers are too cold to open the buttons."

"Do not try my patience, St Clair. You wear gloves. Just do it."

Darcy took a step towards him. "*Do as I say.*" He hissed rather than shouted the words. He did not want Fitzwilliam to hear and blunder over ready to strike St Clair.

St Clair groaned and started to slowly fumble with the buttons of his coat. He seemed to be shielding what was inside with one arm. Darcy kicked his arm aside and St Clair squealed like a pig. Darcy saw the dull gleam of iron. Another pistol. Also, if Darcy was not mistaken, another knife.

"Throw out your second pistol and that knife and then continue to unbutton your coat."

St Clair slowly did so and again Darcy kicked them away. Satisfied, Darcy walked to the horse and patted the animal's neck to reassure it. He then examined how St Clair's foot was trapped. The leather strap was twisted. The horse had remained remarkably still, probably a good thing. Much movement would very likely have caused further damage to St Clair's foot. As it was, the ankle was bent at an odd angle. It was either broken or at least twisted.

Darcy decided that he should get it over with and free the foot quickly. St Clair cried out as he did so, but was free within seconds. Darcy picked up and pocketed the fallen weapons and caught the horse's reins.

"Get up, St Clair."

"God, Darcy, my foot," St Clair gasped, but struggled upright, holding his injured foot off the ground.

"Now, walk with me to the gate as I said. I will lead the horse."

And to the soldiers he yelled:

"Meet us at that gate and bring my horse."

St Clair made slow work of it, limping and hopping, but in addition the horse hampered them, its feet sinking into the deep snow drifts in the field.

"You'd better search him for any more weapons," Darcy told the officers, immediately they were on the road again.

Harvey started to go through St Clair's clothing. Fitzwilliam produced a pair of gyves.

"Hold hard," said St Clair, "you will not cuff me."

He took an aggressive lurch towards Fitzwilliam. Fitzwilliam hit him hard on the side of his face with the gyves, producing a spray of blood and a scream from St Clair who put his hands up to his head.

"Be sensible, St Clair," said Darcy, while glaring at Fitzwilliam. He did not, however, protest at the assault. He did not wish to demonstrate to their captive that his captors were at odds with one another.

Fitzwilliam roughly grasped St Clair's hands and dragged them to his front, fixing on the gyves and locking them quickly.

St Clair spat blood from his mouth and bloody objects, probably teeth or bits of tooth.

"Show me the money," he spluttered, "before I take you anywhere."

"What money?" asked Fitzwilliam.

"Would you guard St Clair?" Darcy asked Harvey.

"Of course, Darcy."

Darcy walked away with Fitzwilliam and lowered his voice.

"He only gets the money if he leads me to Mr Bennet—and alive at that. Without some incentive, especially if he believes Mr Bennet to be dead, St Clair could have us following him around fruitlessly for the rest of the day and night. The money should concentrate his mind and I hope he will take us straight to where he left my father-in-law."

"Is that why you did not want constables accompanying us? Since you propose to let him go if we recover Mr Bennet?"

"Partly, though I do not know if I would let him go. But they would have held us up as well."

"How much?"

"I would prefer not to say. But as you will see it when I show it to him, I will tell you it is two hundred and fifty guineas."

His cousin went red in the face and breathed hard. Darcy thought he was about to explode but at length he sighed. "It seems a very foolish plan to me."

"All right. If it does not work, we can adopt your preferred course and you can have the pleasure of half-killing him. I may well join you."

"Very well."

ELIZABETH had settled her family with refreshments, in their rooms if they wished, but her mother preferred to stay in Elizabeth's sitting room. Therefore she dined early with her mother, and Mary; Kitty and Georgiana joined them. They were all exhausted from lack of sleep but they had to eat and Elizabeth took the opportunity to relate to them what she had found out from Mrs Scargill.

The Philipses dined in the small dining room as did the Gardiners with their children. She would have to tell the Gardiners and the Philipses tomorrow. She had not the energy to go down to the dining room today as the light faded and Darcy and the soldiers did not return.

Perhaps, reflected Elizabeth, it would have been better if the whole family had left Pemberley as Darcy had suggested they might a week since. Then her father would not have been taken. He would have been safe at Longbourn by now. Presumably.

THE mouth of the old mine was some way up a steep hill and was hard to make out, more so since snow had built up around the entrance. It was dark now. The side of the hill faced north and a stiff northerly wind was blowing, lowering the temperature even further. A track of sorts led to the opening. As a result of the snow, it was marked only by the remains of old fencing poking out of the snow either side together with furze. It was too steep for the wagon which had accompanied them from the old millhouse. Darcy, the soldiers and St Clair were walking, almost scrambling in places, up the hill, with St Clair slowing them down and making a great deal of fuss about his injured leg.

Therefore Darcy went up ahead of the others with a lantern. He turned before moving off.

"Are you quite sure this is the place, St Clair?"

"It must be."

"That is not what I asked," Darcy snapped.

"Then yes, I am sure as far as I can be. You see it has been snowing."

"How far in did you leave him?"

"Not far. I tied him to a stout prop with some thick rope which...I found."

Darcy had to be content with that and he went with a heavy heart. All his instincts told him that his father-in-law must by now be dead.

It took him little time to reach the opening. He pitied the poor devils who had to work in these places, fearing being trapped if there was heavy rain and the mine flooded. He had to fight his way in through a drift of snow which penetrated some yards into the cave until he found himself in a large cavern although the weak light from his lantern did not reach the walls and ceiling of this place. He walked about the large space but there was no sign of anyone. He walked back towards the entrance where the roof of the cavern was lower and there was a framework of solid-looking beams and uprights half buried in snow but no one was tied to them.

The freezing wind whistled through the entrance. The cold ate into him. A night in here would kill anyone.

He was wondering whether he should walk further into this hellish place when he heard the sound of the soldiers' swearing echoing through the cavern as they negotiated the snow drift with St Clair and at last they appeared and swung their lanterns about.

St Clair was looking at the wooden framework.

"That is where I left him." He pointed to one of the uprights. "Though there was no snow in here last night. Right there. I swear it was."

Chapter 27

WITH Darcy's return, Mrs Bennet, Georgiana, Kitty and Mary left Elizabeth's sitting room. Kitty and Mary went with their mother to her room; Georgiana to her own room. Elizabeth felt sorry for Georgiana having to be on her own. She hoped that Mrs Annesley would provide some companionship.

Darcy's report that Mr Bennet had not been found cast a heavy shadow over Pemberley House. He spoke briefly to Patterson and Mrs Reynolds and told them the news. He requested that they and the servants should carry on with their routines and duties as usual. The guarding of the house was not so vital now that Paul St Clair, the brother of Mrs Scargill, thought to be the cause of all the recent trouble, had been apprehended and was in custody.

He talked to Elizabeth for a few minutes and asked her to relate the latest position to the family. Then he went into his dressing room and did not re-emerge. Elizabeth was left to cry her tears alone and, when she was sufficiently composed, to seek out Colonel Fitzwilliam and ask him to assist her as he of course was entirely seized of the day's events.

She found him in the saloon having a drink with Lieutenant Colonel Harvey. Doubtless they needed it. The Gardiners and the Philipses were also there, but the children had gone to bed. The lieutenant colonel asked after Kitty.

"As well as might be. It would seem sensible if I call my mother and sisters, and of course Bingley, to this room and we can all be together here," Elizabeth suggested.

While waiting for them to be brought to the saloon, Elizabeth familiarised the Gardiners and the Philipses with Isabella Scargill's visit and what she had said. She also told them of the confusion caused by the letter received by the Reverend Wilde, having been signed 'Isabella Scargill formerly Helen St Clair'.

"Helen has actually had nothing to do with all this."

After the others arrived and everyone was seated, Elizabeth gave a brief account of the failed search today according to Darcy's intelligence. She was glad of the soldiers' presence when various family members started to ask questions which she could not answer, most particularly what was to happen next.

"Handbills are to be printed and posted about Lambton and the surrounding area and left in taverns and shops. Darcy has offered a reward of eighty pounds," said the colonel.

"Will you continue to search?" Mrs Bennet wanted to know.

The soldiers looked at each other.

"Possibly. That is for Darcy to decide," the colonel replied.

They all wanted to know what fate the soldiers thought had befallen Mr Bennet.

The colonel shook his head. "Darcy, I am sure, will discuss that with us tomorrow."

Mr Philips cleared his throat and asked: "Has St Clair confessed though? If not, is there clear evidence against him?"

"I regret not a great deal save that Paul St Clair had been identified as the unknown man seen loitering about outside the Assembly Rooms last night. And, no, he has not confessed."

"But he took you to this place," insisted Mr Philips. "That is surely confession enough."

Again some unspoken message seemed to pass between the soldiers.

Lieutenant Colonel Harvey spoke. "Darcy was insistent that St Clair should not be ill-treated. But...we all had weapons. I believe he is now saying that he was frightened and took us anywhere to satisfy us at the time. We all clearly saw him point to where he said he had tied and left Mr Bennet and heard him swear that that was the place. Now he appears to be saying that that was a sham on his part, because he was frightened of us; what we might do to him I suppose. And there was no sign that anyone had ever been there."

Mr Philips glared at the soldiers. "This is very unsatisfactory. I take it that St Clair was not actually injured by any of you."

Harvey swallowed. "At one point after we first apprehended St Clair, it looked as though he was going to attack Colonel Fitzwilliam. And...er..." He stopped.

"I had gyves with me and was about to cuff St Clair when he came at me. I hit him round the mouth with them. There was a little blood. That was all."

Elizabeth turned away, unable to disguise her anger. That Colonel Fitzwilliam, by hitting St Clair, may have given the man the ammunition to be able to avoid his guilt was intolerable. Had not Darcy implied to her that the colonel was impetuous and acted ill-advisedly? He had been right about that.

Colonel Fitzwilliam continued, oblivious evidently of any-one's disapprobation. "He is to be questioned tomorrow." He rubbed his eyes. "Now, if you will forgive us, Lieutenant Colonel Harvey and I must get some sleep, for we do not know what will happen tomorrow, whether we will be called upon to carry out further searches. Or to speak to Mr Standing the magistrate in charge."

When everyone had left the saloon to retire to their beds, Elizabeth remained behind for a few minutes to think, but when Mrs Reynolds came in to ask if anything more was needed, she decided she should leave the room for the servants to clear up.

A hundred questions started to bombard Elizabeth as she climbed the stairs.

— Surely St Clair having been found with the stolen horse was proof of his having been involved in Mr Bennet's abduction?

— Should she write to Mr Wilde and ask him for the letter he had received so that the hand-writing could be compared with that of St Clair?

— Were local people to be questioned? People must have seen St Clair, a stranger, loitering in the area, on the Pemberley estate even?

— Would Mrs Scargill be questioned? Could she even be an accomplice of her brother?

— Considering what Bingley had implied earlier about the feeble motive for the abduction being a possible refusal by Mr Bennet to recommend St Clair for the benefice, if indeed he had been approached and refused, would some effort be made in and about Longbourn or Meryton for some further motive?

— Her father may have made a note of St Clair's request. He

probably did. Although he hated letter-writing, he was quite scrupulous at keeping records. Would someone be sent to Longbourn House to check this point?

St Clair, Elizabeth was adamant, should not be allowed to get away with it. She would put these points to Darcy tomorrow and any others which occurred to her.

DARCY quite clearly had retreated into himself. The bright sunshine when Monday dawned did nothing to lift his mood. A black gloom had settled upon him and although he must know full well that Elizabeth needed his full love and support, he appeared quite incapable of offering it. Elizabeth begged him to at least talk to her about what had happened but he would not.

"Darcy," she said to him, "I know you bitterly regret not being able to save him, but it is not your fault. We know whose fault it is. Paul St Clair. He may have had his reasons, as yet unknown to us. Doubtless warped and twisted reasons. Wholly unjustified but possibly valid in his mind. We have been wondering whether my father refused to recommend him for the benefice at Longbourn, and that it may be to do with that. But you certainly are not to blame. You did everything you could, Darcy. You—"

"You call me Darcy now, I see," he said, his face expressionless.

She had. In truth, the name suited him and always had. Even during his more relaxed period since their marriage, he looked like Darcy, his bearing was all Darcy, his correct speech, the remnants of his reserve, his tendency to be economical with words. It was all Darcy. His strength, his determination to do things the right way, Darcy's way.

That stern, silent man whom she had first encountered; was Darcy now going to revert to his former self? Unsmiling, rude at times, aloof, disapproving of those he felt were beneath him? It was too much. Elizabeth had to try to resurrect the kind, loving husband she had come to depend upon.

Darcy rose abruptly.

"You are mistaken. I do not in the least blame myself."

Elizabeth did not believe him. She knew her husband's nature well enough. As he had determinedly arranged Wickham's marriage to Lydia, taking everything upon himself, he would now see it as his duty to protect her family.

"I am going to my room to dress," he told her, "then I must go to Lambton to see the magistrate, Standing, to assist in any way with the enquiries. I expect that the soldiers will accompany me."

"But I have questions, Darcy. If St Clair will not admit to having taken my father, there must be things which could be investigated which would prove his guilt. May I not speak these questions to you so that you can put them to Mr Standing?"

"I feel sure he will be quite capable of conducting a thorough investigation without assistance from...without others' help. He has done this before Elizabeth. As indeed have I."

He swept from the room.

Elizabeth had been effectively dismissed. But she would not give up. She sat at her escritoire and pulled a piece of paper towards her. Quickly, she listed all the questions which in her view needed to be answered. She pulled the bell-pull while sealing the note and addressing it to her husband and to 'The Honourable Terence Standing'. She was not confident that Darcy would hand the note to Standing or pose the questions to him. She would have liked to have given it to Lieutenant Colonel Harvey or even the colonel to hand to the magistrate, but Darcy would have been furious.

She decided that she had to trust Darcy. He was nothing if not correct. He would know it was her wish to have these questions entered into the investigation and he was unlikely to suppress them and humiliate her.

When a maid knocked, Elizabeth handed her the note with instructions to take it straight to Mr Darcy.

THE air of doom which had descended over Pemberley was dispiriting. The uncertainty was unnerving. Would her father ever be found? Why did St Clair take Darcy and the soldiers to the wrong place if that was what had happened? If so, was it deliberate or accidental? If it was the right place and St Clair's protestation that it was all a sham was itself a fiction, then what in heaven's name had happened to her father? There were no wolves now to take a man. Perhaps St Clair had been lying all the time and had killed her father and disposed of his body somewhere it would never be found.

Elizabeth gave up thinking about it and went to find out what the others were doing and whether they were being well attended to and had all they needed.

People chose their different ways of trying to deal with the uncertainty. Mary was the easiest to find. The sound of her practising on the piano carried quite a long way. She found Kitty with Georgiana. They were both in the library poring over books about Staffordshire, where Lieutenant Colonel Harvey had his house, which was immensely sweet and poignant.

Mrs Bennet was with her sister and Mr Philips in the saloon. The sisters in particular could turn any subject inside out. She hoped that her mother was not already anticipating her future if Mr Bennet was dead. It was far too early in her view to give up hope of his recovery, even if that prospect seemed, admittedly, to be growing more remote.

Jane was resting. Bingley was in the billiard room practising shots. Elizabeth was about to go out for a walk and try to find the Gardiners, their children and the dogs, when Patterson announced that the Reverend Carmichael had called to see her. She asked for him to be shown into the blue room.

He had come, of course, to commiserate, to offer his deepest sympathy with their plight. Elizabeth was thrown back to the visit by Mr Collins last summer after Lydia had run off with Mr Wickham. It had seemed to Elizabeth that his main purpose in coming to Longbourn was to gloat at his own good fortune and to gleefully emphasise the misfortunes of the Bennet family. There was no such false condolence, of course, on the part of the Reverend Carmichael who was all genuine sympathy but Elizabeth could not cope with it at this time.

She was further reminded that her father's death would mean Mr Collins and her friend Charlotte taking over Longbourn. Would Mr Collins give up his ministry to come to Longbourn and oversee the estate? Probably he would. Charlotte would be near her parents. It would be ideal for them.

Lady Catherine would have to find another humbly grateful, obsequious neighbour to reside in the rectory at Hunsford and pay constant court to her. Such images were at least amusing enough to hold back the flood of tears which had been threatening all day to break out and send her off to her room.

Elizabeth made an effort to push such thoughts from her mind. There would be plenty of time to consider the family's future later. *And*, though she hated to contemplate it, if her father was never found, it would place legal obstacles in the path of Mr Collins.

Banishing these most unsettling thoughts, she thanked Mr Carmichael for his kind consideration and brought the interview to an end as soon as possible.

AT LAST, coming upon her Aunt and Uncle Gardiner, with the children, the dogs and the footman Michael, she walked with them a way and threw sticks for the dogs as necessary. She dearly hoped for some time with her aunt alone. Her aunt was one of the most sensible people she knew and she badly needed to be able to talk to someone of that ilk, to receive advice which could be relied upon, which would not be affected by the advisor's own prejudices and preconceptions. And to simply talk over her own fears and ideas in a logical fashion.

Uncle Gardiner seemed to sense this in due time and declared that they had been out long enough. The puppies would be tired and the children ready for refreshment.

"Would you walk with me a little farther, Aunt? I would welcome your company."

"Of course, my dear."

The children cheerfully waved goodbye to her and she did her best to smile. Mr Gardiner and Michael called the dogs and soon they were all out of sight, round the bend in the path.

"I must say," Aunt Gardiner began the conversation, "that your mother bears hardships now with far more equanimity than formerly she did. Perhaps it is your married state and that of Jane which enable her to feel more secure."

"Yes, indeed. But she is also in great awe of Darcy, even though he has been so kind to her. Now I am not so sure."

"I do not understand. What can you mean, Elizabeth?"

"Oh, Darcy is...you said yourself when he was with you in London while arranging to pay off Wickham, obstinate. On this occasion he has been unsuccessful in effecting my father's return and he now turns in on himself. He will scarce talk to me about it and denies blaming himself, but I know he does. If he reverts to the taciturnity and actual rudeness which he exhibited in Meryton before he spirited Bingley off to London last year to take him out of Jane's way, then I...he will not be the man I married."

Elizabeth allowed a tear to run down her cheek.

"Oh, my dear! I do not believe I was aware that Darcy tried to separate Bingley from Jane, but you can tell me more of that at another time perhaps. What is so clear to all of us now is that he loves you. Once all this is over, one way or the other, I am sure that he will be the same as before."

"I wish I could believe it, Aunt. I sometimes think," she said bitterly, giving vent to feelings held hidden from all others, "that he would have been better off with Caroline Bingley. She desired him well enough and he would not have had to bear the unpleasantness which I have somehow visited upon him." Her voice rose. "This wholly unpleasant episode regarding my father, the curse it seems of the St Clairs. His estrangement from his Aunt Catherine de Bourgh, for example. The scandal even of Lydia's elopement with a man he hates so much. What have I done, Aunt, to have presumed that I could be a good and proper wife to him? And—"

"Lizzy, stop, please." Aunt Gardiner halted, forcing Elizabeth to cease her strident pacing. "He didn't *love* Caroline Bingley. He would have been miserable with her. You must not torment yourself with alternative marital possibilities for Darcy. Lizzy, for him to have paid off Wickham has to mean that he loved you then, very deeply. Quite obviously loved you even before he met you again at Pemberley. I can't say how far back that love goes, but it must be so. As Colonel Fitzwilliam said at luncheon a week or more ago, Darcy found nothing wanting in you as far back as Easter when you were at Rosings. Lizzy, he will always love you. Do not imagine otherwise."

"Aunt, he also knows something of my previous regard for Wickham. *And* of my friendship with the Reverend Wilde. He has had to bear that knowledge."

"And yet he still loves you, Lizzy."

Elizabeth swallowed, feeling tears welling up irresistibly. Listening to her aunt, she knew all this to be true. And she must remain true to his love for her; must resist the forces of mendacity; must wait for Darcy to recover his equilibrium, whatever was her father's fate.

Her tears, suppressed all day, could not be contained. There was no strong husband here to comfort her. Her aunt, knowing her passion more keenly than any other, wrapped her arms around her niece and let her weep for her marriage, for perhaps a lost father, for a family so close thrown into turmoil and all else that could trouble her passionate niece.

BUT that evening was no better.

Darcy would not talk to her. Elizabeth rushed to him and threw her arms around his neck.

"Darcy, I am trying hard myself, we all are, to retain hope," she cried. "Without it, I feel lost, that my life is at an end. The prospect that we shall never know what happened to him, whether he is alive or dead. It is like losing someone at sea whose body is never recovered. Imagining that he may be alive somewhere and we will never know. Or," she cast about for another example, "someone being reported dead in some far-away land with no burial record, who again is not brought back to this country. Never knowing. Never knowing..."

Her voice trailed off but no tears came. Her sisters and mother were the same. They had cried oceans but now they were numb. If she only had Darcy's love and comfort, she could bear the grief, but he was somewhere else, in a dark pit of his own making.

He at least encircled her with his own arms. His body was stiff, but it was some comfort.

"I perfectly comprehend what you say. I feel exactly the same. I will see you tomorrow after my return from Lambton to enquire after any further news."

"May I accompany you?"

He released her and she let him go. He disappeared into the dressing room and shut the door.

It should have been the happiest of times for them. She had said nothing to Darcy or anyone else, but her menses were late and she had begun to feel, very slightly, the symptoms which Jane had described. It struck her forcibly that while one life was being lost, probably had already been lost, another life was forming inside her. A single tear ran down her cheek. It was all she could muster. She climbed cold and alone into her bed and clutched her pillow, knowing that sleep would very likely evade her tonight as all previous nights since Saturday.

Chapter 28

"DARCY, I am coming with you to Lambton today."

"That is not a good idea, Elizabeth. I am riding there. It will be quicker."

"Good idea or nay, I intend to go and if you will not take me, then I will order a carriage myself."

Darcy knew that the servants, or some of them, would follow Elizabeth's orders even if they conflicted with his own. The servants liked her. She was kind and fair, as they perceived. But nonetheless he continued to try to dissuade her.

"I am going to see Standing. If there is any news, he will have been told. You do not know where he lives."

"Then I will find out."

"Elizabeth, do not be troublesome."

"Troublesome! *Troublesome!* How dare you? It is my father, *my* father we are hoping to hear news of. I am as entitled as you are to news of him."

"Whatever I am able to ascertain, I will of course return here and relate it to you."

"Darcy, how can you be so hard? So cruel?"

A look of genuine surprise crossed his face.

"Cruel? Cannot you imagine that I wish to spare you as much distress as possible? It may be the very worst of intelligence. He has been gone..."

"If it is, then I have to find out. At least if we find out that he is dead, we can start to grieve properly. But not to know is intolerable."

He shook his head. "I am not sure."

"Neither am I. It is not a circumstance with which I am familiar, Darcy. As though one encounters this sort of situation every day! But if my father *is* dead, then we must try to become...easy with it."

She regarded him a little more sympathetically.

"Darcy, your own parents died. I have not yet had that sadness forced upon me. But it has to happen at some point and I suspect that a natural death is as difficult to bear as a violent death."

Darcy did not reply immediately. Instead he drew a deep breath and walked over to their sitting room window. He stared out silently at the frozen vista. At last, he turned.

"Elizabeth," he said, "all this," he waved his hands towards the outlook, the park, the lake, the nearer and the distant woods, "is of no matter if we have not our family, if we have not happiness. I was unable to deliver your father safely to you. And," his mouth drew a thin line, "he is as a father to me." He lowered his head. "I have no other father."

And suddenly, Elizabeth understood better. He loved her father as she did. He was deeply hurt by the huge change to their lives. And, of course, it was a matter of honour to him that he should have somehow saved her father from whatever fate Paul St Clair had visited upon him. Paul St Clair, a damaged, inferior person. Darcy had imagined that his own superior station in life, his greater moral strength should have overcome the unworthy efforts of a fellow like St Clair.

And so they should in any fair contest. But fate, in all its iniquitous forms, could intervene at any time and introduce a random event rendering all logical expectations futile.

"Darcy, Fitz," she said abruptly, "something unexpected must have happened between Paul St Clair leaving my father in a cave or a mine and leading you there. Papa cannot just have disappeared."

"All right. Come with me, then."

THE Honourable Terence Standing lived in a vast mansion several miles outside Lambton. The parkland surrounding the house was considerable but, compared to Pemberley, its appearance was artificial, with trimmed hedges, a rose garden, an Italianate garden with a fountain, all now of course overlaid by a layer of snow.

Darcy had driven the curricle for himself and Elizabeth with no accompanying footman. On their arrival, they waited and at length a footman came out to meet them. Darcy announced his business and jumped to the ground, then handing Elizabeth down. Another footman ran out and took the horses' reins and the first man accompanied Darcy and Elizabeth to the house. They entered and were immediately greeted by Standing himself.

Elizabeth had not met Standing before. He had been invited to the shoot out of courtesy, but had been unable to attend. She had gathered that he kept to his own society where possible. He was a small man compared to Darcy, about the same age, as yet unmarried she understood and the second son of a viscount.

In the large hall, Darcy introduced them.

"May I present my wife, Mrs Elizabeth Darcy. The Honourable Terence Standing."

Elizabeth curtsied and Standing bowed.

"Mrs Darcy," said Standing immediately, fixing her with kindly concern. "I am very sorry at the disappearance of your father. But I have today received intelligence which may be of interest to you. Come to the drawing room and I will explain."

Tell me now, Elizabeth longed to scream at their host.

But she followed him into a cosy, panelled room with a hearty fire burning in the grate.

She had forced down that morning a little breakfast of fruit but was still hungry.

"Do take some refreshment Mrs Darcy," said her host. He indicated a range of appetising foods.

Elizabeth was disarmed by their host. He was both charming and vague. Why he was not yet married, she could not imagine. But she had to know what news he had and whether it pertained to her father.

"Er, my father, Mr Standing? If you have news of him, I would be eminently in your debt if you would disclose it to us."

"Yes. I apologise." He turned to Darcy.

"Darcy, I was in the middle of writing a note to be taken to you. Reports have been received of an old man being cared for by a midwife in Cressley since Sunday. I am sorry. I have no further intelligence."

"Being cared for! Is this man alive?" Darcy asked, his expression desperate.

"I am so sorry. I do not know."

Darcy clutched at Elizabeth's arm and he looked earnestly at her.

"We must go there immediately," he said.

Elizabeth nodded and they rose to leave.

"I apologise, Standing, that we cannot take any refreshment with you."

Standing stood.

"Darcy," he said. "Do not you know what day it is?"

Chapter 29

Two days earlier

SUSANNAH, who lived in the village of Cressley somewhat to the north-west of Lambton, opened the connecting door and hobbled through from her warm kitchen into the freezing parlour whence the man had been carried and laid roughly on a bed made of raised wooden planks with a straw mattress. The floor of the room was of earth strewn with more straw. She carried with her from the other room a lighted candle, the flame of which she guarded with her free hand. Hitching up her skirts and hunkering down near the hearth where she had laid kindling twigs atop of dried moss, she applied the flame to the moss and thereby produced a meagre fire as was her intention.

Susannah, a childless widow who earned her living principally from midwifery, had been told many years ago by a physician that, to have any chance of causing a frozen person to recover full health, the person must be rubbed vigorously all over to enable the blood to begin to flow again and must be brought back to a proper degree of heat very slowly indeed. The doctor had been particular in that regard, that this had to be done slowly. Hence the fire was low. She kept the room principally for women who came to her for their confinements and also for the laying out of bodies when she was asked to do so.

In time, Susannah had gained a reputation for her ability to bring beings back from the brink of death due to being frozen. In truth, she had only ever practised this craft on animals, in the main dogs, whose desperate owners would pay handsomely to get back their beloved pets when all was thought to be lost.

In most cases, dogs did not seem to suffer from the cold. They had thick coats. If left out for the night in freezing conditions, they rarely succumbed. They may come to suffer from painful, swollen joints, but they did not die. The ones brought to her had oft-times fallen through the ice on a pond or lake or river and somehow been rescued. These were the ones which Susannah worked on which may or may not recover.

It was not a skill with which Susannah was untroubled. She knew exactly what she was doing and how her results came about, but others may decide that her art was arcane. In earlier times, she may have been in danger of being judged to be practising witchcraft, not simple animal doctoring. Some nights after she had cured an animal which the grateful owner had borne off after paying her a large fee, she lay awake waiting for a band of jealous neighbours to enter her home and take her and kill her in whatever way best presented itself to them. It had never yet happened, she suspected, because all or any of them might one day need her skills to treat their child or wife or husband or other relation. But it could happen nevertheless.

Of course, her efforts were not always successful. Some of the animals failed to come back to life at all. Others did so, but were clearly muddle-headed; slack-jawed, drooling, unable to walk properly, not responsive to commands. Folks would mutter darkly that the Devil had entered their souls, even though animals were not thought to possess souls. And yet, owners sometimes still wanted these poor, afflicted creatures and were prepared to pay. Some, however, abandoned the animal. She had no more use for an addle-headed dog than its owner and had ways of ensuring its swift, painless demise.

Looking down at this old man, almost a corpse already, she observed that his clothes were of good quality and that, apart from his moribund appearance and that most of him was black or shades of black, he was in a reasonable condition; that was to say not dropsical or excessively plump or engorged or scrofulous or affected by a wasting disease. She pulled back the lips of his mouth and found teeth in reasonable condition. He had a nasty gash on his head with a large swelling which perhaps accounted for his failing to respond to any touch.

She determined that if she was able to effect a recovery, he would be able to pay well. The features of his face were fine so far as she could tell, though the face was swollen. He was probably once a handsome young man. He was, she was sure, of the gentry, if not higher placed. There may even be a reward which would secure her future and the futures of her sister and her sister's children whom she loved.

Therefore, despite the cold in the small parlour, and despite the hour and her fatigue and wish to sleep, she returned to the kitchen and made sure there were warm towels for when they were needed and dry blankets and bed linen. She then went back to the parlour and, disregarding her aching joints, she bent over the old man and commenced to strip every stitch of his wet clothing from him, covering his manhood with a cloth, and, when she had done so, settled her aching backside on a low stool and began to rub and rub at his arms and legs and hands and feet until her own arms were nearly seizing up and she continued to do so through her pain for hours following, lighting a new candle when necessary, eschewing the sleep which chased at her.

Periodically, every hour or so, she added more fuel to the fire, slowly bringing the temperature of the room up to a little over freezing. As she worked, she ignored her tiredness and discomforts by turning over in her mind the circumstances which had brought this man into her care.

Hereabouts, unsettling talk had arisen concerning a young man, a stranger, who had taken to loitering in the many caves near Danemill, possibly living in the caves, the disused lead mines and other workings. Whatever he was doing, strangers were not welcomed. They had no call to be here. The parish would not support a person from outside, therefore the person must be persuaded to move on. No one wanted a stranger who would be a burden on the parish and may steal to survive.

Therefore the men had to act. And they had chosen the early hours of this morning, four nights after Christmas and a night when the weather had turned from merely cold to freezing and the blanket of snow which laid everywhere had transformed into a surface as hard as stone, to do so. They had formed a small army, including some who were still cave-dwellers hereabouts living in the vile hovels at the mouths of lead workings, disfigured beings with fingers and toes and ears missing, and taken staves and cleavers and any weapon to hand and had marched to the caves near Danemill intent on seeing off the stranger.

There was a disused millhouse too at Danemill, but it was held to be haunted by the ghost of a murderer who had killed several girls fifty years ago and been killed himself by a group of their fathers and brothers. They had torn him limb from limb and buried his heart in a hole in the dirt floor of the mill. The heart was still there. The stranger would not have lived in the old millhouse and they would not go near it themselves by night.

But they had found no young stranger, or at least they had found no person living roughly in the vicinity. Instead, they had come upon this nearly dead, ageing, member of the gentry, or maybe the aristocracy, tied to a post in an old mine working and they had brought him to her, she being the only person they knew of who may be able to effect some cure.

A hammering at her door some hours before dawn had caused her heart to race. To be woken in the middle of the night usually spelled some sort of trouble. Her distress was only partly allayed to find that the bedraggled army of men had brought her a frozen man to attempt to revive. She had shaken her head. They had no thought for what was ahead for her.

In their excitement at their find, they had then wasted her time showing her the thick rope they had brought back with them which had been binding the man, telling her, as though it made any difference to her, that it was of good quality and valuable, even if it had probably been stolen.

Someone, Susannah knew as she worked away through the rest of the dark hours, would be missing this man and, if her efforts were successful and word went out about him, would rush to claim him and appropriately reward her for her efforts.

She worked as long as she was able but, when at last fatigue threatened to overcome her some four hours after this man arrived in her parlour, she made up the fire, covered him in a blanket and took one for herself and succumbed, falling into a slumber on the straw-bestrewn floor beside her comatose patient.

THE rising sun this Sunday morning brought little change in the man's condition. But she would not give up. He was elderly, she could tell. And he had a substantial injury to his head. There was no point trying to speed up the process. When Susannah awoke, she tested the man's vital signs within the scope of her very limited knowledge and decided that he was still alive. Importantly, the blacks of his eyes were not big (she had witnessed that, with many dead bodies, the cloudy blacks of the eyes seemed to cover almost the whole eyeball) and her mirror placed under his nose produced a slight covering of misty droplets.

Therefore, after sufficiently making up the fire in the kitchen, and then that in the parlour to be a little warmer, she hastened to resume the rough rubbing of his arms and legs of the previous night. She thought she felt that his limbs and body were a little warmer, a little less stiff, than before but there was no reaction from him as she hoped there might have been.

But if it took her all day to continue to work on this man's body until some movement signalled an improvement or until it was obvious that he was dead, then she would not stop. When curious neighbours peered through the window, she ignored them. When the more adventurous crept into her house and into this room, she scared them off with a torrent of foul-mouthed curses. Given her reputation as the worker of magic, most were not slow to beat a retreat. Some of the more courageous expressed their doubt that there was any hope for this man and she treated those to the worst of her tongue.

One neighbour, though, brought her a pot of gruel and fresh-baked bread which she gladly consumed, asking for more to feed to the man when and if he was able to take some food. It was brought in later and left on the cast-iron plate in the fireplace of her kitchen.

She missed church of course. She stopped her rubbing at intervals, resting for ten minutes on her kitchen chair, through the window watching the snow falling quickly at an angle, and rubbing her own arms and hands to relieve the stiffness or going outside for more wood or making up the fires or brewing tea. Otherwise, she steadfastly kept up her work. She fancied as the afternoon dark descended that she could detect the man's chest rising and falling, but the shadows, she knew, often played tricks.

She looked greedily at the gruel and bread given by her neighbour, but held herself back from eating it. Instead, she ate stale bread from her cupboard washed down with weak ale. She had nothing else. She continued rubbing the man's limbs long past nightfall until her head was drooping onto her ample old breast and her eyes were closing of their own accord.

Before she fell entirely into a slumber, she pulled herself to her feet, made up the fires and covered the man with a blanket. She could not spare another candle for the night. She must hope that if the man regained his senses, he would not start blundering about. Her experience with dogs suggested that this was unlikely. Any brought back from the near-dead by her ministrations took some considerable time to recover the use of their limbs.

MONDAY, too, brought little change, save that a knock on her door produced her nephew Tom, a strong lad of fourteen.

"Mother sent these." Tom held out a basket of bread and a flagon of fresh ale. "How is he...?"

Tom jerked his head towards the parlour.

"Thank you, Tom. He is not much improved. Perhaps a little. I cannot stop to talk, Tom. I have to get back to him. If he is not moving by the end of today, then, I do not know..."

She felt grim. You couldn't put a man down like a dog. What were you to do? She began to think it would have been better to have turned the man away.

"Let me do it for you, Aunt Susannah."

"What?"

"You rub them all over. I have seen you before, although with a hound. You will by now be tired as a fox at the end of a hunt. Have a rest. I can spare two hours."

"But you have to work, Tom."

"Not till this afternoon."

"Tom, if you will do that, it would be a blessing. My hands, you see, are almost useless, my arms knotted."

"Go and have a rest and a brew of tea. I would take a little tea myself, Aunt Susannah."

Returning with the warm drink, she watched him drag his strong arms and hands over the man.

"Do it more roughly, Tom," she told him. "That's the best thing for this job. The rougher, the better."

Tom increased his efforts.

"And rub his fingers and toes. More gently, mind, else they may fall off if they are that far gone."

Tom pulled a face.

"Why is it so bloody cold in here, Aunt?"

"Tom, mind your tongue. The cold is how it has to be. The person may be killed if warmed too quickly. I will put a little more wood on the fire."

"I should say he is dead already."

"'Tis as well you are not charged with the care of others. Now get on with it and if we have success, I will share my reward with you."

"Tomorrow is New Year's Day, Aunt Susannah. Maybe we will have a visit from a first-footer. And then, good fortune will result."

"Get away with you! You talk a lot of rubbish sometimes, Tom."

Chapter 30

STANDING rose.

"Darcy," he said. "Do not you know what day it is?"

Darcy halted. "Tuesday, I believe," he said impatiently. "two or more days since our relation was taken."

"It is New Year's Day, Darcy."

"Oh, well, I am sure you are right."

"Do you have a silver coin with you?"

"I usually do."

"A tall, dark-haired fellow like you," Standing looked up, smiling, at Darcy, "if you do not take gifts with you, they will think you bring bad luck."

"What *are* you talking about, Standing?"

"You must recall the tradition of first footing on New Year's Day. It isn't widely practised in Derbyshire but it is still in some parts, and that the visitor should take gifts or else his coming will spell bad luck to the house visited. You have a silver coin. Let me give you other gifts for the household."

Darcy nodded wearily as he received a basket containing cake, bread, cheese, cold meat, a flagon of spirits, a peck of salt and, oddly Elizabeth thought, a piece of coal to take with them.

Elizabeth was ignorant of the custom. Darcy explained the ancient tradition as they drove on to Cressley.

"It may go back to the invasion of the Vikings. They were flaxen-haired which is why a dark-haired man brings luck but a yellow-haired person does not. The gifts signal good luck too."

"A tall man as well, Mr Standing said."

"I hope I fulfil that requirement, Lizzy."

Elizabeth was happy to hear him use the shortened version of her name again.

"Without any doubt," she said. Then it occurred to her to ask:

"Fitz, yesterday when you came home, I saw you riding with Lieutenant Colonel Harvey, but Colonel Fitzwilliam was not with you. Did he go somewhere else?"

Darcy frowned. "He left Lambton earlier. He wanted to go and visit Harriet Layham and apologise, he said, for the confused and abrupt end to the evening on Saturday and the lack of attention to her on Sunday. I suppose it was a courtesy to do so. It is a pity in a way that she came with us but of course no one could predict what would happen."

"No." Elizabeth paused, then said "Do you think he is very interested in her? If he is, I would hope it is for herself, not for any fortune she may inherit."

"I suppose it would be a good match for him, and for her also as he is the son of an earl."

"Are those good reasons to marry though?"

Darcy turned towards her and took her hand. "Not everyone is like us, my love."

Elizabeth smiled her happiness at having her loving husband back. She had misgivings about the colonel, but would not voice them now.

A YOUNG man opened the door to Darcy's knock.

"Aunt Susannah, you have a visitor," he called.

Susannah emerged from the back room and came to the door. When she saw the tall, dark-haired man holding up a silver coin, the blood left her face. She swooned and Tom caught her before she fell.

A dark-haired young woman bearing a basket of food left her speechless.

Darcy cleared his throat. "We believe you may have a man here since Sunday. We are looking for my wife's father." He indicated Elizabeth. "Lost since about midnight on Saturday night."

His words appeared to be having no effect on the young man and the older woman. They stood staring at him and Elizabeth.

"Er, I am Mr Darcy of Pemberley House, and this is my wife, Mrs Elizabeth Darcy. If you have her father here, we would be most obliged if we could see him."

His name produced a gasp from Susannah and Tom, but no further reaction. He might have been a vision, come to haunt them, a spectre, not real.

Elizabeth stepped forward, breaking the spell. She smiled uncertainly, and extended the basket of gifted foodstuffs.

"If you have my father, Mr Bennet, I must see him."

Her short speech ended in a small sob which she could not contain. Darcy took her free hand.

"Please. May we see my father-in-law, if it is him," Darcy said.

The young man and the old woman suddenly came to life.

"Please, follow me," said the woman.

In the next room, which was passably warm, Elizabeth saw a skeleton, almost, on a rough bed, covered in a towel, with pillows, sitting up at an angle. His hands and feet were black, his face and other parts of him less so.

"He has come better this morning," said the woman. "Yesterday, I would probably have given him up for dead."

"Papa," sobbed Elizabeth, "is it you? Oh, Papa."

The skeleton opened one eye and croaked. If he was trying to talk, it was unintelligible.

The woman looked alarmed.

"He should not be caused excitement," she said. "Besides the cold, someone has hit him on the head very hard. He is not well."

"May we not take him away with us?" said Darcy.

"I would not advise it, sir. Much as I see you wish to. If you come back tomorrow, it may be possible to take him if he is better. But," the old woman fixed Elizabeth with a piercing stare, "is this your father or nay?"

Elizabeth felt helpless. "I think so. It is difficult to say."

"Then come again tomorrow. And we will see."

"Yes," said Elizabeth.

Chapter 31

HOW to convey their news to the family?

"We think we have found Papa!" Elizabeth told everyone. "He was taken during the night on Sunday to Mrs Susannah Harris who lives in Cressley. A band of men had gone forth to find a stranger they wished to frighten out of the area. We think they were looking for Paul St Clair, but they found instead in an old mine a man tied to a post. We think it is Papa, but it is difficult to be quite sure until he can talk...properly."

"Lizzy," exclaimed Mrs Bennet, "surely you can recognise your own father."

"I am sorry, Mama. He is...Mrs Harris called it frost-bit. It affects the way people look...she said."

"Who is this woman?" Aunt Philips asked. "Is it some bawdy-house she keeps?"

"Oh, sister!" cried Mrs Bennet.

Darcy intervened, having just entered the saloon where everyone was gathered to hear the latest intelligence. He had been writing a note to be delivered to Standing, telling the magistrate of their findings.

"Mrs Harris," he said somewhat tersely, "is a respectable village woman, a widow who acts as a midwife, and also knows how to treat people affected by exposure to extreme cold."

The colonel spoke. "I understand now. When we had to train once in an inhospitable place, a man became lost and succumbed to this condition. It turned his body and face black, so that he looked like an ebony carving, his face bloated, his tongue swollen, not human at all—"

Mrs Bennet whimpered. The others regarded the colonel with horrified expressions.

"Thank you, Fitzwilliam," Darcy said. To Mrs Bennet he said: "Try not to worry, mother. We will go back tomorrow and bring him home if it is possible. You will all agree, though, that the most important thing is for my father-in-law to be well again, and it may take a few more days before he is able to travel.

"I think it is almost certainly Lizzy's father from what we know. Everything points to it being him."

"Why, Darcy, did not the men seeking a stranger go to the old millhouse?" asked Fitzwilliam.

"Evidently, they think that it is haunted and would not go near it. They assumed the stranger would not be there either for the same reason."

"It is as well they did not, for then we would never have found St Clair and those men would not have taken Mr Bennet to the midwife."

Elizabeth and several of the ladies gasped at the realisation.

"Quite," said Darcy brusquely. "For now, I suggest that we rejoice in the good fortune and enjoy our evening together. Our dinner, followed by music, singing, dancing, cards if you wish. All that we have been missing this last three days."

"Splendid, Darcy," said Mr Philips, and the others variously smiled and laughed their relief.

A HAPPY household it was that retired to bed that night.

"So what of St Clair?" Elizabeth asked her husband as they climbed the stairs. "If my father recovers, St Clair may still hang for what he has done. He may not even have intended for my father to die but events got out of control."

"Oh, I think he did want your father dead. Perhaps he did not plan it, but once he had gone so far as to cause a head injury, steal a horse and take him to that mine, he left himself with very little option than to leave him to die. We still don't know why he had a grudge against your father, but his actions made it inevitable that your father would die. If it had not been for those men finding him and taking him to Susannah Harris, he would be dead by now."

"Even so, to be hanged... That seems terrible. His father was Papa's good friend. And although Mama was not a good friend of Mrs St Clair, Mama offered to write to her to try to find out what had happened to Helen. That was the evening you rode off to Nethermill with the soldiers and we still thought that Helen must be Isabella Scargill and must have poisoned the dogs. For her son to be hanged would be unconscionable."

"Well, perhaps I can arrange things with Standing so that he is merely transported."

Elizabeth wanted to say that the Reverend Wilde's opinion was that the colony would soon become more civilised and that convicts might live useful lives once their initial sentences had been served and they would be freed, perhaps even better lives than they could have lived in England. But it was impossible to say this to Darcy.

Instead, she told him that she had composed a letter to Mr Wilde, telling him something of the recent events and asking him to send her the letter he had received which they had at first thought was from Helen St Clair, so the writing could be compared with that of Paul St Clair's.

She had also written to their butler at Longbourn House asking him to search her father's records for a note he might have made that St Clair had asked him to recommend the young man for the benefice and he had refused.

She had not posted either letter yet.

"I gave your list to Standing," said Darcy. "Whether he will act upon it, I do not know. But it sounds as though you *do* wish for a noose to be placed around St Clair's neck. Such evidence of a threat and a motive would surely be damning."

"Well, he should be found guilty. I just don't want him to die."

"Of course, Lizzy, your father would be able to tell us more if he recovers as we hope he will. He can also say whether he wishes St Clair to feel the full effects of the law or, instead, see a reduced sentence."

In their sitting room by now, Elizabeth gazed at her husband. He did seem to be able to reduce everything to its most logical, to cut out the irrelevant and calm most situations. She could not help but smile.

"What is it, Lizzy?"

"Oh. Just you. How you make everything seem so clear. And how glad I am to have you back. I thought I had lost you."

"Lizzy! You will never lose me. I am so sorry that I have these black moods sometimes and that I make you feel the effects of them. It is unforgivable of me."

"Well, still, it is you. And I would not have you different. So, will you sleep in our bed again tonight?"

"Nothing could be more welcome, Lizzy."

ELIZABETH and Darcy journeyed to Cressley the following day, travelling in the carriage with a footman and a groom in case Mr Bennet could be brought home. But while he was much improved, his colour returning and his voice almost intelligible, Mrs Harris insisted that he was not safe to be moved. However, he was now visibly recognisable as Mr Bennet.

Of course, they took food and drink to Mrs Harris's cottage and fresh clothes for Mr Bennet and stayed a few hours.

They returned on Thursday and Friday and at Mrs Harris's suggestion, they helped Mr Bennet from his bed to take some gentle exercise. By Saturday, he could walk with a stick.

During their travels, Elizabeth and Darcy were able to discuss all the subjects which had been set aside throughout their crisis or left in abeyance; the woman Elizabeth had seen in the woods collecting kindling; what Mrs Scargill had said about the steward, Campbell's, affair with a Wirkworth girl, the condition in which he had left her and whether they should find her and take some steps to help her; Kitty and the lieutenant colonel and the visit Harvey hoped the family might make to his home after the soldiers had departed; whether Kitty should be invited to stay on when Mr and Mrs Bennet and Mary had left Pemberley; the colonel and Harriet Layham.

"I know Lizzy that I have not always been the most considerate in my speech. Far from it. But," Darcy cast about for the right words, "Fitzwilliam has a tendency to be very…literal at times. One must hope that he curbs his tongue when dealing with Sir Peter and employs a degree of finesse if he is not to upset the man."

"Darcy, if anything is to be said, I think it must come from you. I have already interfered too much in Harriet's marriage prospects."

Darcy quickly turned the conversation to his expedition to

Matlock and the mill there and his tentative plans for his own mill; his intention to discuss such a commercial venture with Uncle Gardiner and seek his advice.

"You probably know," said Darcy, "having visited Buxton, that the Duke of Devonshire was responsible for the building of the resort at Buxton."

"I believe we were told something of it. It is an amazing place. We enjoyed it so very much."

"Well, I believe he has a copper mine which made him a fortune at one time and it is said that that was how Buxton was paid for. So you see, if a Duke can engage in commerce, it would not be so very unacceptable for a member of the gentry, such as I, to engage in industry."

"Perhaps I can help, in some way."

"I did so hope that you would want to be involved. You must be present when I talk to your Uncle Gardiner, and come and visit Matlock with me again when we have time to do so."

Elizabeth was thrilled to think that she and her husband could be working together.

Darcy looked at her shining eyes. "Oh," she cried. "How exciting it is."

As the carriage bore them on, they talked in more detail and Darcy described the mill at Matlock to her.

"I was thinking," he said, "of the extra men taken on to guard Pemberley House? It would seem very harsh for them to be sent away now they are no longer needed at Pemberley. The mill is in very poor condition. They could perhaps be usefully employed repairing it for the present, with suitable supervision. Indeed, there are a number of unoccupied dwellings, large and small, on the estate which have fallen into disrepair. The men could help to renovate those and thereby learn new skills."

"What an excellent idea, Fitz."

"I thought so."

They rode on in silence.

"You know, Fitz," she said after a time. "if Kitty does remain at Pemberley, if she wishes to, Mrs Annesley is going to be somewhat redundant."

"I was thinking the same thing. Another innovation I had in

mind was to start a school. You told me of the school opened by your farm manager's wife at Longbourn. It was an excellent thing to do. In the beginning it could be for the children living on the Pemberley estate, but later perhaps other children. I thought that Mrs Annesley might wish to turn her hand to teaching and managing a small school."

"What a wonderful idea. Kitty may wish to assist too."

"And then probably Georgiana."

There was much to think about. A most interesting and stimulating period lay ahead.

A pressing question was what reward should be given to Mrs Harris for she had without doubt saved Mr Bennet. They settled on the two hundred and fifty guineas with which Darcy had tempted St Clair. And the men who had found Mr Bennet and taken him to Susannah; how much should they be paid? They decided on thirty pounds for each man. Darcy hoped they would spend it on their families and not drink it all away.

"Now we know," said Elizabeth on Friday as they were driven home, "what was St Clair's true motive. A dead mistress and baby. It seems very sad."

That day, in a still hoarse voice, Mr Bennet had been able to converse with them about his experiences.

"As your father said, St Clair knew he was unable to provide her with a home and yet embarked on a liason with her. However, he could have attempted to obtain some form of employment and he could have married her. For all we know, he might have simply used her and abandoned her to the workhouse when he discovered she was with child."

"And then chose to blame my father."

"Your father being able to testify does mean that there is firm evidence against St Clair of the abduction."

"Yes. I was pretty angry that Colonel Fitzwilliam, having hit and wounded St Clair, gave St Clair the opportunity to say that he had fabricated the story of abducting Papa because he was frightened of you and the soldiers. I suppose it does not matter now."

"Well, I did kick him myself more than once when his leg was still trapped in the stirrup because he would not give me his name and then gave a false name and would not hand over his weapons."

"You know, Fitz, I rather gained the impression that Papa does not wish to testify against St Clair. Of course it would be an ordeal for him to have to do so, though I think it is more a question of wishing to show some leniency despite what he has been through. And he would have to travel back here from Longbourn at the time of a trial. He is still by no means in full health."

"There is little doubt that St Clair will be charged with the theft of a horse. That may have to do. I can give evidence of having apprehended him with the horse. The soldiers will not be here, of course. And others saw him loitering near the Assembly Rooms. He may yet be deported for that."

"Hanging is not a subject I wish to think about presently, Fitz."

And Elizabeth told Darcy of her growing belief that she was with child."

"Lizzy! What superb news." He hugged her and they laughed together through the jolting of the carriage. "We will have to take great care of you. Although, not too much care."

She hoped that he would not react as Bingley had done with Jane. It seemed unlikely when, on their return to Pemberley, at his urging they went straight to their bedroom.

On Saturday, they gave the money to Mrs Harris before they took Mr Bennet away. Mr Bennet bowed and kissed her hand. She wept, whether because of the kiss or the money or because of Mr Bennet's departure, they could not be sure. She certainly said that she would miss him. She had never had a patient for so long, nor with such kindly relations. She excused the accommodation. Mr Bennet told her that it had been delightful and that there was nothing wanting in her hospitality.

EPILOGUE

THE two carriages rattled up the drive towards Brownham Hall, every person's neck craned for the first sight of Lieutenant Colonel Harvey's house. Catherine Bennet in particular held her breath, having oft pictured the Tudor mansion in her imagination, now hoping that the house they were nearing would match her ardent expectations. She gripped Georgiana's hand and the other returned the pressure and hoped, too, that Kitty would not be disappointed.

Mature beech trees lined the drive, their bare branches overhanging as the drive curved this way and that, obscuring the view of what lay ahead. Overgrown scrub, possibly hawthorn, filled the spaces between the trees. A family of crows rose from their perches, cawing their disapproval at having been disturbed. And indeed, it did look as though this way was not frequently passed.

At last, the house came into view, a large, three-storey Tudor manor house with a wide open area to the front. The initial impression was most pleasing.

Darcy, Elizabeth, Kitty and Georgiana alighted from one carriage. Bingley jumped down from the other and he and Darcy helped Mr and Mrs Bennet down with the aid of the mounting block brought round by the footmen. Mr Bennet, largely now recovered from his ordeal, was still a small amount unsteady on his feet.

At length the family stood regarding the impressive house with its stone mullioned windows, its several attractive gables, and its numerous tall chimneys with their elaborate brickwork. A two-storey wing stood to the left of the main house and a single-storey to the right. The glass of dormer-windows in the roofs winked at them in the last of the late afternoon winter sunshine.

No doubt the house, like many others, could do with some attention, but Darcy judged that the description of it being run down was quite an exaggeration. It was indeed charming and a perfectly fit dwelling for a country squire and his family.

Kitty appeared delighted. They all knew the purpose behind this visit; whether Kitty would like the house and whether Mr and Mrs Bennet would consider Brownham Hall to be a suitable home for their second-youngest daughter should the lieutenant colonel in future make more serious overtures towards Kitty and should she show a strong inclination towards the young man. So far, Kitty seemed innocently impressed with her young suitor and why would not she be with her extreme lack of prior experience?

She was not, fortunately, cut from the same cloth as Lydia and, freed from Lydia's influence since the other's marriage, her behaviour was much improved. She was too shy and modest to be flirtatious and certainly she had not thrown herself at Lieutenant Colonel Harvey, qualities which appeared to have appealed to him, as the men in the party could fully understand.

The sturdy, studded oak front door opened suddenly and an older man and woman hurried down the couple of steps to the gravel driveway; presumably the Barratts, as Harvey had informed them, who took care of the house. They came forward to welcome the visitors, smiling broadly.

"Do come in," said the woman. "'Tis cold out here. We have fires blazing in the large hall and dining parlour and also your bedrooms and other rooms. Mr Harvey wrote to tell us you would be coming and gave this date. I hope you had a pleasant journey. We have been waiting for you."

"Come in, come in," said the man.

"We thank you," said Darcy.

"You are very kind," said Mr Bennet.

They were led through an enclosed porch, rather like a church porch, into a vast hall. The house did indeed seem cosy and warm as they walked through the hall which boasted ornately carved panelling and a huge ornate staircase leading to a handsome galleried landing. What must be old family portraits lined the walls, and a recent painting of Lieutenant Colonel Harvey in his regimental uniform. Kitty gazed at it in admiration.

Mr Bennet introduced his family. Mr Barratt inclined his

head, his expression mellow, and his wife dropped a curtsey, smiling and looking quite avidly at Kitty, more so than the others, Elizabeth thought. Lieutenant Colonel Harvey must be close to this couple to have told them of his interest in Kitty. As they were led upstairs to their rooms, this became clear when Mrs Barratt said:

"We have looked after the family these thirty years. We were here when Master James was born. Oh, I was that worried when he chose a career in the army. If he were to settle down, then he may perhaps leave the army and come to live here full time." She stopped for a few seconds and pointed at the portrait of Harvey. "His uncle had that painted. Very fond he is of Master James. He has no children."

She spoke with the local accent, very similar to Derbyshire's.

Elizabeth smiled to herself, assuming that 'settle down' was a euphemism for getting married. And the uncle spoken of must have been the one to set up the trust for 'Master James'. These servants were obviously on more intimate terms with their master than were servants usually. Longbourn House was not known for its great formality but none of the servants would have spoken thus to visitors, and nor certainly would the servants at Pemberley.

Mrs Barratt sounded almost like a mother when she spoke of her worry for Master James in the army. Little wonder perhaps when he could only have been seventeen years old or thereabouts, just a boy, when his parents died. Though of course Darcy had been only a few years older than that by the time he had lost both of his parents and he had been obliged to take on the running of such a vast estate *and* the joint guardianship of his sister. But then, *he* was Darcy. She smiled again to herself, affection for her husband flooding through her. She must help and support him in any way that she could in his new venture. A paper mill, amongst other industries had been mooted.

She wondered idly how big was the estate here. Within seconds her father was posing a similar point to the Barratts.

"This is a large house for you to have to look after, Mr and Mrs Barratt," he said. "Do you have any help with it?"

"Oh, aye," replied Mr Barratt this time. "I can manage most

jobs, but for building work we get in craftsmen. I do what I can in the garden. For the farms and land, Mr Harvey shares a manager with another estate about the same size."

"And, of course, I clean and cook for Master James," added Mrs Barratt. "Though I have taken on a girl from the village to help me this next two days. Some of the house is shut up as the rooms are seldom used. We do have a groom who also acts as a footman. He will be showing your men the stables and where to stay. And Ned," she nodded towards her husband, "will show you round the house before dinner."

"That would be splendid Mrs Barratt, Mr Barratt. By the by, Mr Barratt, how much land is there?"

"Near on twenty-five thousand acres, all told, I should say, sir."

A not inconsiderable estate then, thought Elizabeth, though the Pemberley estate, she understood, ran to fifty thousand acres. She glanced at Kitty, who was exchanging happy smiles with Mrs Barratt, and at her mother who was listening intently.

She found herself locking eyes with Darcy, wondering what he was thinking. Her own view was that Kitty would be fortunate indeed to make a match with Lieutenant Colonel Harvey, and was glad that she would be able to report back favourably to Jane, the Gardiners and the Philipses.

IN THEIR room a few minutes later, Elizabeth sat down on their bed, an ancient four poster which looked as though it was of the same period as the house, and Fitz joined her. He put his arm around her and they shared a warm caress.

"How are you feeling, my love, after that jolting ride?"

"Very well, Fitz. I am not in the least indisposed. I think I like being with child."

"And I like you being with child too." He kissed her hand, then her cheek and then her mouth, and he gently rubbed her abdomen through her dress.

"And, what do you think of the house and what we have been told?"

With her hand still to his lips, nibbling lightly at her fingers, he said: "I should say that that couple have more than enough to do on their own. If Kitty and Harvey marry, then they will have to take on more servants. That said, it would seem to be an ideal match if they continue to be partial to one another."

"Good. It would be nice to see things settled in due course. And I will be glad once St Clair's trial is over."

"Yes. I do not relish testifying against him. But I must. It is difficult to see how his abduction of your father can be kept out of it since I apprehended him as a result of your father's disappearance. Nor do I see how I can avoid giving evidence of his sister's intelligence that he was staying somewhere around Danemill which enabled the soldiers and me to track him down. But even the theft of a horse may be punishable by hanging. Still, once Standing decided he should be indicted for the theft of the horse, it was out of my hands. It seems to me that it is best not to think about it at all until the date of the trial is upon us, whenever that may be."

"Let us not think upon it, then. There is nothing we can do. Mama and Papa are shocked, of course, that their friends' son may face execution. It is one of the worst things that has ever happened to us, I think. We can only hope that he is deported instead or is sent to prison."

She paused. After a moment, she expressed her sorrow that her family were to quit Pemberley within the week. The soldiers had already left. It had been cautiously suggested to Kitty that she may care to remain at Pemberley, but she seemed to have fixed it in her mind that she would be returning to Longbourn.

"Your parents, I am sure, would have been disappointed had Kitty wished to stay and, in any case, they may not have agreed. As Bingley said, we can visit Hertfordshire at Easter. 'Tis barely two months away. And, Lizzy, he did tell me during the walk he and I took together late yesterday afternoon that he was thinking of employing an agent to enquire of estates in Derbyshire or adjoining counties which may be offered for sale in the near future. He thinks that Jane would be in agreement. You were tired last night, otherwise I would have told you."

Elizabeth's face broke into a smile.

"That is excellent news, Fitz. Doubtless, Mama would not see it in that light, but at some time she may have to be willing to move herself, as we know."

She was referring to the entail and the eventual inevitable loss of the Longbourn estate.

"As you say. But we had better go down now, Lizzy, for the tour of the house and hope that it all turns out well for Kitty and the lieutenant colonel."

They rose together and went out, down the wide staircase to meet the others in the grand hall.

THE END

Author's Note and Sources

This sequel to *Pride & Prejudice* was born out of the great pleasure I had writing *Intrigue At Longbourn*, my *Pride & Prejudice* prequel, and my wish to continue the exploration of the characters and events in Jane Austen's classic love story.

I especially hoped to expand on the character of Darcy. Portrayed initially in *Pride & Prejudice* as a stern, proud individual, I think it is possible to see glimmers of his more admirable side even before the alteration of his manner apparent to Elizabeth when they met at Pemberley during her tour of Derbyshire with her aunt and uncle Gardiner. In particular, his tendency to be measured in his discourse and economical with words was not necessarily an undesirable quality. It spoke of a person who would not exaggerate, who would not usually speak and act impulsively and who could be relied upon in a crisis.

He seemed to me to have a great deal of potential to be a kind and considerate person and a devoted, caring husband and so he is in *Menace At Pemberley*.

His first inept marriage proposal to Elizabeth at Easter 1798 while she was staying with her friend Charlotte Collins at Hunsford may have seemed disastrous at the time, but actually such an event would probably thereafter play on the mind of any woman. In Chapter 17 of *Menace At Pemberley*, Elizabeth analyses the effect it had had on her and concludes that it had probably sown the seeds of her eventual marriage to Darcy later that year.

Another character from *Pride & Prejudice* given more exposure is Darcy's cousin, Colonel Fitzwilliam, whose disposition is examined by Elizabeth who finds she has doubts about the colonel. In *Pride & Prejudice*, Darcy and the colonel are shown to be on familiar terms and this relationship is continued in *Menace At Pemberley*.

As with *Intrigue At Longbourn*, the sequel took a great deal of research, a lot of it already in place and outlined at the end of *Intrigue* therefore I won't repeat the sources here. It was a case of refreshing my memory from having written *Intrigue*, while also continuing to concentrate on the language of the day, trying to avoid the use of words and phrases not in use in 1798 and researching fresh areas.

The sorts of subjects I had to research include vets in the 1790s, how to poison dogs, apothecaries, ladies' attire, Chatsworth and the 5th Duke of Devonshire's likely income and his copper mines, Christmas traditions in Georgian times, the effects of exposure to extreme cold, courtesy titles, coins then in circulation (not much in the way of silver coins apparently), the tradition of first footing, bell pulls and historical events.

In *Menace At Pemberley*, two dogs are poisoned and I wanted to find out what means of diagnosis and, if relevant, treatment would have been available. My husband was convinced that someone of Darcy's stature would have had the means to employ experts to ascertain the cause of the dogs' deaths, that there must have been experts whom Darcy could employ. I doubted that this was the case and indeed his assumption turned out to be quite wrong.

I was lucky enough to come across a long work whose short title was *A Domestic Treatise on the Diseases of Horses and Dogs* by Delabere Blaine, Veterinary Surgeon, Professor of Animal Medicine and author of a number of works on animals and animal diseases. It was first published in about 1802 and was subsequently added to. Delabere Blaine was one of the first students of the Veterinary College of London founded in 1791.

The Treatise referred to above was said to have been written with the express purpose of providing information on veterinary medicine because 'even large towns have no regular veterinarian while smaller towns, villages and the country at large are all of them deprived of any other assistance than what can be gained from the neighbouring smith'.

One has to go to page 237 of the Treatise to learn that the most common poison is the vegetable called crow fig, which produces its deleterious effects by robbing the nervous system of all its energy in a few minutes. The treatise refers to the experience of Professor Blaine of having witnessed the death of a very strong Newfoundland dog destroyed in five minutes by half a dram of crow fig.

Crow fig is said in English to be the name of a plant 'defined with STRYCHNOS NUX-VOMICA in various botanical sources', what we would probably call strychnine.

The Treatise also tells us that, at least at that time: 'Dissection cannot detect this poison with any certainty; and unless an emetic is given within three minutes after the poison has been taken, provided the dose has been a full one, no benefit will arise from any medicine.'

I only provide the above details because it illustrates how much research can be necessary to answer seemingly simple points, in this case how would dogs be efficiently poisoned in 1798 and whether it would have been possible to effectively establish the reason for their deaths. It is just one example of the extent of research necessary to produce a reasonably accurate and authentic novel. It goes to show that one cannot, as a writer, make assumptions (or rely on one's husband's assumption!).

Gill Mather

Please turn the page for a message from the author and an excerpt from the next novel in the Elizabeth Bennet series.

Thank you for reading *Menace At Pemberley*, the second book in the Elizabeth Bennet series. *Intrigue At Longbourn* is the first.

I hope you enjoyed it and would be delighted if you could spread the word about this book and other books of mine. Online reviews, so important for authors, would be particularly appreciated on Kindle/Amazon, Goodreads, Library Thing, other sites for book readers and/or your favourite book provider's website.

The titles are available as ebooks and paperbacks all over the world. Just search by my name, Gill Mather, and the book title.

Try out the Roz Benedict Detective Novellas series. The short books are cozy-crime mysteries with more than a dash of romance in some of them. They all feature Roz Benedict, a detective inspector at the outset who becomes a private sleuth, and Guy Attwood who tends to act in an advisory capacity. Roz's neighbour, Kate Sampson, appears in the third and subsequent novellas.

Compromised – A noir tale of love, suspense and guilty secrets

Cut Off – A fascinating cozy crime caper in a country commune

Conflicts of Little Avail – A stunning yarn arising from brotherly love and official arrogance

Conjecture Most Macabre – A cautionary tale of how suspicion can take extreme forms

Subsequent to *Conjecture Most Macabre*, Roz and her friend Kate form a private detective agency carrying on business under the name of Cops & Roz's. Guy continues to act in an advisory capacity. The first two cases for the Cops & Roz's Detective Agency appear in:

Le Frottage – An intricate web of hidden pasts, religious orthodoxy and young love

Confounded – A sophisticated novella about a property fraud causing serial frustrations for a pair of female private sleuths.

Gill's other book series is called the Colchester Law World series. They are all romantic novels and feature crime or criminal activities. One, the second novel, *Threshold*, is an adventure novel too and the last, *Beyond The Realms*, is a paranormal romance. There are five books in the series available as ebooks and paperbacks. All of the novels can be read alone. Here are the titles of the novels:

The Ardent Intern

Threshold

Relatively Innocent

Reasonable Doubts

Beyond The Realms

***

Other novels by Gill are also available as both ebooks and paperbacks. Check them out below, read a sample on Kindle and see what you think.

AS THE CLOCK STRUCK TEN

Have you ever experienced a life-changing event, after which nothing will ever be the same again? Has anything totally out of your control ever happened to you which, within just a few short hours, robbed you of your assumed place in the world and challenged your preconceptions? A person in *As The Clock Struck Ten* was the unlucky object of such an occurrence. It started when the clock struck ten and, by the end of the day, the consequences were irresistible.

This gripping contemporary thriller takes the reader into a dark and murky subject. This is the perfect lockdown, Christmas or holiday read in which secrets accumulate, white lies yield unwanted results, blackmail is ruthlessly employed and family relationships are tested.

Don Morrison has a new live-in girlfriend, Grace Bennett. His eighteen-year-old daughter, Emma, newly arrived home from university for her first summer vacation, isn't happy to have her home invaded, as she sees it, by this other woman, especially so soon after the death of her mother, Carol, who was very ill for many years and was cared for by Don.

Grace's twenty-year-old son, Luke, lives at home with his father, Greg, Grace's husband.

The five main characters progress through the hot, rural East Anglian summer, some rather haphazardly, others with a more definite purpose. A young woman, Alex, known to some of them helps things along.

The law takes over at one point, its effects quite devastating for the unprepared.

THE UNRELIABLE PLACEBO

A hilarious and powerful romantic comedy.

Funnier than Bridget Jones's Diary, more bizarre than Fleabag, Anna Duke's clumsy attempts to re-join the couples club after the Arsehole – sorry, her husband Alfie – has left her, result in various embarrassing events, and lead her to some strange places and into some weird situations.

Her theory is that some foreknowledge of a man she's dating would help to bring about a positive result, like placebos affect medical outcomes. But it doesn't necessarily work out that way.

Is it possible that one person will have the courage to manfully hack through the thorny thicket of Anna's mind, circumventing the muddled hopes, dreams, fears, musings and speculations, to reach the perfect ending?

CLASS OF '97

In the summer of 2019, 'Greta' has fetched up in South Yorkshire on land owned by Francis. They both have secrets, more entrenched and harder to shake off for one of them than the other. Nearly two hundred miles to the south in Ipswich, Oliver continues to labour as a criminal solicitor, unaware of the consequences of earlier events in his life and, as we all are, of what is yet to come.

Francis doesn't put pressure on 'Greta', nevertheless she ups and disappears anyway, returning to her real life. And yet, is that life any more real than her sojourn with Francis?

She becomes friendlier with Oliver and, despite having serial problems of his own, he helps her with a serious and distressing difficulty. While doing so, he discovers something sinister, though he can't quite believe it.

Their romantic entanglements with others don't run entirely smoothly and, for both of them, the past rakes up some unexpected issues. Gradually, and from various sources, the truth emerges, less palatable in some respects than others…

The twists in the plot will keep you guessing right to the end. Class of '97 is the ideal book club novel, providing food for endless questions about the characters' circumstances, difficulties and life-changing events.

Send me a message any time through my website: https://www.gillmather.com and you can follow me on twitter @gillianmather

With my best wishes,

Gill

An excerpt from Easter At Netherfield

To be published shortly

 *Prologue*

THE salon of the large house in a fashionable part of London was hot and stuffy. The furnishings were over-decorative, quite flamboyant to Darcy's taste, and the air was thick with the scent worn by the ladies in the room, and probably the men too. The effect was almost overpowering. The chairs were over-stuffed and there were so many people in the audience tonight that, should he have chosen to leave the room for just five minutes to cool down, he doubted if he could have forced his way towards the narrow aisle between the two banks of chairs in the crowded room.

They had all come to witness a performance of the violin by a Prussian prodigy, a mere child of nine or ten called Max, who was a virtuoso despite his tender years and was presently astonishing and delighting audiences all over London, including King George and Prince George. It was also said that he had been composing since the age of five. Darcy had never heard of the boy, but one of Bingley's sisters had procured the invitation to this private recital.

Darcy wished he had not accepted the invitation, but it would have seemed churlish to have refused, especially as it was known that he would be in London anyway to see his lawyer about letting his London house and that he was staying in Bingley's London house for the few days' duration necessary to complete his business.

The performances so far had been mediocre. The interval was thus very welcome.

Darcy forced a hand between his neck and his stock in an effort to cool at least a small portion of his anatomy, while Bingley beside him chatted happily with his older sister Margaret sitting on his other side. His sister Caroline sat to the right of Margaret and another sister Susan to the right of her.

In truth, both Darcy and Bingley had been happy to leave Netherfield for a few days, Bingley because he enjoyed London society, and Darcy because he was bored with the sudden leisure, having spent the last two months directing improvements about his estate and in particular making plans for his mill. Furthermore, Bingley had amassed no significant library in which Darcy might have profitably spent his time and it would be at least another week before Lizzy's relations, including her extended family, would be descending on Netherfield for Easter. It was an invasion to which he was bizarrely looking forward, finding that he quite missed the society of the Bennets, the Philipses and the Gardiners who had been at Pemberley at Christmas.

His cousin Colonel Fitzwilliam probably wouldn't be coming. As Darcy understood it, he was hoping to secure an invitation to the home of Sir Peter Layham in Derbyshire, to whose daughter Harriet he was actively paying court. Lieutenant Colonel Harvey, an admirer of Kitty, might possibly be able to visit Netherfield. He had been invited, but it was not yet certain.

Darcy would far rather have returned to Longbourn and to Lizzy once he had seen his attorney. Lizzy had preferred not to venture to town. While her husband was away, she had wished instead to stay at Longbourn House with her family, accompanied by Jane and Georgiana. Lizzy's great friend, Charlotte Collins, would be coming to Lucas Lodge, may even be there now with her odious husband, Mr Collins, the heir to the Longbourn estate on Mr Bennet's death. But Lizzy still fervently wished to see her friend.

An expectant hush had suddenly come over the salon and Darcy's attention was redirected to his immediate surroundings when the boy Max — presumably that was who it was — emerged from behind a curtain to a roar of wild applause. Darcy had to admit that he was a good-looking boy with his dark curls and sweet face. He smiled at his audience, took up his instrument, gestured to the supporting string quartet that he was ready and started to play.

The boy played for an hour without music. He played pieces which Darcy had never heard before, strong, complicated, tuneful music. The audience was enthralled, as would have been Darcy, had he not been so hot and uncomfortable and increasingly stiff at the inability to move more than an inch either way.

At last the performance ended. Max and the quartet took their bows and disappeared behind the curtain. This, Darcy understood, signalled the end of this evening's recitals.

"Thank the Lord for that," he muttered to Bingley, who laughed. The audience was still clapping and calling for an encore.

Please, God, no, thought Darcy as he stared dolefully out of the window. Mercifully, the boy did not return and the audience rose and painfully slowly shuffled towards the next room where refreshments were being served and where the gathering would spend further hours no doubt praising the boy's performance to the heavens.

The glass of wine with which he was served was, at least, welcome and now it was necessary to make conversation with Bingley's sisters. Caroline Bingley wasted no time before addressing him.

"Mr Darcy, I trust you have enjoyed this evening's treat. It was a great coup to have secured a recital by Max for my great friend Octavia Brandreth's soirée."

She spoke as though she knew Max personally.

"We are much obliged to you, I am sure, Miss Bingley, for the opportunity to witness such a wondrous performance."

"Indeed, our thanks should go to Viscount Cedric Morley. You will recall him, Charles, Mr Darcy. He was at Cambridge with you. He knows Max's mother and I am honoured to say that she has become a good friend of mine in the short time she and Max have been in London."

Vague misgivings started to stir in Darcy's breast at that point. At Cambridge, Morley had been a known mischief-maker, ready to play a prank or queer anyone's pitch.

"And it is hoped that Max and his mother Frau Schreiber will come in and mingle with us before the evening is out."

Just then, Caroline Bingley's attention was taken by another of her acquaintance standing nearby and she, Margaret and Susan turned to the woman. Susan introduced her to Darcy and

Bingley after which the four women became engaged in close conversation. Darcy and Bingley turned away and Darcy was about to make a plea to leave when movement near a side door caught his attention.

The boy Max came through the door and looked about, followed by a slender, flaxen-haired woman. Bingley noticed too. His sisters and their friend for the time being failed to observe the prodigy's entrance.

Darcy recognised the woman immediately. He looked at Bingley who stood with his mouth open. He, too, knew who she was. It was Clara. They had known her as Clara Kohler.

"Bingley, how old is that boy Max said to be?"

"I think Caroline said earlier before you arrived that he is between nine and ten years old."

Darcy's eyes met his friend's. Some unspoken meaning passed between them and, his heart racing, he strode away towards the main door, leaving Bingley to make their excuses.

"I AM most truly sorry Darcy. I had no idea it would be her."

"It is not your fault, my friend. How could you know?"

"I have seen little of Caroline since our arrival in town. I could have visited her before tonight."

Caroline was living in London with another sister, Mrs Hurst and her husband, at the moment.

"But Darcy, I have to tell you that Caroline was talking earlier of coming to Netherfield for Easter and, she said, bringing with her a friend and the friend's son. Now, I assume she meant Clara and Max."

Darcy turned and stared at his friend. "Bingley, please tell me you jest."

"Honestly, Darcy, I thought nothing of it. I don't see how I could turn her down. She said that her friend, who is visiting England, would delight in a sojourn with an English family on an English country estate and that her son would benefit and gain from the experience. I thought she was probably talking about an Irish or perhaps and American friend."

"What is Max's surname?"

Bingley dug his hand in his pocket.

"Here," he said. He handed over a playbill which Darcy scrutinised. He saw at the top of the bill in large letters the name 'Maximilian Kohler'.

"I don't believe it." Darcy crumpled the bill and slumped in his Hackney carriage seat. "How long have you and I been married, Bingley?"

"Four months? A little over?"

"Yes. And this has to happen. You must not let them come to Netherfield, Bingley."

"But that would be very difficult. You know how it is."

Darcy did know. That a son, such as Bingley, would inherit the majority of the wealth, but was expected to provide for unmarried sisters who had to be hospitably housed if they needed it. He himself now had duties to Elizabeth's sisters should they need a home in the future, indeed to her mother, to say nothing of his own sister Georgiana, although she had a fortune of her own. Of course Bingley, married to Lizzy's sister Jane, had the same responsibility towards the Bennet ladies.

Caroline Bingley had thus far failed to secure an offer of marriage. She was not yet an old maid but the fear must always be there. It was somewhat pitiable but at this moment, he could not afford to exercise compassion for her.

"Yes, but..." Darcy cast about for some reasonable excuse to turn Caroline Bingley away. What possible credible reason could there be?

He swallowed down his alarm to say: "Can you not tell her that you have received a report that servants at Netherfield have been struck down by some contagious infection so that it is not safe to invite visitors there for the time being?"

"What about Elizabeth's family? Would you put them off to support the fiction?"

"Well, by the time your sister found out that the infection turned out to be short-lived, it would be too late. Bingley, I cannot subject Elizabeth to three weeks in the same house as Clara and her son. It would be unconscionable. And do you think that Caroline is not entirely innocent of the history here? She referred to Morley. You will recall his propensity to play tricks on people."

"Darcy, it was only a few days in Cambridge."

"Bingley, I can't take the risk."

"Very well. I will see what I can do."

———◆———

Printed in Great Britain
by Amazon